JUST AS A GENTLEMAN OUGHT TO BE

BRANDON DRAGAN

Copyright © 2024 by Brandon Dragan
First Edition

Cover Design by Rafael Polendo (polendo.net) and Derik Hobbs (derikhobbsillustrations.com)
Cover & Interior Illustrations by Derik Hobbs (derikhobbsillustrations.com)
Interior Layout by Matthew J. Distefano

ISBN 978-1-964252-18-6
Printed in the United States of America

 QUOIR

Published by Quoir
Chico, California
www.quoir.com

ALSO BY THE AUTHOR

THE WAGES OF GRACE

 Thierry Laroque, war hero and retired mechanic in rural Tennessee, would like nothing more than to live out his days in peace and quiet, but a dark secret buried in the distant past continues to haunt him. When his Wall Street power-broker brother-the person he blames for the loss of his one true love-shows up destitute at his door after decades of estrangement, Thierry comes face to face with the ghosts of a life frozen in time.

THE RESURRECTION OF JESSE BARROW

 When the mayor of a small town in rural Alabama is murdered, the desperate search for answers leads the police to Jesse Barrow, a young drunk with an axe to grind. Despite professing his innocence, Jesse finds himself accused with only one way to keep himself out of the electric chair: to betray his one true friend.

The Resurrection of Jesse Barrow is a fast-paced novella in a distinctive voice, that confronts miscarriages of justice and age old misconceptions about privilege, all the while managing to be thoroughly engrossing. Jesse's story will take you to the grave and back, and leave you with hope that a better world is within our reach.

ACKNOWLEDGMENTS

For my own Mrs. Dragan: My feelings will not be repressed. You must allow me to tell you ardently I admire and love you.

For my girls, two of the silliest in the country: I love you more than everything. And if you are good girls for the next ten years, I'll take you to a review at the end of them.

Special thanks to Joana Starnes. This novel would not exist without her post-laughter encouragement in a Tesco café some years ago, her kind and thoughtful suggestions for revision, and her extensive knowledge of Regency history, culture, and custom.

Thanks to my parents, Derik Hobbs, Rafael Polendo, Matthew Distefano, Keith Giles, Crystal Kuld, Dr. Glen Olsen, Jamie Jean, Elliott Davis, Elizabeth Adams, Crispin Bonham-Carter, my extended family, all of my friends, and every reader who has given me a chance.

In Memory of Dr. Sandra Hutchins. Without her knowledge, encouragement, and kindness, so much of what is would not be. She believed in me at a time when I did not believe in myself, and for that I am forever grateful.

In honour of Jane Austen, whose words were witty and wise beyond her years and far ahead of her time. Miss Austen's work will forever make us laugh, cry, and cherish every jot of perpetual hope this life may offer.

PART I

CHAPTER ONE

IT IS A TRUTH universally acknowledged that the violence by which a man's heart may be consumed must be in want of catharsis. However little known the feelings or views of such a man, consumed by such darkness, may be on his first encounter with slaughter, the truth is so well fixed in the minds of the public that he is assumed to be a blackguard, a scoundrel, and a degenerate, though his true identity and even his motivation be, as yet, unknown.

"*Master Fraser?*" called Jackson in a raised whisper from the hall.

He crouched beneath the light of his outstretched candle and peered into the dressing room, through which he was accustomed to entering his master's bedchamber when summoned. There was nothing out of place. As he rounded the corner and crossed the threshold of the outer room, he again observed nothing amiss—the liquor and glassware were in their proper places, the master's outer coat and buckskin breeches were laid out as he himself had left them in preparation for the morning hunt.

"*Master Fraser?*" the old valet called again.

Jackson had been stirred from his slumber not ten minutes earlier by Dingham the footman, who had been roused by Watson the groom, who was jostled by the sound of the house dogs barking as he prepared Sully, the master's finest horse, for chasing foxes. There had not been a prowler in the county in decades. Certainly not one so impudent as to attempt to loot from one of Britain's most illustrious and well-known swordsmen, to say nothing of Mr. Fraser's baronial collection of muskets and pistols.

Naturally, the old valet suspected a stag had approached the house, or the dogs were otherwise alarmed by the howl of the wind.

Upon reaching the master's door, Jackson found it slightly ajar in the longstanding habit of Mr. Fraser, whose many nights spent huddled in pup tents the world over had left him permanently stifled by stagnant air. In fact, it was his custom to sleep with an open window for the better part of nine months per annum, precipitation permitting. However, as this particular night in early October found the weather seasonally wet, yet unseasonably frigid—even for the north of England—the fires had been lit and the windows shuttered before the master retired to his chamber.

Jackson peered in through the crack but was unable to make anything out in the moonless night. He knocked quietly and pushed the door back gently. It creaked ever so slightly on its hinges. The valet was quite cognizant of his master's fierce temper, particularly when awakened—even at first light after a full night's repose. The room was dead silent, aside from his own footsteps, until a blast of glacial air, carrying on it a fine mist, blew his flame straight from the wick. The old man struggled to light it again in the dark, particularly since the fire in the hearth had completely expired.

Surely, the master would not have left a window agape on a night like this, he thought, fumbling across the room to close it as quietly as possible. Once he had shuttered it, he noticed the latch on top was broken in two, as if by force. Alarmed, he turned toward his master to who was on his side, facing the opposing wall, and motionless in the dark.

Just then, a brilliant flash of white caught the corner of his eye in the courtyard below—a black-hooded rider, bolting from the house on the back of the finest white stallion that had ever graced Derbyshire—

"Sully!" Jackson gasped.

He spun on his heels to rouse his master but slipped on something wet near the bedpost and landed rather heavily on his left shoulder.

"Master," he started with a grimace. "Someone is riding off with Sully!" The master did not stir. "Master!" wailed the old servant again.

With some effort, Jackson sat up, cradling his injured arm across his chest. A slick liquid dripped from his hand to the floor, though he could not make out its essence in the black of the night. *"Master Fraser,"* he called again, standing carefully to his feet. He made his way carefully around the foot of the bed toward Fraser's still face. Just as he pulled the covers back, Mr. Edwards, the butler, swung the door wide, illuminating a scene of carnage that caused them both to gasp in horror. "Murder!" Jackson cried aloud. *"Murder!"*

CHAPTER TWO

Constable Gallagher reacted in a similar fashion when he was shown the corpse of Mr. Fraser. "*Lord Almighty,*" he moaned as the groundskeepers carried the gentleman's pallid cadaver down the stairs and out into the garden toward the chapel. "You must excuse me to fresh air for a moment—I believe I may cast up accounts."

"Certainly," Mr. Burton, the steward replied. Mr. Burton was typically a man of little emotion, though he had been observed dabbing at his eyes throughout the morning. Over the course of ten or twelve minutes, he waited patiently as maids and footmen passed to and from, all with red eyes cast down. When the constable reappeared, Mr. Burton was taken aback by the drastic change in the pallor of his appearance. "Are you unwell, Constable?"

"Very much so."

"May I fetch you water or—?"

"No, no, I thank you." The two men stood in silence for a moment as the Constable pressed his handkerchief over his mouth.

"If you will grant me the courtesy, may I ask what are your impressions of the crime?"

"My *impressions*?" Gallagher answered. "I have never seen such carnage in the whole of my life."

"Nor have I, sir."

"Of course not."

"Did it appear to your eye a crime of passion?"

"How could it not? His throat sliced from ear to ear; more blood let than I was aware was contained within the human body."

The steward nodded quietly. "Is there any chance that this heinous deed might have been committed—and I shudder at the very thought—by a member of this household?"

"I would not think it so, Mr. Burton," Gallagher replied, patting drops of sweat from his brow. "Have we established that all workers were accounted for last night, and are at this moment accounted for?"

"Aye."

"Then it would follow that the horse thief is the culprit, and as the horse in unaccounted for, the—" he struggled with the very word, "—the *murderer*, is also unaccounted for."

"In one sense, I must say, I am relieved. Mr. Fraser was not—" this time the steward grasped for precise words, "—he was not the easiest master to appease."

"It appears clear to me, Mr. Burton, this abhorrent crime was most certainly not perpetrated by a member of this esteemed household."

"You are most kind to declare it so, Constable," Mr. Burton answered with a bow. "It is still difficult to imagine that any person might murder a gentleman in such a savage manner only to abscond with his horse, fine as Sully may be. Particularly with such considerable difficulty—climbing to the second storey, breaking the latch on a window, and subduing a man such as Master Fraser, able-bodied and strong himself."

"To my mind, Mr. Burton, the very circumstances of this event surely point to a more personal motive—a *vendetta* of some sort. Though Sully may have been the prize, Mr. Fraser was the object."

Two footmen carried the blood-sopped mattress past them. Constable Gallagher mumbled something like a prayer under his breath. Mr. Burton wiped his eyes.

"And upon such a fine horse, may I ask, Constable, what are the chances that this murderer will ever be apprehended?"

"Sully may yet be our best hope, Mr. Burton," Gallagher answered. "A pure white steed of his stature and beauty will not be easy to conceal. I have already sent post riders ahead to all inns and taverns within twenty miles with a detailed description. Any rider atop Sully will be stopped and detained on sight."

"That is a most comforting notion, indeed, that the savage might still be brought to justice."

"I assure you Mr. Burton," Gallagher continued with growing confidence. "When Sully is found, the perpetrator of this most barbaric deed is found, as well—"

"Mr. Burton!" called Dingham from the courtyard. "*Mr. Burton!*"

"Yes, Dingham?"

"Sully has been found!"

The steward and the constable gazed at each other, the first in astonishment, the second in self-assured conceit.

"Allow me to venture a conjecture—he was found in Buxton?"

"Buxton?" answered Dingham. "That's nearly ten miles."

"That would have been my first estimate, being a larger village where the fiend could presumably hope to blend in with the locals, but as I said, find the horse and you've found your—"

"No, not Buxton, sir," Dingham continued. "Sully was found not two hundred yards from the gate."

"*What?*" the steward and the constable replied in unison.

"He was in the grove some twenty yards from the road, tied to a tree. Even had a bucket of water left for him."

CHAPTER THREE

TWO GENTLEMEN SAT ACROSS from each other in what would have been at that precise moment, and by no small measure, the most expensive coach in Hertfordshire. Both men were as rich as they were handsome and unattached. The first, his back pressed to the rear of the well-apportioned box, was lean and of greater-than-average height. His dark eyes, straight nose, and square jawline were softened by lips that curved delicately at the corners when he smiled. A tuft of hair the colour of chestnuts wafted across a broad and masculine forehead. This man carried himself with an air of confidence which was nearly as intimidating as it was attractive. The second man was an affable and lively man and also tall—though not as noticeably so as his friend. This one's untamed and sandy-coloured curls matched with a winning smile to naturally draw the eye and may have had the unavoidable effect of masking a deceptively sturdy build. In the current moment, the second man found his naturally amiable disposition tested by his prudent friend's calculated line of questioning.

"Darcy, for the life of me I cannot understand your constant aversion to all things quaint and charming."

"And I cannot understand your insistence on taking a country home that will not suit you as a settled, permanent estate, particularly in a county such as Hertfordshire."

Bingley sighed heavily and glanced out the carriage window. "The choice of an estate is an axial task for the future of my family, and great care must be exercised in its selection. I would be immensely regretful in my later life, had I made the selection of a heritable estate based upon youth and imprudence."

"You may be *young*, Bingley, but you are certainly not *imprudent*," Darcy answered him.

"I am well aware that the two may, in fact, be intimately connected."

"Be that as it may, I still say I am not persuaded by your selection of this particular location. Certainly, the society cannot be much... *refined*."

"I have heard, my dear man, that this county is home to some of the most splendid beauties in the whole of England—"

"And so that is your *design* in settling here—to find yourself a bride among the unconnected and bucolic ladies of the countryside?"

"*Design!* Nonsense, how can you talk so? However, I've always felt kindness and charm as particularly attractive qualities, and country girls are quite celebrated for both. *Design!* My aim at present, is to find a place where I may settle comfortably *for a time*, and the distance from here to town is not nearly as great an imposition as it is to Derbyshire. You must remember, Darcy, my father may have left me a fortune, but he did not leave me *Pemberley*. Thus, I feel it is my familial duty to make a sober and fully informed selection when I decide upon a permanent estate."

Darcy only shifted in his seat and turned his gaze out the window.

"In addition, Netherfield has been vacant for some time, and if it lives up to its billing I may endeavour, with your aid of course, to achieve quite a bargain on its price."

"A cheap house and pretty girls," Darcy summed up his friend's motivations such.

"An appealing price for a country home where I may," Bingley shifted in his own seat, a strained smile quickly fading from his lips, "*take refuge* from the...*demands* of my business. And while the girls are not my *specific* cause for taking the place, there is the possibility that I *may* very well fall in love with one of them."

"I might dare to predict it so much as a likelihood."

"And you would censure me for falling in love?"

"Of course not. However, I would hold you to account if you were less scrupulous in the choice of a bride than you were in the selection of a family estate."

The two friends locked eyes momentarily before turning their respective gazes out their respective windows as the carriage rumbled forward over bumpy country roads.

"Well, I thank you, yet again, for coming from town to see the place with me."

"You need not thank me. It is my pleasure to accompany you."

The carriage pulled round a bend and from Bingley's seat the house came into view. "Oh, there it is—and what a fine prospect!"

Darcy turned and looked out the glass on Bingley's side. He had not expected to be affected in such a positive manner by the home's appearance, but he was genuinely pleased by it on first sight. "Very fine, indeed." Bingley looked quickly to Darcy's face to measure his friend's sincerity. He was rather pleased that Darcy seemed to genuinely admire the place, and for this reason his unparalleled smile appeared.

The gentlemen toured the grounds first on horseback and were quite impressed by the size of the garden, relative to the size of the home, and Bingley, in particular, by the row of tall hedges that ran from behind the stable nearly to the edge of the wooded acreage which bordered the property. It was his habit to come and go as he pleased, and preferably without being noticed. The layout of Netherfield and its property would allow him a measure of privacy that was simply impossible to attain in London. There were several outbuildings that, though they may have fallen into a degree of disrepair due to the property's vacancy, were nearly out of sight and would not cost but a few dozen pounds to return to working order.

Equally impressive was the interior of the home. The well adorned parlour, sizable music room, and prodigious ballroom—again, relative to the size of the house itself, not say, in comparison to the ballroom at Pemberley—all particularly delighted Mr. Bingley. Mr. Darcy, however, seemed more concerned with noting imperfections in the home, as he perceived them, mostly with the intention of leveraging for a better price at the leasing table. The bedrooms were more commodious than Bingley had anticipated, and the master chamber was particularly impressive to his mind. The large corner windows granted a clear prospect both of the lane, and of the gardens. Through an alcove in the closet, a most convenient staircase had been constructed, leading directly to a door which opened to a portico near the garden. In but a few steps one might be, say, from the portico door to the gravel behind the hedge, and completely unnoticed from any vantage within the home.

"It is perfect!" Bingley declared. "Darcy, what say you?"

Darcy felt along the outer doorframe with two fingers. "It seems that there may have been some damage caused by water. It will take some repair."

"Darcy, give me your opinion," Bingley said.

"Depending on the scope of rot, perhaps ten pounds to repair properly."

"The *house*, Darcy, not the door frame!"

"Oh, well, yes," Darcy stammered. "It is a fine house, but there is work to be done, which, no doubt, will cost upwards of—"

"Shall I take it?"

"Are you asking my approval?"

"Not your approval, *per se*, but your opinion—as a *friend*," Bingley answered him.

"I would personally not take a house in this county at all, particularly not one that has been vacant for all this time."

"But I *like* it," Bingley said. "It suits my needs perfectly."

"Then why ask my opinion?" Darcy asked, eyes still attentively searching wood and stone for signs of age or disrepair. Bingley's shoulders heaved and he looked toward the earth beneath his feet. "I would not lease it at asking price, that is a certainty," Darcy continued.

"And I would not let it slip away over a hundred pounds of repairs."

"Fine, then," Darcy replied. "Let us be off to Meryton and make the arrangements."

"Splendid," Bingley answered, a rapturous smile pasted across his face.

The two set off in near silence. When they arrived in the village of Meryton, Bingley had full intentions of taking the house outright. He was, however, met with some resistance in the solicitor's office, and that resistance was all on the part of his friend Mr. Darcy. However, by the time all the business was concluded, Bingley had an agreement in hand and, thanks to some shrewd negotiation on the part of his friend, had paid twenty percent below the asking price.

CHAPTER FOUR

WHEN THE GENTLEMEN ARRIVED back at the Bingley residence in Grosvenor Street in London the following afternoon, they were dismayed to discover that their return was to be marred by some shocking news out of the British Morning Post. Bingley had come directly to Meryton from the north, where he had been tending to business affairs. It can be surmised, then, that he was somewhat disenchanted by the sullen greeting from his sisters, whom he had not seen in more than a fortnight. Darcy, on the other hand, had met Bingley in Hertfordshire from London, hence the dearth of overwhelming affection in the greeting of Caroline Bingley and Louisa, Mrs. Hurst, did not slight him in the least. In fact, he quite veritably preferred it.

"Would you have preferred if I *stayed* in Derbyshire?" Bingley appealed.

"No, of course not, Brother," Caroline answered solemnly. "Have you not heard the news?"

"Have you not heard that I have leased a country home?" Bingley petitioned.

"Yes, and a very fine home, we envisage it must be," Louisa answered. "But you see, Charles, we have all been dreadfully affected by such horrid news from Derbyshire."

"*Derbyshire?*" Darcy asked, suddenly drawn into the conversation by the mention of his home county. "What's happened in Derbyshire?"

"Sir Andrew Fraser is dead," Caroline stated flatly.

"Andrew Fraser?" Darcy repeated.

"Three nights past," Louisa said. "In his bed."

13

"How terrible," Bingley remarked. "I had not known he was in ill health."

"He most certainly was not," Mr. Hurst suddenly spoke from the sofa. "Fraser was vigorous and in fine health!"

"Yes, I now remember he was an acquaintance of yours. I'm terribly sorry," said Mr. Darcy.

"He was a friend, and a damned fine one at that," Mr. Hurst slurred, his words dangling somewhere between emotion and inebriation. "I hunted partridge with him not a month ago." Louisa gently patted her husband's knee.

"Have they published the cause of death?" asked Darcy.

"He did not *die*, Mr. Darcy," Caroline answered.

"Pardon?"

"He was *murdered*."

"Murdered?" Darcy echoed.

"Yes—*butchered*. And in his own bed, in the dark of the night."

"Unfathomable."

"Why do you say the word *butchered*?" Bingley asked.

"That is what the papers have called him, the murderer—Derbyshire's Nobleman Butcher," replied Louisa.

"There is no real flow to it... but still, rather grim," remarked Bingley, somewhat under his breath.

"Quite," Mr. Hurst blurted.

"Have they any idea as to the butch—err, *perpetrator?*" Bingley inquired abruptly.

"Not in the least," said Louisa. "Supposedly a prized horse was stolen, presumably by the murderer, and then returned the next morning."

"Shocking," Bingley replied.

"*Abominable*," remarked Mr. Hurst.

"And the paper does not mention any knowledge or theories as to who might have committed such a fiendish act?" asked Darcy.

"Only to say that all members of the household have been eliminated from suspicion," replied Caroline.

"Naturally, that would be the first thought, would it not?" Bingley posited. "Such a heinous act must have been realized by a personal connection, no?"

"Or a draw-latch rum-padder who happened upon the house," Darcy postulated.

"Oh Mr. *Darcy*, your expressions! You have been in town too long," Louisa retorted with a subdued chortle, immediately looking toward her mourning husband to be sure she had not offended him.

"Simply terrifying," answered Caroline. "To think, any passing highwayman with murder on his mind, breaking into the bedrooms of noblemen, and—"

"Calm yourself, Caroline," Bingley broke in. "If it were a highwayman he would have simply poached the horse. No, there must have been more personal reasons for such an act."

"Were you acquainted with him, Charles?" Caroline asked.

Bingley looked up suddenly and looked as if he'd swallowed a mouse. "With whom? Of course not. Why do you ask?"

"You seem to have such a strong inclination toward the slayer's motivation," she answered teasingly. "And, if I'm not mistaken, you were present in the county at the time of the act."

"Ha!" Bingley laughed suddenly. "I was but twenty—that is to say, I was at least twenty-five miles from Grantley Manor, if that is what you mean to know."

"No doubt the constable might like to have your expertise on the subject," she retorted.

"I merely asked about the *horse*," Bingley countered. "If the act in question was a robbery and not a personal vendetta, why would the pirate leave the horse? I am sure it is not anything the constable hasn't already considered."

The room fell silent for a moment.

"You are right, Charles," pronounced Darcy. "It doesn't make sense—"

"None of it makes sense!" With that outburst Mr. Hurst was up off the settee. He snatched a carafe of wine from the table on his way out of the room and proceeded rather unsteadily and quite nosily, mumbling all the way, up the stairs and out of sight.

"He's been *exceedingly* upset," said Louisa after another moment of reticent quiet. "I've never seen him take to drink like this." Bingley raised a single eyebrow in bewilderment before approaching the table to pour a drink of his own.

"I do think *too* much grief over someone so barely, if at all, acquainted with us is a fruitless manner in which to conduct ourselves," Caroline eventually stated.

"Aye," voiced Louisa. "Especially at a time when we celebrate our dear brother's establishment of a household."

"Yes, brother, do tell us all about Netherfield Park!"

CHAPTER FIVE

CONSTABLE GALLAGHER SAT IN the tavern and imbibed all that evening. The pile of shoes in disrepair strewn across his workbench could be neglected in favour of drink for one night. His wife and four sprightly children would be momentarily neglected, as well. He sat alone, the grisly image of the deceased gentleman burned into his memory, a portrait of a such vile obscenity more dreadful than he might have ever imagined in a hundred lifetimes. Being that there was no professional police force in Derbyshire—or anywhere in England, for that matter—it would ultimately fall upon the shoulders of Sir Andrew's relations to track down his killer. Gallagher was simply a volunteer, who felt it was his duty to town and country to serve in whatever small capacity he might. To this point in his five-year term as Constable, he had made but a single arrest—a meddlesome youth from a destitute family who was caught poaching chickens from the Darcy estate at Pemberley. The boy, who was not yet fourteen, had fled when confronted, and was arrested days later by Gallagher after he was spotted hiding in an outbuilding near Andrew Fraser's estate. The young man was subsequently adjudged to be whipped by the cart's tail, until his sentence was commuted on the supplication of Mr. Darcy, himself, who upon learning of the wretched condition of the boy's family, made arrangements to secure the father and his son a small living on the Pemberley Estate itself. Needless to say, this singular experience had not prepared the good Constable for the gruesome scene he had earlier witnessed, nor for the feeling that he might in some capacity be responsible to aid in bringing the depraved killer to justice.

As he sat and found the bottom of yet another lager, an elderly coach driver walked through the door and sat a couple tables over. The driver was well-dressed and cheerful, but worn and stiff-limbed. A drink was brought to him by the barmaid, who received a toothless grin in exchange. It was immediately evident to the Constable that the elderly coachman was in want of society, most likely having travelled a considerable length of time in no one's company but his own thoughts. The old man leaned this way and that, attempting to eavesdrop and thus insert himself into any conversation that might have allowed it. His success was rare, aside from the occasional cordial gesture or civil rebuff. It was not until he overheard Dier, the hog farmer, and Hedge, the post rider, recounting details of the prevalent topic of the murder of a nobleman in the county the previous evening, that the aged traveller realized the feat of conversance which had to that point eluded him.

"A murder? In *Derbyshire*?" he queried in disbelief.

"Aye, sir," answered Dier. "Sir Andrew Fraser, lord of Grantley Manor."

"A gentleman?"

"Aye," Hedge replied. "And one of the most prominent in the county."

"What abhorrent news!"

"We concur," Dier added.

"Has the murdered been apprehended?" asked the driver.

"No, sir," said Hedge. "I am unaware of any suspects in the matter whatsoever."

"How odious," cried the old man. He then continued on before another party could add a word. "I'm curious, if you possess the knowledge, and do not object to say—what was the manner in which the crime was carried out?"

"The lord's gullet was cut from ear to ear whilst he lie own bed," Hedge responded with a shiver.

"Ghastly," declared the visitor. "Ghastly, and in every respect, *ghastly!*"

"Aye," the swine breeder answered. "From what I've heard, it was an adept and single slash—nearly identically how one might slaughter a pig."

"Is that so?"

"Aye."

"And you've experience in that field?"

"Near this time every annum," Dier answered.

"Can you account for your whereabouts last night, in that case?"

"What are you, a travelling constable?"

With a hearty laugh, the old man replied, "Funny thought, indeed! I drive the coach for Sir John Walters of Northumberland. He reposes as we speak, and we continue on toward London on business at first light."

Hedge laughed boisterously and slapped his mate on the shoulder. "Don't be so serious, Dier!"

"Do you mean to intimate that I am involved in a murder simply due to my occupation?"

"I do not mean to suggest any such thing," the driver answered. "I apologize for any offence I may have inflicted to your pride, sir. I am sure that you are the most respectable and law-abiding sort of man."

"And you, sir, mustn't be so high-minded as regards our friend, Dier," Hedge bellowed. "He was far too tap-hackled to have any kind of slaughter on his mind last night!" Dier chewed the inside of his cheek. "Poor bastard hardly made it home and he lives but a stone's throw up the lane!"

"That's enough," Dier spoke harshly. "I accept your apology, sir, but I refuse to be party to another word of your bag of moonshine, particularly as I don't know you from Adam—"

"Rawden Acton, at your service," the driver interrupted, extending a hand. Dier shook it reluctantly. "Please do pardon my intrusion into your evening, I have been alone atop a coach for nearly ten hours, with no companions but the horses, and they are not nearly as fond of conversation while being whipped as one might imagine."

"Pleasure," Hedge said, extending his own hand.

19

"Pleasure," Acton answered. "I merely breached propriety and intervened in your conversation because I believe that it may, in fact, hold an uncanny interest to my master."

"How so?" asked Dier.

"Allow me a moment's courtesy of, at once, ordering another cider and also asking one further clarifying question."

"Certainly," said Hedge, who was by this point growing simultaneously curious and half-sprung.

Once the barmaid fetched the driver a fresh mug of cider, the driver continued: "Did the devil by any chance steal a horse?—and before you answer, let me pose a guess—a fine horse, a stallion?"

"By God, yes he did!" Hedge blustered.

"Not precisely," Dier stated. "He—"

"Discarded it in the wood by the road," Acton said, eyes suddenly illuminated and halcyon.

"How did you—?"

"Did he leave it a bucket of fresh water?"

Hedge slapped the table, nearly flinging their drinks onto the patrons at the neighbouring table.

"How the devil did you come by such knowledge, sir?" Dier demanded.

"My first master, the late Eoin Walters, was murdered *in the very same fashion* not twelve months past."

Constable Gallagher suddenly found the table in front of him sliding out and his own derriere crashing to the stone floor. He looked up in befuddlement at the post-man, the coach-man, and the swine-man from his posterior.

CHAPTER SIX

THE WIND HOWLED AND spat gusts of rain across the faces of those unfortunate enough to be outdoors. What had been a warm, breezy day of clouds mixed with sunshine had devolved into a moonless, algid evening. The temperature had not been nearly as frigid when Thomas Abbott had departed the Customs House headed west on Lower Thames Street. He had turned right onto Botolph Lane and dodged into the Hare and Hounds Tavern just as the drizzle began. Upon leaving after a period of nearly three hours, he shivered and turned his outer coat collar up around his neck. He had not been quite prepared for such a drastic change in the weather, and particularly not to be outdoors in it. He turned into Monument Street in the direction of London Bridge.

His meeting at the Customs House had reassured him that his business dealings were intact and would remain profitable, despite the rather sudden and shocking development of the murder of his partner, Sir Andrew Fraser. Abbott would be happy to relate the former news, in spite of the latter, to his financial guarantor, Lord Bertram St. John, the Earl of Canterbury. Lord St. John was undoubtedly among the ten richest men in all of England, and had achieved such status largely through ruthless enforcement of his financial dealings.

Bad news in the ears of St. John in an affair such as this would certainly lead to Abbott's downfall, the end of his political career at the least. While a downturn in the particular sort of trade these men were engaged in would mean ruin for Abbott, there certainly would be other Members of Parliament clamouring for the opportunity to take his place in such an arrangement, far beneath the salt as it might be. Thomas Abbott was not a man of great fortune and relied on his ability to bend the ears of political allies and even enemies occasionally, to further his prospects. This talent had served him well in establishing himself as a conduit for political favours, particularly in the fields of appropriations and customs. It was, in fact, this peculiar aptitude that had caught the eye of the Earl of Canterbury, who alongside Sir Andrew Fraser, sought in their business dealings uncommon degrees of blindness of eye and deafness of ear in certain quarters of the civil power structure. It was thought that Abbott, given his position among those powers in addition to his unremitting avarice, would be the perfect candidate to conceal and further such illicit business dealings. The eerily conspicuous death of Sir Fraser, however, had the potential to unhinge the enterprise as a whole, and to bring the full force of the law crashing down around the remaining members of the cabal.

Once he had reached the bridgehead, it was with such thoughts contesting for his mental energies that Abbott failed to hear his name being called from a stoop behind him. Finally, he turned as the voice shouted loudly enough to cut through the tumult in his mind.

"Yes?"

"Thomas Abbott?"

"Yes," answered he. "Who is there?"

"A messenger," came the steely reply.

"Reveal yourself," he called into the shadows.

"I carry a message from Aileen Clarke," came the steely reply.

Abbott pondered the name for only an instant before the blood froze in his veins.

"*Aileen Clarke?*" he muttered.

"Yes, the very same."

Abbott began to back toward the bridge slowly. "You can't have a message from Aileen Clarke—"

"And why is that?"

"It's impossible," he muttered to the figure behind the shroud of darkness.

"Is that so?"

"Quite so—show yourself, I demand it!" A hooded figure emerged from the shadows. "Who are you?"

"A little bird," came the frigid reply.

"Show me your face," Abbott demanded as the figure approached him.

"Do you wish to hear her message?"

"Tell me and be gone."

"She wishes you to join her beneath the earth."

With that, Abbott turned and ran, his lungs burning with every inhalation. The bridge was deserted, aside from a lone drunkard lying face down under a gas lamp. "Help, help," cried Abbott as he approached the prostrate indigent. The rapid footsteps of the cowled messenger neared until suddenly the lights of the city all flared and then faded to black. Abbott could feel the cold pavement under him but was unable to move. He heard heavy breathing atop him for what seemed like a lifetime. The dark figure began pulling at Abbott's coat, finally rolling him over onto his back to get the overcoat out from under him. Abbott shivered and sobbed quietly from where he lay. Suddenly, the phantom stood atop him, only the whites of his eyes visible through his mask.

"You, Thomas Abbott, are a *murderer*," the caliginous voice stated through steady breaths.

"I don't—"

"In fact," the apparition continued. "You are much worse than that. I dare say there is not a name for the form of evil to which you have been a party."

"Pray—"

"Miss Clarke sends her regards," and with that, his throat was slit.

The shadowy figure deposited the Minister of Parliament over the railing and down into the frigid Thames before covering the sleeping inebriate with the coat of the former man. With a look in both directions, he was off toward Tooley Street and back into the darkness from whence he had come.

CHAPTER SEVEN

"*MUST* WE ATTEND AN assembly this evening?" Mr. Hurst asked in a much-agitated fashion.

"My brother has been invited and escaping introductions is, *regrettably*, unavoidable," Louisa replied.

Her husband chafed at the thought of spending an evening in the company of country-town simpletons as he had earlier branded the people of Meryton. Though he had, as far back as he could recall, been fond of drink, he had not to this moment in his life felt as though he must depend upon it simply to endure an evening—any evening, but particularly one so unpalatable as this. The news of Sir Fraser's gruesome demise had shaken him deeply, for more reasons than one. It was, firstly, the death of a friend, however removed the period of their true closeness had been. Secondly, such an unthinkable crime was an affront not simply to humanity, but particularly to the known social order—to natural law itself. Gentlemen, say nothing of members of the nobility, were not victims of lower-class crime. In an age of manners, modernity, and reason above all else, such a barbaric act was illogical at best, and a symptom of some dark and chilling derangement at worst. Mr. Hurst simply could not wrap his mental faculties around a deed of such brash contempt for the civil and sacred authorities that govern the universe itself. To his mind, if something such as this were possible, what form of evil was impossible? A world like this was certainly not one that Mr. Hurst had the fortitude to navigate in sobriety.

"I understand quite fully the grief under which you now subsist my dear, but it will pass, I assure you," Louisa said with every effort at sincerity.

"It is not simply grief, Mrs. Hurst," he barked back. "It is a matter which shocks the conscience completely—who on earth could commit such an act of depravity?"

"I would not know, Mr. Hurst."

"And there will be no justice, will there?"

"Again, I could not possibly answer your question with any degree of surety," answered Louisa while adjusting the glove on her left hand. "There is a constable investigating, is there not?"

"A *village* constable, who spends his days repairing *shoes*," he quipped with a sneer and a swig of wine.

"But a man who will be dedicated, for the near future, anyway, to the task of apprehending the fiend."

"Grantley Village is not half the size of Lambton," Hurst stated with disdain.

His wife chortled and jeered, "It is a wonder there is anything there at all, then. It must make Meryton seem like Vienna by comparison."

She walked to the window as he attempted to suppress his laughter. "You understand me well, Mrs. Hurst."

"Come, darling," Louisa called, walking back to where he sat. "The coach is at our service."

"I consent to this evening only on your bequest."

"I know Mr. Hurst, and I thank you," answered she with a kiss on his ruddy cheek.

CHAPTER EIGHT

BINGLEY COULD SCARCELY CONTAIN his excitement as the evening approached. He had been settled in Netherfield but a fortnight and had already been visited by such pleasant gentlemen and met with such handsome young ladies as he might have ever imagined. He had been called back to town by business for a brief spell, and had returned at once relieved and heavy-hearted. The very thought of a dance—an opportunity to forget his troubles, along with the sadness and corruption of the world—no matter how provincial, delighted him to no end. With the burdens of the darkness of other men upon his shoulders, a pleasant evening dancing with charming maidens offered just the respite for which his weary soul pined. His delight was tempered, however, not only by the brooding countenance of his friend, who as was well-established, thought rather lowly of the company in which the evening would be spent, but also by the line of questions Mr. Darcy had seemingly prepared for him as they waited in the drawing room for his sisters and Mr. Hurst.

"What happened in London, Charles?"

"What ever could you mean, Darcy?" he replied with a hint of sarcasm.

"I hesitate to believe you were called away on such urgent business that could not be expediently handled by your steward."

"Mr. Wilshere is most trusted, you understand, but I had to attend to a matter of particular detail and importance which dictated a swift and singular response," answered Bingley.

"One which Mr. Wilshere is not authorized to give?" Darcy asked.

"A response I would not *require* him to give," Bingley said, casting a grave and ironic look in Darcy's direction.

"Your singular response did not, in any way result in the body of Thomas Abbott floating in the Thames, did it then?"

Bingley looked as if he might be sick. "You've never asked in such depth about my ventures before, Darcy. Why do you take such an interest so suddenly?"

"Because you have never killed a member of Parliament before, Bingley."

"Thomas Abbott may have been in the House of Commons, but his connection to Sir Andrew Fraser and his... *dealings,* was rather particular."

"You have yet to explain those dealings to me, Charles, and I do not ask out of morbid curiosity or any such trifle of the sort, but only because dispatching members of the nobility and members of Parliament potentially raises the profile of your mission significantly. You may continue to count upon my silence, but I must ask: you are unequivocal in that these acts have no connection to the poor treatment by these men of your late father?"

"Poor treatment? Darcy, had it not been for the influence of your own good father, may he rest in peace, they might have ruined him completely."

"You must understand that your mission ceases to be a noble one when it crosses into personal vendettas and a thirst for revenge. I will always be your friend, but I could not support such endeavours."

"How can I answer you, Darcy?" Bingley shifted in his seat and then stood quickly. He remained in thought, arm propped on the mantle for some time.

"Do not mistake my meaning—"

"My personal feelings of betrayal and animosity were certainly principal motivating factors for my investigation of Walters in particular, I would not wish to deny it. However, the severity of the crimes that I—or rather Mr. Wilshere—discovered that these men were engaged in is my *sole* motivation for their elimination."

"You swear it, Charles?"

"Darcy," Bingley said, turning to face his friend. "You did not object to the *dissolution* of Eoin Walters once you learned what kind of man he was, did you?"

"Certainly not," Darcy answered. "His character was more wretched than I could have ever imagined."

"You must, then, allow me the benefit of your continued confidence in my mission," Bingley replied. "Eoin Walters was a choirboy in comparison to the coterie of Andrew Fraser."

Darcy glared at him gravely. "I am hard pressed to believe such a thing could be possible."

"Believe it," said Bingley. "And if you cannot believe what your mind cannot conceive, then at least believe in your friend. You know my character better than anyone on earth. I have always been honest and candid with you, Darcy, and I do not cease to be so now."

"I do believe you, Bingley," Darcy answered. "I only hope that you are cognizant of your own personal prejudices when it comes to this rather necessary, albeit unpleasant, business to which you have been called by the just arm of heaven itself."

"I take no pleasure in it whatsoever, I have you know. The only satisfaction I take is the fact that such horrible men have ceased their capacity and their propensity to contrive the most grievous injury upon such defenceless victims."

"I am glad to hear it," said Darcy. "And I take no pleasure whatsoever, I have you know, with such vapid and agrestic persons in whose company we are, no doubt, to spend the evening."

Bingley laughed and shook his head. "Your perspective on these things is, in truth, utterly preposterous."

Darcy stood as Miss Bingley and Mrs. Hurst entered the room, followed by an unsteady Mr. Hurst.

"Prepare yourself to be disappointed, then," Bingley stated nonchalantly. "For I believe, despite your best intentions to the contrary, something splendid may result from this dance."

"I shall be quite disappointed either way, I believe."

"At the very least," said Bingley. "I shall have a grand time and will not allow your contemptible demeanour to dissuade me in the least."

"I would not have it so," Darcy answered with a half-smile, Caroline taking his arm as they turned toward the door.

"Let us do what we can," she half-whispered to Darcy. "To allow my dear brother some mirth and levity. He is but a gentle soul and deserves at least one evening's diversion."

"I rather agree," Darcy replied.

She smiled and squeezed his arm as they descended the steps toward the coach.

CHAPTER NINE

BINGLEY DID NOT ARISE in time for breakfast the next morning. He had not slept so hard in weeks, as the stresses of establishing his house in Netherfield, the abhorrent business that kept his evenings often occupied and nearly constantly occupied his thoughts, as well as the improvement of the family business which his late father had left in his care, often denied him repose. This night's slumber, however, was filled with the aroma of perfume, the rhythm of the dance, and the delicate figure and angelic smile of Jane Bennet, with whom he had been quite captivated immediately upon being introduced. When he awoke after eleven, he sent for tea and rolls to be brought to his room, and instructed the footman to request that Mr. West, the butler, inform his sisters and Mr. Darcy that he was, indeed, in good health and even better spirits, and that he would join them shortly. While eating in bed, musing over the many pleasant images of the past night imprinted upon his memory, he heard a courteous knock at his door.

"Come in," Bingley called.

The heavy door turned slowly on its hinges and his steward, Mr. Wilshere, entered.

"Ah, Mr. Wilshere, top of the morning to you," Bingley said cheerfully.

"And to you, sir," the steward replied. Wilshere was a man in his late thirties, as of yet unmarried in large part due to the strain his work put upon him. He was, as always, immaculately dressed.

"Do you care for some bread?"

"No, thank you, sir."

"Well, what business is at hand that requires my attention from bed?" asked Bingley jovially.

"I believe I have discovered the third and fourth members of the Fraser cabal," stated Wilshere.

Bingley sat up and placed a half-eaten roll on the silver platter resting atop the duvet. "Tell me," he demanded, his mood suddenly transformed.

"First, let me prepare you, sir—"

"Tell me, man."

Wilshere put up both hands. "Patience, sir, I beg you. The development at hand is, while not certain at this moment, *rather sobering*."

"Wilshere, out with it."

"I am in no doubt whatsoever that the third member of the scheme is Lord Bertram St. John."

"The *Earl of Canterbury?*" asked the bewildered Bingley.

"The same, sir," responded the steward.

"It cannot be."

"As I stated earlier, sir, of this I am completely certain—"

"Complete certainty does not persuade me, Mr. Wilshere."

"I am waiting on particular confirmations, Mr. Bingley. You will, as always, inspect the evidence yourself and make your determination."

"Yes, I certainly shall," Bingley answered. "Bertram St. John is one of the wealthiest men in Europe."

"I am aware of it, sir."

"He has personally advised the King's Treasury on several occasions."

"Indeed, he has," confirmed Wilshere.

"King George *himself* summoned him personally during the American War—"

"You commissioned me to gather information, sir—to track down those responsible for the unthinkable evil being committed under the noses of our countrymen, *by* our countrymen. I have faithfully executed this task, with great effort and personal risk, I might remind you. You will consider the evidence yourself at your leisure, but it most certainly leads to the door of Lord Bertram St. John, the Earl of Canterbury."

Bingley picked up the half roll and tossed it haphazardly at the window. "How sure are you, Wilshere?"

"Comprehensively."

"As certain as you were of Andrew Fraser and Thomas Abbot?"

"Aye."

"Unthinkable," Bingley answered calmly.

"Again, sir, you will inspect the evidence yourself."

Bingley nodded. "And who is the fourth?—No wait, let me guess, the Prince Regent himself?"

"I should not entertain such a thought, sir, not even facetiously."

"Of course not, Wilshere; forgive me."

The steward nodded. "The fourth, and I would submit to you that of this person's involvement I am slightly less convinced, although only slightly less so—"

"Please, end this misery and tell me already."

"We have eliminated the military muscle—Sir Andrew Fraser. We determined the political favours were purchased by the late Thomas Abbott and have recently dealt with him. The obscene operation itself is financed by none other than Lord Bertram St. John. And I believe, Mr. Bingley, that the legwork, the real and daily work of the devil, is carried out by none other than *George Wickham*."

CHAPTER TEN

THE REST OF THE party was put out by his sleeping-in. They had already been in sour spirits after enduring a gathering in the most unrefined society of Meryton's residents the previous evening. Upon hearing the news brought by his steward, however, Bingley's sullen mood practically outmatched theirs by the time he joined them in the music room after lunch.

"Brother," began Caroline. "Are you unwell?"

"Did not West inform you that I am perfectly well?" Bingley replied rather curtly.

"He did, but you hardly ever sleep so late, and—"

"I was quite fagged by the dance—well, the dance and the drink together, I suppose," he answered unconvincingly.

"No," she remarked. "Something else is amiss. Do you not agree, Darcy?"

Darcy turned from the window. "We know your brother dipped rather deep, as is perhaps not his custom—"

"I dare say, Louisa," Caroline called to her sister who sat at the piano. "Should we call for Mr. Jones?"

"Let us have no more of this fustian nonsense, sister."

"I do believe that my opinion is in accord with yours, Caroline," Mrs. Hurst declared, ceasing her playing mid-chord.

"Darcy," Bingley pleaded. "Speak for me, man."

"He may have been a trifle disguised at the assembly, but I believe your brother when he says it has had little to no ill effects on his health this morning."

"*Thank you*," cried Bingley. "My usual countenance may be slightly put off by business with my steward, but I affirm to you that I am not in the least physically unwell."

"If Mr. Darcy endorses such a declaration, then I shall leave it be," said Caroline. Darcy nodded his accession. "But do be so good as to reassure me that your business dealings have not left us destitute," she remarked with a facetious smile. Louisa burst into laughter at the thought.

"I can assure you, sisters, that our father's fortune is on firm footing," he answered flatly. "The business with my steward which has for the moment vexed my temperament is of a more intimate nature."

"I dare say," Louisa called from the piano. "You have not learned anything unfortunate about a particular Bennet girl, have you?"

"Whatever could you mean?" asked he in genuine perplexity.

"Your attention to Jane Bennet would not have escaped even the casual eye," Caroline answered.

He looked to his friend by the window for support. "Darcy, you do not blame me for my attentions to her?"

"Certainly not," replied Darcy coolly, moving toward the centre of the room. "At first glance, she is, I grant you, very pretty."

"At first glance?" Bingley asked indignantly. "I imagine she may be the most beautiful creature on which I have ever laid eyes."

"What Mr. Darcy means, brother, if I may be so bold," Louisa broke in, her fingers nimbly playing on. "Is that the eldest Miss Bennet's connections and fortune are rather beneath your touch."

Bingley stared at her, mouth agape.

"I might not declare it so *categorically*," Caroline interjected, sensing the need to smooth over her sister's flat declaration. "Jane Bennet is a sweet girl, and very pretty, I grant you. But a cursory knowledge of her circumstances *must* alleviate any discomfort you may feel this morning..."

Louisa nodded deferentially from the piano.

Bingley suddenly perceived an outlet for his distemper on account of his nocturnal affairs. He had, indeed, found Jane Bennet extraordinarily pleasant, but his mind had not been made up in any particular fashion in her regard. He imagined, however, that if his sisters believed him to be in agony over what they might consider to be a forbidden, but harmless, example of calf-love, he might escape any further pressing on his more furtive activities. Should he pursue this course of action, he must find opportunities to spend more time in the presence of Miss Bennet, which delighted him also. She was a remarkably charming young lady and though, at present, he had no designs on marriage, any perceived pursuit of her would undoubtedly fix his sisters' thoughts and would offer him more leeway in pursing his other and more pressing interests. Bingley was surely too honourable to intentionally lead Jane toward an outcome he did not desire outright, so he declared to himself that he would remain open to any possibilities and would not be dictated to by the will of his sisters. He also wondered with some mystification as to the hand of providence, and its, perhaps, placing such a fine and agreeable young lady in his path. Her connections aside, even on first acquaintance he was sure that she would make a most desirable object to any sensible man. He was soundly convinced that, to this point, he had never met a finer young lady in all his movements in society.

"I do hope that, while you may have a decidedly unfavourable view of her circumstances, you would not object to my desire to become further acquainted with her," he said, feigning concern over their good opinion.

"Of course not, brother," Mrs. Hurst answered. "In fact, Caroline and I would have you know that we also desire her further acquaintance."

"Certainly, I do agree," Miss Bingley added. "From our vantage yesterday evening, though her manners may be unrefined and rather informal, Jane Bennet may, in fact, be the most sensible and agreeable person in the county."

Bingley furrowed his brow at this. "You are very harsh on a society with which you are hardly acquainted."

"Bingley," Darcy started. "You cannot, in good faith, assert that you were impressed by the manner of dress, discourse, or even the particular breeding of the company with which we dined last evening."

BRANDON DRAGAN

"I thought the company was pleasant and the manners were precisely what I might have expected at any country gathering," Bingley declared. "They were absolutely charming, every last one of them."

With this, Mr. Hurst awoke with a start from his podgy stupor.

"And now," Bingley continued. "I assume you will censure him as harshly as you have me?"

The piano fell silent. "Brother," Louisa began sombrely. "He is grieving the loss of a friend—"

"And how long may we expect that will he carry on in such a fashion?"

"You do not comprehend the *depth* to which he has been *afflicted*."

Bingley rolled his eyes and turned toward Darcy. "Do you fancy a ride into the village? An hour of fresh air would do my constitution much good."

"I shall ride with you, if the ladies would permit it," Darcy answered, deferring to Bingley's sisters.

"I think it is a splendid idea," Louisa answered.

"Why don't you take Mr. Hurst with you?" Caroline requested. "I am sure the fresh air would do him well."

"Are you *quite serious?*" Bingley demanded.

"Why not?" inquired she.

"Because he cannot even *stand*."

"I'll stand enough for two—" the bosky gentleman bellowed from the parquet floor.

Bingley glared at his sisters.

"Then go alone," Caroline muttered with a dismissive wave of her hand.

"Darcy, shall we?"

The two friends bowed and quit the room.

"Insufferable," Louisa remarked from the piano bench.

"I heard that," Bingley called from the hall.

"Do take care on your ride," she answered quickly before striking up the piano again.

CHAPTER ELEVEN

OVER THE COURSE OF several weeks, Constable Gallagher had managed not only sobriety, but had additionally secured an investment of funds on behalf of the Fraser estate which would allow him to temporarily shutter his cobbler shop and, in lieu of mending soles, pursue the course of inquest which he believed—and had been efficacious in persuading the inheritors of Grantley Manor to believe—would lead to the capture of its late owner's killer.

The chance meeting of the Constable and the driver, Rawden Acton, had spurred a frenzied conversation and an even greater frenzy of cerebral activity within the unpaid officer of the peace. He could not accept, after seeing the slain corpse of the departed and having the associated carnage impressed firmly in his mind's eye, that such a barbaric act could go unanswered by the law. Then, hearing in explicit detail of the murder of Sir Eoin Walters from Mr. Acton, he could not escape the conclusion that the slayings, as eerily and inexplicably similar in manner as they were, must have been committed by the same fiend.

He spoke at length a second time with Dingham, Mr. Fraser's footman, who had recovered Sully, the horse, in the wood near the road. Dingham related the events of the evening, from his perspective, with much candour and excessive, and largely superfluous, detail. The footman was quite affected at being summoned for a second interview and evidently thought himself honoured that he should have been to be so singled out amongst the house staff. Through a series of burrowing inquiries, Constable Gallagher was able to determine that the surprisingly astute footman had, in addition to discovering Sully tied to a tree, bucket of water left for him, also noticed a set of footprints in the mud, diverging from that spot in the direction of the road. He had initially failed to report this finding due to the euphoria of recovering his late master's prized stallion.

The day following the aforementioned second interview, Constable Gallagher accompanied the footman to the place where the horse was found. The woods were, even in the midday hours at that point in the autumn, fairly dark, which was a boon to the law-man's hopes, as the two were able to readily retrace the horse's steps in the now dry mud. When they reached the place Dingham had described, they located the perpe-trator's boot prints still intact. The coppice floor had been particularly wet that evening, as rain had been falling steadily for some time prior—so wet, in fact, that the prints were deeply fixed. Gallagher sent Dingham back to the estate while he followed the tracks in a south-westerly di-rection toward the main highway where, naturally, he lost sight of them at the road. He took particular care, however, to sketch the footprints, which, to his trained cobbler's eye, happened to be particularly unique.

On nothing but a hunch, Gallagher set out the next morning by horse on the road toward the west. He was not able to sleep most of the night, and rather than employing his restlessness in some prudent endeavour—such as shining his muddied boots, as he should have—he simply tossed and turned. Once he departed, he came through the towns of Buckstone, Holly Springs, and Hillingshire, stopping at local inns and petitioning their proprietors for information. None had seen a suspi-cious rider during the evening in question. He was nearly about to give up his hope in this direction, when some small voice inside him pried him to continue on toward just one more village, a mere eight miles to the west. It was already nearly dark, and he would most likely have had to take up lodging anyway, so he resolved to persist.

To his chagrin, at the inn at the small market town of Lambton he also garnered no such hope from the innkeeper. Frustrated, cold, and by this time very hungry, he ordered a room for the night and a meal. Once he had paid with funds allotted to him for expenses by the Fraser estate, he went out to make sure his horse was seen to properly. In the yard, he introduced himself to Robert Toomey, a local who worked in the stable. Toomey was something near fifty years of age, but at least seventy in appearance. His posture was fixedly hunched forward, and he approached with a limp as he took the reins.

"My, you must have come a great distance," Toomey pronounced.

"Why do you say so?" Gallagher replied.

"We have not had rain in a full week."

"I am afraid I do not discern your meaning."

"Your boots," the stableman pointed with a crooked finger. "Caked in mud. You must have been somewhere along the coast where it rained."

"I comprehend you now," answered the Constable. "Nay, I am from not but thirty miles toward Sheffield."

"And have you had rain in that direction?"

"Not recently, no. I had a walk through a rather damp wood yesterday."

"I see," Toomey answered. "It must have been some walk."

"Yes, indeed, and not for the pleasure of it, I can assure you."

Toomey laughed heartily and then coughed into his sleeve. "I have not seen boots that muddy in nearly a month!"

"Have you not?"

"No, sir. And I would remember such a time."

"Why is that?"

"The last time I laid eyes on boots in such a state was under very peculiar circumstances."

Gallagher took him gently by the elbow. "Peculiar—how so?"

"I rose at three-thirty in the morning, as is my custom, and began checking the stables and polishing saddles, when lo, with a great uproar, a carriage came thundering up the lane."

"A carriage?"

"Yes, sir. And a costly one at that."

"Please, go on."

"As I neared the front gate, the horses reared to a halt. The coachman dismounted, rounded the back, and opened a trunk. He approached me with two of the soggiest, muddiest boots I had ever laid mine eyes upon. Then, he offered them to me!"

"Do you have them?" Gallagher asked excitedly.

"Nay." The Constable let out a sigh. "Astonishing quality as they were—I most certainly have never seen a pair their equal in my lifetime—they were a bit too large for my frame, so I declined them." Gallagher groaned in displeasure.

"And what of the carriage—in which direction did it depart?"

"Off toward Pemberley," came the flat reply, crooked finger pointing the way.

"*Pemberley?*" Gallagher asked in astonishment.

"Aye, sir."

"The *Darcy* estate?"

"The very same."

"It was not Mr. Darcy's coachman, was it?"

"No, sir. In fact, it was not even one of the Darcy's coaches."

"Are you sure?"

"Positive, sir."

"How can you be positive?"

"There are not so many carriages in this part of the country, aside from Mr. Darcy's. Additionally, I have never met with that coachman before. Mr. Darcy's driver is Edward Dalton. He lives just up the lane."

"I see," Gallagher contemplated. "Is it possible that the driver went on to Pemberley directly?"

"I suppose it is possible, sir, but not likely," came the courteous reply.

"And why not?"

"The Darcys were all in London at the time. I doubt very highly a guest of such means would be staying at Pemberley in their absence."

"So, if not to Pemberley, where might they have gone?"

"To the seven seas and beyond, sir."

"I beg your pardon?"

"Headed in *that* direction," Toomey said, jabbing the air with his gnarled appendage, "a man could take a road to Manchester, Liverpool, Glasgow, Bristol, or anywhere in between." The lawman hung his head in disappointment at the impasse he had seemingly reached. "What's your horse's name?" asked the servant.

"Abacus," replied the Constable. "But he is not my property."

"What a shame—beautiful creature."

"That he is."

After a moment's silence, Toomey suddenly asked, "Would you like to see the boots?"

"Excuse me?"

"The boots—would you like to see them?"

"You have them? I thought you declined them?"

"The coachmen told me to give them away or dispose of them on his behalf. He said they belonged to his gentleman, but he had no further use of them, and wished not to weigh the carriage down—silly thought indeed!"

"What did you do with them?"

"Cleaned them up nicely and gave them to my son."

"And he has them?"

"Certainly. Wears them every day."

"And he lives *here*—in Lambton?"

"Aye, sir. He can bring them to you in the morning."

The Constable had a few pints inside before proceeding to his room for the night. He slept heavily in a serene medley of exhaustion and delighted inebriation.

CHAPTER TWELVE

IF KEEPING HIS SISTERS' prying eyes occupied was his aim in lavishing more attention on the eldest Miss Bennet than was at that point genuine—and it was—Bingley took to heart after several meetings that he could not have tasked himself with a more gratifying diversion. Each occasion in her presence granted him more and more pleasure and consequently, more regard for her. Jane was not, perhaps, as lively, or as quick-witted as her sister Elizabeth, but she was certainly a vast deal more level-headed than her puerile and callow youngest sisters. The eldest Miss Bennet was indeed pleasant, undoubtedly beautiful and, perhaps most importantly, she had a calming effect on his nerves. He had not yet the opportunity to spend hour upon hour in her presence, but when he found himself able to speak with her, detached from the prying ears of the rest of the party—whoever it might be—a sense of tranquillity flowed over him that allowed him, for that time at least, to be liberated from his more worldly troubles.

It was not, however, until the party at Lucas Lodge that he began to suspect that he had genuine feelings for her. Even if he was too cautious to believe himself in love, he found that he was not opposed to the idea altogether. At the same time, her countenance was so tranquil, that while she received his attentions most amiably, he felt that he could not be sure of her true affections. Was there, in fact, any sincere regard for him at all, or had she been acting on instructions from her mother to receive his addresses with civility in order to induce him toward matrimony? Mrs. Bennet was certainly a scheming, though somewhat comical, woman. Yet he believed her capable of influencing her daughter's affections—or at the least, her various charms—in his direction as the means of achieving an advantageous match.

The seeming indifference which Miss Elizabeth Bennet exhibited toward his friend, Mr. Darcy, caused him even more consternation. Bingley could not reconcile the courteous and agreeable reception his attentions received from Jane, with the aloofness with which Elizabeth treated Darcy, particularly if Mrs. Bennet was engaged in so directly prescribing the behaviour of her daughters. He could very well comprehend Mrs. Bennet's feeling slighted by Darcy's perceived lack of tactfulness. However, he could not reason that such meagre affronts to her sensibilities would utterly disrupt her stated—and quite publicly at that—purpose to see her daughters married and, expectantly, far above their situation. If Miss Elizabeth was indeed playing the role of the dutiful daughter as her elder sister might be, Bingley could imagine no slight—real or perceived—that Darcy could commit that might induce Mrs. Bennet to drop all designs on a man of his stature.

Even more mystifying, however, was the attention that Darcy had subtly begun to pay to Elizabeth. She was, to Bingley's eye, also remarkably handsome—and he told Darcy as much. Naturally then, he could not fault his friend for finding her so, as well. However, his concern emerged from his knowledge that his friend was far less likely than he to be taken in by the charms of a pretty young lady. Darcy was more resolute in his attachments, and most certainly more judicious in his consideration of a lady's situation and standing in the society in which they moved. While Bingley recognized his own proclivity to be swept under the buoyant current of enchantment and felicity, he believed that Darcy would more certainly retain his self-control with a mind to his duty as a son and an older brother.

That evening, after his sisters and Mr. Hurst had retired, he sat with his friend and a fine glass of brandy by the fire in the drawing room.

"Darcy, may I ask you a peculiar question?"

"Certainly."

"What is your sense of the eldest Miss Bennet?"

"Very handsome," Darcy stated. "Her manners are quite genteel—far more than her sisters or her mother."

"Yes, yes," stammered Bingley. "But more specifically, how do you perceive her attentions toward me?"

"Are you concerned that she may be developing an attachment?"

"I confess, there is certainly a part of me that thinks she may be growing fond of me."

"And you are concerned that your attentions may be perceived as a courtship?"

"Perhaps," answered Bingley.

"I would not profess to know the true feelings of a woman, particularly one with whom I am hardly acquainted, but I would caution you that to *use* her, whilst she might believe that you may actually be forming an attachment to her, for the sake of keeping your sisters unaware of your vocation, would be using her ill, indeed."

"I cannot argue on that point. However, I find there may also be another factor at play, and I cannot make it out."

"And what is that?"

"Is it possible that she only shows me the attention she does in order to please her mother?"

"That her mother is hoping you will fall in love with her?"

"Precisely."

"Miss Bennet does not strike me as guileful, but again, I cannot be the judge of her character without the benefit of being better acquainted."

"I agree with you," said Bingley. "Though it is difficult to be certain—she presents nothing in her countenance that suggests she is capable of deceit."

"From my vantage, Bingley, I will say, there does not currently seem to be a great affection in her demeanour toward you. She may receive your attentions with charm and civility, but at this time, I would not pronounce her as greatly attached to you."

"That is a comfort to hear," Bingley said circumspectly, a pang of regret at the very notion displaying itself in a small grimace at the corner of his mouth.

"Do you suspect yourself of forming an attachment on her?" Darcy suddenly asked.

Bingley hesitated, sipping his drink. "I cannot say with any degree of conviction," he finally answered. "She is undoubtedly the most handsome creature I have ever beheld, but more than her beauty, it is her serenity, or rather, the effect her serenity has had on me that gives me cause to ponder my own feelings."

"And what is the great effect that her demeanour has had on you?"

"In her presence, and in her presence alone, I seem able to be at peace with the world."

"Is that so?" Darcy asked with a hint of condescension in his voice.

"Yes, it is," Bingley replied. "There is not a moment of the day or night that I cease to cogitate on my plans. I am not at peace for a single minute—I cannot escape thoughts of the things I have seen and the things I must do, until I am with that dear girl. The anxiety, the nerves, my racing thoughts all seem to abate in the glow of her company. If *that*, my friend, is not a reason to fall in love with a person, what is?"

"I would caution you again, Bingley," Darcy started seriously. "Her family connections, her situation in life *must* factor into your feelings. She may indeed be guileless in her attentions toward you, but that does not mean she does not consider you to be a very eligible match for her, and indeed, you would be. She may be showing more affection than she feels with that design in mind."

"I would not pronounce that I am *in love* with her—"

"And I hope to not hear you say it."

There was then a stern silence in the room, save the crackling of the fire.

"As I stated before, on the day you decided to let this house," Darcy continued, "you must take as much consideration—*even more*, in fact—in the selection of a wife than you do of a familial estate. An estate will affect generations to come, most assuredly, but the choice of a wife of proper breeding and advantageous relations will put your family on a firm footing, and will greatly increase not only your fortune, but your influence."

"Your point is well taken, Darcy, but is a man's *felicity* in marriage not a matter of concern?"

"Of course, it is, but a man of your situation will not be happy with a wife whose condition in life is decidedly beneath his own."

"You seem quite certain on that point."

"In particular matters such as these, I am," answered Darcy. "It is best not to doubt the design of nature in these things. A man of consequence is suited for a fine horse and would not deign to ride into town on a donkey."

"And these ladies are but donkeys to you?"

"It is an inarticulate comparison, I freely grant you, but the analogy holds—a man must endeavour in matrimony to do himself and his family credit, and position in society certainly plays a role."

"That is very harsh, indeed," Bingley rebutted. "Especially when I believe I have detected a certain endearment on your part toward her younger sister, Miss Elizabeth."

"On that point I give you credit," Darcy replied flatly. "She is, indeed, very handsome... *her dark and fine eyes, particularly.* And her figure is light and pleasing on the eye... but I take great care in forming attractions and can assure you that I am of no mind to form one on her."

"Did I not, though, overhear you asking for her hand in a dance this very evening?"

"I do not wish to deny it," Darcy responded coolly. "Though you are obviously not aware of the circumstances."

"Enlighten me, then," Bingley quipped playfully.

"I asked for her hand after having it thrust in my direction by Sir William Lucas. I could see the uneasiness in her eyes after he dared to entreat us both when neither of us had to that point showed an inclination to dance. I acquiesced out of deference and politeness to her, and that is all."

"Though you would have danced with her?"

"I would have."

"In *that* room?"

"Do not assign feelings or motivations to me that I do not declare. I spoke truthfully when I said that I had no designs to dance this evening—with Miss Elizabeth Bennet or anyone else."

"Yet you nearly did," Bingley chuckled, taking a sip of his brandy.

"And she declined my hand," said Darcy. "It was, therefore, an acceptable result for us both."

"How so?"

"I behaved in a gentlemanlike manner, and yet, neither of us danced against our inclinations."

"And you did not feel slighted by her refusal?"

"Not in the least," Darcy answered calmly.

"Then I believe you may have feelings which you, yourself, may be unwilling to acknowledge," Bingley stated.

"I beg you not to tire me on the subject, Charles. I have been in the presence of Bennet girls all evening and am more disposed to be in your company at present."

Bingley watched the flickering flames in the hearth and sipped his brandy with a smile.

CHAPTER THIRTEEN

THE GOOD CONSTABLE MET Mr. Toomey's son the following morning and was able to secure the boots in question on a loan. They were in good condition still and had been meticulously cleaned. There was some wear, but given their rare quality and obvious expense, the cobbler-turned-policeman was satisfied that a positive identification as to their origins might yet be made. The leather was fine and the craftsmanship greater than any he had ever seen. Only a handful of men in England could afford boots of such quality, and he hoped deducing their origin might aide his quest to find the killer.

Small perpendicular etches on the underside of each sole caught his attention, and he hoped they would identify, at least, the shop in which they had been crafted, if not the signature of the boot maker himself. He left Lambton in the direction of his home in order to pack for a longer journey and to hire a coach. After two days' time, the Constable was headed in the direction of Manchester to query the boot makers there with hopes of identifying the origin of such exquisite boots. Upon his arrival, he sought out the best-known and most expensive shops in towns, but to no avail. Time after time, the boots were admired for their peculiar quality, but no shopkeeper or boot maker had ever seen their design before. He spent two full days attempting to ascertain anything which might be helpful but was rebuffed at every turn.

Having given up hope, he decided to return home to rethink his next options, and perhaps make plans to travel to London to continue his present line of inquiries. There was, however, a delay in his travels, as coming back through the village of Holly Springs, his coach was forced to a halt due to the collapse of the small wooden bridge which crossed the stream to the town's southwest. Being but ten miles from home, he ordered the driver to find an alternate route which took them out of the village to the north. However, Gallagher happened to glance up from his newspaper at precisely the moment he passed a small cobbler shop that he had never seen before. He ordered the driver to stop the coach. He introduced himself to the owner, a Scotsman by the name of William Dow who had recently moved his family from Glasgow, after inheriting a small house in the village from an uncle. He and his son had been employed in a cobbler shop in the city but took the opportunity to open their own shop there in Holly Springs.

"Fine boots," the Scot drawled. "Don't believe I have ever seen their equal."

"Neither have I," replied the Constable. "Do you have any thoughts as to their origin?"

Dow shrugged and scratched his red beard. "Could be French, perhaps."

"French?"

"Possibly. They are expensive, that's for sure."

"Could they be London-made, then?"

"'Tis a thought."

Just then, Dow's son Gregory entered the shop, carrying a bundle of bread under his arm.

"Boy, have a gander here," William said, while passing the boots on.

"Aye, would you look at those!" exclaimed he.

"Fine, are they not?"

"Finest boots mine eyes have ever beheld—except for that one time in York," Gregory added.

"York?" the father asked.

"Aye—remember when old man Logan sent me down there to pay what he owed to that specialty tanner in the Shambles?"

"Aye, I recall it."

"Well, I stopped in a shop in that street and met a man that crafted the finest boots in all the kingdom, I might say," said the son, turning one of the boots in his hand and eyeing it carefully.

"Were they similar in make?" the Constable queried.

"Very similar," Gregory replied. "And ah, yes—there is his mark!"

The young man pointed to the small etchings on the sole.

"Are you quite serious?" Gallagher asked, bewildered. "Those are the marks of a boot maker in *York*?"

"Undoubtedly. These shoes bear the workmanship and the signature of Xavier Prichard, the finest boot maker I've ever met." Gallagher left the town with the name of the shop in York, thankful that a trip all the way to London would not be necessary.

PART II

CHAPTER FOURTEEN

"SHE ARRIVED ON *HORSEBACK*?" Bingley asked, incredulous.

"We could not have been more surprised, ourselves," Caroline answered, taking her place across from Darcy on the settee in the drawing room.

"There was rain for nearly six straight hours," said Bingley, while uneasily stirring the burning timber in the fireplace.

"She was thoroughly sodden when she arrived," Louisa interjected. "We were quite taken aback by her appearance, although to her credit, she displayed some degree of poise in attempting to gather herself."

"She did indeed," Caroline continued. "However, by tea it was quite clear that she had taken ill."

Bingley looked toward Darcy worriedly; his friend returned his glance with a concerned sigh.

"Mr. Jones has seen to her, Bingley," Darcy began. "Every attention is being paid to her. Most likely, she caught a chill and will be mended in the morning after being allowed to rest."

"I certainly hope so."

Bingley thought his sisters might be alarmed by the level of concern he showed for Jane's illness, and then realized that he had not feigned concern whatsoever. In his genuine anguish over the health of the eldest Miss Bennet, he again began to suspect that he was developing feelings toward her that might soon grow beyond his control. Oddly enough, he had no wish to curtail them, either.

"How did you enjoy dinner with the officers?" Louisa inquired suddenly, as if to change the subject.

"Fine enough," her brother replied.

"And Mr. Darcy—did *you* enjoy the company this evening?" Caroline asked, leaning forward in his direction.

"I would hesitantly say it was among the finest society I have experienced since our arrival," he answered flatly. "Colonel Forster, particularly, is a pleasant and agreeable man. Would you agree, Bingley?"

"Yes, indeed," came the haphazard reply.

"Certainly, the company of regimental officers could not hold a flame to the lofty society of *Lucas Lodge*," the younger Miss Bingley teased. Darcy raised a brow and cocked his head toward her. Caroline leaned back and snickered under her breath.

The following morning, to the shock of the entire party, Elizabeth Bennet was announced in the breakfast parlour, having received word at Longbourne that Jane had fallen ill. Elizabeth was vexed by her sister's absence from breakfast, as it served as a poor augur of her state of health.

"Miss Elizabeth," Darcy murmured in surprise, as all three gentlemen stood in her presence, Mr. Hurst most unwillingly, a piece of ham dangling from his mouth.

She curtsied and replied, "Thank you all for your kindness in receiving me and for your attentions to my sister. May I inquire after her condition this morning?"

"Unfortunately," Bingley began with genuine concern, "she is a great deal unwell. I am afraid she slept very ill."

Darcy watched Elizabeth and was struck by the handsome ruddiness of her complexion, having walked several miles at a quick pace.

"She is awake, but quite feverish," said Caroline.

"Sister," Bingley called, "would you be so kind as to take Miss Elizabeth to Miss Bennet—unless of course you would like something to eat first?"

"No, I thank you," answered Elizabeth. "I would be exceedingly grateful to be taken to her at once."

"Of course," replied Bingley, motioning toward his sister. Caroline tepidly stood from the table and led the way toward Jane's room.

Elizabeth spent the better part of the day with her sister. Miss Bingley and Mrs. Hurst for their part, dutifully paid the occasional visit to the room, but spent the majority of the day japanning and speaking French to each other. Mr. Hurst silently brooded by the window, thinking damnable thoughts about the French, brought on by he could not imagine what. Bingley paced from room to room, occasionally picking up a book, only to throw it down disinterestedly after reading but a few lines. Darcy observed this, thinking his friend's concern for the eldest Miss Bennet had moved past feigning mild attraction in a direction which could not be suitable for a man of his position. Bingley's sisters were not nescient to their brother's demeanour either and, being ignorant of his plan to use Jane as a ruse against them, drew much the same conclusion as Darcy.

What each of them utterly failed to notice was Mr. Darcy's unrest. He sat going over ledgers for his business ventures but was distracted enough by the competing sensations of weightlessness and heaviness which he had been experiencing since the unexpected appearance of Elizabeth Bennet that morning, that he struggled to perform basic arithmetic, often arriving at sums that made him either far richer or far poorer than his true circumstance. Indeed, he blotted out several calculations altogether, and did his best to conceal his discomposure. When it was announced that Elizabeth would stay the evening, he was at once concerned for her sister's wellbeing, and oddly delighted that he would be granted the occasion to dine with her.

CHAPTER FIFTEEN

WHEN THE LADIES ENTERED the dining room, Bingley immediately inquired after Jane's condition. His expressions morphed from an expectant smile to a distressed grimace upon learning that she was still, indeed, quite infirm. He was adamant that she would continue to receive the highest levels of attention, and that Elizabeth should not hesitate to allow him the honour of every courtesy he might bestow, in the case that she, herself, might require anything at all. His sisters may have echoed their brother's generosity several times over, at Miss Bennet's unrelenting ill health. However, once they had, to their minds, discharged their duty of the barest civility, Mrs. Hurst and Miss Bingley were quickly onto other subjects, without any continued regard for Elizabeth, or her ailing sister.

Lizzy was sat next to Mr. Hurst and immediately became aware he had been drinking for several hours at least and was more than a trifle disguised. Several fine courses were served, and when she quietly declared that she preferred a more plain dish to the ragout that was served, he announced that he would have nothing more to say to her during the course of the meal. Miss Elizabeth, upon hearing his bellicose pronouncement, thought she might have won a small victory in having to endure Mr. Hurst's conversation no longer. Between his stupor and impertinence, the pretentious declarations of the sisters on many a subject, and her concern for her own dear sister, Elizabeth also failed to notice the modest, but intentional, attentions Mr. Darcy paid her. Bingley, on the other hand, could not help but regard his friend's absorption with the younger Miss Bennet. He began to consider that Darcy's feelings toward Elizabeth might be also growing, in spite of his friend's ambition to temper them.

After dinner, Elizabeth immediately returned to her sister, and directly the well-documented abuse of her by Louisa and Caroline commenced. Somewhere between playing the part of starry-eyed lover and his actual feelings, Bingley heard himself, to his own astonishment declare, "If they had uncles to fill *all* Cheapside, it would not make them one jot less agreeable." Given his belief about Darcy's own growing infatuation with Elizabeth, and after hearing him so compliment her "fine eyes" having been "brightened by the exercise" of her long walk to Netherfield, Bingley was equally shocked to hear him declare so callously in reply: "But it must very materially lessen their chance of marrying men of any consideration in the world." Bingley was aghast enough at the fervour of Darcy's proclamation as to make no reply himself. His sisters took the opportunity to heap praise upon Darcy for his steadfast temperament and affirmed his statement with verve. They then made it their sport to make levity in mocking the relations of the Bennet sisters, one of whom was, by their own admission, a *dear friend* to them both. Bingley could not make out how much was an act on their part—an attempt to dissuade him from any earnest pursuit in the direction of Jane—and how much was the ugly flaw of their own conceited vanity.

When Elizabeth returned to the room, the entire party was at loo. Although it vexed him to learn of Jane's continued discomfort, Bingley was relieved to hear that she was finally sleeping peacefully. The night continued with conversation back and forth—his own sisters attempting to assert their superiority over the Bennet sisters under the cloak of breeding and manners, while simultaneously tossing themselves embarrassingly in Mr. Darcy's path. Then there were Darcy's backhanded compliments of Elizabeth, particularly after she quit the room to attend once more to Jane. By all this Bingley was agitated, and only more so to learn as the evening went on that the eldest Miss Bennet's condition had continued to deteriorate. It was decided that an express would be sent to town to fetch a renowned doctor, and that Mr. Jones, the apothecary, would be sent for at first light if Jane's illness had not markedly improved. At this moment, Mr. Bingley experienced a sudden disquietude—he had not considered the possibility that Jane might actually be in some danger. His sisters sang duets to pass the time while he added order upon order to his housekeeper that every possible attention be paid to the sick lady and her sister.

The next days passed in a famous manner. The household welcomed Mrs. Bennet and the remainder of her daughters, of which many remarks were made once they had departed. Bingley could not fathom the genteel and polite manners of the eldest Miss Bennet, in comparison with her mother and younger siblings, save Elizabeth, who due to her devotion to Jane and her lively disposition, he had come to greatly admire. He admitted to her mother that he felt quite settled at Netherfield presently but was plain in his admission that if he were to quit the place, he would most likely do so suddenly. He had particular business dealings in mind when he said this, having heard from his steward Mr. Wilshere, just that morning, that Lord Bertram St. John, the prime object of his work, was in the process of preparing a trip abroad. Bingley had in the meantime, however, promised a ball at Netherfield, much to the distaste of his sisters.

When Jane was finally well enough to join them in the drawing room, Bingley could scarce contain his delight. He had not laid eyes upon her in less than a fortnight, yet he found his remembrance sorely lacking in comparison to her beauty at present. He stoked the fire over and over and removed her to the side of it away from the door that she might be warm, and also, to some extent, out of earshot of his sisters. Her grace and her charm were not lost on him, and within but a few moments, he had ceased to remember that there was anyone else but her in the world, let alone the room. He slept that evening without anxiety, without thoughts of panic or guilt or the gravity of his mission in ending a barbaric crime against humanity. For the first night in many, he did not hear the screams of his victims or theirs in his dreams—he only felt the serene aura of Jane Bennet.

CHAPTER SIXTEEN

THE NEXT FEW DAYS he endured in torment. Once the Bennet sisters departed Netherfield for Longbourn, Bingley found himself afloat in a deluge of pompous insinuations about the entire family, all accompanied by absurd and two-faced declarations from his sisters of Jane Bennet's sweetness and their mutual desire to know her better. He also observed Darcy to be restless, which was quite unusual. Bingley could not quite apprehend where his friend stood regarding Eliza Bennet, but he was certain that there was something more than met the eye. He was keen to notice, over those few days, his sister Caroline's undivided attention to Darcy, and her frequent comments disparaging Elizabeth's relations, or lack thereof, undoubtedly with the intention of calling his admiration from the younger Miss Bennet, and onto herself.

In addition to all this, news continued to pour in about Lord Bertram St. John's imminent departure for the continent, and all in a jumbled and seemingly hurried manner. Bingley wondered if the deaths of Sir Andrew Fraser and Thomas Abbott had rattled the ringleader's cage. He was not opposed to the object of his plot living for some time in fear, but he felt he himself could not bear a prolonged resolution to this nasty business. For all Bingley knew, St. John was traveling in an effort to reorganize, or perhaps even expand, his devilish operation. There was no further word from his steward's network of contacts regarding George Wickham's involvement, nor was there any word regarding even his whereabouts, other than a report that he had recently enlisted in the militia. He was careful not to share such news with his confidant, Darcy as even though Bingley had never personally met Mr. Wickham, he was fully aware of the strength of his friend's feelings toward him, specifically regarding the infamously foiled plot to ruin Darcy's sister, Georgiana. He did not want to muddle Darcy's mind with such details until Wickham's involvement in the sinister business was incontrovertible.

Even more upsetting to him was learning from Mr. Wilshere of another young girl of not sixteen gone missing from her home in Birmingham under the guise of an elopement, only to be found deceased on the rocks in Southampton. The details of this incident fit the pattern that Bingley had unintentionally uncovered and was so fixated to stop—young maidens from poor families gone missing with a handsome young gentleman, only to be found murdered several days later in some far flung part of the country. The latest young victim's name was Letitia Yates. Her father was a chimney sweep and her mother had died of typhus when she was but twelve, leaving Letitia to care for her five smaller siblings. The particulars of her attachment to the handsome young man with whom she fled were murky, but he was said to be rather charming, and promised her a great fortune and a life abroad. Her broken body was discovered by a boy and his dog walking along the shore.

Over three nights these factors caused Bingley to sleep but nine hours. He felt guilt at not having done more and sooner, to curtail such evil occurring right under the noses of Britain's most powerful men—or, as daunting as it was to imagine, with their direct entanglement. That was why, on the fourth day since the Bennet girls had departed Netherfield, he persuaded Darcy to accompany him to Longbourn to call upon Jane and enquire after her health. He had again been pressed by his sister to take Mr. Hurst, but they had been unsuccessful in multiple attempts to rouse him from his slumber.

The two gentlemen rode at a leisurely pace, enjoying the unseasonable warmth of the sunlight that afternoon. When they entered Meryton, they crossed the central lane where they were surprised to come across a group of redcoats conversing with every Bennet sister, save Mary. There was also in their company a rather swarthy and dour-looking young man who stood near Elizabeth. Bingley went directly toward them and dismounted before bowing and commencing his usual and enthusiastic civilities. Darcy remained astride his horse and greeted them but said very little otherwise.

"And how, Miss Bennet, is your health?" Bingley beamed.

"Much improved, I thank you," Jane answered.

"I very am glad to hear it," he said with a radiant smile.

She smiled back at him and that sensation of light-heartedness and tranquillity which had been so lacking in his mind the previous days washed over him. He nearly forgot completely that her sisters, another gentleman, and several officers were standing about. After a minute of continued inquiries after Jane's health and assurances of his happiness in her recovery, he observed a look of confusion on the face of Elizabeth, who was doing what she could to avoid glancing in the direction of Darcy. Bingley took his leave quickly and rode on with his friend.

"Very good to see her so well recovered, I dare say," stated Bingley gleefully as they turned in the direction of the glade outside Netherfield Park. "She looked very well indeed."

Darcy hardly acknowledged his friend's comments and when Bingley glanced over at him, he saw Darcy's face was ashen. His teeth were clenched together, and his brow was furrowed most fiercely.

"Darcy, what on earth is the matter?"

"It is nothing of consequence," answered Darcy decisively.

"How can you say so? There is obviously something amiss."

The two riders slowed their horses to a halt. The sun was beginning to set over the ridge, bathing Netherfield Park in a golden late autumn dusk. The temperature was also noticeably dropping with the ebbing of the day.

"You must tell me," Bingley appealed. "Are you unwell?"

"I am quite well physically," Darcy replied through deep breaths.

"Then what can it be?"

"That man in Meryton, with the Bennet sisters—"

"The youngish, surly one?"

"No, no—the one who stood with the officers."

"I did not see a man with them," answered Bingley.

"You were too engaged with Miss Bennet to notice."

"What about him?—Was he rude or vulgar toward you?"

"Not just then," Darcy replied, squeezing the horse's reigns with a finely gloved hand.

"I do not follow—"

"It was George Wickham," Darcy blurted.

"George Wickham? What on earth is he doing in Meryton?" Bingley inquired.

"I had heard that he enlisted in the militia—"

"Was he wearing regimentals?"

"No," answered Darcy. "But I have been told that he meant to seek a commission, although I assumed it would have been with a company in the north."

"Perhaps he is only visiting in Meryton?"

"I would doubt that very much," said Darcy flatly. "From what I understand, he owes debts everywhere he has been. Moreover, he is not the type of man who would be content in the country if he could lead a life of dissolution in town—there are far more opportunities for debauchery and gambling there. I cannot see a reason for him to be anywhere near this place unless, of course, he has secured a commission in Colonel Forster's regiment."

Bingley felt uneasy for his friend but was himself vexed by the presence of Mr. Wickham, the fourth potential perpetrator in the malevolent plot he had uncovered, now right under his nose. His thoughts then drifted to the upcoming social engagement of the ball he had offered at Netherfield Park. "Darcy, the ball—"

"What of it?"

"I invited the entirety of the regimental officers. If he has obtained a commission, he has obtained an invitation to the ball." Darcy stared sedately at the pink and orange and the wispy clouds above the house and said nothing. "Shall I renege the invitation?" Bingley inquired.

"I would not dare ask you to act with incivility on my behalf."

"What then? Will he attend, do you think?"

"I cannot say with any measure of certainty," Darcy answered, looking his friend in the eye. "His actions have, doubtlessly, shocked me in the past, but it is not for me to be driven away by Mr. Wickham. If he wishes to avoid seeing *me*, then *he* must go."

"It is settled, then?"

Darcy nodded. "Back to the house, shall we?"

The two friends rode off toward Netherfield Park in the last rays of twilight, both troubled by the unanticipated arrival of Mr. Wickham, though for vastly dissimilar reasons. Darcy hoped that he might have never seen that man again, whilst Bingley had hoped that he might not have to kill him in such close proximity to his friend. This would certainly raise Darcy's suspicions that Bingley's mission was more driven by personal factors than by an appeal to justice, which had hitherto gone unanswered. Wickham's involvement in the ongoing and organized crimes was also, still in doubt, to some extent—at least to Bingley's mind. In the ten minutes of silence that accompanied the conclusion of their ride back to the stable, Bingley decided that judgement would have to be withheld on the Wickham subject. At least for the time being, he would do what he could to avoid the problematic young man's company, and certainly to keep him from Darcy's attention, as difficult a task as that might be. After all, he thought, Lord Bertram St. John was the remaining leading figure in the design, and perhaps *the* leading figure—therefore, eliminating him must be the first priority. If, indeed, George Wickham was involved, it must have been at a very low level. And if St. John was departed from the earth, he reasoned, the whole nefarious machination would fall in on itself.

CHAPTER SEVENTEEN

THE EVENING OF THE ball had arrived. Bingley took more care than usual in dressing, issuing rigorous orders to his valet and footman regarding the manner of his pantaloons and tailcoat. He made his valet, who was quite skilled indeed, untie, disentangle, and retie his cravat at least six times in order to have it perfectly knotted. A man of fashion as he was, the particular precision with which the master directed them this particular evening was something of a shock to those who normally dressed him. As he brushed the lint from his master's shoulders, the footman shot quizzical glances toward the valet, who was having none of it. Just as he was buttoning the front of his lawn shirt, Mr. Wilshere entered quietly.

"Wilshere," Bingley began in exasperation, "if you're not going to give me good news, for the love of all things sacred, please do not say anything at all."

"Pardon me, sir?" the steward stuttered.

Bingley waived the valet and the footman off and turned to face his steward. He brushed the front of his pantaloons with both hands, then looked up. "This is destined to be a night of revelry, jubilance, and dancing with the prettiest girl I have ever laid mine eyes upon—grant me the consideration of not laying waste to it with bad news before it has even begun." Wilshere looked directly at him and held his tongue. "Well man, you have come all this way," spoke Bingley with a frustrated wave of his freshly manicured hand. "And now you stand there like a figure in marble. Tell me."

"His voyage is delayed," replied Wilshere flatly.

"Delayed?" The steward nodded. "Well, that's fantastic news!"

"It is indeed," commented Wilshere. "A storm in the Celtic Sea is headed toward the Channel. Too unpredictable for private charters. Looks as though he might be delayed in Brighton a week."

"If you weren't my man, I would kiss you, Wilshere!" Bingley declared.

"Thank you, sir," came the adroit response. "There is one more detail which might further amplify your delight."

"Do tell."

"I have it from Colonel Forster's man that Mr. Wickham has been detained by business in London."

"Fine news indeed, Wilshere! This puts a real spring in my step," the master said, glancing at himself one last time in the mirror and smoothing out a few curly locks, "and I hope to use it to full effect!"

With that, Bingley flashed his grand smile and passed by Wilshere, who bowed, and out into the hall. He hurried down and through the gallery into the ballroom, directing servants thither and fro with a meticulous eye. He passed through the dining room and the stag parlour into the drawing room. His staff had done fine work preparing for the ball, but little things such as a curtain askew or a crooked vase caught his regardful eye on this particular evening. He snapped his fingers toward housemaids and footmen alike, pointing out minuscule flaws in each room that were apparently in urgent need of correction.

What might have set Bingley apart from young men of his age and situation, among other things, was that he did all these things with great cheer. No servants were berated; no abuses were shouted. In fact, on this night in particular, he felt like he floated through the house two feet off the ground. Nothing could scuttle his sunny disposition at that moment, which would explain why, although perhaps he should have expected nothing else, he was taken aback by the look of agitated complacency on the face of his friend whom he happened upon in the library.

"Darcy," started Bingley, "whatever is the matter *now*?"

His friend looked up from his fingernails. "You know I take little pleasure in balls."

"There are many things from which you derive little pleasure," Bingley countered.

"Bingley, you have been aware of my view on such matters for some time," replied Darcy. "I am quite surprised that my disposition seems to constantly take you by surprise."

"I am not surprised, *per se*, but I find myself, at the moment, in such a grand state of suspense over this evening, and your sulkiness tempts me toward melancholy."

"I would never wish it," Darcy answered. "You must not allow your mood or your enjoyment to be tempered by mine."

"It hardly is," quipped Bingley. "But it is difficult to have a friend who takes no pleasure in the very things by which I am so excessively diverted."

"You do not wish me to be here, then?"

"Of *course,* I do. What I wish is that you would allow *yourself* some diversion."

Darcy smiled wryly. "I cede your point."

"Plus," Bingley began, "I have some news which might lighten your mood."

"Go on, then."

"Mr. Wickham will not be in attendance tonight," Bingley stated with glee. Darcy drew in deep breath and managed a half-smile. "Does even this not invigorate you?"

"To be frank," Darcy said slowly. "I had not even thought of him. My mind had been more agreeably preoccupied."

"Well, you may put him out of your mind once more. The coward has fled the scene of battle."

Just then, Mr. West, the butler, entered to announce that the first invitees had arrived.

"I must go down to greet my guests," Bingley said with delight.

"Of course, you must," responded Darcy. "Take heart, Bingley—I am resigned that for *your* satisfaction, I will endeavour to derive some pleasure from this evening." Bingley smiled broadly, thoughts and heart racing alike. Darcy, for his part, had only one thing on his mind at that moment—the fine eyes of Miss Elizabeth Bennet.

CHAPTER EIGHTEEN

THE BENNETS KEPT HIM waiting in anguish for nearly an hour. Bingley greeted each guest who entered, from the Lucas family to Colonel and Mrs. Forster to the Robinsons, all with great mirth and civility, and all the while watching the door for the arrival of Jane. When at last they were announced, he had trouble concealing his delight, for Miss Bennet was more dazzling than he could have ever dreamed. After greeting her parents with delightful regard—and being accosted by the perpetual cordiality of Mr. Collins, who he recognized as the swarthy young man who had accompanied the sisters in the village—he took Jane's arm and led her toward the ballroom, leaving his sisters and Mr. Hurst to receive all who entered thereafter.

"Good evening," was all he managed.

"Good evening," she answered with a smile as sweet as honey.

After several dances spent in pleasant conversation and rapt attention to the grace of her movement, they sat and drank punch together. "It appears that your sister has drawn the attention of your cousin," he remarked under his breath, with a glance toward Mr. Collins.

"Oh," Jane answered with a chuckle, "to her mortification, it seems that she has. I must thank you for extending an invitation to him."

"Naturally," said Bingley. "A relation of yours must always be welcome."

She then looked up across the room and caught Lizzie's disenchanted glance and a quick shake of her head. Jane had hoped that her sister's burden of Mr. Collins's attention would be eased by the prospect of dancing with Mr. Wickham, but it appeared that he had, perhaps, not been invited, but certainly was not in attendance. In the midst of her delight in Mr. Bingley's presence, she wondered if she might not take an opportunity to, perhaps, alleviate Lizzie's curiosity.

"I do believe my sister is more presently and agreeably diverted by the attentions of another," said Jane with a smile.

"You do?" Bingley looked up only to see Elizabeth with Charlotte Lucas.

"I do not mean at this present moment," Jane clarified. "We met the most delightful young man in town on the same day that you happened upon us. He is a recent addition to Colonel Forster's regiment."

"I see," he replied with delight.

"Are you at all acquainted with George Wickham?"

"Is he here?" he asked with sudden agitation. His eyes searched the room, only to be drawn to the shocking sight of Mr. Darcy querying for the hand of Miss Elizabeth Bennet.

"No—at least I do not believe so."

"Oh," was all he could muster.

"Did you expect him?"

"He was attached to the invitation of all the officers," he answered with slight hesitation.

"Then you have met him?"

"No, in fact," answered he, "the only time I have ever seen him was in Meryton just the other day."

"Have you any idea what kind of man he is?"

He took a sip of punch and mulled over his thoughts. He certainly wished to put any of the Bennet girls off the trail of Mr. Wickham, but he also baulked at the thought of coming across too strongly on the subject, as he had already conceded not knowing the man in question. He thought, perhaps, giving an inclination of his dastardly character on the basis of Darcy's late interaction with him might serve his purpose with a balance of delicacy and forthrightness.

"I would not wish you to believe me to speak ill of a man with whom I am not acquainted," he started, checking her face for a signal, "but I would think myself less than dutiful not to caution you in regard Mr. Wickham's character."

Jane looked stunned for a moment before regaining her composure. A couple passed by them and nodded politely. Jane and Bingley smiled back in their direction as they passed.

"What kind of man is he?" asked she, when she was sure there was no one within direct earshot of their conversation.

"I am afraid that I have not the particulars of the circumstances," he began. "He grew up at Pemberley, my dear friend Darcy's estate—"

"Of this I am recently aware," she injected.

"Yes, well, it is my understanding that Mr. Wickham treated Mr. Darcy in an egregious manner. For his part, Mr. Darcy's actions in the matter were irreproachable."

"I would not consider anything else of Mr. Darcy, being that he is a dear friend of yours. But the incident you speak of was more than a mere misunderstanding?"

"I dare say it was rather a... *pattern* of behaviour," Bingley answered.

"Shocking!" Jane replied quietly. "And it is your opinion that Mr. Darcy was within his rights to revoke the living that had been promised to Mr. Wickham?"

"I confess, I am not privy to the exact circumstances which caused their falling out, but to my knowledge, the living left by the late Mr. Darcy to Mr. Wickham was conditional."

"And Mr. Wickham did not meet those conditions?"

"I am afraid not." He thought perchance he had spoken too definitively on the subject and sought to reel his declarations back slightly. "I fear demeaning a man's character without first-hand knowledge of the events—"

"You are very agreeable, Mr. Bingley," she said suddenly, catching herself as soon as the words left her mouth. He looked up at her and beamed. "What I mean is that, you are very sensible to both the feelings and reputation of others. It is a very respectable trait."

"Why, I thank you."

She smiled and blushed, feeling that she, herself, had said too much.

"You find the good in men and are content not to demean or cause harm unduly."

"But if there was no good to be found," replied Bingley slowly, searching her eyes, "you would not have it that I would settle."

"Do you speak of Mr. Wickham?"

"No—" he stammered. "But *if* a man was truly vile, you would not think well of me to overlook his character."

"Of course not," she answered. "But I am afraid I do not grasp your meaning."

"I admit, I struggle to make sense of it myself." The master of ceremonies gave the order for the cotillion, so Bingley stood and offered his hand, again, to Miss Bennet. "I mean to say that," he began again, "if I were witness to a truly evil act, you would not wish me to stand idly by, even if a response would be... *disadvantageous*?"

"On the contrary, I would think less of a man who did not act in response to evil," she responded slowly as she rose to her feet.

"Even if that response required what would normally be reprehensible conduct?"

"If the evil was so egregious as to require such reprisal from a man of character, then I would be inclined to respect him all the more. A man who would not act on behalf of good would not be worthy of much regard." He smiled and heaved a sigh of relief as they crossed the room, speaking softly to one another. "May I ask," she began, "to what does all this refer?"

"One day, Miss Bennet, I should very much like to tell you," he answered quietly.

"You must at least satisfy me that this line of inquest has not the least to do with Mr. Wickham," she posed.

"No, of course not. My musings are merely philosophical in nature, I suppose," he answered with some discomfort. He hoped beyond hope that his response would not prove to be a lie. Bingley found relief, however, in her reply to his question—certainly his mission might be viewed as a just one in light of the circumstances.

They took their places in the dance line. It was only then when he noticed Darcy standing across from Miss Elizabeth Bennet. The guileless smile for which Bingley had gained much local notoriety reappeared on his face, due to both of these happy developments, as he saw them. They danced two more dances before he felt obliged to ask for the hands of other young ladies, though he took relatively no pleasure in dancing with them after Jane. He certainly took no pleasure in seeing her dance with other gentlemen. He was jubilant, however, to stand with Jane for the final dance of the evening, just before dinner was served.

CHAPTER NINETEEN

Breakfast at Netherfield was held even later than usual the morning following the ball. The household and its guests were exhausted and somewhat traumatized by the evening, although it is safe to conclude that Mr. Bingley was significantly less traumatized than his sisters. The house servants were grateful for the reprieve, as they were afforded a whole extra hour of sleep after several days of preparations for the event, and a night of cleaning and restoring the house to its proper condition. In recognition of their fine and resolute work, Mr. Bingley had been sure to send the leftover food and wine down to the servants' quarters as a token of appreciation.

When breakfast was served, only Bingley and his sisters were present. Mr. Hurst had been peculiarly jug-bitten the preceding evening, and was not in any condition to be seen, let alone decamp from his bed. Mr. Darcy's truancy, on the other hand, was certainly a bit more remarkable.

"The evening seems to have got the better of our friend, Mr. Darcy," Mrs. Hurst jested while buttering a hot roll.

"I dare say it did, Louisa," answered Miss Bingley, "And he was not even half-sprung by the end of it." The two sisters giggled in unison.

"Might he be unwell?" Bingley asked guilelessly.

"Oh, brother, I would not think so," Louisa answered. "Though I believe you might have been more pleasantly distracted than the rest of us by the manners of certain number of our guests."

"I was not ignorant of what we might consider to be certain *faux-pas* that may have occurred. You must remember, there is a distinction between country manners—"

"Barnyard manners, you mean," Mrs. Hurst cut in. Bingley frowned and laid his silverware down.

"Ill-breeding, I would argue," Caroline added.

"Well, you will have to argue it until you're blue in the face," Bingley declared, "because to my sensibilities, the entire evening was exceedingly merry."

The sisters glanced at each other and then thought the better of continuing their scarcely disguised line of attack on the Bennet family. Their point had been made, surely, and more would no doubt be said on the matter at a later time. Caroline thought she might diffuse the situation by sending for Darcy's valet to check on his condition. Louisa took the opportunity to have hot chocolate and rolls sent up to her husband's room. The three siblings ate in relative silence until Ridley, the footman, entered once more to inform them that Mr. Darcy was not in his room.

"Not in his room?" Bingley inquired.

"No, sir," replied Ridley. "Mr. Perry advised me that Mr. Darcy did not *go* to bed, but rather, lingered in the library until dawn, whereupon he asked for his coat and went out walking."

"Walking?" Louisa cried. "*At dawn?*"

"Yes, ma'am," the footman answered.

"Very peculiar, indeed," whispered Caroline.

"*Poor* Mr. Darcy," Louisa continued, "the fiasco of last night must have impacted him greatly."

"Yes," her sister answered, "he must be excessively unnerved."

Neither Bingley nor his sisters were of the mind to mention what they were all thinking—that Mr. Darcy was thoroughly smitten by Miss Elizabeth Bennet. The brother reflected upon the thought with a contented smile, the sisters, with affrighted disbelief.

Just then, Darcy himself entered the drawing room looking dapper and sanguine. His appearance was both a shock and a comfort to Louisa and Caroline. For his part, Darcy bowed slightly in their direction, then set about arranging his plate with French bread and boiled eggs, before calling politely for tea. He sat next Bingley, who grinned as he wiped the corners of his mouth with a napkin.

"Mr. Darcy," Mrs. Hurst uttered. He looked up from his plate at her and smiled. "Good morning," she mumbled after an awkward moment.

"Good morning to you, as well," he responded amiably.

"Are you quite well?" Caroline queried.

"Most assuredly. Perhaps a bit fagged, but that is all," he quipped. The sisters glared at each other in disbelief. They had never heard him utter such a low word.

"We heard from your valet that you did not sleep," stated Louisa.

"He spoke truly," answered Darcy after chewing a bite.

"But you were not unwell?" Louisa asked slowly, her mind unable to process the near absurdity of this normally rational and habitual gentleman.

"I assure you I am perfectly well. These weeks in the country have granted me, perhaps, more tranquillity than I have been lately accustomed to. Yesterday evening was a fine gathering, certain social blunders notwithstanding, but it excited me more than I may have given it credit. The thought of sleep was dreary in comparison to the music in my mind, and when the sun began to rise, the notion of absorbing its rays seemed marvellous. The woods were quite enchanting this morning."

With that declaration, he nodded again and with an affable smile, resumed his breakfast. Bingley and his sisters glared at him with such astonished silence, frozen in place like Grecian sculptures, until the fork unwittingly fell from Caroline's hand. The sound of silver clattering on porcelain roused them all back into reality but did not inspire a resumption in conversation.

When the meal was over, the ladies retired to their separate parlour to continue working on the screen they had begun previously, while the two gentlemen were left in the drawing room. Darcy had his ledger brought in and began energetically poring over his accounts. Bingley sat with a book in hand, watching him the entire time. Once or twice, his friend would look up from his journal and make eye contact with Bingley, as if he felt he was being watched. The two would smile and nod at each other and then go right back to their tasks with rigid interest—actual or feigned. Eventually, Bingley could hold his tongue no longer: "What on earth has gotten into you?"

Mr. Darcy finished a calculation and jotted some quick notes before making his response. "I gather you mean to inquire after my quite unusual behaviour."

"*Bizarre* behaviour, yes."

"I do admit, it has been many years since I have spent a sleepless night with no physical ailment to hinder my repose."

"Then what is the matter?"

"Can you not guess it?"

Bingley thought for a moment, when an idea so simple that it seems preposterous popped into his mind. "You're in love, aren't you?"

Darcy smiled. "Not *in love*—I do not regard myself quite so imprudent. However, you are correct in a sense, and I have no shame in admitting it to a friend such as you—I have taken *quite* the fancy to Miss Elizabeth Bennet."

"You *are* in love, Darcy," Bingley exclaimed. "You are simply so rigidly pragmatic that you do not know what to call it."

"*Bingley*," Darcy began calmly, "I am honest enough with myself to acknowledge my own feelings. I have, no doubt, been *smitten* by Miss Elizabeth Bennet—her eyes, her vigour, her intelligence—however, I must square my feelings with the reality of my situation, and hers."

"I do not follow your meaning."

"We have been over this several times—her connections, or lack thereof, her—"

"Yes, yes," Bingley interjected, annoyed at having to broach the old and familiar subject again. "But if you *love* her, Darcy—"

"Even if I did, and I contest that I do not, it seems to me that a recent development has settled the question entirely."

"What—Mr. Wickham?"

"No, Bingley," answered Darcy. "*Mr. Collins.*"

"The vicar?" Bingley demanded. "The obsequious—" he struggled for a word—"unctuous, little man—"

"Bingley," Darcy cut in with a near-chuckle, "do not tell you me you were so enamoured by the eldest Miss Bennet that you failed to notice the attention that Mr. Collins paid to Miss Elizabeth Bennet?"

"It did not fully escape my notice, no."

"And you, no doubt, can easily guess the intention of his particular fawning over her?"

"You don't think—"

"It is an eligible match for both of them," remarked Darcy casually. Bingley felt slightly piqued at the thought. "Bingley, look," Darcy stood and walked to the mantle. "I admit to you freely that I was quite enamoured with Miss Elizabeth. In fact, those feelings, and the violence with which my rational intellect assaulted them, were the reason I could not go to bed last night. I felt more comfortable pacing the library than I would rolling around in bed, wrestling between my feelings and my better judgement. Now, mind you, I am of firm enough resolve, as I hope you would expect, to never act on such flighty and spontaneous sentiments, but they would have to be conquered either way. Then, just as the dawn began to make itself known through the easterly windows, the thought struck me—she will certainly soon be engaged to Mr. Collins. And so, the question was settled. In spite of the way she makes me feel, she is surely soon to be betrothed to another in what would truly be a more sensible match for all involved. When I realized this, the tension in my soul was lifted and I felt a freedom from attachment as I have not since I first met her. Therefore, I went walking and whatever ill-feeling in my heart still lingered on her behalf was lifted with the ascent of the sun."

After a moment's stunned silence, Bingley said, "And I suppose this is to be a lesson for me—to suppress my feelings in a similar fashion?"

"Your *feelings* will be what they are, Charles," replied Darcy. "You must act on what your *reason* informs you—and you certainly cannot be ignorant of the disgraceful manner in which her sisters, her mother, and even, to some extent, her father, conducted themselves yesterday evening."

"Darcy, I don't—"

"It would give me great delight, my dear friend, if we *together* could disregard any endearment to *either* of the Bennet girls."

Bingley slumped back in his seat and sighed. He felt as though he had been lectured—again—but knew, or at least acquiesced to the idea that Darcy was right. It was, however, as if the glow emitted from Jane still surrounded him—he had not given a moment's thought that morning to the ugly business that laid ahead.

"Last night was a fine night, Charles. Let it be that, but do not commit an error which you might regret the rest of your life. Besides, you have business to attend to, do you not?"

CHAPTER TWENTY

IT WAS CONSIDERABLY WARM for the last day of November. Constable Gallagher left the inn where he had spent the night in Skeldergate and crossed the River Ouse. He walked up Market Street and turned into Jubbergate, as he had been directed. Several turns and alleys later, he found himself into the centre of the Shambles, shops and inns to each side. Having turned himself around admirably, he asked a young boy for directions to Xavier Prichard's cobbler shop. He was informed that he was standing directly outside its door. Once inside the dark, musty shop he rang the bell, as not a soul attended the front. Crumpled papers littered the bespattered floor and dust floated listlessly through what light the murky windows allowed to pass.

"Yes?" called a feeble voice from the back.

"Pardon me, but I am in search of Mr. Prichard," asked the Constable.

"Which one?"

"Xavier."

"May I tell him who is calling?"

"Constable Luther Gallagher, from Grantley."

"A constable?"

"Yes, sir," Gallagher answered as a cat nimbly jumped to the counter in front of him.

"Is Mr. Prichard in trouble with the law?"

"No, of course not—"

"Well, that's surprising!"

"Excuse me?"

"Tell me truly—what's the old man done now—*murdered someone*?"

"May I ask with whom I speak?" Gallagher called, a bit perturbed by what seemed to be insolence. He petted the cat mindlessly and looked about him—in truth, it was hard to believe such fine boots came from a shop such as this.

"Mr. Prichard," the frail voice answered.

"Which one?"

"Now you're learning!"

A door creaked open and an old man, decrepit and skinny, emerged hobbling from around the corner. Gallagher winced instinctively. The man with whom he'd been speaking was dressed poorly, both in style and in substance. His breeches were ripped at the knee, his shirt untidy and stained, and his hair uncombed and greasy. One eye was brown while the other was clouded by a cataract, and his eyebrows were long and wild.

"Xavier Prichard, at your service," he said, extending a limp hand.

"Xavier Prichard?" Gallagher repeated in disbelief while observing in full the slovenly shopkeeper. The old man looked around the shop in confusion. "Are you quite alright?" asked Gallagher.

"Yes, but you asked for Xavier Prichard!"

"I only repeated what you said."

"And what did I say?"

"You said that you were Xavier Prichard."

"And so I am," he remarked with a giddy chortle.

Gallagher glanced down at the old man's hands—liver spots, oddly spaced patches of hair, and filth under his fingernails. "You are the *cord-wainer*—Xavier Prichard?"

The cat suddenly hissed.

"Ah!—be gone with you, Dillweed!" the old man shouted as he pushed the cat indelicately to the floor. "Petulant little hellion. Yes, I am the cordwainer, Xavier Prichard—why do you keep asking me?"

"Please infer no offense, sir, but," Gallagher struggled to find a deferential way to express his thoughts, "to be frank, I would never have imagined that a shoe as fine as yours would be fabricated in a shop such as this."

"You believe my shoes are fine?" the old man's eyes widened.

"I am a cobbler, myself, sir, and your product is amongst the finest I have ever seen in the whole of my experience."

"Why, I thank you. It is very kind of you to say so. Now, may I ask, to which part of your statement might I have taken offense?"

Gallagher's eyes drifted around the unkempt room before, with a raise of an eyebrow and an obliging smile he said, "Nothing at all, sir. From one craftsman to another, your work is simply marvellous."

"Thank you once more," answered the old shopkeeper. "Now, may I fit you with a pair?"

"Thank you, sir, but no. I am here on official duty."

"Sounds serious," Prichard murmured, leaning forward on the counter. "Are you *sure* that I am in no trouble?"

"No, of course, not. I need to learn if there is any chance you could inform me of who might have purchased a particular pair of boots from your shop."

With that, the Constable reached in his bag and pulled out the suspected killer's boots. He placed them on the counter. Prichard smiled broadly. "Ah, my boys," he declared fondly, "I see that you have been well cared for." He took the left boot in his hands and twirled it around, observing it from all angles.

"Can you tell me who might have purchased it?"

"It is from the Marylebone Collection, though I am not sure why I would have picked such a silly name," he mused. "An order of fourteen pairs of boots—you see here?—" asked Prichard as he peeled back the inside of the boot's tongue. The Constable nodded. There was a mark he had hitherto not observed—a Roman numeral twelve. "This is pair number twelve of fourteen—you see?—this is how I mark the pairs, so I remember how many I have made! Ingenious, is it not?"

Gallagher smiled and nodded politely. "Can you tell me who ordered them?"

"For the life of me, I could not remember that. It would have been spring or summer, but beyond that I cannot recall." The Constable bit his lip in frustration at this news. "I suppose we might have some luck if we went down to records."

"Records?" Gallagher repeated.

"Yes, the records department, why do you ask?"

"You keep records of *all* your transactions?"

"Naturally," Prichard replied. "They are just through here," the old man said, waving an arm as he walked round the counter to the side where the Constable stood. Prichard knelt down and began sorting through a heap of loose parchment crumpled about the floor. "Help me, help me," he called, "but not over there—those are last year's books."

Gallagher knelt down and began opening and smoothing the crinkled papers. Dillweed, the cat, even managed to lazily paw through some of them. To the Constable's astonishment, the eccentric old man kept meticulous records of every pair of boots sold, repaired, or even inquired after, on sheets of paper which he then crinkled and tossed about his shop floor. What appeared initially to be random piles of rubbish on the floor were, in fact, organized by quarter and even by month.

"Here it is, here it is," declared Prichard. "Marylebone collection, fourteen pairs."

"And does it say for whom they were ordered?" Gallagher asked excitedly.

"Chambers Cordwainer, Limited, in Marylebone, London," he responded, moving the paper closer and further from his eyes to help bring it into focus. Then, with a giddy laugh he said, "The silly collection name makes more sense now."

"So, you produced these for a shop in London?"

"It appears so. Chambers is not a *proper* cordwainer, I tell you. He's more of a merchant now than a proper shoemaker—caters to the rich, even to the royals."

"Fascinating," Gallagher answered. "Well, thank you very much. You've been ever so helpful."

"No trouble at all," Prichard laughed. "From one shoe enthusiast to another!"

"I thank you again," replied Gallagher, collecting the boots he'd brought from the counter.

"Please latch the door on your way out. I don't want any dust to blow in—I have had to sweep the floor twice already this annum!"

Gallagher shook his head and made sure to firmly close the door behind him. He walked up the crowed lane with a smile on his face, even though it was now apparent that a trip to London was in his future after all.

CHAPTER TWENTY-ONE

SCARCELY A WEEK AFTER the Netherfield Ball, Bingley and his party quit the house for London. Bingley had further news from his steward, Mr. Wilshere, that Lord Bertram St. John's travel abroad had been once again postponed, due to his wife's falling ill in Brighton. Her condition was not severe, but it did prevent the couple from traveling. Therefore, Bingley allowed his sisters to believe that they had convinced him to consent to spend Christmas in town, while his true intention was to travel to Brighton to deal with the delicate matter of the life of Lord St. John, before the demon was allowed to depart for the continent. In Bingley's plan, he would return to Netherfield the week after Christmas, and spend the winter in the most pleasant surroundings and, particularly, the most pleasant company he had ever enjoyed.

So, a fortnight before Christmas Bingley and Mr. Wilshere left London by landau carriage. Their journey was delayed at every turn by mud, broken vehicles, and other hazards until a full eight hours later they reached Crawley and elected to dine and stay the night at an inn there. The following morning their campaign progressed much more smoothly, and they arrived at the hotel in Brighton at half past two in the afternoon.

Bingley was anxious to be apprised of the current whereabouts of Lord St. John and perhaps even drive by his home along the coast. Mr. Wilshere, however, was adamant that they keep a low profile at the hotel, in part because he expected news from one of his hired investigators regarding St. John's location, itinerary, and more. Bingley had lunch sent to his room and penned a note to Darcy to try to pass the time. Following his hastily written letter, however, he spent the remaining time pacing the room like a caged lion. It was only thoughts of Jane Bennet which allowed him to settle down, but even then, only momentarily. Finally at a quarter till six that evening, Mr. Wilshere's messenger, a young man by the name of Maitland rang and was shown to the room by the steward.

"What have you to say, boy?" Wilshere asked.

The young man, tall and lean with eyes the colour of emeralds held his hat in his hand. "Lady St. John is lately on the mend. In regard to their travel plans, their vessel leaves two mornings from now, at nine. Everything looks to be running bang up to the mark in that quarter."

"Thank you, Maitland," answered Wilshere, turning to Bingley: "Do you require anything else, sir?"

Bingley sat pensively for a moment, then looked up at the young man and asked, "Have you been into the house?"

"Of course, sir," answered Maitland. "Mr. Wilshere gave me a sham recommendation—with a set of Banbury stories like you've never heard—a chimney sweep that's come to clear some birds out the chimneys."

"Did you clear out the birds?"

"Aye, sir. What ones there were."

"If you were to try to sneak back into the house, how would you do it?"

Wilshere gave Bingley a cautionary glance. His network of informants and couriers was well apprized that their activities were not strictly for legal ends, but none of them were aware of any more serious crimes that might take place due to their investigative work. He was even careful to hire such free-traders, those who would have direct contact with the targets at hand, from varying parts of the country. By the time the act was finished, they were a hundred miles away and certainly not likely to keep abreast of the news. Maitland, for example, had been sent to Brighton ten days preceding from the same street as Letitia Yates in Birmingham. Wilshere thought it fitting that inn a small way, the information Maitland had acquired would serve to avenge his fellow Brummy.

"It depends on which part of the house you'd like to end up in, I suppose," the hired man replied.

"It's a large house, then?"

"It's a fort, to my mind," declared Maitland with a laugh.

"Walls?"

"Fifteen feet high."

"All the way round?"

"Yes, sir. And a moat."

"A *moat*?" Bingley asked flabbergasted, glaring at Wilshere. Maitland nodded.

"It lets out into the sea at low tide, though," the secret agent offered. "Around the back there's a spot where you can walk clean across the rocks. A man could probably use the vines and what tree limbs there are to get over the wall without hardly a soul every seeing him. It is awful dark back there and it's only the pigs and horses inside the yard."

"Is that so?" Bingley inquired with interest.

"Would put you into the kitchen, but at least you're in the house," Maitland offered with a curious smile.

"Does he have any protection?"

"It isn't the King's Guard, but—"

"But, what?" Bingley demanded.

"Five men, round the clock," said the young man, measuring the questioner's disappointment. "I never did see one at the kitchen door."

Bingley's face lightened drastically at hearing this. "No one watches the kitchen door?" Maitland shook his head. "Into the kitchen or into the house?"

"Into the kitchen," stated Maitland. "There's two who stand inside the main hall outside the dining room."

"I see," Bingley quipped.

"But the hall might not be how I would get in—if it were *me* getting in the house."

"Whatever do you mean?"

"Lord likes a nibble before bed it seems. There is a staircase that leads directly from the kitchen to the master's sleeping chamber, but it takes a keen eye to find it."

"Why is that?"

"The door is made to look like regular stones in the wall—a bit of a secret passage, you might say."

"How do you identify the door?"

"A burlap bag hangs down to about the height you might expect to find a knob. Push on that bag and the door opens."

"Excellent information."

"Thank you, sir," answered the servant proudly.

"What time does he go to sleep?"

"Not sure, but his room is lit until at least one each night."

"You have done very well, Maitland."

"I take my work seriously, sir."

With that, Bingley stood and crossed the room. He opened a bag and pulled from it his money purse. He turned and handed the young man a couple notes. Maitland's grew wide and he quickly thumbed through the money.

"Sir, I have already been paid... for *reconnaissance*," he said glancing at Bingley nervously, fearing he might be asked to partake in something truly nasty.

"And you've done fine work," Bingley replied.

"But," Maitland muttered, staring down at the hard cash in his hands, "this is *two pounds*." Bingley nodded solemnly. "Who are you, sir?"

Bingley glanced at Wilshere and then back to Maitland. He read the young man's eyes and considered his words carefully. "I am a *ghost*," he said slowly.

"Sir, I have never held this much money in the whole of me life."

"Then use it well—enjoy it and do good with it. And forget about me—forget my face, forget the sound of my voice."

"I could never forget you, sir," said Maitland calmly, "but I will *forever* be in your service."

"You are a good man, Maitland," replied Bingley. "Mr. Wilshere may very well call upon you again."

"I would be most pleasantly obliged, sir."

"Thank you and goodnight."

With that, Wilshere showed the young man out. When the door was closed and the two were alone again, Bingley stood up and accusingly said, "You did not inform me that I would be storming a bloody *castle*."

"I did not know, sir—"

"You did not know?" Bingley demanded incredulously. "With all the information you have managed to gather from the four corners of the globe, this particular, and *highly relevant* detail somehow escaped your attention altogether?"

"Mr. Bingley," Wilshere answered stoically, "I cannot know every detail. The young man's correspondence over the last weeks indicated nothing about a wall, or a moat, or guards whatsoever."

"Then what good was the information he gave?"

"He told you how to get into Lord St. John's bedroom undetected, did he not?"

Bingley turned and shook his head in irritation. The steward remained silent and serene. "What other options do we have, then?"

"You could kill him in broad daylight in view of a hundred onlookers." Bingley glared back at him. "Or, like our initial plan dictated, since we have now heard from the informant, we could drive by the house and survey it ourselves."

"This business will be the death of me."

"Let us hope not, sir," said Wilshere calmly. "You have more than halfway accomplished the mission. Granted it is a dark mission, but a noble one, and I am better acquainted with your character than to believe that you could at the first true obstacle abandon it so easily. Your conscience would not allow it."

Bingley watched his hands as he flexed his fingers into a fist and then stretched them out. "How far is the *castle*, then?"

"But six and a half miles, sir."

"Be ready in ten minutes time. We shall ride on horseback."
With that, and a bow, Mr. Wilshere quit the room.

CHAPTER TWENTY-TWO

BINGLEY AND HIS MAN took a circuitous route to the shore home of Lord Bertram St. John. Over the final patch of road, they discreetly crossed into the thicket, taking great care to ensure they had not been observed, and made slow progress toward the house through the thick brush. The night was still and frigid, the moon only sporadically making its presence known through cracks in the cloud cover overhead. At the edge of the coppice, they paused and observed. The house was, indeed, built like a castle, though far too modern to have been there very long. Wilshere soon informed Bingley that the house had been erected within the last ten years. Bingley surmised that Lord St. John must have been something of a medieval-period enthusiast. Wilshere did not contradict him. But what was the purpose of so large a house, fortified as it obviously appeared to be, for a man who was, by all outward appearances, an upstanding and gentlemanlike citizen in the empire.

"Perhaps they bring their victims here," Bingley mused gravely.

"Perhaps," the steward replied solemnly.

"Gives me a shiver in my spine to think on it."

"It certainly is formidable."

"Can we be sure that Maitland was right about the number of guards and where they are stationed?"

"His report was rigorous enough in detail to earn my confidence," answered the servant. Bingley looked toward the house soberly. "Does my confidence not inspire?"

"Wilshere," Bingley began thoughtfully, "I do not believe I have to mention how utterly you have gained my trust—in your hands, I have laid my reputation, my fortune, and even my very life. However, this particular portion of our mission does not inspire confidence in my *own* abilities."

"Sir, do not doubt yourself, now—"

"Stealth I can accomplish, and in ruthlessness of purpose I shall not falter, but the physical and mental demands of this objective are vast, indeed, and the chances that innocent bystanders may enter the fray are significant enough to give me pause."

"May I speak bluntly, sir?"

"As always, good man."

"Are you certain that the rigors of the task at hand are what cause you trepidation, and not the situation of the target?"

"Explain your meaning."

"Mr. Bingley," Wilshere said as the two turned from glaring at the house to face each other, "Lord St. John is, after all, the Earl of Canterbury."

Bingley did pause. He turned his gaze back toward the imposing fortress beyond the clearing. "If your information is right, Wilshere, this man is involved in acts so gruesome, so evil, that I would not hesitate to slaughter the king himself—"

Wilshere raised a hand: "I would not dare to question your character in such a way, sir."

The two men sat astride their horses in silence for another few moments before Bingley spoke. "Let us ride through the thicket and skirt over to land's end and see what we might observe."

They trod on in silence, both of them scrutinizing entry points, guard positions, and the general layout of the place. By this time, it was after midnight and to their sight, only a single lamp burned in the whole place—in the tower window overlooking the channel. They made some calculations, discussed various scenarios—pointing and motioning and speaking in near whispers until they had exhausted themselves. The two men witnessed the extinguishing of the lamp in the tower shortly after one, just as Maitland had reported. With that sight, they began their slow and furtive movement back to the main road, from whence they galloped back to Brighton in record time. Back in Bingley's room, they drew up their plan, replete with contingencies and alibis, had a few drinks, and then slept—the master in the bed and the steward on the sofa. Had it not been for the wine, neither would have slept well, as both their heads were full of all the possible outcomes, including the dreadful ones. They were determined, more than ever though, to bring the mighty and evil scheme to an end, and if all went according to their projections, would be able to accomplish the daunting feat in less than twenty-four hours' time.

CHAPTER TWENTY-THREE

THE FOG HUNG THICK like a blanket over the city. His lungs burned and his heart pounded as if it might leap from his chest. Sweat flecked from his forehead and his boots clapped the paving stones at a sprint. Down the alley and cornering out onto the lane, he was nearly struck by a barrel of sherry that had flown off a cart. His legs underneath him began to feel like rubber and his side began to cramp, but he darted on in panic. Somewhere in the race from the docks to the inn he had lost his cap, but not to worry, he still had the money in his pocket. The information at hand was too valuable, anyway, and might, after all, save his mysterious benefactor's life. Through the empty pub he raced toward the stairs and up two flights. He found the ghost's room, paused just momentarily to acquire some semblance of decency, then proceeded to knock vigorously.

"Good Lord, what is the matter?" came a shout from inside.

"Sir, please, open the—" he struggled to catch a breath, "—it's Maitland, sir."

The door flung open and there stood Mr. Wilshere, dressed already for the night.

"Is... is the master in?" Maitland panted.

"No," stuttered Wilshere, "he's gone out for the evening."

"He's not gone to Lord St. John's, has he?"

"Why would he—"

"Mr. Wilshere," the agent interrupted, "I may be young and poor, but I'm not thick."

Wilshere peered both ways down the hall and ushered the boy inside. "Keep your voice down. What have you to say?"

"St. John is departed."

"Departed?" gasped the steward.

"Aye, sir—but not that way!"

"Then which way?"

"*Decamped*—he has left Brighton," stuttered the young man.

"He is gone?"

"Aye, sir," gasped Maitland. "He and Lady St. John sailed for Le Havre this evening."

"Well, then," Wilshere stammered as his mind raced toward France.

"But, sir," Maitland said, his breath finally catching up with him, "I am afraid that our master shall not find the house empty."

"Whatever do you mean?" Wilshere snapped.

"I happened to be down the wharf in search of a trollop or two—oh, I should not have said that—" Wilshere waived his hand to dismiss the young man's indiscretion, "—when I saw the most massive barouche I have ever laid mine eyes upon roll up the lane. There was not a doubt in my mind as to who it could be and sure enough, Lord and Lady St. John themselves emerged by the dock. As their luggage was unloaded and they directed their servants this way and that, I managed to work myself within ames-ace of the gangplank to eavesdrop on Lord St. John and his steward, Mr. Trippier—"

"Was your presence detected?"

"Not in the least," declared Maitland.

"You are sure of this?"

"Between the fog and the dark and my silence, there is no way I could have been detected."

"All right, what transpired next?"

"The Lord told his steward to have a ship dispatched immediately to meet them in Le Havre with what he called, 'the outcome of the evening's entertainment.'"

"The evening's entertainment?" mused Wilshere.

"Sir, I believe Lord St. John has been properly startled by the untimely deaths of several other members of... well, I believe they have laid a trap for our master."

"We must go at once!" Wilshere proclaimed.

CHAPTER TWENTY-FOUR

BINGLEY HAD TIED HIS horse in the thicket beside the road and walked what was a distance of nearly half a mile through the brush to the edge of the clearing on the westerly side of the massive abode. As was his usual practice, he would pilfer a horse from the stable and ride it to that point, where it would be tied in the same place as his horse. The only catch in this plot was that, because he rode in on horseback and not by carriage, he was unable to leave the stolen horse a bucket of fresh water. This he lamented.

He peered out into the moat and sure enough, the tide was ebbing toward the sea, but what must have been nearly a foot of water still swayed to and fro in perfect rhythm. He checked his watch and saw that it was nearly half-past midnight. In timing the movement of the waves, he calculated, roughly, that the tide would be at its lowest—and most crossable—point at quarter after one. He bided his time listening and watching what he could. The night was moonless and murky, his movements would be advantageously obscured by the low cloud cover.

At ten minutes to one Bingley observed the extinguishment of the single lamp in the master suite. Glancing down at the moat, or what was left of it, he concluded that two to four inches of sea was all that remained. By the time he climbed the vines over the wall, down the stable roof, and made the appropriate observations in terms of security and his exit strategy, the Lord of the house would be fast asleep, and surprise easily had. He swallowed the massive lump in his throat, and after pulling his cloak's hood over his head, checked the surrounding area once more, then darted for the castle's outer rampart.

His exquisite boots splashed across the rocks under fog so dense he nearly ran straight into the wall—only his arms broke his stride. He clenched the ivy while he caught his breath. Looking up he could scarce see the peak of the wall due to the haze. Once he collected himself, he began his ascent. His climb was an arduous one as, having no footholds to utilize, he was compelled to use, ostensibly, only his upper body. His arms and shoulders strained with effort, and he nearly exerted all his strength when, with one enterprising stretch, he felt under his fingers the top of the wall. Buoyed by the nearness of the apex, he was able to raise his entire body onto the barricade, which incidentally, was at least four feet thick. He panted and laid motionless in a pool of his own sweat; his muscles pulsed with relief.

Within a few moments, he regained his self-possession and crept toward the interior edge of the bulwark to observe the circumstances into which he would fling himself. The stable was but twenty yards from him, and—just as Maitland had recalled—had a perfectly sloping roof that would be simple to descend from his current position. There was not a sound, save the lapping of the waves; no movement in the yard, save a pig settling in its sty. This sight caused a momentary reflection on a summer some time past, when a very skilful peasant in the north with an anfractuous understanding of swine and their slaughter, had helped him prepare—unbeknownst to either of them at the time—for the greatest task of his life. He drew a long breath and scrambled toward the ledge, leaping onto the stable's roof. The startled sounds of horses and pigs gave him a moment's hesitation, until he realized that in his current position, he was in full sight of half the yard and several windows in the tower. With great stealth and even greater dexterity, he flung himself toward a tall bale of hay, which broke his momentum. He landed rather inelegantly on his feet, thankfully with no damage done to either himself or the hay bale.

Bingley adjusted his hood and quickly took cover behind the stable. Peering around its corner, he observed the empty yard, devoid of human activity. The animals had quieted back to their slumber, and nearly all was still, aside from the bare and breeze-blown tree limbs. Perhaps fifty feet across the yard he identified the kitchen door, which appeared to be latched. He bolted toward it and was shocked to find it unlocked. Having cracked it open only enough to peer inside, he found the large room empty, last embers dying in the hearth. Once inside, he closed the door quietly behind him. To his left the long servants table drew his eyes toward an opening that was, no doubt, an entry into the bottom floor of the house. Across the room from his vantage point, just as Maitland had described, was a burlap bag hanging from a rafter. Bingley clandestinely cross the room, taking great pains to ensure that his footsteps were nearly silent. He pushed on the bag and, just as reported, the stones creaked forward and to the right on a hinge. Before him was a stone stairway, spiralling up and out of sight.

As he entered the stairwell the door closed silently behind him and, save for the light of what must have been a window some distance up, Bingley found himself in nearly total darkness. Using his palm as a guide, his hand followed the wall, and his feet cautiously took each step. He came to a small window, which because of the moonless night, hardly illuminated the path, after he had climbed forty-three steps—he had been sure to keep count. He began to wonder if there was a secret opening into the bedchamber that, perhaps, Maitland had failed to recall or never even discovered. The staircase ended not at that point, so he continued his ascent. After another forty-three steps exactly, he came to another window, this one under a landing. The subsequent steps narrowed drastically. He assumed these led to the roof, although he couldn't be positive. Out the window the bay was visible, shoreline lit here and there by lamps from homes, and the beginnings of a shower spattered against the glass. Having his bearings roughly in place, Bingley searched the wall to his left for a door, and to his surprise, found a proper handle. He turned it quietly until the door opened just a crack. Putting his ear to the opening, he listened intently. All he heard was calm breathing. He furtively nudged it open and looked round it into the room—an enormous chamber furnished with a regal canopy bed. Across the room, a dresser stood under a large window—atop the dresser sat a single unlit lantern.

Bingley unsheathed his knife and entered slowly. He made his way silently toward the bed, taking care to suppress his accelerated respiration. Aside from the blood coursing through his ears and his own stifled breathing, he only heard the sound of his victim's sleep. At the edge of the bed, he lifted his knife in his right hand while taking hold of the corner of the thick duvet in his other. He flung the cover back to find the bed empty. His mind had not time to process his shock when he was suddenly and forcefully grabbed from behind. He swung his blade down instinctively. His attacker let out a bestial howl as Bingley's blade ripped through the flesh of the man's right buttock. In the ensuing scramble, Bingley freed himself from the grip, only to find himself entangled with another stranger in the dark. He swung his knife wildly, connecting with flesh only occasionally as he felt himself being pummelled from all angles. He suddenly realized he was grappling with more than one man, as the mass of them spun in circles, crashing into other bodies, chairs, and articles throughout the room. In the skirmish, Bingley's feet became tangled in the mass of humanity, and he felt himself spin toward the stone floor. He landed crudely atop one of his assailants, and with an audible crack of his spine, all his breath left him. Gasping on the unforgiving floor, his knife was pried from his hand, and he was gripped firmly around the neck. Rolled onto his stomach, his face was pressed into the cold stone and his hands were tied behind him.

One of his attackers attempted to attend to the man Bingley had stabbed, though it seemed from his waning moans that not much hope could be held out for him. Bingley deduced that, aside from the dying man on the floor, there were three additional combatants with whom he had vied. Those who remained alive—Bingley included—panted and struggled to regain a normal breathing pattern.

"Who are you?" one of the figures in the dark barked. After no response was given save his rapid respiration, the man demanded: "You are the *butcher*?"

After a moment's hesitation and a deep breath, Bingley growled defiantly, "I am but a ghost."

"That is all that will be left of you soon enough," another man answered.

Bingley's mind raced distractedly between his pain and his astonishment at the situation in which he found himself. The bedchamber should have been empty, save Lord St. John. The light went out at one. The moat was easily traversed by foot. He had been, with minimal inconvenience, able to use the vines to scale the wall. The stable was exactly as he had pictured it. Even the location of the secret door from the kitchen was where it was supposed to be. So why had this mission gone so wholly and abominably awry? Every vital element had been described perfectly in minute detail by—

That was it—he had been betrayed by Maitland. *That low-born Brummy bastard has made a May game of me,* Bingley fumed. *How could I have been so trusting, so naive?* Even Wilshere had been hesitant to cover the complete details of the castle's layout with the newly hired young man. Surely his steward had been the wiser man. But that was his own greatest weakness, was it not? He was too optimistic, too agreeable, too guileless for his own good—and where had it got him? Here he was, sure to be publicly disgraced in the worst way by one of the most powerful men in the kingdom. His sisters would be abased and cast out of the society of which his father had toiled his entire life to grant them access, and in the course of not five years, he would have undone it all. There was also the good chance that he would be hanged as a common criminal. Certainly, there was no proof that he had been involved in the murders of Andrew Fraser or Thomas Abbott, but he had been caught in the act of attempted murder. He was, no doubt, bound for the gallows, and that low-born knave he had relied upon had sent him there.

As his captors pulled him to his feet, he censured himself for his selfish ruminations. Surely, he thought of his sisters and their place in society, but even if he were gone, their fortunes would be intact, and perhaps even enhanced. In his initial brooding over his current scrape, he had forgotten completely the innocent maidens, who would not only go unavenged by his failure, but who would continue to be victimized by such a diabolical plot. Young ladies would continue to be hunted, lured away from their families, ravaged, and ultimately dispatched as if their continued existence was nothing more than a nuisance.

"Am I to be disgraced publicly?" Bingley demanded.

"Who are you, but a nightcrawler, a blackguard with a penchant for murdering the wealthy?" answered the man behind him.

"Rubbish like you don't deserve the public recognition," declared another of the men as he moved toward the window. He pushed it open and set the lantern on the ground beside the table. "No, you shan't be disgraced. Up you go."

Bingley was hoisted onto the dresser and made to stand before the open window.

"What is to become of me, then?" Bingley queried.

"To become of you?" laughed the brute who climbed up with him. "You are going to disappear."

More gruff laughter echoed through the chamber.

"But first, you are going to break your neck."

Bingley was nudged until his toes were over the ledge. He glanced down and quickly closed his eyes—the distance from the tower window to the rocks below was at least sixty feet. Suddenly, his thoughts turned to Jane Bennet. If only he could have, at the very least, told her who he was, what he was trying to accomplish. A revelation of his brutal mission would have surely startled her and may have even driven her away, but at least he would have been fully known. Even now he held out the hope that she might have understood that his character would never allow him to be a bystander while pure and undiluted evil flourished. Surely this she could have accepted, and perhaps, it would have allowed her to ascertain his true nature and maybe even respect him all the more. But finally, his last torture would be going to his watery grave without telling her that he loved her—*he loved her*.

"Now would be the time to say a prayer," the ruffian behind him growled.

He may have managed a word to the almighty before his thoughts hurried back to Jane, and then, to his horror, to Wickham. George Wickham would now have unconstrained, unchallenged access to the

Bennet family, and perhaps, with his own body feeding the fish of the Channel, that fiend would vie for the attention of Miss Bennet herself. At this reprehensible thought he began to struggle, writhing to and fro until his shirt was firmly gripped by a second guard.

"To the devil with you now!" cried the ruffian.

Just before he felt himself completely overpowered and tossed to his death, a loud sound like a cannon burst his ears and a flash of muzzle illuminated the room. He spun and ducked clumsily, and in doing so one of the men who had subdued him tripped and vanished from the ledge and out of sight with a caterwaul. The thud of his body on the stone below was heard but a second later. The other man who had been with him on the dresser simply slumped to the tower floor, having been shot through the heart. Bingley knelt and heard the unmistakable sounds of a struggle, then of a man's shrieking diminishing to a low wheeze.

"Master!"

"Wilshere—is that you?" Bingley gasped into the darkness.

"Master Bingley!" heaved the worried reply. The steward rushed over and unbound his master's hands. "Are you hurt, sir?"

"No," sighed Bingley, "not critically."

"Thank God!"

"Why on earth did you come here? Did you discover that Maitland betrayed us?"

"Maitland—*betrayed*?" Wilshere asked dumbfounded. "He is right here, sir."

"*What?*"

"He is the one who learned of the trap, disarmed the guard at the front gate, and... finished off that one there."

Bingley panted heavily. "I do not—I do not comprehend you. I was nearly certain that St. John must have greased him in the fist to set up this trap."

"No, sir," Maitland finally spoke up, "I could never do such a thing. I swore that I would forever be in your service, and I intend to keep my word."

"Let us flee this place and we will regather our bearings at the hotel."

"Are you fit to ride, my Lord?" Wilshere asked.

"I assure you, my man, I am unhurt and alive, thanks to you both. I owe to each of you a debt which I can never hope to repay."

"There shan't be a need, sir," answered Wilshere.

With that, the three men escaped to the woods where they untied their horses and absconded back into the hotel under the cover of thick darkness.

CHAPTER TWENTY-FIVE

HE SAT THERE SHIRTLESS, a reddish-blue bruise rising on the skin under his arm and a cold piece of meat pressed against his cheekbone, listening to Maitland recall the circumstances under which he had learned of the trap that Lord St. John and his odious steward, Mr. Trippier, had sprung for him. These wounds aside, Bingley had only small cuts and bruises, mostly across his arms and torso.

"Should I fetch a doctor, sir?" Wilshere inquired once Maitland's story concluded.

"No, I thank you, Wilshere," Bingley answered, shifting delicately in his chair. "It may be a few days, but I do believe I shall recover tolerably."

"Would you have me reserve our lodgings through the week?"

"That would be fine, I suppose."

"I will make sure it is in order first thing in the morning."

"Thank you," said the master before turning back to the young man who had saved his life. "So, you are *sure* that they have sailed to France?"

"I am sure that is what he discussed with Mr. Trippier," retorted Maitland.

"Explain yourself," Wilshere insisted.

"I cannot be absolutely positive, but I also think their plans to sail for Le Havre may have been a gammon."

"A gammon?" Bingley asked.

"A ruse, you might say," answered the young man. "It was too large a vessel to be chartered for nothing more than skipping the channel."

"Too large even for Lord and Lady St. John?"

Maitland shook his head. "It was carrying cargo, as well as their person effects. Truth is, sir, I was in a tavern along the waterfront and overheard some of the deck hands talking about the journey. They are bound for Valencia."

"Valencia?" Bingley asked. "You are sure of this?"

"That's what the word was in the tavern. The size of the ship, the length of the journey, that would seem reasonable to me."

"And you know much about overseas travel?" Wilshere asked.

"I confess, I do not, sir. I've an uncle who is a shipbuilder in Liverpool, but building ships is far different than sailing them."

"You seem to have a knack for casually learning very useful information, Mr. Maitland," Bingley spoke up, tossing the meat from over his eye into a bowl on the table next to him.

"I suppose so. But then again, is that not the reason I was hired in the first place?"

"Have you done this kind of work before, Mr. Maitland?"

"Not on such a scale," the young man answered. "You could say I have made a little name for myself around the neighbourhood, perhaps."

"What kind of name?"

"As a man who can figure things out when he puts his mind to it."

"And why, sir, have you put your mind to this task with such vigour?"

"You pay very well."

Bingley shook his head. "What do you know about Lord St. John?"

"He's the Earl of Canterbury—he's one of the richest men in the kingdom."

With a grimace, Bingley leaned forward and toward the seated Maitland. "There is more than meets the eye with you. Do not pitch the gammon with me, son."

Maitland's top lip curled into a wily smile. Wilshere watched him intently, then glanced at Bingley who met his gaze.

"You are very intuitive, sir. I should have expected nothing less."

"You know what they are up to, do you not?" Wilshere asked.

With that, Maitland's smile dropped. He bowed his head slightly in affirmation.

"How are you connected?" inquired Bingley.

"Letitia Yates—" the young man's voice trailed off and he lowered his head before strengthening his resolve and his moist eyes met Bingley's again: "Letitia Yates was my betrothed, sir."

Wilshere's jaw nearly touched the floor. Bingley reached across the small distance between them and put his hand on Maitland's shoulder.

"Wilshere? Be good enough to pour the man another drink."

CHAPTER TWENTY-SIX

"I GREW UP JUST a few streets over from her family. Saw her here and there in the neighbourhood but was never familiar on personal terms. My father passed away when I was nine—croup—and my mum was never the same after. I was quite nimble and never afraid, so one of my father's friends brought me to Mr. Yates, who was a chimneysweep, and he took me on as an apprentice."

"Do you have any siblings?" Bingley asked.

"An older brother who was killed at Trafalgar, two sisters who died very young."

"I see. I am very sorry to hear it."

"Thank you. I worked with Mr. Yates to try to support my mum. He was a very good man and treated me like a son. When Mrs. Yates passed on—nearly four years ago, now?—Letitia, who was still but a child herself, took over all the house duties, caring for all her young siblings, as well. She was always a pretty girl, but the death of her mum and other hardships induced a maturity both, I suppose, emotionally as well as physically. She was kind and patient and understanding with the little ones. She worked from the first light of day to nearly midnight, mending clothes, cooking, cleaning. Through all of that she had a serene, I would almost dare to say confident, temperament. And she certainly blossomed into quite a beauty, during that time, as well. Each day I saw her, over the course of those four years, after her mum passed, I fell in love with Letitia more and more." Bingley could not help but be stirred to thoughts of Jane. "Ours was not a high romance, but it was love, nonetheless. She loved me, and I made great sacrifices to be sure that once she was sixteen, we could marry, and I could care for her properly."

Maitland's voice trailed off and he took a swig of wine before looking off out the window contemplatively.

"How did things then go awry?" Wilshere probed. Bingley glanced at him and glowered.

"Pardon my man's callous indifference. I can assure you that he is most interested in any information that you can share."

"Of course," replied Maitland, still staring off. He looked back at Wilshere and nodded.

"When you are ready, please continue," said Wilshere politely.

"I asked Letitia to be my wife."

"Was her father aware of your intentions?" Bingley asked.

"Of course," Maitland responded. "I asked him for her hand before I ever thought to ask her. He gave his consent and seemed quite relieved, it seemed. As I already mentioned, he treated me like his own son. He even cried when he gave me his blessing. I did not have a ring for her, and though she agreed when I proposed, she made me swear that I would wait for her, until she could be sure that her siblings would be cared for. After all, the youngest was not yet six years old. This was very difficult for me—I was just turned twenty—for several reasons, as you might well imagine. She assured me that all would be well and that the best days of her life would be spent caring for me. I believed her in earnest and dreamt night after night of the day which I could call her my bride—" His voice trailed off once more. His eyes fluttered about the room as if to find some object of comfort that might steady him. "—But that day never came."

"Take your time," Bingley said reassuringly, tapping the top of his glass for Wilshere to pour the wine again.

"One day, when we had finished working, we returned to Mr. Yates's home like we always done. Letitia had dinner cooked as usual, and even a pie for me to take home to my mum—this is before she, herself, passed—but Letitia was... *distracted*. While she did not seem distressed, her usual attentions to her father and to me were hardly paid. After dinner, I heard from her nine-year-old sister that a man spoke with them outside the butcher's shop that afternoon, and that he was charming and handsome. I said, 'charming and handsome?' and asked if she had ever seen him before. The little one then giggled and ran off. I went home and gave my mum the pie but laid in bed unable to get the thought out my mind. The next day being Sunday, I thought to myself that I would meet her at church—her whole family faithfully attended—and we'd have a talk after. And sure enough, next morning I got gussied up, which basically meant scraping the soot from my fingernails, as best I could manage and headed to St. Benedict's, but alas, the entire household was in attendance save Letitia, who had stayed home with a headache. I bolted out the church and raced over there, when I come round the corner to see a man leaving the house—"

"The man she met outside the butcher's?" Bingley prodded.

"The same."

"And you saw him?"

"With both mine eyes."

"Can you describe him?"

"Tall and thin; dark haired. I would characterize him as very handsome."

"Anything else remarkable about him?"

"Other than that, he was wearing regimentals, I could not say—he turned his back to me and was off before I had the chance to catch him."

"Regimentals, you say?" Wilshere implored.

"Aye," answered Maitland.

Wilshere and Bingley exchanged solemn glances.

"Did you speak with Letitia?" Bingley asked.

"Naturally," Maitland continued. "I knocked on the door and she was quite surprised to see me when it opened. I demanded the identity of the man who left, and she started to cry—I thought she might faint. I sat her down at the table and she wept into my chest. She kept saying that she was sorry. I asked what she had to be sorry for—really, what had she done? After what seemed to me to be a lifetime of this, she looked in my eyes and told me that she could not consent to be my wife. My mind could not... *grasp* what she had spoken—I could not understand a word of it—it just hung in the air like a winter fog.

"Eventually, I asked her why, and if it was because of this other man. She implored me to believe that she loved me and would always love me. I asked her what that had to do with her refusal to marry me; she answered that her situation was untenable and that she might well never recover from her broken heart. She stated through her tears that he had made her an offer of marriage, and that she had accepted him. 'How long have you even known this man?' I barked. She had met him less than a fortnight earlier, but he had apparently had his eye on her for some time.

"As you might imagine, by this point I was quite despondent and wholly baffled. I asked her on what basis had she accepted him, and she told me that he could provide for her family—even that her father would never have to work again. With that I was crushed, as you could well understand. But for all the betrayal I felt, for all the carnage she wreaked on my poor heart, I cannot but remind myself that my dear, sweet girl, had chosen not only her family's wellbeing over me, but even over her own feelings. She was not flighty; she was never impetuous. Her decision was based on how she might best care for those closest to her. She went on to tell me that he was a young man from Derbyshire who had recently inherited a fortune from a great uncle on the coast."

"From *Derbyshire*, you say?" Bingley asked with great anticipation.

"Aye, from Derbyshire," he answered slowly.

"Did she give you his name?" Wilshere entreated.

"No. Well, perhaps she did. I was too...devastated."

"That is not surprising, given the news you had just received," stated Bingley. "Can you recall, did she tell you anything else about him—anything at all?"

"Only that he was from a great estate in that part of the country. He ostensibly informed her that it was his desire that she should be the mistress of his own great home, and that her siblings receive a proper education. She implored me not to tell her father—that she would tell him in due time. Taking my hand and kissing it, she apologized, and asked for my forgiveness. She wished for my happiness—that I might soon forget her and take a wife in whom I would be forever enraptured. I was too befogged to even imagine how to respond. I believe in my heart I wished her to know that she was indeed forgiven, and that I did not hold her in any kind of disregard, but I am not sure that I was, in fact, able to say anything at all. She held my rough, blackish hand in her pale, delicate fingers—drops of her tears splattering my skin. At that moment her relations entered the home with the usual ruckus that accompanies the arrival of small children. Her father was startled by her state of emotion. He asked her what on the earth was the matter, and before I even knew it, I was I was outside and down the street."

A sympathetic smile morphed into a grimace across Bingley's face. He glanced at his man and then back to Maitland.

"I never laid eyes on her again," spoke the young man before he was no longer able to control his own emotions. He wept vigorously for an extraordinarily brief moment before nodding and regaining his typical air of quiescence. "Mr. Yates tells me that she left the house under cover of dark, leaving behind all her belongings and a note, explaining that he should not worry. She declared that she would be married in those early hours in the private chapel at Sir Andrew Fraser's country house outside Coventry, and that she and her new husband would return for the family within the week. That Thursday, her body was discovered in Southampton, and three days later, her father heard the news."

"Sir Andrew Fraser, you say?" Bingley mused, casting a sideways glance at his steward.

"Yes, and I nearly killed the man myself," uttered a stone-faced Maitland, looking up and directly at Bingley. "But *you* had got there first."

"How on earth—" Bingley began, nearly rising from his seat.

"Mr. Bingley," Maitland interrupted, "please be assured that I am your friend—nay, your servant. When I pledged you my devotion, I did so not because of how well you paid, but because of your devotion to a thankless, but essential undertaking."

"But how—I do not understand," Bingley muttered looking back and forth between Maitland and Wilshere.

"The methodical details are not vital," Maitland said. "The evidence that led you to Sir Andrew Fraser, Thomas Abbott, and ultimately, Lord Bertram St. John was all there for anyone willing or, perhaps, *daring* enough to look at it. Many of the same methods that led me to those men led me straight to you, sir. And I cannot thank you enough for the work you have done, Mr. Bingley. You are a vengeful angel from God, bringing judgement upon men whose hearts are so vile, that hellfire itself may not purify them."

Turning toward his steward, Bingley said: "Now Wilshere, I am a bit concerned that it was so entirely simple for a person to discover not only my work, but my identity, and even to come so close as to infiltrate—"

"Mr. Bingley, please," Maitland inserted again. "Have no harsh words for Mr. Wilshere. I will not say that it was *exceptionally* difficult to locate, and even identify you, sir, but a firm resolve and dedicated effort *were* required, and I would doubt very much that anyone is looking as hard as I did."

Bingley rolled his eyes and sipped his wine. "What about Lord Bertram St. John? Does he not have a vested interest in learning my identity at this juncture? And he certainly possesses the means with which to do it!"

CHAPTER TWENTY-SEVEN

IT WAS DECIDED THAT very evening or, perhaps it was early that morning, that Mr. Bingley and Mr. Wilshere would return after the week to London for Christmas, while Mr. Maitland was to set out immediately for Valencia in pursuit of Lord St. John. Maitland's mission was one exclusively of reconnaissance, as firm direction was given him not to encounter the Lord or Lady directly in any way. He was to attempt to ascertain their travel itinerary and report back to England. For his part, Mr. Bingley would spend a few days nursing his bruises, and then return to the company of his sisters, Mr. Hurst, and naturally, the Darcys for the Christmas festivities.

The day after his nearly untimely death, Mr. Bingley discovered that at some point during the course of his venture his right boot had been severely damaged, the sole being nearly torn from the heel. Once they had returned to town, he sent Mr. Wilshere directly to Chambers Cordwainer shop to have it mended.

Upon entering the shop, he was greeted with a courteous wave by the man who normally oversaw the steward's requirements, Mr. Chambers's son Alfred, who was at present tending to another patron. By the look of Alfred's glance, Wilshere ascertained that the other guest must have been somewhat tiresome. The man was of medium build and more commonly dressed than was usual in a shop of such high standards.

"Mr. Gallagher you must excuse me," the shop owner's son spoke up. "I have gainful clients that I must attend to. I have done everything in my power to satisfy the demands of your most unconventional inquiry, and at this point, I do cordially request that you take your leave."

"You will not have heard the last of me," Gallagher declared with a finger pointed toward the sky. He turned in Wilshere's direction just as the steward lifted his Lord's broken boot from the canvas bag around his shoulder. The Constable's eyes were immediately drawn to it as he passed and exited the door.

"What the devil was that about?" Wilshere queried, placing the boot on the counter.

"Hard to say," replied Alfred, taking the boot in his hands. "Oddly enough, he was asking about this very collection of boots—and my, what a problem have we here!"

"Yes, indeed," Wilshere answered, chuckling as the sole dangled from boot.

"How did this happen?"

"A riding accident, I suppose you could say."

"Oh dear, I hope Mr. Bingley is not hurt," Alfred exclaimed.

"No, not nearly as badly as the boot," quipped Wilshere.

With a courteous laugh, Alfred said, "Unfortunately, Mr. Wilshere, our cobbler is not yet in. I can have him mend it this evening, and have a boy run it to your address first thing in the morning, if that does not inconvenience you."

"Of course not," Wilshere answered. "And what is the charge?"

"For a patron like Mr. Bingley, I would happily repair this gratis, along with a wish for his speedy recovery. After all, this is not the first shoe your master has purchased here."

"And shan't be the last, I can assure you."

"In fact, if I recall correctly, Mr. Bingley purchased several of the pairs in this very line, did he not?"

"Yes, sir," confirmed the steward.

"And the rest are in fine condition, I do hope?"

"Yes, perfect condition. He rather has a habit of muddying them, but nothing a good polish does not solve."

"Ah, that suits me very well," said Alfred as he extended his hand. "Please give my regards to Mr. Bingley and expect this repair to your door by nine in the morning."

"Of course, and thank you again."

Wilshere left the shop and departed down the lane, his thoughts occupied with other errands and more pressing matters. The Constable lurking in the shadows by the shop windows escaped his notice completely. Presently, Gallager slunk back to the inn where would lodge with questions and ideas heavy on his mind.

Next morning, he waited on a stoop near Chambers Cordwainer, and watched the early morning hustle and bustle when, at ten minutes to eight, he saw a young boy enter the shop, collect a box big enough to hold a boot, and exit heading in the direction of Mayfair. Gallagher followed the unwitting errand boy through throngs and down alleys, artfully evading oncoming carriages and mounted riders alike. Finally, rounding the promenade of Grosvenor Square, the young boy stopped, looked down at his package and checked his whereabouts. The Constable seized this momentary pause as the opportunity to make his move.

"To whom does this package belong, lad?" He asked, gruffly gripping the young lad by the shoulder.

The boy looked up in terror: "I do not know sir—I was hired by Alfred Chambers to deliver it to this address." He pointed at the label on top of the box. "I believe it's located right across the way, sir, in Grosvenor Street."

"And you have no name attached to it?"

"No, sir," squared the frightened youth.

"Give it here," Gallagher demanded, taking it brusquely from boy's hands.

"But sir, I shan't be paid until I bring a receipt of delivery."

"How much is your charge?"

"Five pence, sir."

"Well, here—take twenty," Gallagher scratched the coins from his coat pocket. "And you never met with me."

"Thank you, sir," the lad quivered as he ran off with his exponentially inflated wages in his dirt-stained hands.

The Constable checked the box over and even peaked inside it—sure enough, a single boot from the Marylebone Collection of Xavier

Pritchard's making. It was polished and gleaming—a near exact replica of the number twelve boot which Gallagher held in his inn room as critical evidence. He quickly checked the underside of the tongue and found the Roman numeral fourteen etched into the leather. This boot was of the last-made pair in the collection, and only two digits off from the pair recovered in Lambton, the pair doubtlessly worn by the killer of Sir Andrew Fraser. A thrill of excitement and nerves shot up Gallagher's leg. He went on to find the address and knock at the front door of the appropriately numbered row-house—it was ten minutes to nine.

"Good morning, sir," a most formal voice announced as the door opened a moment later. "May I help you?"

"Yes," the Constable started, checking his voice for nerves, "I have a delivery from Chambers Cordwainer."

"Thank you, sir," asked the servant, extending his hand for the box. Gallagher kept it closely tucked under his arm. "I apologize, but are we in arrears for the delivery?"

"No, of course not," the cobbler-constable-courier stuttered. "But I have strict orders to release it only personally to your master—is he home?"

"Mr. Bingley is not in at present, sir."

"Ah, and what is your name?"

"I am Ridley, the footman."

"Pleasant to meet you, Ridley—is the master's steward at leisure?"

"Mr. Wilshere?"

"Yes, of course—Mr. Wilshere."

"May I ask your name that I may inform him who is calling."

"Naturally—I am Constable Gallagher from the village of Grantley."

The footman looked him over with apprehension. "Since when does a cobbler send a constable to deliver a boot?"

Gallagher nearly choked on his own stupidity but was able to regather himself and even managed to bluff. "Mr. Ridley, I say that I am a constable, though in truth, I only volunteer as such. My profession is indeed as a cobbler, and I was in town inquiring as to some of the finest boots in England, and came across the Chambers shop. Well, in only what detail is vital, I convinced Mr. Chambers to allow me to conduct a little... *surevy*, you might call it, of some of his finer patrons."

"A survey, you say?"

"Yes—a survey! That I might learn the particular tastes of London's finest and most fashionable gentlemen, in the hopes of...of improving my *own* humble trade."

"You will have to wait here," the footman answered sternly.

"May I come in?"

Ridley nodded and held the door open into the marvellous townhouse. "I will see if Mr. Wilshere is available to speak with you."

"Thank you very kindly."

"Wait here, please."

Once the footman had gone down the hall and out of sight round a corner, Gallagher began to observe the town home of the gentleman. *Could this man, whoever he was, be capable of the sort of butchery he had witnessed at Grantley Manor?* The home was lavishly adorned in the latest fashions; there was not a hint of the steady, voluminous acquisition of wealth which was commonplace in homes such as the late Sir Andrew Fraser's. Taking into account that this was but a town home, he still could not but ponder that there were no portraits, no heirlooms, no antiquities. Everything about the place from the style of the carpet runners to the Egyptian-theme sofas betrayed the vain self-importance of the *nouveau riche*. The Constable wondered at what kind of man this Mr. Bingley could possibly be, though he did find himself conceding that the man's choice of boots surely was more sensible than his choice of furnishings, even if they might have been equally extravagant.

At this moment, he detected footsteps from the direction whereby the footman had disappeared, and abruptly perceived that he was in far beyond his depth. His knees quivered beneath him, and his mouth was suddenly devoid of moisture. Glancing up the curling staircase, his eye catching the gleam of sunlight in the cut-glass and ormolu chandelier over his head, he lost all nerve and was across the street before the steward approached the hall.

Wilshere stood for a moment, then peered out the window and saw the cobbler-constable timorously crossing the park back in the direction of Marylebone. He had dropped the boot inside the front door before his hasty departure.

"What name did he give, Ridley?" Wilshere asked with a scowl.

"Gallagher," answered the footman. "From Grantley."

"We shall have to make inquiries."

"Yes, sir."

"I surely hope the good constable is mindful of the imbroglio into which he has just thrust himself." Ridley said not a word. With a hardly concealed snarl, Wilshere turned and disappeared back down the hall.

CHAPTER TWENTY-EIGHT

THE BINGLEYS WERE JOINED for Christmas by Mr. and Mrs. Hurst, Mr. Darcy, his sister Georgiana, and his cousin Colonel Fitzwilliam, among others of the genteel and wealthy class to which they belonged. In the bustling of the holiday festivities, there was hardly time for Bingley to enlighten his closest friend as to the near disaster at Brighton, nor of the mission of the newly attained services of Mr. Maitland in Spain. Aside from the multitude of visitors and the furore of the holiday, Bingley thought he detected an uneasiness in Mr. Darcy, though he could not reckon as to its cause. Mr. Hurst, for his part, had descended even further into dissipation, to such an extent that he was unable to attend the Christmas Mass. Georgiana delighted the party nearly every evening with her playing and singing, which really were quite proficient for a girl of her age, and spent much of each day with Caroline Bingley and Mrs. Hurst, though she was far less pompous in her manners than they.

Often during the evening, Caroline would make it a proper aim to ensure that her brother and Georgiana were seated within close enough proximity to converse. Bingley was well aware of his sister's machinations, as well as he was of her own intentions upon Darcy, who seemed as time went on, and despite his superior manners and perhaps even condescension, that he would not be prevailed upon in that particular regard. In respect to his sister's schemes of marrying him to Georgiana, Bingley was equally resolute. For as long as he had known Darcy, Bingley had considered Georgiana as a younger sister of his own. As eligible a match as she might have been, her charm and handsomeness aside, Bingley would not be prevailed upon to think of her in those terms. His feelings, particularly after the incident between her and George Wickham, in addition to the information he now possessed, induced him to see himself as more of an additional guardian over her well-being and happiness. He knew not whether to share the exact nature of his feelings with Darcy, but he had done so much as inform his friend that he would have no intentions toward his young sister. For his part, Mr. Darcy was truly thankful to have an upstanding man of such integrity and valour as a friend to Georgiana.

The second of January that year was a Thursday, and Bingley met with the officers of the companies his father passed to him, as had been his habit upon the dawn of each new year. The financial statements were strong from all quarters, despite temporary shipping woes produced by the New Madrid earthquakes in America, which had temporarily reversed the flow of the Mississippi River. A long day of meetings, figures, and calculations under his belt, along with what he sensed might be the beginning of a cold, Bingley was none too enthused to have his steward enter his bedchamber at half past eleven that evening.

"What news is so vital, Wilshere, that you shan't allow your master to sleep until morning?"

"News from Spain, sir," answered Bingley's man.

"Let us have it," the weary master said through a yawn.

"Maitland writes that Lord and Lady have quit Valencia for Barcelona, where they intend to spend five nights."

Bingley rubbed his eyes and sighed. "What good does this information do, Wilshere? If I had set out last night, I could not have made Barcelona in time."

"There is more, if you will allow me, Mr. Bingley," the unaffected steward pronounced. Bingley rolled away and hugged the duvet, but with his right hand waived his acquiescence. "They intend to spend the following fortnight in Marseille."

With those words, Bingley sat up and wiped his nose with the sleeve of his nightshirt. "Now there is something, finally, worth waking for."

"There is one additional piece, sir, that is not quite so pleasant."

"There you go again—"

"A constable hailing from Grantley recently paid you a visit, sir—"

"A *constable*?"

"Aye, sir."

"From *Grantley*?" Bingley exclaimed and then sneezed.

"Aye," Wilshere answered in his typically placid manner. "Three days before Christmas. He was the one who delivered your boot from Chambers'—" Wilshere held up his hands before Bingley could break in. "—He said he was a volunteer constable, and by trade was a cobbler, interested in learning the particular preferences of the wealthy in regard to their shoes."

"What the devil?" the master stated with a shudder.

"I had a man look into it, sir. Seems the lad has been tracing your muddy footprint across England but lost his nerve when it came to confronting the man himself."

"What does that mean?"

"He went *home*, sir. He is currently piddling about with shoes in his village shop."

"Then this, too, is good news; is it not?"

"It is, except that I do not believe he has given up entirely."

"But why wouldn't he?—he has no actual evidence of any kind to link me, does he?"

"Not that I am aware of, sir, but his family stands to be well compensated by the estate if he were to bring Sir Andrew Fraser's... *killer* to justice. And I do not believe that a man who so diligently traces a single boot print across an entire nation simply gives up. He *saw* the remains of Andrew Fraser. He *saw* the bedroom. I do not believe a decent man can walk away from *that* and not have a stain on his conscience until the day he dies."

"So, what is he doing at present?"

"Gathering his strength, or perhaps he is attempting to formulate a plan to approach from another angle. I have had it confirmed that he has not informed the estate that his investigation is closed."

"What then is *our* course of action?"

Wilshere shrugged, the shadow of a single candle's flame tossing across his face. "We will have to alter his pursuit, by one means or another."

CHAPTER TWENTY-NINE

IN THE TEN DAYS that followed, Bingley hardly left his bed. While his life was never in danger, he suffered constant headaches, fever, chills, and sore throat. He found it nearly impossible to stay awake during the day light hours but was maddeningly unable to sleep during the night. A diet of vegetable soups, sweet cakes, and tea with honey sustained him for nearly a fortnight.

Two days after the initial onset of his symptoms, Bingley's sister Caroline took ill, herself. She had him informed that her symptoms were undoubtedly as severe as his, and quite possibly much more so. Wilshere sent for Mr. Fletcher, the local apothecary, who prescribed saline draughts and barley water. Incredibly, these treatments, which had little to no effect upon her brother, caused miraculous healing in Caroline, so much so, that she was recovered enough to attend a noteworthy ball just two days after declaring herself—to her lady maid only—unfit to call on Jane Bennet, who had written her to announce her arrival in Gracechurch Street after the new year, with her aunt and uncle, the Gardiners.

In the meantime, Mr. Wilshere, at his master's approbation, dispatched a man to Grantley to keep a close eye on the volunteer constable. Wilshere's man made rounds about the town and sat for hours in the alehouse—undoubtedly he was more than willing to fulfil this particular duty—casually gathering information on the man who mended shoes. He was also able to learn that, while Sir Andrew Fraser was distinguished locally with respect to his rank, the village's population was not particularly enamoured by him personally. The reason for this qualm was two-fold: firstly, he was notoriously severe in his collection of past-due rents; and secondly, he was reputed to be a violent, and even profligate, drunkard. The rumour was that he, in his younger years, had been in the rather rakish habit of administering carte-blanche offers to young ladies, only to dismiss them unceremoniously once their corsets had been untwisted. This gossip circulated very much in hushed murmurs, though it seemed that the entire village was aware of such stories. It could then be concluded that whatever mourning had taken place in the village on behalf of his death was largely superficial, and that most of the people considered Gallagher's self-appointed investigation as merely an act of self-aggrandizement.

The cobbler, for his part, had the reputation as a quiet family man who, perhaps, had taken to thinking himself more important than he was due to his role as volunteer constable, particularly following the murder of the estate's lord. Since fleeing the house on Grosvenor Street, however, Gallagher had been racked by a nagging concoction of guilt and self-doubt. He repaired shoes in his shop during daylight and went straight home to his family in the evening, rarely appearing out of doors otherwise. It was all that he could do to forget the horrible thing he had seen, as well as the pieces of the puzzle he had yet assembled, but he feared wandering into a world of wealth, intrigue, and danger that he had not anticipated. In his mind, he had always, on some level, believed that the killer was a maniac. It was difficult then for him to confront the idea that such an act of ruthless barbarity might have been committed by one of England's own gentlemen—that a knowing, calculated crime had been committed, rather than one of madness. Having concluded this, the thought of Sir Andrew's murderer escaping justice haunted his every waking moment, but the thought of confronting that butcher haunted his dreams.

However, when pressed by Grantley Manor's steward, Mr. Burton, on behalf of the heirs of the estate, Gallagher asserted that he had not at all relinquished the undertaking which he had initially persuaded them to finance. Mr. Burton was advised that there had been some progress but was at present stalled. Additionally, Gallagher requested a suspension in his payments while he tended to his family for a time, though he assured the steward that after a short respite, his work would resume. Throughout this time, the business of the estate went on as usual, with no new inhabitant taking up occupancy. Mr. Burton took care to deal with the estate's tenants in much the same fashion as he had previously. It was nearly as if life in the village went on as normal.

By the time Bingley recovered from his illness, it was too late for him to attempt a trip to Marseille, and Maitland had had some difficulty in procuring further intelligence as to Lord St. John's travel plans. In the cold, dark of winter, it seemed the waiting game was on. Bingley began to reappear in society little by little, although not nearly with the pleasure that normally accompanied it. He thought of returning to Netherfield, if only to be in the company of Jane Bennet, but his sisters, as well as even Darcy, had spent weeks attempting to convince him that, as pleasantly as she might have received his attentions, it was abundantly clear to them that she had no real attachment to him. It seemed that Caroline, in particular, never let an opportunity go to waste toward the aim of detaching him from Miss Bennet, and in many cases, attempting to attach him to Miss Darcy, despite his feelings on that particular subject which have already been expressed at length. All this increased his vexation and his impatience to hear from his man in France.

Eventually, word arrived from Maitland that Lord and Lady St. John were to journey to Genoa for a duration of four nights, moving from there by sea to Naples, where they would be entertained by Cardinal Ignazio Endrizzi, with whom Lord St. John apparently conducted some form of business, apparently unrelated to Bingley's interests. They were to linger in Naples for a period greater than a fortnight. Bingley then resolved that this would be his best opportunity to bring St. John to proper justice, and hopefully bring the vast and wicked plot to an end, with the added benefit of escaping attentions from investigators or meddling constables at home. Wilshere arranged for a ship to be hired from Portsmouth to Naples. The journey, complete with a stop in Marseille to collect Maitland, would take just over nine days, which would put them into port five nights into Lord and Lady St. John's stay. He also sent word ahead for a man to be hired and begin to gather intelligence on the Cardinal and his home.

It was quite another matter for Bingley to ensure that his sister stayed behind. Caroline was quite adamant that she take the holiday with him, despite his entreaties that the voyage would not be one of pleasure, but rather of business, and a further opportunity for him to collect his health in a warmer climate. She protested at this, as well, claiming to have been far more dangerously ill than he, despite her malady having lasted only a fifth as long as his. He took the measure of enlisting Darcfy's aid in convincing her that the middle of January was not an ideal time to travel abroad, and that she would have much more opportunity for leisure if she remained in London. Bingley believed that it was the prospect of spending more time in the solitary company of Darcy that was the factor weighing most heavily toward her eventual resolution to stay behind. She wished her brother Godspeed and turned her attentions entirely back toward her own self.

Bingley was thankful for Darcy's intervention and, naturally, confided in him the true reason for his sudden excursion. However, there still lingered something in Darcy's manner that Bingley struggled to resolve. His friend was at once steady in his good wishes for the journey and the desired outcome but was also oddly circumspect. In fact, Darcy seemed to be in conflict within his own self, which Bingley found not only peculiar, but downright troubling. Such, however, were the mental demands of his imminent departure that Bingley determined that there would be no solving the dilemma until his return. He and Wilshere were meticulous to ensure that their domestic affairs were in order before boarding their ship and departing into the unknown.

PART III

CHAPTER THIRTY

DESPITE THE BITTER COLD and cutting wind, Bingley spent much of the journey on the ship's deck. This was, in part, because his steward became violently seasick within thirty minutes of leaving port and gave no indications that he would improve over the course of the voyage—and he did not. Their landing in Marseille gave Wilshere a first measure of relief, and even persuaded Bingley to take a hotel for two nights out of compassion for his man. Though the journey be slightly delayed, their landing in Naples would still allow ample time to survey the situation and, most hopefully, the opportunity to plan a strike. During their brief respite, Bingley took the chance to be brought to speed by Maitland on the details of Lord and Lady St. John's trip—their preferences and habits. His lower-class breeding notwithstanding, Bingley was impressed by the young man's intellect, discretion, and attention to even the smallest details. Wilshere, during this time, recovered remarkably well, though his anxiety regarding the completion to their voyage to the Italian coast caused him grave concern. The ship sailed from its berth in Marseille for a further two and half days before docking in Naples. Unfortunately for Wilshere, the additional sixty or so hours on the sea quite lived up to his worst expectation, as he continued to cast up accounts in utter misery. Dry land was, once more, his saviour.

Though the weather was seasonally cool for the coastal Mediterranean city, it was yet a welcome reprieve for the three travellers who were accustomed to more severe winters in the north. As contemplative and focused as Bingley had been on the daunting task at hand, he struggled to restrain his more vivacious spirits in light of the additional sunshine and warmth. He remarked to Maitland that he felt he had not seen a clear blue sky in well over three months' time. The party spent their first afternoon on shore locating their lodgings and settling in. Wilshere would order soup to his room and then sleep, while Bingley and Maitland ventured out for forage. Down the lane and around the corner in the direction of the sea, the pair were overwhelmed by the most singular and seductive fragrance.

"My God," Bingley cried, "what on *earth* is that smell?"

"It is unlike anything I have ever taken in," proclaimed Maitland, with his nose in the air.

"It must be nothing short of the aroma of heaven; it is the incense of the gods."

"The perfume of Venus herself."

"There!" Bingley exclaimed. "It emanates from that shop down the way."

They pushed through the throng of passers-by, drawn on by the scent which had them thus enraptured. A crowd was gathered round a large stone oven. There was shouting and laughter and sudden movements and white sheets tossed overhead. Before they knew it, they had been pressed into a sort of makeshift line and were squeezed ever closer to the fire. The wonderful fragrance enveloped them more and more, until they were nearly drunken on its blissful veil. When they finally reached the front, they were confronted by a man, rather gruffly, in Italian:

"How many?"

"How many *what*?" Bingley asked naively in his limited Italian.

"*Slices*—how many slices?"

"Slices?" Bingley looked nervously at Maitland and then back at the man. "What is that celestial smell?"

"The smell?" asked the man in disbelief. "The pizza. How many slices do you want?"

"Can I try just one, please?" Bingley inquired.

"Va bene, one slice—and you?"

Maitland pointed his finger at himself and shrugged his shoulders. "I do not speak Italian."

"Yes, one for him, too, please," Bingley replied to the oven man.

"Dodici cavalli," the man stated.

"Oh yes, we must pay," answered the gentleman as he fished in his pocket for the correct change. "Here you are."

"Grazie," came the reply. The man tossed the coins in his own pocket, turned, and then shoved a large wooden plate of sorts into the fire and pulled out two enormous slices of thin, glorious pizza, and served it to the two Englishmen. They walked off with their dinner, leaning their noses in and inhaling every few seconds, making "ah" sounds, and smiling giddy smiles back and forth. Finding a bench near the waterfront, they sat and ate, eyes aglow with ecstasy.

"Never in my entire life have I tasted anything so delectable," declared Bingley.

"Nor have I," answered Maitland through a mouthful of cheese. "I do believe this may be the finest meal of my entire life!"

"The very same thought just crossed my mind!"

The two went back to the line and ordered again, and again, eating until they were nearly in pain as the sun faded over the ridge to their west. Even after their last bites were taken and darkness crept in, a sense of euphoria lingered still in the air. Bingley wondered if he should have felt guilt for such enjoyment on such a serious and disagreeable mission.

"We must eat," said he out of the blue.

"Of course, we must," replied Maitland.

Bingley nodded. "I need some wine."

"I need some whiskey."

The pair set off for the hotel and ordered drinks up to Bingley's room. Bingley wrote a letter to Darcy and one to his sister, detailing the experience of the journey and in particularly intimate detail, the culinary experience of the evening. During this time, Maitland sat with his legs propped near the fireplace, smoking a cigar, and sipping from a fine crystal glass. He was thinking that he might become accustomed to luxury such as this; then cautioned himself to enjoy the fruits of Mr. Bingley's generosity with gratefulness and humility.

"Tomorrow," Bingley began without looking up from his letter, "we shall locate the Cardinal's residence."

"Aye, sir," answered Maitland with a puff of smoke.

"From there, we shall formulate our plan."

"Are you concerned that Cardinal Endrizzi may also be involved in some way?"

"Endrizzi and St. John are partners in business, that much we do know. What business they conduct together remains to be seen."

"You must not really suspect that a holy man such as that could be involved in the kinds of evil we are attempting to eradicate, do you?"

"Maitland," Bingley looked up solemnly, "at this juncture, I do not believe there is *anything* that would surprise me."

The young man took the last swig of his drink and placed the glass down gently on the table beside him. "You and I are in accord in that regard."

"I would suspect as much."

"Good night, sir," said Maitland as he rose to his feet. "And thank you... for *everything*."

"You are a good man," Bingley replied. "I will see you at ten in the morning, then."

"Aye, sir."

"Goodnight, Maitland."

With that, the door was closed. By himself in the candlelight, Bingley paused and contemplated writing to Jane Bennet, but his propriety got the better of him. He finished his wine, washed his face, and crawled into bed. He was just enough distracted by the beauty and wonder of this new place that he drifted to sleep easily.

CHAPTER THIRTY-ONE

THE MORNING CAME TO see Mr. Wilshere in much higher spirits. A couple of bland meals and sixteen hours on land had made a world of difference. At breakfast he was surprised by the cheerfulness of his master who, it seemed, could not stop recounting the splendour of a lately discovered Italian dish. In time, the steward was able to settle his master enough to get down to the details of their aim for the day. Maitland had been out early on Wilshere's instructions to get word of the location of the Cardinal's residence. Once he returned, they would hire horses and ride out to make their initial observations. Wilshere had hesitantly hoped that Endrizzi might keep a humble apartment somewhere in the city so that an easy escape into a crowd might be possible after the strike took place. He also wondered if Endrizzi himself might be embroiled in the dirty business of St. John, though for all his worldly knowledge, he still found it difficult to accept that a man of the church would be so debased. It was one thing to be rich or powerful, and iniquitous; it was wholly another, to his mind, for a man devoted to the Lord to be involved in such duplicitous malfeasance.

Maitland entered at half-past ten. Bingley waved him in and toward the buffet which had been laid out. The young man wholeheartedly obliged and began rather unceremoniously piling bread with butter and jam, fresh fruit, pastries, and various cheeses onto his plate. The attendant brought him a glass of Chianti which he also accepted eagerly. Wilshere looked keen to begin discussions, but his master motioned for him to wait until Maitland had had a chance to eat. Once he was sure that their new underling was very near completion of his meal, Wilshere commenced: "What have you learned?"

Maitland nodded his head and wiped his mouth with a cloth napkin. "Much to tell, sir."

"Well, let's have it," said the steward.

"Endrizzi keeps a town home—"

"Excellent news—" Wilshere cut in.

Maitland shook his head. "But he is never there, save three nights per week, and then only for an hour or two." Bingley rolled his eyes. The circles he moved in back home prepared him patently for the declaration Maitland was about to make. "He sees a 'light o'love' there, as one might say."

"Oh, I see," a slightly dejected Wilshere replied.

"Now, where he *lives* is a much more interesting dilemma. His home was appointed by the king but is owned by the church."

"And what does that mean?" Bingley inquired.

"*Protection*—and lots of it," Maitland answered as he took a last swig of his wine. "Gates, walls, soldiers, and the like. The way my man explains it, the Cardinal's residence makes gaining entrance to the castle at Brighton look like opening the door to a sweet shop."

Wilshere and Bingley exchanged glances. "Mr. Bingley, please—" Wilshere tried to head his master off at the thought.

"We may be forced to address the problem publicly."

"Sir," Wilshere started, "with all due respect, there would be hardly time to plan; their movements have been difficult to discover, and—"

"Not quite so fast, Mr. Wilshere," Maitland interrupted. "My man has learned where they are to dine on Thursday evening."

"You keep saying 'my man,' Maitland," blurted Wilshere. "You have been in this country not forty-eight hours—how have you come to develop a trustworthy source in such a short amount of time, pray tell?"

Maitland shrugged and glanced toward Bingley, then back at the steward. "I learned from the best, I suppose."

"You do not even speak Italian!"

"The language of love is universal," the lad countered with a chuckle.

"Maitland, my man," Bingley laughed, "your information may be sound, and no one can discredit your zeal for your work, but the last thing we need is for some trollop to tip you the token."

"Mr. Bingley?" Wilshere asked quizzically.

"To give me the clap," Maitland clarified.

Bingley winced slightly and nodded. "All right, Maitland, well done. Where are they to dine on Thursday evening?"

"A little place called '*Volpe e Cane*.' I am told it overlooks the piazza."

"It will be *very crowded*," uttered the steward.

"*Noted*, Wilshere," Bingley quipped.

"I did not mean to disregard the fact as a negative, sir."

"How so?"

"A large crowd would make for a quick strike and an even quicker exit," explained Wilshere. "Perhaps you use a pistol—fire your shot and disappear into the chaos. You would hardly be noticed at all."

"What if there are two targets, though?"

"Lord and Lady?" Wilshere asked, appalled.

"Lord and *Cardinal*, is more in line with my thinking."

"Mr. Bingley, we have two days' time—I am almost positive we will not be able to ascertain whether or not the Cardinal is involved. Assassinating as high a ranking church official as Endrizzi and on his home ground, no less, would be paramount to a declaration of war between nations if our activities were ever discovered."

"Then we would need to provide proof, if he were involved."

Wilshere exhaled sharply. "And where do you supposed we get this proof?"

Bingley took a bite of an apple and pointed toward Maitland. "He seems to have a knack for that kind of thing."

"Sure, sure," Wilshere started. "Why doesn't he just wait until tonight so that he can interrogate his source again? What was her name?"

"*Carlotta*—at least that is the name she gave me," replied Maitland casually.

"And what name, may I pry, did you give her?"

132

"I told her my name was Robin Hood." Bingley could not help but chortle under his breath, particularly at how cross his steward looked during that moment. "If I hurry, though, I do not believe I will need to wait until this evening."

"And why is that?"

"When I left my room, she was still sleeping."

Small chunks of apple flew from Bingley's mouth as he burst into laughter.

CHAPTER THIRTY-TWO

THAT SAME MORNING, THE bell chimed as the door swung open into Mr. Gallagher's cobbler shop. The Cobbler-Constable glanced up from the work in his hands to see a well habilimented gentleman enter slowly, as if unsure he was in the right place. The man disinterestedly tapped a thin layer of snow from his shoes on the mat just inside the door.

"May I help you, sir?"

The gentleman nodded slightly as he removed his hat. He was portly and balding; and for all his apparent wealth, was rather dishevelled in appearance.

"Are you Gallagher?"

"Aye, sir."

"The Gallagher who has been investigating the mur—or shall I say, *death*?— of Sir Andrew Fraser?"

"I am he."

"Fine," the stranger pronounced, while looking about with obvious distaste for his surroundings. "May I ask why you have taken such an interest in the case?"

"Erm, well, sir," the cobbler stuttered, "it is a matter of justice."

"*Justice*, you say?"

"Aye, sir."

"Tell me then, have you been compensated for your troubles?"

"I have, to an extent," Gallagher answered. The man chewed the inside of his cheek and looked around again before walking closer to the bench where the shop keeper was seated. "I have primarily been reimbursed for expenses."

"Primarily?"

"Aye, sir," replied the cobbler. "I do have a family to feed."

"Understood," the imposing visitor said flatly, still avoiding eye contact completely. "Then why has your inquest ceased?"

Gallagher grappled with his reply. "May I ask, sir, what is your interest in the whole affair?"

"*Justice.*"

He finally looked down at the seated cobbler and locked eyes with him. Gallagher was slightly intimidated; at the same time, he repressed a sudden urge to laugh at the grandiose display of gravity. Now that the man was close enough, he wondered if he smelled of drink. It was only ten in the morning.

"I will ask you once more," the serious stranger continued, "why have you halted your investigation?"

"It seemed to be nearing a dead end."

"It did?—Or you *wished* it to be at an end?"

The cobbler swallowed the lump in his throat. "May I help you in some way, sir?"

"I would like to compensate you for your time," said the man, looming over the shop owner. "I would like you to *finish* the investigation."

"I do not mean any offense or insult at all, but before I answer, I would like to have a plainer understanding of your interest in the case. Are you a relation to Sir Andrew?"

The man's head shook. "A friend."

"I see."

"Is it possible, in your estimation, for the task to be completed within six months?"

"I believe so, sir, but—"

"Is fifty pounds per month sufficient?"

"Fifty pounds per month?" gasped the cobbler.

"In addition to your expenses, and of course, a handsome reward at the proper conclusion of your inquiry." Gallagher stared up at him with eyes aghast. "Naturally, you would follow the investigation *wherever* it might lead—to the very end of the road, and within six months' time."

"I must have your name, sir."

"Hurst."

"It would be my honour, Mr. Hurst."

CHAPTER THIRTY-THREE

BINGLEY AND WILSHERE HIRED a carriage to take them to the piazza where they could survey the layout and features of the landscape. Maitland would meet them in the early evening for dinner and discussion of the latest information on the Lord and the Cardinal. He had, additionally, been charged with the task of locating a pistol. It was early afternoon before Carlotta left his room and left him with all the intelligence he would require.

The piazza was, even at that early hour, as crowded as Wilshere had anticipated. There were lots of buildings surrounding the rectangular-shaped common, with two major lanes leading in and out, but lots of small alleys and corridors that broke off in every imaginable direction. A large fountain adorned the centre and the church loomed menacingly on the south side. The street was cobbled, and a few restaurants and cafes dotted the scene, along with a flower market, tannery, and jewellery shop.

Bingley and his steward located the '*Volpe e Cane*' restaurant where the target—*targets*, potentially—were to dine the following evening. They sat inside and ordered drinks. Bingley was mildly irritated to learn that they did not serve pizza. He had an excellent pasta e fagioli instead. The space was cramped with tables situated in very close proximity to each other, and even during the daytime, not much light penetrated the room. The two men quietly remarked that this was ideal. Once they had finished, they walked round the piazza several times and made endorsements and criticisms about each possible point of exit. It was eventually decided that an alley on the north side, between the flower stall and a leather shop, would be the ideal point of flight once the act was accomplished—it led directly down into the ancient catacombs under the city. They followed the maze of passages out onto a main thoroughfare with intersections along the way. From that point, it would be simple to disappear into a carriage and be off in nearly any direction. Notes were copiously drawn on each detail of their exercise and what elements would be required to make the plan into an actuality.

Eventually, and perhaps not entirely by chance, they found themselves at the same pizzeria where Bingley and Maitland had eaten the previous night. In fact, he was already there awaiting their arrival. They ordered four slices of pizza each and sat at a table across the lane.

"What news have you, *Mr. Robin Hood*?" Bingley quipped.

"Lots," Maitland answered. "Though I am afraid that what I have to say may complicate our business slightly."

"Be so good as to enlighten us."

"Endrizzi is most definitely *not* involved in the particular plot for which we have hunted Lord St. John thus far."

"That simplifies matters, does it not?" Bingley supplicated.

"To an extent, only," retorted the reconnoitre. "There is reason to believe that Napoleon Bonaparte is scheming an invasion of Russia, as you may well know. The Kingdom of Naples, as you are also aware, is nothing more than a French satellite state. While our current situation of war against the Russians in the northern seas is ongoing still, we as British citizens, are appalled by the thought of a further expansion of French power across the continent. The information I have gathered makes it clear that St. John and Endrizzi are in the war munitions business together."

"Are they supplying the French or Russians?" Wilshere asked.

"Neither—they are supplying the *British* navy."

"I do not follow you, Maitland," remarked Bingley.

"I should have been more clear. They are plotting to use St. John's name and status to enter the business, while Endrizzi supplies *faulty* canister shot. The balls do not open when they hit their target—they open when they are *fired*."

"Good Lord," muttered Wilshere.

"St. John becomes even more enriched while the Cardinal means to destroy the British fleet in the northern seas on behalf of his French overlord," said Bingley.

"Do you have proof of this?"

Maitland shrugged. "If you mean to ask if I have notes or letters or purchase orders or agreements, then no, regretfully. Do I have it on reliable information?—I believe so."

"Your whore?" Wilshere demanded.

"Her *uncle*—the foreman in Endrizzi's munitions production factory."

"Well, this is a complication that puts me in a dudgeon from which I am afraid even this heavenly repast may not lift me," declared Bingley, tossing his final slice of pizza down.

"Is it safe to presume that Sir Andrew Fraser was also involved in this particular plot?" Wilshere asked suddenly.

"I think it is," Bingley replied. "An arms deal of that sort would most likely require an endorsement from a respected military figure like Fraser."

"Which means he has been replaced as a figure in the cabal," asserted the steward.

"I believe wholeheartedly you are correct," Bingley said with a cringe. "However, while that detail certainly does complicate our work all the more, it cannot distract from the reason we are here at present, nor can it divert us from settling on the cardinal question of the Cardinal. Do we eliminate both targets?"

"Mr. Bingley, it is *far* too risky," Wilshere chimed up. "The Cardinal is an important figure, and extremely well known locally. The uproar would be tremendous. If you were sighted, I fear we might not ever leave this city alive."

"What say you, Maitland?"

"To my mind," he started slowly, "it is both or nothing. If you eliminate Lord St. John but allow Endrizzi to live, he will simply contact the new military wing of the operation in England and the machination will go forward largely as planned, and our own men and boys will die as a result."

"Mr. Bingley I would strongly advise against such a—"

Bingley put up his hand. "I shall think on it. In the meantime, Maitland, were you able to procure a pistol?"

"Aye, sir—a Francotte. Made in Belgium; quite reliable."

"Good man."

CHAPTER THIRTY-FOUR

WILSHERE SPENT THE BETTER part of the evening detailing plans with his master, while simultaneously reasserting his position that the Cardinal should be left in peace. His continuing overtures to the effect included arguments concerning caution and the difficulty of adjusting their plan at this late hour—how, for instance, would Bingley manage to shoot *both* targets with a single pistol? The steward additionally inserted his distaste for eliminating a clergyman—no matter how morally bankrupt the man might be. Wilshere believed the more prudent course would be to gather more evidence of the plot to sell rigged munitions to the British navy and then return home—possibly, as a national hero. Bingley stirred the fire and sipped his brandy in silence as these diatribes went on. He had looked over the pistol and it was, to his taste, quite satisfactory. He pondered that he might even keep it for his collection at home. At half past one, Bingley sent his man to bed, once again assuring him that his recommendations would be fully and carefully considered.

The next morning the three men shared pastries and tea in a cafe near the water. Their noses were accosted in equal measure by the fresh baked confections and the salty mist from the sea. It was a chilly morning, but the intensity of sun's early rays carried the promise of a warm day. From the bake shop, they had walked through a public park and down to the edge of the sea where they sat while Wilshere once more recounted every detail of their plan as formed.

The Cardinal would travel from his offices separately from the Lord and Lady and reach the restaurant at eight that evening. It was expected that St. John and his wife would arrive to the '*Volpe e Cane*' from an engagement with a countess a quarter-hour later. Maitland had managed to learn, in exchange for five cavalli from a beggar who sat near the fountain in the centre of the piazza, the most valuable intelligence—that the Cardinal's favourite table was the first near the window on the left, if one were facing the establishment. The three then inferred that this table would be reserved for him and his foreign guests that evening. Wilshere had, accordingly, made a reservation at ten to eight for two under the name William Collins. He thought he might have known someone by that name at home in England but could not put his finger on *who*—it had just popped into his mind. Bingley would take the seat facing the front window—and therefore facing his target—order a glass of wine and wait as if he were anticipating the second half of his party. Once Lord and Lady St. John arrived, Bingley would allow them time to be seated and order drinks. At precisely eight-thirty, Maitland was to cause an apparently drunken commotion outside, which would serve as enough distraction for Bingley to fire a single shot into St. John's head and be outside in nearly a single stride. From there, he would break through the crowd and meet Wilshere, who was to be waiting with a lantern at the entrance to the catacombs. A hired carriage would be ready on the surface at the main road; from there, they would be dropped off at the back door of the hotel. One last piece of forethought by Wilshere was to hire Carlotta to stay in Bingley's room and order food and wine on the account. He hoped that if somehow his master was implicated in the shooting, the room bill and the woman's testimony would be enough to establish a consequential alibi.

Maitland spent the afternoon in his room in the company of Carlotta and, presumably, had a nap. Wilshere familiarized himself more closely with the catacombs, walking the dark and anfractuous passages back and forth, again and again. His concern was that he would be well enough acquainted with them to guide his master through them and to safety quickly and efficiently. Bingley returned to his room where he composed a letter to his friend Darcy, though he did not mean to send it. He sealed it and left it on his writing table with the intention that Wilshere should send it if he, Bingley, were apprehended or worse. He had a glass of wine and then found that he could not quiet himself enough to sit still. He spent several hours walking the city aimlessly. At half-past five, he even came across Wilshere outside the entrance to the catacombs along the main thoroughfare which would serve as their exit route. They nodded solemnly toward each other, and Bingley walked on. Once back inside the hotel, he made a point to be seen and noticed, entering with greetings and gestures toward guests and staff alike, before climbing the steps in the direction of his lodging. He returned to his room at a quarter past six to find that Maitland's ladybird had already taken up occupancy in it. He left the room door open after calling down the hall for Wilshere.

"Oh, how do you do?" he stammered nervously to the olive-skinned woman lying stretched on the chaise lounge.

"Ciao," answered she with a smile. He smiled back and nodded skittishly, hands clasped behind his back.

"Wilshere!" he called down the hall again.

"You do not have to be uneasy," Carlotta said slowly in a thick accent. He smiled back and nodded again. "Though a man as handsome as you is always a welcome sight for me."

"Why, thank you," he muttered, looking back down the hall for his steward.

"You have una moglie?"

"Excuse me?"

"Do not worry, I see many married men."

"Oh, no, no," sputtered Bingley. "I am *not* married, though I hope to be, and someday soon."

"So, you have one ragazza—oh, how do you say in English?"

"Lady?"

"Yes! Maybe... *girl*?" replied the courtesan, her dark eyes widening with excitement that she'd stumbled upon the right word. "You have one *girl* you love?" He hesitated to speak, though his thoughts fixed immediately upon Miss Jane Bennet. "I can see that you do from the way you smile now," she said gently.

At that moment, his steward entered. "Oh, I see you have found Miss Carlotta."

"Indeed, I have, thank you," came Bingley's agitated answer.

"I apologize, sir," Wilshere began. "She needed to be seen to come in before you arrived."

"I see. Please bring my clothes to your room, Wilshere. I will dress there."

"As you wish."

"Good luck," called Carlotta just before he left. "You are a man of much virtue—unless you simply find me unattractive?"

"On the contrary," Bingley replied. "You are far too handsome to be in your line of work. I would wish much better for you."

"And I would wish you to marry the girl that you *love*!"

"Thank you," he said with an unaffected smile before turning down the hall. Wilshere bowed and closed the door behind him, following behind Bingley toward his own room. He helped Bingley dress for the evening, making sure to have his master insert the Francotte pistol into the hidden pocket Wilshere had sown inside his jacket once they had loaded and inspected it. Bingley also insisted on carrying his knife in its sheath. "Sir... to what end—"

"If anything were to happen and the gun were to misfire or something worse," Bingley replied slowly, "you know that I am much more comfortable—"

"Say no more, sir," the steward answered. At this moment, he was tying his master's cravat and their pair of eyes were a mere six inches apart. They fell silent after this. In another moment there was a knock at the door. "Yes?" Wilshere called.

Maitland opened the door and looked inside. "It is quarter-past seven. The carriage is waiting downstairs."

"Thank you, Maitland," Bingley answered.

"And Carlotta?" Wilshere inquired.

"She has ordered a bottle of wine and fish of some sort."

"Good," the steward answered as he put the finishing touches on Bingley's cravat. He looked up at his lord, who stood several inches taller than him. "Godspeed, Mr. Bingley."

"Godspeed, Wilshere."

Bingley followed Wilshere down the steps which led to the rear exit of the hotel. The carriage had been situated as close to the door as could be arranged to allow as little chance of him being seen leaving the building as possible. The two men joined a waiting Maitland inside the closed coach. Wilshere shouted toward the driver, and they were off. The three men rode in silence for most of the journey, Wilshere wiping his forehead occasionally with his kerchief. Bingley and Maitland occasionally held eye contact which would be broken by a subtle, but confident nod. At twenty-minutes to eight, the coach entered the piazza and slowed to a stop outside the '*Volpe e Cane*'. Bingley shook hands with each man before he the door was opened, and he departed. From there, the driver slowly crossed through the crowd and allowed the two servants to decamp near the alley between the florist and the tannery.

Upon entering and giving the name William Collins—*why had Wilshere picked that name?*—Bingley was seated directly behind the Cardinal's choice table. He ordered a glass of wine and waited. In a matter of a minute's time, an enormous barouche arrived and from it an enormous man in ecclesiastical regalia emerged. Bingley thought the man must have weighed nearly twenty stone, but as impressive as was his heaviness, his height surpassed that of any Englishman he'd had ever seen. The Cardinal was truly gargantuan. Bingley swallowed a lump in his throat as Endrizzi entered, ducking as he crossed the threshold as to not strike his forehead against the stanchion. He was greeted ardently by the Majordomo who proceeded to kiss the Cardinal's enormous ring. Endrizzi was seated at the front table—just as anticipated—facing the window, hence with his back to Bingley.

Even seated, the Cardinal was a full foot taller than Bingley, who was himself not uncommonly the tallest man in a given room. The Neapolitan's shoulders were square and exceedingly wide, though they tapered to a slim waist. His hair was oiled and combed back, his skin olive and bright in complexion. Bingley glanced down and caught a glimpse of the man's shoes which were so large that they must have been custom fitted. Just at that moment, Bingley's wine arrived at the table. Suddenly, the colossal shoulders turned, and the Cardinal shifted in his seat, glancing directly at Bingley.

"Buonasera," he said in a deep and resonant voice. His chin was square and large, his eyes dark and confident. The black moustache on his lip had obviously been combed and neatly trimmed. Bingley nodded and muttered something nervously.

"Inglese?"

"Sì."

"I am meeting an Englishman here in a few minutes," Enrizzi answered, nearly without accent. "What wine have you ordered?"

"Gaglippo," squeaked Bingley.

"*Excellent* choice," he boomed, cupping his hand and kissing his fingertips. "Had you not ordered it, I would have recommended it. *Here*, they only serve Gaglippo directly from Calabria. If you get it from Marche or Abruzzo, *it's...*" he cocked his head and tilted his hand from side to side. "I hope you enjoy!"

"Thank you."

The Cardinal turned back toward the door just in time for both men to witness Lord Bertram St. John enter the establishment. He himself was a rather bookish man with beady, narrow eyes and a short, up-turned nose. Bingley guessed that he might be exactly half the size of the Napolitano. His hair was grey and thin. In essence, he was very much the opposite of what Bingley had expected he would appear—particularly after becoming familiarized with his imposing portrait. With a bow and a handshake, he sat across from Endrizzi, facing Bingley; although he could not see the Earl, once he was seated, due to the enormous Italian in his path of vision.

Bingley took a sip of the wine and momentarily marvelled at its apparent paradox of structure and lightness. He thought he detected hints of plum and rosemary. It was quite a pleasant experience. He made a mental note to have Wilshere procure several bottles before they departed for home.

"Grazie for coming Lord St. John," Endrizzi spoke. "Is your wife to join us this evening?

"Unfortunately, she has a headache," St. John replied in a shrill voice.

"I am sorry to hear it. I always relish the company of Lady St. John."

"I thank you, and I apologize for her absence."

"There is no need to apologize," said the Cardinal cordially. "It will allow us the chance to discuss business. May I order the wine? The Gaglippo is wonderful, in my opinion. Is it not?" Endrizzi asked suddenly, twisting his massive frame again in the direction of Bingley, who found himself, at that moment, in St. John's direct line of sight.

"Yes, yes," he stammered in reply. "It is superb."

"It makes me very happy that you enjoy it. And I must apologize for my rudeness earlier, sir, I failed to even introduce myself. I am Ignazio Endrizzi, and this is my guest, Lord Bertram St. John, Earl of Canterbury—an Englishman like yourself!"

St. John bowed his head ever so slightly. Bingley was in a near panic—he had not anticipated thus conversing with his target. In a moment of befuddled, near-absent mindedness, Bingley nearly had the "ch" at the beginning of *Charles* on his tongue before he blubbered, "William Collins."

"William *Collins*?" St. John asked in astonishment.

"Aye, sir," answered Bingley hesitantly.

"Of the Hunsford Parsonage in Kent?"

Bingley could hear the blood rushing in his ears. His tongue went numb, and he suddenly felt himself unable to speak. For some mystifying reason unknown to his conscious self, he observed himself to be nodding his head.

"What a peculiar coincidence!"

"Are the two of you acquainted?" Endrizzi queried.

"Yes," replied St. John suddenly. "Though I do not believe we have ever *met*. Instead, I have heard such a marvellous account of your faithful and modest service from Lady Catherine de Bourgh herself. Our families' estates are not but thirty miles apart, and we both summer on occasion in Ramsgate, though I, myself, fancy several locales on the south coast."

Bingley smiled and nodded again.

"And I believe congratulations are also in order," declared St. John.

"Are they?" Bingley inquired.

"On behalf of your recent nuptials."

"Aye, thank you."

"Are you expecting Mrs. Collins?"

"Yes," declared Bingley. "Yes, she is due any minute."

"Wonderful. May I dare say that it is a testament to your service that Lady Catherine would allow you and your wife to accompany her to Naples for your honeymoon—and a tribute to her generosity which, I must admit, surprises me the least bit."

"Lady Catherine... *in Naples*?" Bingley mumbled.

"She is ever so attentive to her daughter's health—is she not?—to holiday each winter in a much warmer climate such as this."

"Yes, she is very attentive," came the stuttering reply

"Well, Mr. Collins, it is very pleasant to meet you at last. Please be sure to introduce me to your wife when she arrives."

"I shall," Bringley answered with a queasy smile.

Endrizzi smiled from ear to ear. "Fantastic! What luck! And you are also a servant of the church?"

"Sì," blurted Bingley.

"I have always marvelled at how simply the English clergy dress—I do not mean to say that your clothes are simple, in fact, they are quite exquisite," the Cardinal mused, looking Bingley over with admiration. "This Lady Catherine must be generous indeed."

At this, St. John squinted and eyed Bingley askance. For his part, Bingley could do nothing but grin uncomfortably. The large churchman then turned back toward his table guest, and to Bingley's relief, their private conversation began. Bingley clutched his knees under the table to halt them from shaking. He took another swig of wine but was not nearly as distracted by its delightfully rounded flavour as he had been just five minutes earlier. After several minutes of ceremonious discourse, particularly regarding Lady St. John's wellness, the conversation between Lord and the Cardinal turned to business. Their tone was cautious, but not particularly reserved, as if they were so well insulated from any type of consequence of their deeds that anyone might hear their words to no effect. Eventually, Bingley managed to overhear the following:

"Ignazio, I am grateful for the opportunity."

"I wondered if you would hesitate on behalf of your loyalties to crown and country."

"My *primary* loyalties are to pound and shilling, as you are well aware."

"We find once again a commonality across language and borders."

"A few dead sailors are a small price to pay for what it will afford us both. And if, in addition, it perhaps prevents England from entering into full-fledged war against France, there is a secondary benefit."

"I could not agree more."

The two men raised their glasses and drank.

"And you have been able to secure the military advocate who will ensure our contract?"

"After the unfortunate death of Sir Andrew—"

"*Che Dio lo riposi*," the Cardinal said while crossing himself.

"Certainly," St. John said dismissively. "I have been able to procure the support of an *active* commander. He will soon move his troops closer to one of my estates, where the details of the contract with the crown will be finalized."

"And this man is trustworthy?"

"He is also a new partner in my *other* venture."

"Very good," Endrizzi said, lifting his glass once more.

"Now, as concerns my offer with regard to the *ragazze*," St. John began again, "are you decided on the matter?"

Endrizzi shifted his massive form in the comparably tiny seat. "There are not many lines that I would not cross. However, and this not a *moral* judgement, of course—I care not how a man provides for himself—I do not believe I would have interest, personally. Having stated that, I would not oppose introducing you with some Turks who would savour the opportunity to buy pale young English girls, and as you know, the virgin kind are their *particular* favourite."

"I assume your normal fee would apply?"

The Cardinal's mountainous head shifted back and forth, his brawny fingers tapping on his chest over his heart. "Because of my *conscience*, I would charge one hundred-fifty percent."

"I accept," the Earl answered, lifting his glass. "*Saluti*."

Without warning, a large bang was heard against the glass, followed by shouting and general ruckus. Endrizzi leaned over the table to get a better look out the window, while St. John turned in his chair to do the same. Bingley rose quickly and unsheathed his knife. He stood beside St. John and said, "Letitia Yates gives her regard." St. John's head swung around quickly, his formerly small eyes as large as apples, suddenly full of comprehension and fear. Bingley slit his throat in a single motion. He gargled and gasped for air as bright red blood spurted across the table, bespattering the Cardinal's white frock. Endrizzi rose with astounding agility and grabbed Bingley's wrist with the strength of a colossus. It was more evident than ever, the two men standing face to face, how herculean the Italian truly was. In his grip, Bingley felt like his bones would snap. St. John meanwhile flailed to the floor, his blood-soaked hands clasped round his gullet in desperate futility. The enormous Cardinal raised his right hand above his head to strike, while Bingley fished frantically for his pistol. Through his coat, he aimed and fired. A blast like a rocket and then the top of Endrizzi's skull spattered against the ceiling. His teeth gritted together, his massive arm still dangling above his head, before he slowly crumpled to the floor. The Cardinal's grip on Bingley's wrist was so tight that even after the man expired, it was a struggle to pry the massive fingers from his arm. Bingley dropped his coat, sheathed his knife, and was outside in a moment.

In the piazza, not fifteen paces from the door of the '*Volpe e Cane*', a tussle was ongoing, and it was but a second before Bingley saw Maitland being choked mercilessly. With the butt of the pistol, Bingley struck his man's attacker. The stranger collapsed and Maitland gasped for air. Through the dense crowd, the din of screams and shouts and chaos, Bingley lifted Maitland by the shoulder and hurried him toward the far corner where Wilshere would lead them through the catacombs. Just before they reached the alley, Bingley caught sight of Lady Catherine, seated beside her daughter Anne, in a cafe. The gaze of both ladies, fortunately, was focused across the way, toward the uninterrupted bedlam outside the '*Volpe e Cane*'. Bingley lowered and turned his head as to not be identified. When they reached the passageway, Bingley perceived a look of shock across his steward's face. He looked down at himself and for the first time observed that his own shirt was spattered with blood.

"Give me your coat," he demanded. Wilshere quickly shook himself out of it and helped Bingley on with it.

"This way, this way," Wilshere directed, lifting the lantern, and leading down a stone stairwell.

The catacombs, flame from the steward's lamp aside, were as dark as the inside of a coffin. Disquieting moans and shouting reverberated from seemingly all directions. Bingley breathed heavily as they moved as fast as the dearth of light would allow. The deeper they descended under the city, the more enveloped in darkness he felt; it was like a cloak around his body and a pillow over his face. When they finally emerged from the depths, the coach awaited them as directed. Once safely inside, Bingley shook uncontrollably while Wilshere held his shoulders and tried to calm him.

"We must depart this very evening," Bingley declared.

"Sir, there are no ships that—"

"The cost is irrelevant. We must not be in this kingdom come sunrise."

"Mr. Bingley," Wilshere started, "I do not understand. Are you concerned that Endrizzi might identify you?"

"Endrizzi is dead."

Wilshere expression betrayed his surprise. "The *Cardinal* is dead? And St. John?"

"Both," declared Bingley calmly. "St. John by the sword; Endrizzi by lead."

"And Lady St. John?"

"She was not present."

"Then it is over, sir. You have accomplished your aim and then some."

"No," Bingley shook his head. "First of all, George Wickham is still alive. Secondly, Sir Andrew Fraser's replacement has been commissioned."

"Who is it?"

"I do not pretend to know with any degree of specificity. He is another military man but not of any particularly great rank. That is all the information I have been able to ascertain to this point. We must work to confirm this man's identity and move swiftly against him."

"But sir, the plot is surely foiled."

"It may be, but that is of no consequence," said Bingley. "I cannot allow a man as depraved as would involve himself in such an enterprise to simply carry on without repercussion."

"I understand sir, but there is nothing to be done about that *tonight*. We must rest this evening and make our departure plans tomorrow."

"Because I may have been seen by Lady Catherine de Bourgh or Miss Anne de Bourgh or both of them!"

"Lady Catherine de Bourgh? Mr. Bingley, whatever do you mean?"

"They are here on holiday—and were eating at the cafe near the alley."

"Good God."

Bingley had, by this point, managed to calm his physical convulsions, but he looked down at his blood-stained hands and trousers in disgust. He glanced over at the silent Maitland whose head rested on the carriage door. There were dark red marks in the shape of fingers around his neck. He breathed slowly.

"Are you hurt, Maitland?"

"No, sir," came the breathy answer. "You surely saved my life."

Bingley nodded. "I could do nothing less."

The coach halted at the back door of their hotel.

"I will see to it that you are washed and comfortable, sir," Wilshere pronounced. "Then I will find a ship that can depart this evening for either Palermo or Cagliari."

"I can manage to wash myself, Wilshere," retorted Bingley. "You must go and see to the ship with great urgency."

Bingley helped Maitland up the stairs and to his room, before sending Carlotta to tend to him. The master then took off his boots from the Marylebone Collection and stripped down completely. He threw all his clothing, save Wilshere's outer coat, in the fireplace and prodded it repeatedly to ensure that it burned. From the basin of fresh water, he washed and dried himself as quickly as he could manage and then donned fresh attire. He poured a full glass of brandy and grabbed a hunk of bread from the bounty Carlotta had ordered up before he sat down heavily in the chair by the fire. He ate nervously and swigged heartily. Then taking up the letter he had written to Darcy, he placed it in the fire, as well, and then stirred it again. Once he had finished his bread and brandy, he began packing what remained of his belongings into his trunks. Though he was not at all accustomed to putting his own things away, he felt that every advantage toward readiness of flight would be beneficial. Just when he was nearly through, his door flung open without a knock. Wilshere entered; his face was covered in sweat.

"Mr. Bingley, we must make haste this instant," he panted.

"Is the ship ready?"

"Yes, but also, the gendarmerie has arrived downstairs."

"*What?*"

"*Now* sir, I beg you. The coach awaits at the rear exit."

"Have you got to Maitland?"

"Not yet, sir. But we must not linger a moment longer."

"Take this," Bingley said, handing him a trunk. "I shall carry the other two then come back for your trunks. Get Maitland and get to the coach."

"Mr. Bingley, there is not—"

"There is not time for you to question me, steward," Bingley snarled.

Wilshere took the chest and spun back out into the hall in the direction of Maitland's room. There was a mad rush down the stairs, up the stairs, and back down. Commotion could be heard in the direction of the foyer and Bingley even caught sight of a uniformed officer mounting the front stairway. He dashed out with the last of Wilshere's trunks and had the driver hastily mount them before he climbed into the coach. Anxiously Bingley peered out the windows, waiting for his men to appear while simultaneously keeping watch. Just as he began to consider the very real possibility that his men had been arrested, Wilshere and Maitland burst from the exit. Bingley opened the carriage door, and they shot inside with Maitland's trunk, all the while Wilshere shouting at the driver to be off. Bingley only managed to close the door as the coach sped off, leaving a gaggle of running gendarmes in its wake.

"Wilshere?"

"They have traced you to the hotel, sir, but no further, I assure you."

"How can you be certain?"

"The room was reserved under the name Boykov. I left Carlotta with another twenty cavalli to confirm that we are Russians and are heading across the country for the port of Bari. As long as we get to our ship and set sail, we are safe."

The ride was maddeningly long. Bingley continued to nervously spy out the small back window to discern whether they were being pursued. After what seemed an eternity, plus some, the coach stopped at a pier and the three men inside disembarked, gathering their trunks with the help of the driver and a member of the ship crew. The boat was alarmingly small for overseas travel, but was ready for immediate departure and was, additionally, had at a price reasonable given the circumstances. After being reassured that the crew of four and the captain routinely made voyages of such delicate nature back and forth to Sicily, Bingley and Maitland sat in the mess room where, to their pleasant surprise, they were offered rum and salted fish. Wilshere stayed atop the deck, and once they were but sixty meters from shore, began to heave into the sea.

The voyage of roughly one hundred and seventy nautical miles progressed slower than they might have hoped, and the total journey spanned just over twenty-two hours. However, once the party had alighted onto the soil of the Kingdom of Sicily, the three fugitives felt an enormous sense of relief, Mr. Wilshere in particular. They took a hotel just across the lane from the port, which had been recommended by the ship's captain. Once their various belongings were situated in their various rooms, each man collapsed onto his bed. None of the three stirred until after noon the following day.

CHAPTER THIRTY-FIVE

WHEN WILSHERE FINALLY AWOKE, he sat up slowly and parted the curtain by the bedside window. The sky was grey and what tree branches he could see fluttered and swayed in the wind. It did not appear to be raining at present, but a misty spray hung on the street side of the glass. The steward's head pounded, though he felt much better being on dry land. He rang the bell and ordered tea and rolls from the man who came to attend him. The small breakfast helped further settle his stomach and calm his pounding temples. He washed and dressed, then walked to the window that overlooked the harbour. At first glance he merely enjoyed the view, but he then noticed a solitary figure seated under a canopy near the water's edge, and after squinting tender eyes, became quite positive it was his master.

Wilshere wondered at the toll all this nasty business was taking on Mr. Bingley—the hunting, the hiding, the secrecy, and of course, the act of killing itself. For a man of such breeding, character, and gentle kindness, even the ends could not possibly alleviate any anguish caused by the horrendous nature of the means. His master—a wealthy, cultured, and sophisticated man—truly was at heart, a servant of the least connected and most vulnerable members of society. Wilshere reflected on the personal cost of this journey to his master, in not only sterling, but in mental and emotional throe. Mr. Bingley, by all accounts, should be enjoying the advantages of his rank and his youth. He was the most agreeable man Wilshere had ever met, let alone worked for. He was handsome and tall, affluent and easy-going—he should be, at this time in his life, consumed with thoughts of marriage and starting a family.

His master was universally admired for his generosity, his gentility, and his easy manners. It was, unfortunately, these very qualities that suited him, perhaps above all others, for the grotesque calling into which he had been unwittingly hurled. He was equal parts selfless, capable, and just. Wilshere could only hope the vile plot, and its loathsome culprits could finally be dismantled—and quickly.

The steward donned his coat and walked down to where his master sat near the dock. "Mr. Bingley," he said calmly.

"Mr. Wilshere," came the weak reply.

"Are you well, sir?"

"Aye," he answered. His face was turned down and away from his steward, his collar flipped up over his neck to block the wind.

"Have you eaten, sir?"

"I have not."

"Shall I retrieve something for you?"

"I thank you, no." Bingley looked up at him and sighed deeply. His eyes were red; his cheeks tear stained. He sniffled and wiped his nose with his kerchief.

"It is nearly over, sir," stated Wilshere.

Bingley nodded solemnly, then turned his eyes back toward the sea. "Does a man ever become accustomed to killing?" he asked, nay, pleaded.

"Many do, sir," replied the steward. "But to your credit, *you shall not.*"

"That does not make the task any easier."

"If the task were easy, Mr. Bingley, it would not have fallen to you."

"I do not grasp your meaning."

"Your mission is a just one, sir. If you were the kind of man whose conscience could become callous to taking life, you would no longer be worthy of it—it would cease to be just. I am convinced, sir, that you are among the very best of men, and such acts of justice can truly fall only to a man of stalwart character and decency like yourself."

"Will it ever end, though? Will there ever *be* justice?"

"One day, there will, and it will not be retributive, it will be restorative. But until that remarkable day, you have been tasked with defending the innocent, the assailable, and that is a holy duty, indeed."

"Thank you, Wilshere," answered Bingley, wiping his eyes with his sleeve. Looking back toward the open expanse of sea, he said, "I believe that we should avoid Marseille."

"Why is that?"

"I have just committed double murder on territory controlled by the French. I do not suppose it would be entirely safe to put into shore there."

"I see. I will inquire about a boat that might take us straight back to England."

"Inquire about Lisbon," Bingley said. "I have always desired to journey there, and I believe we are due some time in ease and repose."

"Aye, sir."

"Also, have thirty pounds sent to the father of Leticia Yates as soon as possible, and anonymously, of course."

"As you wish."

The party stayed on in Palermo for four days before boarding the Portuguese vessel named *Senhora Sagrada*, which Bingley came to learn translated into English as *Sacred Lady*. The journey to Lisbon took six days—six miserable days, in Wilshere's case. The three men stayed in a seaside hotel for more than a fortnight before setting off for London. From the dock along the Thames, Maitland was given a fortnight's leave to Birmingham, while Wilshere and Bingley arrived at the house on Grosvenor Street that same day—Friday, the fourteen of March.

CHAPTER THIRTY-SIX

ALTHOUGH, OR PERHAPS BECAUSE, he had not seen his sister in nearly two months, Bingley struggled to cope with her oppressive bearing. Caroline assailed him for hours on end about the details of his travels, while impeding, by her own self-absorption, each of his attempts to apprise her of said details. Often, he would have only just begun to speak, when she would launch into a lengthy oration about the latest fashion trends for ladies, the balls and soirées she had attended in his absence, and even occasionally a disingenuous gibe about the provinciality of those long and tedious evenings spent in and around Meryton. He inquired timidly if she had been in correspondence with any of the Bennets or other families from Meryton, to which she replied in the negative. She did, however, remember that she had received a rather dull reply from Miss Jane Bennet, after inviting her to visit in London, in which she had stated her strong aversion to travel of any type. "Miss Bennet," Caroline recalled with effected indifference, "does not wish to take leave of her mother. Jane is *very attached*, you see, and has no desire, *in the least*, to leave her side."

Through a squint of his eyes and a tilt of his head he had a strong notion that she was lying—at least about *something*, though naturally he could not infer about what in particular. Had she indeed been in further contact with Jane?—or were there other extenuating circumstances that prevented Jane from being in town, other than close familial bonds? His immediate instinct was to depart for Netherfield that evening, but he knew he would be hedged in and berated at the very suggestion of it and lacked, at present, the energy to deflect such a tirade. There was too much merriment to be had in town yet, and with the weather still quite in the grip of winter—according to his sister—he was sure to be reminded of miserable travel conditions and more. It did enliven him to recall, however, that he would have the opportunity of seeing Darcy for at least several days before he and his cousin, Colonel Fitzwilliam, departed for their aunt's house in Kent—

Lady Catherine.

A cold shiver racked Bingley's spine at the mere mental recollection of her name. Surely, she had not seen him that night in Naples—*what if she had?* He had been in her company but a handful of times in his life, but those meetings were enough to convince him that a woman of her obduracy and austerity would not fail to make note of such an inexplicable chance encounter on the far side of the continent. Perhaps she had only a suspicion that she had, indeed, seen Charles Bingley covered in blood, racing through a public square in the seconds after a notorious double homicide was committed? And if it were more than a creeping suspicion, would it be enough for her to, perhaps, breach propriety and question her nephew Darcy about it? Would she solicit from him the whereabouts of his friend during the winter? He resolved that he must prepare his friend for such a possible interrogation, lest his activities came under further scrutiny on British soil.

On the Monday after he had returned, Bingley spent the better part of the afternoon, and into the evening, attending to his various—legitimate—business ventures. He was advised of the unfortunate news that, while the crew had been rescued, a large consignment of timber, in addition to furs, from Canada in which he had an interest had been lost during the penultimate week of February when the vessel known as "Renown" ran ashore off Penzance and sunk the following morning. The insurance policy on the vessel only covered *cost* of merchandise lost and would take several months to be paid. The singular shipwreck aside, his affairs were still in good order, and he could even expect a marginal increase in his expected income for the first quarter.

When he arrived back at the Grosvenor Street address, he was startled by his steward's insistence that he be immediately granted a private audience. Bingley's coat had hardly been taken before Wilshere whisked him down the hall and into the master's private study.

"We have reason to believe the Constable from Grantley has not yet abdicated his obligation to seek out the killer of Sir Andrew Fraser," the steward said in grim ferment.

"Lord almighty, Wilshere," Bingley replied. "Would you pour me a drink, or at the very least have Ridley pour one, before you start with all this rubbish?" The steward's mouth contorted frenetically for the span of half a second before he turned and was down the hall. Bingley rubbed his temples with his fore and middle fingers on both sides while closing his eyes and inhaling slowly. He only opened his eyes when he heard the agitated footsteps of his man returning up the hall. Wilshere entered with a hastily poured glass of sherry. "When do we expect Darcy?" Bingley asked, taking the glass, and smelling its contents before sipping.

"He shall be here for dinner, sir," replied an exasperated Wilshere.

"And what does Jensen have on the menu for this evening?"

"Pea soup, veal cutlets, asparagus, lamb, and salad alongside apple pudding and pineapples, sir."

"Very good," mused Bingley. "Have Jensen put some pudding back for me. I shall require another serving before I retire for the evening."

"Aye, sir."

"What do you anticipate for the weather tomorrow?"

"Cold."

"Undoubtedly." Bingley idled intentionally, taking a turnabout room and cupping his hands by the fire. "Was there something else that you required, Wilshere?"

"The *Constable*, sir."

"Oh, yes, do remind me about the Constable," Bingley quipped with feigned disinterestedness.

"It appears that he has resumed his inquest into the death of Andrew Fraser."

Bingley ruffled his nose and bit at the corner of his mouth. "Is the estate so troubled by his murder? It would seem to me that whatever distant relation should inherit such a grand domain would be content to take it over from such an odious man."

"The estate continues to finance the Constable's inquisition at a rudimentary rate—which, to my mind, does seem rather more out of obligation than fervour for justice."

"Why then has this Constable of late become so freshly entrenched?" Bingley asked.

"It seems, sir, that there is a private donor to the cause," answered the steward.

"A private donor? And what is his interest?"

"Justice, it would seem—and justice solely."

"This is enough to cut up my peace," the master said, swigging his wine. "And who is this new benefactor?"

Wilshere shook his head quickly. "I do not know, sir. That information has been impossible to come by. I would assume it is a business relation or a close friend."

"You do not think—"

"Mr. Hurst?"

Bingley's eyes darted to and fro around the room as if he were connecting visual dots within his psyche. "Surely they were not so closely connected."

"His reaction, sir," Wilshere began with a shrug, "was rather severe."

"He was dipping more deeply than usual in the weeks after the news, was he not?"

"Most of his waking hours were spent properly shot in the neck, as I recall."

"You must do some digging on the matter," Bingley directed. "But with great care and discretion; he is my relation, after all."

"Of course, sir."

"You would not believe Mr. Hurst could have been *involved* with Fraser's plot, would you?"

"I have never come across anything that would even mildly suggest a connection in that particularly untidy arrangement."

"Was he perhaps a patron of it?" Bingley asked with a look of disgust on his face.

Wilshere paused, considering scrupulously his thoughts. "We have become accustomed to shocking revelations over the course of recent time. Any involvement on Mr. Hurst's behalf would surely give me a fit of the blue devils. He may be a bit of a rube for someone of his situation, but I do not believe him to be a man of ill character."

"Nor do I," stated Bingley, sipping the last of his wine. "Any word on Wickham?"

"It would seem that he now fancies himself in the pursuit of a Miss Mary King."

"Mary King? —was her grandfather Atticus King, of Liverpool?"

"Aye," responded Wilshere. "The shipping magnate. Indeed, he bequeathed her ten thousand pounds upon his passing."

"Surely her fortune is his target, then?"

"She is also very young," retorted the steward.

Bingley cocked his head to one side and fidgeted with the cuff of his coat. "It does not fit the pattern."

"How so, Mr. Bingley?"

"Every young lady who has as yet been abducted and killed has had little family protection to recommend her. Targeting someone of Miss King's situation would be highly imprudent. Her familial connections, not to mention fortune, would expose the entire plot to intense and extremely public scrutiny."

"I see," Wilshere replied. "Then perhaps he truly is no more harmful than your common fortune-seeker."

"Unfortunately, Wilshere, I believe Mr. Wickham to be even more dangerous because he is disposed to seek his fortune at any cost. If he can marry into wealth, he certainly will; if he must murder his way to affluence, I am persuaded that he shall not hesitate on that score, either."

The room fell silent for a moment.

"Shall there be anything else, sir?" Wilshere finally asked, sensing that his master perhaps wished to be left in solitude.

"Yes, Wilshere," Bingley said, leaning against the large mahogany desk. "Have you any word of Miss Bennet?"

"Unfortunately, no, sir."

Bingley nodded and looked down absentmindedly at his empty glass.

"Shall I bring you another glass of sherry, Mr. Bingley?"

"Oh," the master said, seemingly awakened from a dream. "That is very kind of you. And be sure to have one yourself, Wilshere."

"Thank you, sir," the steward answered. "I always have one with dinner."

Bingley smiled sullenly as his man went back up the hall to fetch more wine. He was indeed thankful for the half hour in seclusion before Darcy and Georgiana arrived. His pleasure in seeing his dear friends after what seemed like a long and arduous interval was somewhat curtailed by the overbearing interference of Caroline, who was sure to compliment Darcy's sister in the most hyperbolic language she could muster. It was Caroline's fixed desire to have her brother notice each of Georgiana's perfections, of which, admittedly, there were many. His genteel nature and concern for the feelings of his good friend's young sister compelled him to courteous replies to his own sister's effluence of flatteries. Georgiana, for her part, was all parts humility and good breeding, accepting adulation with grace and even a degree of self-deprecation. She was a good-spirited girl who, despite her lofty and advantageous position in life, thought of herself in a seemingly ideal balance of confidence and modesty.

Once their guests had finally been settled and reacquainted with each other, the party dined. To Bingley's surprise, Darcy was more reserved than usual in his company, and he even sensed in his demeanour a certain restlessness that was quite out of the ordinary. Nevertheless, Bingley devoured his serving of apple pudding before requesting that his friend join him in the study.

"Darcy, you must tell me whatever is the matter," Bingley urged while he poured two glasses of brandy from a crystal decanter.

"What is your meaning?" Darcy asked with an attempt to deflect his disquietude.

"You seem out of sorts."

"As do you, I might add."

"Perhaps I am," countered Bingley, handing his friend a glass of amber-coloured inebriant. "Though my reasons for being forlorn and disconsolate should be rather apparent."

"Are they?"

"For one, I have just returned from a rather abominable holiday abroad."

"It came to my attention that several weeks back that the Earl of Canterbury met a grim end whilst in Naples," remarked Darcy playfully.

"Indeed, he did," Bingley answered in a tone that betrayed the conflict in his soul.

"And what other reason do you have for melancholy?"

"Among your many aptitudes, Darcy," Bingley began with a chuckle, "you certainly possess a talent for averting any discourse on your private thoughts."

"I do not wish to obscure my personal feelings from you in the slightest, my friend," replied Darcy after sipping his brandy. "On the contrary, what vexes me is a concern of the heart that I should hope may be settled in a matter of a fortnight."

Bingley had his glass half-raised to his lips when he put it down on the table next to him. "Surely you are not inferring that your cousin—"

Darcy shook his head. "I shall not enter into an agreement of marriage with my cousin, Anne de Bourgh, despite the most ardent wishes of my aunt."

"I see," was all the answer Bingley could marshal.

"Your friendship is dear to me, Bingley, and I pledge that once my current state of suffering is settled, for better or for worse, you shall be apprised of the matter in all its detail."

Bingley nodded and sipped at his drink.

"What of the other matter of *your* despondency?" Darcy inquired.

"It is difficult to say, even with a friend as close as you."

"If you do not feel inclined—"

"I am in love with Miss Jane Bennet, Darcy, and I cannot be persuaded otherwise."

Darcy's eyes narrowed slightly before he turned his attention anxiously to the glass in his hand. "Charles," he began, with perhaps a modicum of vacillation in his voice, "I would entreat you to be cautious with such declarations. Certainly, you have not forgotten the position of her family, to say nothing of the wanton impropriety—"

"I have not forgotten a thing," Bingley interjected. "My entire life has been an exercise in *caution*—from my upbringing to my time at school to my business practices to the endeavour of staying alive and keeping my neck out of the hangman's knot. For once in my life, I want to feel something *freely*—I want to give myself with abandon to the woman I love."

"Are you, then, convinced unequivocally that Miss Bennet would reciprocate your feelings?" Darcy challenged.

"It is not a matter of unequivocal certainty, Darcy," rebutted Bingley. "My heart demands that I, at the very least, make my feelings known."

Mr. Darcy shifted his weight restlessly on the sofa and drew a deep breath. "Having considered all things, Bingley, you must not be *hasty*—that is all that I ask. Your mission should be completed before the distraction of matrimony weighs down upon you. And even if, as you have declared, you truly love Miss Bennet, would it be prudent to marry with such dreadful business unfinished? What if you were to be killed or captured? Your wife—whoever might be so fortunate as to secure that title—would be *disgraced*. In light of your feelings and your honour this consideration must be borne with solemn gravity."

"I cannot say that I disagree with your reasoning," Bingley admitted. "But it pains me greatly all the same."

"Your feelings are natural," stated Darcy with sympathy. "From all appearances, your vocation of justice is nearly at an end. Take comfort in that, at least. You shall have your happiness, and God knows it will be well deserved."

"Thank you. I dearly hope that you are correct."

The two men sat in silence for a moment, both of them lost in their own thoughts.

"Before the thought escapes me completely," Bingley abruptly proclaimed, "there is a very slight possibility that your aunt and your cousin *may* have observed my fleeing the scene of Lord St. John's murder."

At those words, Darcy's jaw dropped, though he felt a sudden urge to laugh for a reason he could not explain. He listened to Bingley's recollection of the incident and assured his friend that whatever Lady Catherine might have *thought* she had observed, her adulation for her nephew would certainly permit Darcy to convince her otherwise.

CHAPTER THIRTY-SEVEN

BINGLEY SPENT THE REST of the week largely in Darcy's company, aside from his friend's time spent making final business preparations before his departure for Kent. Though there was much that he had learned from Darcy, the most tangible lessons had been in regard to financial affairs. Having inherited his fortune from the man who directly created it, Bingley depended greatly on the advice and example of his friend who had learned the more refined methods of wealth management from countless proceeding generations of men who had inherited, increased, and passed on their prodigious capital. For his part, Mr. Darcy had always been forthright and willing to support his friend by any means possible.

Their meetings that week, however, were marred by what Bingley perceived as an increasing imbalance on the part of Darcy—in one moment he might be dolorous and lost in rumination, the next he was uncommonly exultant and much more talkative than was his usual manner. When further pressed in private about his curious behaviour, Darcy referred Bingley back to what he continually referred to as, "a concern of the heart, which would be soon settled, for better or for worse." Despite his denials to the contrary, Bingley could not help but think his friend was feeling the pressure of visiting his aunt whose singular desire with regard to her nephew was seeing him wed to her infirm daughter. Presumably, he intended to use the occasion of this visit to Rosings Park to settle that score once and for all.

When Darcy and his cousin Fitzwilliam departed London for Kent, his sister Georgiana stayed behind with her recently procured governess for another fortnight and accompanied Bingley and Caroline to dinner and the theatre on multiple occasions. He got the feeling that Georgiana enjoyed their personal company much more than the crowds of admirers and sycophants which made up the preponderance of the populace in larger social settings. Georgiana was amiable, talented, and undoubtedly handsome, but she was hardly noticed for such qualities in the blinding light of her substantial fortune. Though her conversation was erudite beyond her years and her disposition gracious and pleasant, it pained Bingley that these were not qualities appreciated by the young men who courted her, nor by the young ladies who displayed the bare minimum of civility in rather puerile efforts to conceal their envy. These same young ladies were often dealt perceived slights by suitors who paid them attentions only after failing to secure the continued regard of Miss Darcy. Bingley could not help, but in this circumstance, to feel solidarity with her—affluence could be as much a curse as a blessing. It was over the course of those weeks, then, that the two resisted Caroline's best efforts to accept every single desirable invitation they received—and there was no shortage of desirable invitations. He did acquiesce to some of her requests—more than he might have otherwise endured—bearing in mind that having been out of the country for so long, it was prudent for the viability of continued secrecy surrounding his surreptitious ventures, to appear to be the same affable and untroubled young man he had once sincerely been. His time, then, was spent in the delicate balance of appeasing his sister and preserving his own sanity. Additionally precarious was the act of feigning interest in the many eligible ladies to whom he was continually introduced—none of whom in his mind could hold a flame to Jane Bennet. Unfortunately, his tacit indifference to all the most recent young ladies to have been presented at court convinced his sister all the more that his attachment to Georgiana Darcy increased with each passing day. Their attachment, however, consisted still merely in a sense of friendship, born of similar circumstances in upbringing and position.

During this period of counterfeit diversion, Maitland was dispatched to the village of Grantley to accumulate information about the state of the cobbler-constable's ongoing investigation into the murder of Sir Andrew Fraser. Wilshere sent other trusted servants in the directions of Brighton, Kent, and Canterbury, all with the aim of unearthing the identity of the newly appointed military arm of the late Lord St. John's evil plot. The latter assignments were, indeed, two-fold: the second task being to establish whether the nasty business of abducting young maidens for the gratification of wealthy fiends was ongoing in the absence of the Earl of Canterbury. The master and his man had furthermore considered dispatching a man to shadow Mr. Hurst, as he and Louisa had been called to the north to attend to a property they owned near Harrogate, but it was decided that he was harmless enough and was unlikely to be enmeshed in Fraser's repulsive game. For Bingley then, all that was left to do was bide his time and imagine a scenario in which he could return to Netherfield and be at once in Jane's presence without Caroline's endless harassment which would no doubt ensue. All his thoughts and prayers were consumed in wishing that winter, in its frigid indifference to the plight of his heart, would soon give way to the sunny rays of spring.

CHAPTER THIRTY-EIGHT

SHORTLY AFTER THE MIDPOINT of April, Mr. Wilshere received word from Mr. Darcy's steward that he and Colonel Fitzwilliam had departed Rosings Park in Kent directly for Pemberley. Wilshere had also been given assurances that Darcy would write Bingley as soon as the opportunity presented itself. Darcy would either return to London in a fortnight or send for Georgiana at that time if his business in the north detained him further. Darcy did relay that in his aunt's extensive recollection of her trip to Naples—including a full accounting of her vexation at presence in close proximity to a crime of such gruesome and wholly debased nature as murder—Mr. Bingley's name was never averred. No further details accompanied the report.

"Undoubtedly, had she seen me she would have reported it to Darcy."

"Certainly, sir," the steward replied.

"But still, what an *odd* dispatch," Bingley remarked.

"Indeed, sir," answered Wilshere. "It is most unlike Mr. Darcy in its dearth of fraternal timbre."

"It clearly must be related to his visit at Rosings, no?" Wilshere shrugged. "Though the words are his, the intonation is that of a man distressed by... Distressed by what? Surely he did not *propose* to Anne—or perhaps, conversely, he made it plain that he had no intentions to do so, and that greatly vexed Lady Catherine?"

"I have not known Mr. Darcy to be a man excessively concerned troubled by the wishes of his aunt."

"No, indeed."

After several moments of reflective silence, Wilshere began to relate the latest information from their reconnoitrers throughout the country. His men had effectively established that the trade in young ladies had been somewhat curtailed by the downfall of Lord St. John but had been unsuccessful in uncovering the identity of the new appointee who would replace Sir Andrew Fraser. In addition to the fruitful discovery of the dark fraternity's extant operation, Wilshere's men reported another troubling piece of news: that George Wickham's involvement appeared in every report from every direction. It was widely believed he was a low-level operative, but he was undoubtedly responsible for the procurement of innocent young ladies on behalf of the vile plot. Bingley's worried thoughts immediately turned to Longbourn and the Bennet girls. He even imagined that exterminating Wickham would give him cause to return to Netherfield, but this plan was checked by his better judgement. He could not simply return to the area and immediately dispatch with Wickham—such an overt act would be reckless and cause too much suspicion to befall him. After learning from his steward that, though the repugnant scheme was dormant but temporarily, no young women had disappeared since the murder of Lord St. John in Naples. With this information in hand, in addition to the fact that the Bennet sisters' status did not fit the profile of those young ladies who had fallen prey, he considered that they were safe—at least for the time being.

From Grantley Village, Maitland had learned that Constable Gallagher was preparing a voyage to London once the weather had warmed slightly. The young man had attempted to earn the cobbler's trust by offering himself as an apprentice, but Gallagher had patently refused. Though they met by chance—or so it was made to appear—at the local alehouse on several occasions, Maitland had hardly been able to coax any relevant information from him. Even on those evenings where the shoemaker drank too much, he remained resolutely tight-lipped in regard to his investigation. There was hardly a useful word from the entire town on the subject. The cobbler was apparently solemn in the pursuit of his duty.

As the following week wore on in tedium—one soiree after the next on behalf of his sister—Bingley took seriously the thought of initiating correspondence with Darcy but thought the better of it each time he sat down to write. He even briefly contemplated leaving at once for Derbyshire, but again reconsidered on the basis that, though his friend would most likely welcome his company out of civility, he was more likely to consider Bingley's unannounced arrival as an imposition, and a needlessly impulsive deed. He had never known Darcy in such a state of emotional disquietude and was simply bewildered as to how to act.

Fortunately for Bingley, while he and Caroline took tea the following afternoon, Ridley, the footman, introduced Georgiana who presented a letter for Bingley from her brother. He thanked her and then excused himself to his study to read it. He fumbled hurriedly with the seal and unfurled several sheets of Darcy's careful and practiced hand.

Dear Bingley,

Please pardon my recent detachment. I can assure you that my hasty and unexpected withdrawal from society, including your cherished company, was by no means intended as a slight against you, my dear friend. As you will undoubtedly recall, my emotional state prior to my departure from London was visceral and quite beyond the control of my faculties, as much as it shames to me admit. In your position, as one of the more intimate companions of all my associations, it is likely that you observed such uncharacteristic volatility in my countenance. I would like to make an apology for any manner in which my state of heightened inner turmoil may have affected or offended you.

My visit to Rosings began initially quite as expected, though indeed, rather more pleasantly than I had anticipated. Our days were spent in remarkably more sunshine than is usual during that time of year; our nights spent in the most agreeable company I might have ever imagined—my aunt's overbearing fatuity aside. By the halfway mark of my visit, I was nearly convinced that my future would be in large part decided before I withdrew back to town. Oh, what terrible turns our best intended plans can take!

Before I could fully appreciate what was happening, a storm born of my own naivety and ignorance descended upon me like a mighty scourge from the heavenly realms. At present I have finally, I believe, begun to unravel the enigma of my own uncompromising weaknesses, to which I have, perhaps, been wilfully blind. I would by no means intend you any distress, but I hardly feel after such an upheaval of my mind and spirit, that I am half the man I was a month ago. I do not know if I will ever fully recover from such a blow to the image of the man I had aspired to be. For most of my life I have been dutiful to craft my character as a gentleman worthy of my position, worthy of the legacy to which I have been charged by not only my own dear father, but those gentlemen who proceeded him into death. I have never taken lightly my responsibility to my estate, my family, and those within the scope of my influence. I cannot relay the distress I have felt these last weeks in the apprehension that I have let them all down.

As you are aware, it is not at all habitual for me to use such emotive language in my correspondence, but I would have you know that, while I am confident that I shall recover, and ultimately conquer the recently illuminated deficiencies of my character, my heart has, at present, been ravaged and punctured to a degree that I fear a scar shall ever remain.

Please accept my apologies for the unnerving effect I now perceive this letter may bestow. I can assure you that I am in good health, and that I look forward to giving a full account of the circumstances to which I have so clumsily alluded through the course of this letter. I plan to finish numerous, but minor, matters of business before departing for London on the fourteenth of May. I shall be exceedingly grateful for your company at the conclusion of that journey, and do hope you will aim to stay in town until at least that week, unless of course urgent matters of business were to call you away. I am grateful for your trusted friendship, Charles, and do wish to be more mindful of expressing said sentiment.

Sincerely, Darcy.

Bingley sat on the lip of the desk, holding the letter in both hands. His right eye squinted as he did his best to make sense of his friend's nebulous dispatch. The letter did, however, settle his plans to stay in London at least another month complete, rather than scheming an escape to Netherfield Park. He wondered how much of Darcy's fragile state had been conveyed to Georgiana. Certainly, Darcy would not wish to burden her with concern over his wellbeing with such distance between them. Bingley then decided he would lock the note away and return to the company of his sister and Darcy's sister, so as not to give either of them cause for anxiety over the contents of Darcy's letter. He returned to the drawing room to find the young ladies painting contentedly. He sat there with a book he barely feigned to read over the course of the next hour. While they dined that evening the thought struck Bingley that upon his return to Netherfield, whenever that might be, he would conjure a way to have Jane Bennet dine with them and would order Jensen to make pizza—what a night of everything delightful that would be.

CHAPTER THIRTY-NINE

THE FIRST OF MAY had passed, and the air was filled with the bustle of spring—Londoners of all classes taking in the first significant warm stretch that year. The leaves all around gleamed in their freshly birthed hues of light green and flowers burst forth, vivid in both colour and fragrance. Against this backdrop, parked under the low-hanging foliage of an acacia tree just a block from the Bingleys' front door, Constable Gallagher waited patiently for the gentleman's emergence. As his horse snorted and shifted under him, he was careful to stroke its mane and whisper calming nothings in its ear.

At half-past twelve, a young boy led a fine horse up the street from the opposite direction and stopped directly in front of the Bingley residence. Gallagher observed the front door open, and through it emerged a fine-looking gentleman, perhaps in his mid-twenties. He was tall, but not unusually so, and of a lively complexion. Sandy-coloured curls leaked out from the sides of his Wellington cap. Adorning his feet—even from a great distance Gallagher was positive—were the Marylebone Collection boots from Chambers Cordwainer. Before mounting his horse, the gentleman paused and leaned down to the stableboy's level. They shared a fierce laugh over something before the man tousled the boy's hair and flipped him a coin. The lad ran off in the direction he had come from, while the gentleman smiled from ear to ear, massaging the horse's neck while looking all around him in seeming delight. Gallagher turned his shoulder as to be more properly concealed by the shrubbery around him but marvelled at the young man's bright disposition. Surely, from all the accounts he had of physical description, this was indeed Mr. Bingley. But could *this* man be a killer? However unlikely it seemed, Gallagher had sworn a vow to follow the investigation wherever it might lead. He had spent the previous two months ruling out the first eleven pairs—four were shipped to France, three had made their way to New York, one was in possession of George Byng, 4th Viscount of Torrington, who at the time he acquired them, was seventy-one years old and infirm, another three were buried with their owners prior to the murder of Sir Fraser. That left pairs number twelve—the boots used during the crime—thirteen, which were unaccounted for, and fourteen—the pair worn by Mr. Charles Bingley.

After another moment of quiet revelry, Bingley was nimbly installed atop the horse and off at a meandering trot down the lane. With a quick sharp kick to his horse's side, the Constable emerged from his hiding place and began to follow Bingley at a canter. Within several blocks of Hyde Park, Gallagher was able to slow his gait to the point that he gently came up alongside Mr. Bingley, who seemed at the present moment quite diverted, and agreeably so.

"Hello, sir," the Constable called, pulling even with the gentleman.

"Why, how do you do?" Bingley answered cheerfully, turning his gaze from the sky and the trees to the man who had approached him.

"Well sir, and you?"

"Quite well, indeed! Pardon me, but have we been introduced?"

"Unfortunately, we have not. I do apologize for the impropriety—"

"No need to apologize. I gather that you are a proper gentleman. Charles Bingley." With that, Bingley outstretched his hand across his body. The Constable took it in his briefly.

"Luther Gallagher. I am pleased to meet you."

"And you, as well," Bingley said with a quizzical smile. "Do you fancy a ride through the park? Having been in town as long as I, a proper excursion in nature does much good for my soul—particularly in weather as glorious as we have today."

"I could not agree more. I've been in London but a week and already pine for my life in the country."

"Ah, yes—I find that country life is ideal. I would spend all my time there if I was able."

"I feel the same myself. If you do not mind me saying, sir, that is one beautiful stepper."

"Oh, you mean Quinton?" Bingley asked as he patted the horse's neck. "He's a fine one, indeed. I dare say he loves the freedom of the country as much as I."

"I would wager he does," Gallagher answered as they approached the narrowed lanes of the park. "He is much finer than the bone-setters I am accustomed to."

"Your mare does not appear too shabby," complimented Bingley.

"She is rented for my time here in town."

"So, I see."

"I must say, those are stunning boots, as well," Gallagher commented.

"Oh, why thank you!"

"Absolutely top-of-the-trees. Where might someone go about the purchase of such a fine pair?"

"Somewhere in London, from what I am told."

"Is that so?" the Constable asked, feigning sincerity.

"My steward buys them at my behest. He has an intimate knowledge of both my foot size and my preferences."

They crossed a small wooden bridge and into a thicker type of overhang. The sun only peaked through the dense frondescence overhead. Around a small bend they paced, at times, brushing hanging tree limbs away from their faces.

"Your steward does you credit. A man must be fairly flush in the pockets to afford a pair of gems like them, I would say. I bet you've got three pairs of them."

"Sir, I would like to think that I am not so high in the in-step as to boast—"

"Of course, not," cut in Gallagher. "I would not think it so. My allusion to your apparent wealth was meant as a compliment, but I am afraid that I made a mull of it."

"No need to apologize, Mr. Gallagher," Bingley chirped. "No offense taken at all."

The Constable was carefully noting every gesture, every word that came from the gentleman's mouth, and none of it seemed to add up in his mind. Could this man of high breeding, intelligence, and complaisance really be the person guilty of climbing into Andrew Fraser's bedroom window and slitting his throat in the most grotesque way while he slept, only to evanesce with the only trace of him being a single muddy boot print? Why, the sadistic killer had even watered Sully—

A lump rose in Gallagher's throat so quickly than he nearly lost his balance on his horse.

"Are you quite all right?" Bingley queried.

"Yes, yes, I am fine," stammered Gallagher. "Only lost my grip a moment."

The killer had watered the getaway horse. The same monster who had ripped open his Lord's neck had also watered his horse, perhaps out of concern that the creature might not be found immediately. A renewed sense of terror overtook him as he casually glanced across to his riding partner. *This was the type of man who would water the horse.* The Constable did his best not to betray with his visage the frigid chill that ran up his spine. The path took a turn into even deeper brush, though the light into the open area of the park could be seen a few hundred feet down the lane.

"You seem to pay rather more detailed attention to boots than the average man in my company," Bingley said calmly. "Is there a root cause of your peculiar interest?"

"I am a cobbler," he replied with a small gulp of phlegm.

"In London on business, then?"

"Yes, sir."

Bingley nodded silently; his eyes fixed straight ahead. "And how is Grantley Village, sir?" he asked suddenly.

"Grantley... I, uh—"

"If you indeed believe that I am the sort of man to own multiple pairs of the finest boots money can buy, you will allow yourself no surprise that I know full well who you are, and the pertinence of what questions you ask."

"Mr. Bingley—"

"Mr. Gallagher, or Constable Gallagher, as I might more properly refer to you, what is it that you would like to ask me?"

"Where were you on the night of Sir Andrew Fraser's murder?"

"Rather blunt," remarked Bingley with a chortle. "I spent the evening at Pemberley, the estate of my good friend Mr. Darcy. My entire presence the evening can be accounted for, I assure you."

The cobbler tried to gather his wits as their horses slowed to a halt. The gentleman leaned casually forward, crossing his arms on the back of Quinton's neck. His cordial gaze had turned serious—not dangerous or menacing, but exacting.

"Mr. Bingley, you must believe me when I earnestly state that I am unequivocally aware of how outlandish it is for me to even be in your presence under such circumstances. I do not believe in my heart that you are the kind of man capable of such a gruesome crime—"

"And why not, Constable?"

"Because... because I saw the remains of Sir Andrew Fraser with mine own eyes. I inspected his bedroom and observed his blood spewed on his bed linens, on the floor, on the walls. It is beyond my wildest imagination that a gentleman like yourself could ever be suited to such a vile act."

"A gentleman *like me*," mused Bingley. The Constable's eyes were fixed on him, staring through an expression crossed between incredulity and horror. "What kind of gentleman am I, then?"

"Mr. Bingley, having no knowledge of you whatsoever personally, your reputation aside, I would assume that you are a well-mannered, virtuous, and upstanding citizen."

"And that opinion would be based on the bare fact that I belong to a certain social standard?"

"To some degree, yes," Gallagher responded.

"Oh, my poor Constable," laughed Bingley. "How naive you are if that is your opinion of those in society who outrank a simple cobbler."

"Sir, I—"

"Please do not take offense at that," Bingley interjected. "I understand your shop is highly regarded in the county and that you care for your family. That is more respectable than much of the sort of company by which I am surrounded."

"Thank you, sir."

"Why is it that you have taken up the inquest of Sir Andrew Fraser's murder?" Bingley posed, looking sidelong at him.

"For the sake of justice, sir," answered the cobbler.

"You set foot in my house months ago—" Gallagher stared at him, unable to conceal his shaking hands. "—Is this not so?"

"Aye, sir."

"Then you went home?" Gallagher nodded. "You did not confront me in January when you had ample opportunity," stated Bingley flatly. "Instead, *you went home.*"

The Constable closed his eyes and felt his head bow slightly. "It was such a remarkably unlikely scenario, sir, that I simply—"

"Forsook your duty. And where in that, might I ask, was the justice which so motivated your quest, served?"

"It was not," he answered, looking directly into Bingley's eyes.

"Then what has changed since January, then? Could it be that your pockets have been lined with silver?"

"I resent the notion, sir—"

"Resent it all you like," retorted Bingley, suddenly sitting up straight on the back of Quinton. "And you have come here, with what—a boot print? Your grand design was to accost me in the street, badger me about a pair of boots that were not found in my possession, and then what—arrest me in public?" Gallagher chewed the inside of his mouth. "In what court of law would a magistrate convict a man such as me on such evidence such as this? No, you would be thrown into prison for libelling an upstanding citizen."

"I have meant you no personal offense, Mr. Bingley," declared the Constable. "I have simply followed what little evidence that was privy to me to its logical conclusion."

"You are mistaken in your assumptions, Mr. Gallagher, but I give you credit. You made it much further on such little information than most men in your position would have ever dreamed."

"I thank you," he said softly.

"A word of caution, Constable," spoke Bingley, "before I complete my ride in solitude. Whatever sort of man you may think Andrew Fraser was, you are almost undoubtedly incorrect. Bear that in mind as you ponder where your recent benefactor's motivations lie—you may in fact be pursuing something much more sinister than you could even begin to fathom." Gallagher gave an obligatory nod. "Speaking of your benefactor," continued Bingley, "you are not of the mind to give me his name?"

"No, sir. Though I imagine a man of your means and capabilities would not find it troubling to uncover such information."

Bingley smiled and tilted his hat. "Good day, Constable."

With that, he rode Quinton off in the direction of the open field at a gallop. The Constable sat upon his horse, mulling the entire conversation over. He thought he would find a pub and have a drink. A shrewd smile crept across his face. His suspect had put himself of his own accord at Pemberley the night of the murder.

CHAPTER FORTY

WHEN HE ARRIVED BACK at the house on Grosvenor Street, Bingley was a mix of dread and exhilaration. He entered the house with a clamour and proceeded immediately to his study—ignoring entirely the greetings of his sister, Caroline—and rang for Wilshere. Bingley poured himself a glass of whiskey and downed it in a single swig, while pacing around the room. Suddenly feeling flushed, he discarded his waistcoat and cravat on the chair beside the bare fireplace and immediately proceeded to unfasten the window that opened into the private courtyard. Wilshere entered to see him sitting atop the sill and fanning himself with a stack of parchment.

"Mr. Bingley?"

"Wilshere," he began rapidly and with verve, "please be so good as to remind me why we thought it prudent to bestow my riding boots to the stable-keeper at Lambton?"

"Sir, we've been over this more than once—"

"Just indulge me, please."

"As we approached the village, sir, you took them off in the box and said that you wanted to be rid of them because they were covered in sludge and blood. I advised you to toss them into the wood or burn them in the pit at Pemberley, but when you saw the old stable-keep and his bare feet, you ordered the carriage stopped, and bade me to give them to him."

Bingley nodded and asked for another glass of whiskey which his man was dutiful to pour. Once again it disappeared in a single motion. "I met with the Constable earlier," said he.

"I figured you might."

"He has the boots and has matched them to a print in the mud where we left Fraser's horse."

"Is that all he has?"

"And I admitted to him, in a moment of sheer vacuity that I was at Pemberley the evening of the murder."

"An alibi can easily be provided—"

"He also has a witness who can connect my boots to my carriage and observed its departure in the direction of Darcy's estate."

"There are many carriages in the world, Mr. Bingley."

"I want it burned," he suddenly demanded.

"The coach?"

"Aye."

"Burned?" the stupefied steward blurted.

"Immediately," Bingley ordered. "And I want it noted in your records that it happened in an accident last summer."

"But sir, that coach cost upward of three hundred pounds—"

"Wilshere, I have the utmost respect for you and trust you with my very life, but do not dare question me when I make a command in respect to my property. Your duty is fulfilling my instructions, and you are compensated fairly for it."

"I do not argue with you on the latter score, but as for the former, my duty is the management of your estate. Respectfully, I am not a farm hand to be ordered to and fro at your every whim—particularly when your typically sound judgement has been clouded by paranoia and fear." Bingley ceased fanning himself and tossed the papers on the small table beside him. He rubbed his eyes with both hands and mumbled an apology. "There is no way your coach could be properly identified by that old man. It was dark and raining and I would have grave concerns about his mental capacity to withstand any serious type of examination. That coach is a popular style—a lavish one, yes, but not *terribly* uncommon. The road through Lambton may lead a man to countless destinations."

"Does it not trouble you?"

"Mr. Bingley," the steward started deliberately, "that coach is under lock and key and out of sight at Netherfield Park. There may come a time that it becomes prudent to dispose of it, but the present is not that time, and if I may be so direct, I will not obey an order that is not in your best interest."

Bingley glanced up at him. "You are a good man, Wilshere. We have been to hell and back these last two years and I do not know where I would be without you."

"Thank you, sir. As always, I hold you in the highest esteem. I would be unable to work for a man of lesser quality; and men of your nature are far more rare than the coach in storage."

"Pour us both a glass, will you?" Bingley asked with a smile.

His steward obeyed him at once.

CHAPTER FORTY-ONE

IT WAS OBVIOUS TO the Constable as he sat inside the Black Bear Tavern with a third pint of stout nearly drained that Mr. Bingley, for all his amiable qualities and good looks, had a gravity about him that must have been considered uncommon among young gentlemen of his age and station. He was good-natured and jovial, even accommodating—until the moment he felt himself threatened, and alas, a weightiness emerged from just under the surface. Surely, this was a trait of a sadistic killer, was it not?

At the same time, he thought as he swigged the dark porter and put the empty glass down with a clank, *what on earth could be the motivation for such a crime?*

"Another, please?" called the Constable brusquely to the barmaid. The buxom woman of perhaps forty-five glowered at him through straggly strands of salt and pepper hair. He imagined that she was a good deal more handsome in the early evening light than when he had entered an hour and three pints earlier.

He wondered about tracking the carriage down. It was quite possible that it was with Bingley right there in London—though it was equally possible that it might be stashed on any number of properties scattered throughout the county. If perhaps, however, he was able to find it and make a positive identification with Robert Toomey, the old stable keep at Lambton...

Yet again, however, the question of motive gave him pause. In his cursory inquisition, he had not been able to establish a link—personal or otherwise, between Bingley and Fraser, though they both hailed from similar parts of the country. He thought it might be necessary to delve further into any potential dealings between the two, because that, and only that, would allow him to establish some kind of reason for this young and well-reputed gentleman to stoop to commit so low an offense.

From out of nowhere, just as the comely barmaid brought his glass, he remembered the conversation he had happened to overhear so many months ago, in a similar establishment back home in Grantley between Dier, the hog man, Hedge, the postman, and the carriage driver named... *Oh, what was his name*—Acton! *Rawden Acton!* He had mentioned the similar circumstances of the murder of his current master's father, Eoin Walters of Northumberland! Perhaps that was where any connection might lie, and perhaps the two awful slayings were linked by that very connection. He made up his mind that he would finish his drink, find his way to bed, and wake in the morning to call upon the London residence of Sir John Walters in order that he might again interview his carriage driver.

At half past twelve, then, the Constable strolled up the lane and knocked at the door of Walters House just a stone's throw from Kensington Palace. The butler answered and directed Gallagher to the east gate where he was allowed entry by the gardener's assistant and directed toward the stables. In a moment's time he came upon the figure of Rawden Acton who appeared to be spot cleaning an already sparkling barouche.

"Mr. Acton?" Gallagher called from ten paces away.

"At your service," the old man answered, torturously straightening himself to greet his guest. "To whom do I have the pleasure?"

"Luther Gallagher, Constable of Grantley Village," he said as he bowed.

"Ah, yes, from the pub!" declared Acton.

"Aye, we met in the pub."

"Well, 'pon rep, you've come an awful long way to see your old friend, haven't you?"

"I was of the mind that you might be able to give me some further details surrounding the horrible demise of your master."

"You mean, Sir Eoin Walters?"

"Aye."

"A very sad tale, indeed," the coachman remarked as he leaned back against the carriage. "Have you solved the Andrew Fraser matter, and you are now making inquiries here?"

"Not entirely, no. I had hoped that you might offer some illumination which could potentially provide a link between the two crimes."

"You believe the two crimes were perpetrated by the same man?" gasped Acton.

"It is not out of the realm of possibility. After all, from what you described, the manners in which both men were dispatched were extraordinarily similar."

"*Butchered*, I would say. Slit from ear to ear in their beds."

"Horses stolen but left behind with buckets of water in case they were not found promptly."

"Eerie," declared the driver.

"Are you aware of any familial relations between Sir Eoin Walters and Sir Andrew Fraser?"

"None whatsoever, though I suppose it is not impossible, but would most likely be some generations removed. I never heard my lord mention the name Fraser, and had never heard of him, myself, until that fateful day we stopped for respite in Grantley Village—a lovely village it is, incidentally."

"Thank you," Gallagher replied. "Any possible business connections between them, then?"

"Unfortunately, having no true information about Sir Andrew Fraser, I would not know. My master was well-respected in the financial community—a banker with some political sway, I might add—in addition to the operation of his expansive estate."

"A banker?"

"Aye, sir. His son John has taken over in his stead, though I must admit," he lowered his voice as he cautiously scanned the immediate area around them, "he has more hair than he does wit."

"I see," the Constable nodded.

"In what sort of business was Sir Andrew?"

"Arms, mostly, though he had a long and celebrated military career, as well."

"Weapons would be a natural line of work for a soldier, eh?"

"Aye."

"The proximity of the crimes is also distressing, is it not?"

"How so?—Northumberland is nearly two hundred miles from Grantley."

"That it is," Acton answered with a short chuckle. "But Eoin Walters was murdered in his home outside Chesterfield, and *that* is but thirty miles from Grantley Village."

"Why did you not mention this the first time we met?"

"I suppose I was so shocked by the news that I was not struck by the thought. After all, Sir John Walters had the house—it was but a small country house—razed to the ground after the murder."

"Uncanny," gasped Gallagher. "Did your late master have any adversaries?"

"Not truly," retorted the driver. "You must understand that the family's wealth is so immense, that only a handful of men in the country could manage any actual rivalry. Now, there always were the heel-nippers—mostly the *nouveau riche* who imagine themselves much more influential than they are. And there was one in particular, but to be honest, the whole matter was so inconsequential to my master that I hardly remember the fellow's name."

"A man who would have had motivation to attack your master?"

"Oh yes, or at least he would have believed it so."

"But?"

"He was, himself, passed on to the grand secret."

"The man who was disposed toward dislike of Eoin Walters was already dead when Walters was murdered?"

"Aye," the driver said sadly. "I do seem to recall that they enquired after the whereabouts of his son at that time, though."

"And?"

"He was installed comfortably at the Darcy estate at Pemberley."

"The man's son was away at Pemberley when your master was murdered?"

"Yes, I believe it was so."

"And you cannot recall his name?"

"I am afraid not. My memory does not serve me as sharply as it once did—although when I hark back, I am almost positive it ended in a 'lee' of some sort or another."

"Bingley?"

"That's the one!" Acton exclaimed.

"Thank you, sir—thank you! I must be off," Gallagher declared, turning toward the gate.

"Will you not stay for tea?"

"No, but I thank you once more! You have been exceedingly helpful!" he called over his shoulder as his trot became a gallop.

"Best of luck!"

Once he had mounted Abacus, he and his horse tore off down the lane. The Cobbler-Constable was convinced that if he could find the coach of Robert Toomey's description in the possession of Mr. Charles Bingley, he would have just cause for his arrest.

CHAPTER FORTY-TWO

BEFORE HE LEFT FOR Lambton to obtain a more comprehensive description of the coach witnessed by Robert Toomey, Gallagher made careful observations of the coach house where Bingley's carriage would have been stored around the corner from the house on Grosvenor St. The stable boy he had earlier viewed interacting with Bingley led a horse back toward the stable. Unluckily for the Constable, he was, from the vantage point on the street, unable to see down the mew and inside the coach house itself. He decided to return after dark and attempt to gain clandestine entry that he might survey the coaches present.

At nearly half-past two the next morning, he approached again, this time dressed in all black. He carried a small lantern which he would light only once inside. Cautiously, he entered down the alley behind Bingley's house. There was an iron gate at the end of the small lane which he scaled with ease. Inside the yard, he crept past the stables where seven horses slept and on toward the garage. Checking the first large coach stall he came to and finding it locked, Gallagher slunk over to the next and the next—all secure. Finally, at the edge of the building was a small door which seemed to be latched from the inside, but not particularly well. He found a tree branch that leaned over the fence and snapped off a limb, with which he was able to pry the bolt open by leaning against the door and leveraging upward. Once inside, he closed it softly behind him and lit his lamp.

Three carriages were stowed in total, with space for perhaps two more. The first was but a gig in ghastly condition, considering the neighbourhood. The second was a cabriolet; but alas, the third was a massive town coach. Even in the dark, Gallagher could tell it had been washed recently, as his reflection beamed off its gilded sides. It was richly adorned with golden scrollwork; its wheels were painted royal red. The top was flat with decorative posts at each corner. It certainly fit the bill for what had been previously described to him by the stableman in Lambton. The Constable was careful to take copious notes on every detail he could make out in the light of a single flame. When he had made several rounds about the carriage, he extinguished his light and let himself out. In a moment he was over the gate and back on the street without detection. He rode Abacus back to his inn where he slept just four hours before having a breakfast of bread and kippers with tea. Once the horse was watered and saddled, he was on his way north.

When, after a remarkably uneventful ride of nearly four days' time he arrived in Lambton, he took up lodging in the same village inn where he stayed in the first weeks of the investigation. He arrived late enough that the stableboy, a teen by the name of Carl, stalled Abacus as Mr. Toomey was not on duty until morning. After sleeping until just after nine, the Constable ordered tea with bread and jam to his room. Once he was fed and had the opportunity to wash his face, he strolled down to the yard in nervous anticipation. Though he felt confident in the deductions he had made to this point, the description of the carriage was the lynchpin that held his case together.

Unfortunately, after speaking with the stable keeper, it was abundantly clear that the town coach in the house in London was not a match for the coach used in the murderer's flight. The coach that Toomey described was a brougham with a rack for trunks on the back—black in colour, aside from gold trim around the windows and panels. He did add that on the side there was a very distinctive vertical striping pattern that he had assumed must have been a new fashion from London, as he'd never seen such a design prior or since.

A bit dejected, the Constable made notes of his conversation with Toomey and gathered his few belongings from his room in order to start out for home. As he mounted Abacus, the thought struck him that he was but five miles from the estate at Pemberley. On a whim he galloped off in that direction. As he entered the park, he was stunned by the size of it: Grantley Manor, as extensive as it might be, could not compare to the staggering largess of Pemberley. Eventually he came upon the house, and at the direction of a gardener, found his way to the stables and the coach house where he introduced himself to a young man by the name of Vessey who watered the guest's horse.

"Vessey, I assume you are well acquainted with the coaches that frequent the estate, in addition to your master's?"

"Of course, sir."

"May I describe a coach to you and if you think you know it, tell me to whom does it belong?"

"I shall do my best." The Constable proceeded to read from his small book the description of the getaway coach as had been described to him by Robert Toomey. "That sounds like Mr. Bingley's new brougham," replied Vessey. "Are you all right, sir?" Gallagher forced his mouth to close and stammered a reply. "Will you require any further assistance, sir?"

"One more question," he began after he had gathered himself, "when was the last time you saw this carriage?"

The young man thought for a moment. "It must have been six months at least, sir. Mr. Bingley has not been here since at least November."

"And where might he keep this coach when it is not in use?"

"I doubt he would take it to London, as he has a town coach as well. If I had to make a guess, I would say it is stored on the grounds of his home in Netherfield Park."

"Netherfield Park?" Gallagher asked excitedly. "And where is that?"

"In Hertfordshire, sir."

"Thank you, Vessey," the Constable said as he climbed back astride Abacus.

Gallagher rode on through Buckstone, Holly Springs, and Hillingshire practically without stopping to rest and eventually arrived in Grantley Village that evening around midnight. As his arrival was quite unannounced, his wife was pleasantly shocked to see him, and he was glad to see her—especially so that he found her in their bed alone. He spent three days at home and in his shop, catching up on backorders, before departing for Hertfordshire.

On the second day of his journey, just before he crossed the River Trent outside Nottingham, he was set upon by a band of three highwaymen. Thanks, however, to the fine conditioning and robust speed of Abacus, they were able to cause him no harm. In two more days' time he arrived in Meryton and took lodging in the inn. That evening, he hired a horse to save Abacus the exhaustion he did not spare himself and rode out in the direction of Netherfield Park.

While it was nothing to the grandeur of Pemberley, Netherfield was an impressive estate situated in unanticipated seclusion, given its relative proximity to the village. The back half of the property appeared, by moonlight, to be shrouded in woods, with a large hedge dividing the lane from the garden. Gallagher tied the hired horse to the gate and went round toward the hedge, as the property was not walled off. Quietly, he approached the house and saw that it was, indeed, closed up for winter, and appeared that it been for some time. Peering inside the low windows on the ground floor, he observed furniture covered by cloths and rolled rugs. The Constable strolled to the back by the garden and had a look about. There were a few outbuildings beyond the hedge, some of which of the larger variety—likely to be the location of the stables and coach house.

When he found the carriage house, he was confounded once again to find it locked. In the thicket nearby, he found a rock that would, perhaps, serve well to break the latch. After several firm strikes, the lock bent, and the Constable was able to pry open the door. The very first thing his eyes beheld in what moonlight the doors allowed to penetrate was a brougham—black with gold trim and a decorative stripe across the side. A cheeky smile spread on his lips: he had found his man.

He closed the door behind him and, just as thoughts danced before him of the ways he would spend his reward from Mr. Hurst, he was hit squarely as he had not been since scrapping as a young lad. Staggering backwards he was hit again—from where he could not tell—and fell to the ground. A burlap sack was placed over his head and his arms were pulled tight behind his back where his hands were fastened with a cord. Warm blood ran from his nose into his mouth and as much as he wished to question the nature of this assault, a moan was all his battered frame was able to muster. His attacker took a deep breath and then all went black.

When Gallagher awoke, he could not help but perceive a raging headache and at the same moment realized that he was restrained and unable to move. As he shifted in his seat, he let out an inadvertent groan.

"He is awake," a familiar voice remarked. "Maitla—young man, would you please?"

The hood was snatched off his head. Gallagher found himself in a candlelit room with no windows. He was seated in a wooden kitchen chair, his arms and legs secured to it. The man before him was tall and lean and seemed in the candlelight rather young and handsome, too. He bent down near him and carefully blotted the Constable's lip with a cold rag.

"Mr. Gallagher?" asked that familiar voice once more. "How badly are you hurt?"

"Not seriously... at least I think not."

"Your nose is not broken."

"Well thank the devil for that," he answered with a wince as the man pressed the chilled fabric to his cheek.

"Why are you here?"

"Because I was attacked!"

"No, not in this *room* Constable—why are you at Netherfield Park?"

"I am conducting an inquiry into the murder of Sir Andrew Fraser of Grantley Manor and was attempting to identify a coach that had been used in the killers flight."

"I told you we should have burned it," the voice said—the Constable was so certain he had heard it recently but in the muddle of his pained mind he could not place it. There was no answer.

"Where am I?"

"Not twenty yards from where you were discovered."

"Mr. *Bingley*?" he asked in horror.

194

"I warned you, Mr. Gallagher."

"Please, do not hurt me," came the anxious reply. "I have a family—"

The Constable could hear Bingley sigh. With a jolt, a chair slid close to him, as the young man who had tended him moved aside. For the first time, he could make out the face of Charles Bingley, and he was taken aback by the amalgam of sternness and warmth he saw there.

"I try to make out—what kind of man are you?" Bingley mused.

"I confess, I have been trying to do the same with you."

Bingley bit the inside of his lip and nodded. "If you were truly motivated by an inner sense of justice, you would not have abandoned your quest on my doorstep all those months ago."

"Sir—"

Bingley held up his hand. "But if you were only motivated by financial means, you would certainly not be traipsing the country in every direction. You would collect what you might while living a life in London you have only previously dreamt of. At fifty pounds per month, at the conclusion of six months, you would be fairly flush in the pockets and could return home and live on however you wish. Yet here we are."

"How do you know about fifty pounds per month?"

"And your benefactor—Mr. *Hurst*?"

The Constable nearly choked on his saliva.

"Let me be direct with you, Mr. Gallagher," started Bingley. "I have no inclination to hurt you." Gallagher's eyes closed instinctively, and a tear ran down his cheek. "And I shall not, if you will but *listen* to me."

Looking up, Gallagher was relieved to see kindness in Bingley's expression. "Mr. Bingley—"

"*Only listen.* In exchange for your life, I expect that you will agree to cease and desist in pursuit of my arrest, but I dare to believe that you are, at heart, a man of character and a man of true justice, and that upon hearing my word, you would not *wish* to pursue it. I freely admit to you that I killed Andrew Fraser in his bedroom. It was I who used his horse to flee into the grove, and I who left it a bucket of water for the animal. I then entered my coach and rode on to Pemberley through Lambton, where in near-freezing rain I bequeathed a barefoot, old stable keeper the pair of boots which might have ultimately led to my downfall. As you might well know, I am a close friend of Fitzwilliam Darcy, who allowed me to rest at his family's estate during this time, but with no knowledge of my activities. I further confess in your presence that the blood of more men has been shed at my hand—Sir Eoin Walters of Northumberland, Thomas Abbott, Member of Parliament, and Lord Bertram St. John, the Earl of Canterbury." In the dark, Bingley witnessed Gallagher's eyes grow the size of plums. "But though I may be a *killer*, I am certainly not a *murderer*."

"Mr. Bingley... I am completely bewildered," the cobbler sputtered.

Bingley shifted back in his seat and crossed one leg over the other. "Is the hangman a murderer?"

"No, sir—he meets out justice."

"Yet, he kills."

"That he does."

"If the hangman kills in the administration of justice, then, his actions cannot therefore be considered criminal, true?"

"Not if he acts in accordance with the law."

"And what if the law is corrupt?"

"Mr. Bingley, what are you suggesting?"

"That a perversion of the law is paramount to a perversion of justice."

"I do not understand," Gallagher muttered.

"Sir Andrew Fraser, along with the other men I mentioned and several others who live still—similarly powerful men with lofty connections—have been party to an extra-legal cabal, the likes of which I stumbled upon quite unwillingly two years ago. These men had developed an enterprise, dealing under the cover of night and the protection offered by their rank, in the trade of young maidens—persuaded to leave the safe-keeping of their dear families for the prospects of riches and love, only to be violated and murdered in the most heinous fashions imaginable. To date, sir, we are aware of the murder of twenty-seven young ladies at the hands of these gentlemen—though they are certainly unworthy of the title."

The Constable heaved and swallowed. "How is this possible?"

"Mr. Wilshere, here, can furnish you with details of the nasty business," answered Bingley. "Maitland, release Mr. Gallagher and pour him some brandy, please."

When he was freed from his restrains and had promptly downed his drink, Wilshere came forth and presented the Constable with an overview of the whole plot, including evidence that connected each man to particular crimes. Andrew Fraser, for one, had written in an intercepted letters to Eoin Walters, that he personally dispatched eleven young women by slitting their throats after he had ravished them. Their remains were hidden in thickets or dumped unceremoniously in rivers or the sea, everywhere from Grantley Manor to Ramsgate and even Birmingham. More than anything, in reading these letters and documents, Gallagher was left somewhere between enraged and completely numb at the wanton callousness with which these heinous crimes had been committed. None of these men exhibited the slightest regret or even hesitancy. Rather, they boasted in the brilliance of their plan and even the fact that the randomness of their abductions offered little chance that their deeds would ever be detected. They vaunted their rank and their power and bragged of the staggering magnitude of their ever-growing victim count, as if they were keeping a running tally at fives.

"Would you open the door, please?" Gallagher called toward Maitland as he suddenly stood and rushed outside. He barely cleared the threshold of the shed before he was on all fours as if he'd be sick. After a few moments of heaving, he made his way to his feet and back inside. "My apologies," he uttered, taking his chair once more.

"It is a most vile revelation, is it not?" Bingley asked.

"Abominable," replied the Constable.

Bingley nodded, then turned to Maitland: "Would you fetch some water, please?"

"I've some right here," the man answered as he passed his canteen to Gallagher.

"Many thanks."

"So, I will enquire your judgement, having now the necessary information at hand: am I to be considered a murderer?"

The Constable gulped down some water, then levelled his eyes at Bingley and said, "You, sir, are an angel of the Lord."

"Though it certainly does not feel so, at times," answered Bingley with a sigh, leaning back in his chair.

"What am I to do, then?" Gallagher enquired.

"You will go back to your benefactor, Mr. Hurst, and declare that your investigation has been solved conclusively. The killer was a highwayman named Garrett Surman—he was hanged for other crimes a fortnight ago."

"And this is truth?"

"Aye, Gareth Surman was hanged in Doncaster. It is a matter of public record."

"My scruples will prevent me from taking the reward that would be due me."

"Then deny it and let that serve as a testament to your character," responded Bingley. "And be confident that you shall be forever in my favour, and I give you my word that your family shall never be in need."

"Thank you, sir."

"And one last matter I wish to broach with you."

"Of course."

"I should like you to take a month to return to your family and your home—rest and consider a proposition, *carefully*. After that time, and not before, write me to inform me if you would accept a position in *my* employ."

"Mr. Bingley, I am honoured, but I—"

"I do not wish for a response until a month has passed. You have demonstrated the depth and quality of your character, your alacrity, and your perspicacity. It would be my honour to employ your various gifts toward the purpose of ending this evil business once and for all, but again, I wish you only to rest and consider for now."

"Thank you, sir," the Constable answered. "Whilst I will not yet give a reply, I would like to acknowledge that I am honoured by your proposal."

The two men shook hands.

The entire party spent the night at Netherfield Park before setting out at dawn: Bingley and his men for London and Gallagher for his room in Meryton. The Constable had tea and bread ordered to his room and after supping voraciously, slept until late in the afternoon. When he awoke, he laid in the bed for what seemed an aeon, grappling with the discoveries which had been foisted upon him in such strange circumstances the previous evening. Though Mr. Bingley required that he not commit himself for a period of four weeks, Gallagher was indeed a man of virtue and action, and as such would be incapable of standing by whilst such depravation went unchecked. He considered his own position in society; he thought of his own daughters. When he finally arose, he washed his face and proceeded downstairs to the inn for dinner. He was greeted and handed a sealed envelope by the innkeeper. Inside was a note that read: "Rest and nothing else," and was simply signed "B." Beneath the paper were two ten-pound notes.

PART IV

CHAPTER FORTY-THREE

OVER THE COURSE OF the following month several important happenings occurred. First, Mr. Gallagher returned to his home and within a week wrote to Mr. Hurst that his inquiry had concluded. His letter gave a sparingly detailed account of his firm belief in the guilt of Garrett Surman, executed by the magistrate in Doncaster, putting the matter of the murder of Sir Andrew Fraser solely in the hands of God. The cobbler hoped that his chronicle of events would be enough to assuage the interest of Mr. Hurst, who might then declare their business at an end. Gallagher, for his part, made no mention of the reward.

In five days' time, he had his reply. A post rider appeared at his shop at nearly six o'clock that evening with a dispatch from London. Although the handwriting was slovenly and many of the thoughts disjointed, it seemed Mr. Hurst was satisfied with the results of the Constable's efforts. Neither did he make mention of any reward. Just when the cobbler believed the business to be settled satisfactorily to all parties, a single day later, and nearly the same time of day, a different dispatch arrived at the shop, letter in hand from Mr. Hurst. This letter was slightly more coherent but made many of the same assertions and even in the same general order—with no mention, once more, of any type of reward. Gallagher chuckled to himself at the absurdity of his former benefactor's correspondence and was glad to have the whole concern decided.

The second series of events were rather intricate, but ultimately nothing more than a lugubrious exercise in futility. In summary, information emerged from within Mr. Wilshere's network of informants that the evil plot had resumed once more, with a victim who matched the pattern of previous killings being found in Newcastle-Upon-Tyne, her body hidden in a thicket near Hadrian's Wall. Maitland was dispatched to the north and was quickly followed by Bingley himself, when it was learned that a certain captain in the Royal Scots Dragoons called Cairbre Mac-Caig, had connections to Andrew Fraser's black-market arms venture. Further inquiry allowed the discovery that it was not Caibre MacCaig who was party to some of Sir Andrew Fraser's dealings, but rather, a sugar importer named Caibre MacKay whose involvement in any illegal dealings was cursory at best. Additionally, MacKay had died of apoplexy a full seven months prior to Bingley's cessation of Fraser. On the other hand, Captain MacCaig was, from all indications, a fine and upstanding gentleman who was both honourable and kind. Over the course of those weeks spent in the city chasing one dead end after the other, they were finally able to trace down the young lady's lover who, after some stern scrutiny, confessed to her murder out of a jealous rage. He was turned into the local constable who charged him before the magistrate where he plead guilty to the crime. Two days later he was hanged atop the gaol in Carliol Square.

Being convinced that the proper course of justice had been met in this instance, Bingley and Maitland drove south toward Grantley Village, where they would pay Mr. Gallagher a visit. However, during a stop in Harrogate they were met with an express letter from Wilshere that another young lady had been found under similar circumstances in Hull. They diverted course and began to investigate. The victim was a young lady of fifteen named Mary Fenning. Her father was a shipping clerk, and her mother had died in childbirth. She was the youngest of five surviving siblings. An offer of marriage would have yielded a gentleman but two pounds per annum. In speaking with her father and older sister, they learned that she had recently fallen under the charms of a wealthy young man from Derbyshire. Over the course of but ten days, she fell completely enamoured by the young man, though none in her family had been introduced. Miss Fenning left a note to her older sister the morning of her disappearance, writing that she was to be married in Derby and honeymoon in Ramsgate before returning home with her new husband in tow. Naturally, while this was cause for concern, there were no desperate efforts to find her, as her plan, though hastily concocted, seemed to put her in no danger, and in fact, might have been highly beneficial. Her remains were found eight days later, half submerged down the Humber in Hessle.

The similarities between this story and those previously adjudicated were uncanny and could only lead to the conclusion that the dark conglomerate was indeed active once more. Bingley was thorough in gathering whatever details could be recalled about the description of the young man from Mary's siblings who were in her confidence. He was tall, dark haired, and uncommonly handsome. She was told that he grew up on a vast estate in Derbyshire. He was charming, witty, and good-natured. The more he heard, the more it sounded like George Wickham.

Bingley might have flown to Meryton and murdered him as soon as time and distance would have allowed but for another wrinkle in plans. Another corpse was found along the shore in Scarborough. The young lady was yet to be identified but was not believed to be a local. Being in such relatively close proximity, Bingley and Maitland made the journey north from Hull, only to find upon their arrival that the young lady was not a young lady at all, but an old man dressed in women's clothing, who had by all appearances drowned himself by tying weights around his neck and hurling himself into the sea. He had washed up on the shoreline and was initially identified as a female, but upon closer inspection... While this unfortunate occurrence may have no doubt piqued their curiosity, it did not but distract from their mission.

Next, an unfortunate encounter with a cart driver in his highest altitudes caused Bingley to part company with Quinton, and land rather heavily on his backside. He narrowly avoided breaking bones, but was left with severe bruising, and a cooler not fit for travel for nearly a fortnight.

During his convalescence in Hull, he received a letter from Wilshere that three weeks prior that Colonel Forster's regiment—Wickham included—had left Meryton for Brighton. It was by this time, the twentieth of June. Upon hearing the news, Bingley was one on hand, relieved that the Bennet girls were now safely out of the reach of the miscreant, and on the other hand concerned for the safety of vulnerable maidens on the south coast. In light of this, he dispatched Maitland down to Brighton to keep a distant, but watchful eye on Wickham. He additionally hoped that his man could potentially un-cover Wickham's contacts which might lead them to the new power brokers within the scheme. First, though, he directed Maitland to rest for a week in Meryton and gather what news on the Bennet sisters he could—particularly with regards to Jane.

Bingley corresponded with his sister, Caroline, about his condi-tion and well-being, but also wrote a great deal to Darcy. He was disappointed, however, to find his friend still in odd spirits and unwilling to discuss in any form the "matters of heart" which caused him to quit Rosings Park so abruptly. *Poor Darcy must be under a real fit of the blue devils,* Bingley thought as he pondered his friend's reluctance to speak on the topic. He did, indeed, bemoan the fact that he had not been able to see his friend since the spring, and was overjoyed when he received a letter expressing an invitation to Pemberley for the second week of July—once he had recovered, and returned to London. Bingley also lamented the thought of so much travel, particularly because he was already in the north, but it had been over a month since he was in town, and there were compulsory matters of business that must be attended before he could depart for any kind of holiday.

His condition having improved enough to allow for travel, Bingley purchased a used buggy and departed Hull for London. When he ar-rived, he spent three complete days heeding the demands of his various companies and setting plans straight, after which he slept for nearly two more. He dreamt continually of Jane Bennet, as was typical, and felt tremendous anxiety about not only her wellbeing, but her marital status. Surely no woman as handsome and kind and pure of heart could remain unattached for long—particularly after what must have felt a terrible spurning after his hasty and enigmatic departure. *How could I have been so daft as to allow circumstances to dictate the treatment of so admirable a young lady?*

Once he was rested, he dined with Caroline, Louisa, and Mr. Hurst. He inquired—as subtly as possible—whether any of them had been in correspondence with Miss Bennet but received glum responses that she had not been heard from all this time. After the meal, Bingley gave Wilshere a dressing down over the fact that, since Maitland's arrival in Meryton, neither the master nor the steward had received a single word from the young man, though judging from the accounts, it was clear that he was alive and spending his stipend daily. Mr. Wilshere, however, did have a report from Brighton that, recently, Miss Lydia Bennet had joined Colonel Forster's wife as her "particular friend," which only added to the appetence for a report from Maitland.

Once plans had been settled, it was agreed that the Bingleys would dine with the Darcys and depart for the north the following morning from their house on St. James Street. When the Bingleys arrived, they were received into the parlour where they were informed by a remorseful Georgiana Darcy that her brother had been summoned to depart that morning due to urgent business with his steward, Mr. Ballentine. *What the devil has gotten into him?* Bingley wondered. Aside from the absence of Darcy, the evening was merry and anticipatory.

The following morning, just minutes before their departure, Bingley received a note from Maitland, apologizing for his delayed correspondence, but assuring his master that all was well regarding the Bennet sisters—all of whom remained, as yet, unattached—aside from a small tryst within the family, accompanied by patronizing rumours through the village, caused by Lydia's departure for Brighton. Maitland was, by this time, already halfway to Brighton himself, where he would send remarks as to any intelligence he might gain regarding the activities of George Wickham. Once he had read his man's letter, the entire party set out for Pemberley. Bingley allowed himself to fancy the notion that not only was Jane Bennet still unmarried, but perhaps she was even awaiting his return. He thought he would use the days of travel to formulate a plan which would allow him to return to Netherfield Park, and perhaps stay there till the day he died.

CHAPTER FORTY-FOUR

"*HERE*—AT PEMBERLEY?" BINGLEY CRIED.

"Yes, and she is staying at the inn at Lambton," answered Darcy, "with her aunt and uncle, Mr. and Mrs. Gardiner."

Bingley's eyes darted around the room as his mind churned frenetically. "Where do—how do I—"

"She is expecting Georgiana and myself to call on her. Naturally, you may accompany us if you'd like."

"I must find Burke and have a change of clothes!"

"We shall take the curricle, then," said Darcy with a smile. "Will you ride on horseback?"

"Yes, I shall take Quinton!"

"I will have him fetched and ready for you."

"Good, good—now I—" and without another word, Bingley dashed from Darcy's study to his guestroom, shouting for his valet, Burke, to be brought immediately.

Bearing in mind that Darcy planned to invite Miss Elizabeth Bennet for dinner, Bingley chose his second finest available ensemble and rushed his man at every turn. He could see from his window Darcy and Georgiana departing up the lane, which in turn, caused him even greater impatience with the deliberation Burke took in dressing him. In normal circumstances, Bingley was abundantly thankful for the time and careful consideration with which his valet made him fit for sight, but today, it was all he could do not to leap from the window and onto the back of the Darcy's carriage. Once he was dressed respectably, he hurried downstairs and was grateful to find Quinton waiting for him, reigns in the hands of Vessey the stableboy. Bingley practically leapt onto from the second to bottom step, calling a quick, "thank you!" over his shoulder as he galloped off.

In town, he handed his horse off to Robert Toomey and bounded into the inn where he was directed to Mr. and Mrs. Gardiner's chambers. When he was within three steps of the room it dawned on him that he had run up the stairs, so he purposefully slowed his stride before entering.

"Miss Bennet," he said with a bow, trying to control the pace of his breath. "How delighted I am to see you."

"And you, as well, Mr. Bingley," she answered.

Jumbled thoughts suddenly swirled around as he suddenly wondered if Elizabeth might not wish to see him because of the circumstances surrounding his parting with her sister.

"May I presume you to be in good health?" he asked.

"I am, thank you, and yourself?"

"Yes, very good, indeed," he answered, having no recollection, at that moment, of the nasty fall he had suffered so recently. He did think that she appeared to be pleased to see him and he took that as encouragement. "And your family are good in health?"

"Yes, all are in perfect health," Elizabeth replied kindly. "May I inquire after your sisters?"

Sisters? he thought absentmindedly as his brow wrinkled slightly. *Who are my sisters?*

"Oh yes, they have arrived with me just this morning—and Mr. Hurst."

"I am happy to hear it so."

"Is this your first time in Derbyshire?"

"Yes, it is."

"How have you enjoyed it?"

"It is magnificent—stunning, even."

"I do not disagree," Bingley answered. "It is certainly one of the finest counties in the whole of England; although I equally fancy Hertfordshire."

"Do you?"

"Undoubtedly. It may not possess the wild qualities of the north, but its beauty and charm are second to none."

"Bingley, may I introduce you to Mr. and Mrs. Gardiner?"

"Oh, of course," he answered, turning toward Darcy. "My apologies—"

"There is no need for apology," Mr. Gardiner stated after having been introduced. "We understand you have been acquainted with our niece for some time, or our *nieces*, should I say?"

"Ah, yes, sir," Bingley replied a bit awkwardly. "Since autumn, in Meryton."

"And you have come from town just recently?"

"Yes, just arrived this morning," he answered pleasantly.

Darcy and Georgiana sat with Elizabeth while Bingley conversed pleasantly with both Mr. and Mrs. Gardiner. They talked of the road conditions, the itinerary of their holiday, and their various and complimentary impressions of Pemberley at some length, but at every opportunity, Bingley did steal glances toward Elizabeth in order to attempt to ascertain whether she harboured ill-will toward him. He did, additionally, find himself mulling what resemblance there was between her and sister. To his mind, Jane was the most handsome woman he had ever encountered, and though it was undoubtedly true that Elizabeth was a startling beauty in her own right, there was enough dissimilarity between their appearance that the two might have been confused for cousins, rather than siblings.

When the occasion presented itself, he turned his attentions back toward Elizabeth. Darcy and Mr. Gardiner were engaged at present with discourse on fishing, whilst Georgiana and Mrs. Gardiner discussed the magnificence of the music room at Pemberley.

"It has been a very long time since I have had the pleasure of seeing you," Bingley blurted Before she could formulate a reply, he added: "It is above eight months. We have not met since the twenty-sixth of November, when we were all dancing together at Netherfield."

"Yes, I believe it was."

"And your *sisters* are in good health?" Bingley queried, thinking with regret his tone may have betrayed his eagerness.

"Yes, sir, they are all excellent; though one has left Longbourn recently."

Momentarily he forgot that Lydia was in Brighton and panicked at the thought that Jane had been married. "*Which* sister?" He noticed Darcy look over at him in censure. Bingley managed a subdued smile.

"Lydia," answered Elizabeth. "She has gone to Brighton for the summer with Mrs. Forster."

"Oh, how lovely," he panted in relief. "And the rest of your sisters—*all* of the rest of them—remain at Longbourn?" Elizabeth nodded and smiled sweetly. The corners of his mouth darted upward suddenly before he spoke once more with a shade of true lament: "I deeply regret that it has been such a lengthy separation."

He could see that she was hesitant in preparing a reply and he wondered yet if, perhaps, she and her sister did not regret the dis-union between them. His heart quivered with the very thought as he anxiously anticipated her answer. It did not escape his attention, though, through much mental strain, that she continually glanced toward his friend. Eventually, she looked back toward him and said, "It has been too long *indeed*, Mr. Bingley."

"It pleases greatly me that you share my opinion."

In reply, she smiled and then glanced off toward Darcy again, who was still absorbed in confabulation over trout and tackle with Mr. Gardiner. When she looked back to Bingley, she drew breath to ask a question, but stopped herself before the first syllable came out. Rather than press her, Bingley only smiled while she diverted her gaze.

Before they knew it, more than a half hour had passed in discourse of the most pleasant variety. When the visitors rose to leave, Mr. Darcy called on his sister to join him in expressing their desire to entertain Mr. and Mrs. Gardiner as their guests for dinner at Pemberley. Once the engagement was arranged for the evening after next, the party bid their leave.

"It is a great pleasure to have the certainty to see you once more, at least, before you depart the country," Bingley addressed Elizabeth. "I look forward to the opportunity to speak with you again. I still have much to say to you and... many inquiries to make about all of our shared friends in Hertfordshire."

"I would like that a great deal, Mr. Bingley."

When they departed, Bingley rode Quinton at a gallop out of the village and through the park until he sensed the horse begin to tire. They slowed to a gait where Bingley felt himself breathing nearly as hard as his horse. They walked on slowly through the woods until they reached a small pond where the rider dismounted and led the horse to drink. By this time, it was well after noon and the sun was bright overhead. His thoughts swirling all about, from the exhaustion of his travel and the astonishing delight at seeing Elizabeth Bennet so unexpectedly, Bingley dared to hope that Jane still held him in high regard. Her sister certainly did not seem put off by his appearance. In fact, he imagined that Elizabeth had seemed rather pleased to have been reacquainted with him. Bingley was certainly delighted to have confirmation that Jane was not married or engaged, though he wondered yet again how long he could rationally expect her to remain so.

Under the weight of such thoughts and the heat of the day, Bingley suddenly felt faint. Having gained no relief from undoing his cravat and peeling off his coat, in a flash of spontaneous abandon, he further disrobed down to his shirt and drawers—having the momentary flicker of sanity to remove his watch—before scampering toward the edge of the pond and diving in headfirst. The naively unexpected chill caused his muscles to seize momentarily, and he burst through the surface, gasping and laughing. Pondweeds brushed against his ankles, generating a shiver up his spine, as he paddled further toward the centre of the lake. He swam with the giddiness of a child for nearly a half hour before climbing back up the bank and collapsing on his back in the grass. Basking in the sun's warmth, he allowed himself the bliss of imagining Jane by his side and thought that truly nothing on earth could ever make him happier.

Putting his breeches and boots back on, he walked Quinton to the stables and entered the house by the kitchen, grabbing a hunk of bread as he passed, and motioning his thanks to the kitchen maid, whose carrot chopping ceased in shock when she recognized the man. Bingley passed up the stairs in the east wing, with the hopes of avoiding detection, before withdrawing to his quarters in order to wash and change clothing, chewing on the warm bread with vivacity. In the hall of the guest rooms, however, he encountered Caroline whose jaw dropped at the sight of him. He nodded his head, and with an easy grin, breezed past her and into his lodging, taking delight in the fact that he had finally managed to render her speechless.

CHAPTER FORTY-FIVE

SINCE MR. HURST DECLINED the invitation, as had been expected, Bingley and Darcy set out to meet Mr. Gardiner, accompanied by two other gentlemen who had travelled with them, just before noon the following day. The men spent several hours that afternoon in the act of fishing for trout, and quite successfully so. It seemed that Mr. Gardiner had a knack for the activity, though they all caught half a dozen or so from Darcy's stream. The conversation was gentlemanly and cheerful, though it may not have been particularly plentiful, which suited each member of the party. As the afternoon neared three o'clock, Mr. Hurst graciously accepted Mr. Darcy's invitation to take the carriage back to Lambton—along with the other two gentlemen when they were finished—as his wife and niece had called on Georgiana and Mr. Bingley's sisters. After instructing the servants about the tackle, the two friends were left then to meander back to the house.

"It is a wonder, Darcy, that we have not been in each other's company as to converse in months," Bingley began.

"I do agree, between the demands of our business and the injury you took in Hull, it has been far too long since I have had the pleasure of your company."

Bingley sighed through his nose as they strolled through the park. "You must, then, inform me as to the occurrence at Rosings which has had you dejected and aloof all this time, although I must admit, seeing you in such high spirits here at Pemberley these last two days has assuaged much of my concern."

"I once more offer my apologies for my alienation from you these past months," said Darcy, hands clasped behind his back as he walked. "I do believe that I am much recovered from my downtrodden state, or at least recovered enough to converse about my feelings."

Bingley looked over at him with concern. "Are, or rather, *were* you in love with Miss Anne de Bourgh?"

Darcy's head spun toward his friend with a glare so baffled as to be nearly comical. "Miss Anne de Bourgh—my *cousin*?"

"Well, yes," answered Bingley, completely perplexed by the astonishment in Darcy's tone.

"I do apologize indeed, my friend," chuckled Darcy. "It appears I have kept you rather in the dark more than I imagined. Please believe me that it was inadvertent." Bingley nodded his reply. "Being that you have not suspected my true feelings, this will come as a rather great surprise, then: Miss Elizabeth Bennet was visiting her cousin Mr. Collins and his wife at Rosings at the same time which I visited my aunt."

"Miss Elizabeth Bennet?" Bingley gasped.

"Yes, and for quite some months leading up to that encounter I had found myself enraptured by her, or perhaps, *tortured* would be a better description of my state of being. Despite every objection with which I attempted to curtail my feelings, they would not be repressed. I tell you truthfully that from the time we left Meryton I struggled, in vain, to convince myself that it was nothing more than a passing fancy. Yes, as the weeks and even months, dragged along, I found that I could not even conceive the thought of being wed to any other. It had been for quite some time my arrangement with Colonel Fitzwilliam to visit Lady Catherine in the spring, but when I learned that Miss Elizabeth Bennet was near Rosings, I hastened our plans and we left immediately. I deluded myself that spending those afternoons in her presence would confirm to me the absurdity of my feelings, but despite all my efforts at diversion and what I perceived to be rationality, her charm, her wit, and yes, her beauty had left an indelible mark upon me that nothing but her consent to be my wife could soothe. One afternoon I took the liberty of walking down to the parsonage where I proposed to her—"

"You *proposed* to Miss Elizabeth Bennet?" Bingley cried.

"And she quite summarily rejected me."

Bingley's motor functions temporarily departed him as he stood, mouth gaping, next to the man who had cautioned him time and again about the folly of forming designs upon a Bennet sister. Suddenly, Bingley shoved his friend's shoulder with the words, "You *proposed* to her?"

"And I botched it horribly," replied Darcy, tidying his coat. "Are you angry at me for allowing my feelings to get the better of my judgement?"

"You daft, *daft* man," Bingley retorted. "I would wager a thousand pounds that you insulted her."

"Indeed, I did, though in my defence—"

"In your defence?" muttered Bingley. "There is *no defence* for the fixed state of vanity in which you at times operate, Darcy."

"Then you rejoice in my suffering?" Darcy answered solemnly.

"Of *course* not," his friend replied as they began to walk toward the house once more. "It is only that I despair at your blindness to it. I wish you could have been open with me about your feelings."

"I regret not having spoken with you candidly—that, too, was motivated by pride."

They strolled along in silence until Bingley began to laugh under his breath.

"I would wager another thousand pounds that you told her you liked her against your will."

"I did indeed say something to that effect, and how ashamed I am to think of it now," exclaimed Darcy. "And would you hear what she told me? That my vain declarations only spared her any concern she might have had if I had acted, *'in a more gentlemanlike manner.'*"

Bingley glanced up at him, both eyebrows raised. "I bet that one has kicked your backside all these months."

"Verily, it has."

"And so, it should. I hope you have at the very least, endeavoured to learn from it."

"I have acquired a decade's worth of wisdom these last three months, thank you," Darcy answered as they neared the door.

"I also hope that your suffering has at least become easier to bear."

"In some ways yes, it has, but my heart is still very much attached."

"I've observed your cordiality with her and her relations since yesterday, and I would venture a guess that you desire to win her heart still."

Darcy looked at him gently and earnestly: "I desire her to see that I have changed—that her opinion of me cut me to the quick and has caused me to become a better man than I was. But most of all, I desire her happiness above my own."

The right side of Bingley's mouth curled into a smile. "And that is, perhaps, the second-best outcome that might have been achieved."

Darcy nodded and opened the door. "Will you come up with me? The ladies have called from the village."

"I thank you, but no," replied Bingley. "I hardly slept at all last night out of the nervous excitement of it all. Please give my apologies and assurance that I anticipate seeing Miss Elizabeth Bennet tomorrow evening, but I believe I am in great need of a few hours of repose."

"What sort of excitement?" Darcy asked playfully.

"You cannot be so obtuse as to not comprehend *my* feelings," declared Bingley.

"Your *own* feelings toward Miss Jane Bennet?"

"Naturally."

"I have perceived them."

"And you do not blame me?"

"I would only caution you as before, Bingley—your business *must be at an end* before you might even consider marriage. Any design on matrimony, in light of your current circumstances, would be *madness*—surely you must know this."

"What if she marries before I am through?"

"Then you will mourn in private, and in public wish her the best for her health and happiness, and then remember that there are many other eligible young ladies you might take as a bride."

"But I do not *want* any others."

"Then complete the mission with which you have been divinely tasked and see what reward awaits you."

Bingley managed a reluctant smile. Darcy responded by clasping his shoulder reassuringly. With that, they entered the grand house through the courtyard—the master toward his rooms to change and the guest toward his room to repose. Maddeningly, it was a struggle for Bingley to sleep, even as enervated as he by that time was. However, when he was finally in the grip of rest, he slumbered unmoved until it was nearly time for dinner.

CHAPTER FORTY-SIX

AFTER BREAKFAST THE NEXT morning, Darcy excused himself from the party and expressed a wish to ride into the village. Bingley declared a desire to walk the park and enjoy the fresh air, to which his sister Caroline advised him with scorn to be careful not to fall into any ponds, as they might be infested with leeches. He smiled wryly back and took his leave. The day was cooler than any preceding it since they had arrived at Pemberley, thanks in part to a fixed cover of clouds, though they did not seem to portend rain. He took the path round the reflection pool and admired the house from various angles, then took a turn in the garden before strolling through the orangeries. From there, he crossed the path through the wood and into the wilderness to the west. Crossing a rushing stream by dancing from surface stone to stone, his thoughts about Jane rambled along. He mused about how he might assure Elizabeth that he was still fond of her sister without being overly candid, particularly in light of the fact that he still lacked any acute assurance of her feelings toward him.

After an hour or so he roamed back toward the house by way of the stables and coach house. He caught himself reflecting on the night he arrived from Grantley, his hands stained with the blood of that terrible man—how feverishly he had scrubbed them. Wilshere had his clothes burned in the pit; he had nearly wished he could have severed his hands and tossed them in as well. What a ghastly undertaking he had been commissioned for. He only hoped it would not cost him Jane. When he arrived back, he saw Darcy's gig race up to the front step where the man himself quickly dismounted and practically sprinted inside. Bingley approached rapidly and was met just outside the door by Mr. Wilshere.

"I have had word from Maitland," the steward spoke soberly.

"What is it?"

"Come in, quickly," he said, holding the door as Bingley passed through. Wilshere led him to the solitude of Darcy's library.

"Let's have it," Bingley demanded.

"It would seem that we have irrefutable proof that George Wickham is, indeed, the charming young man of large fortune who has been luring young maidens from their families as part of the evil cabal."

"How do we know?"

"Maitland reports that another young lady has disappeared with him," panted Wilshere. "She has left her friends and written that they shall marry in Gretna Green."

"Then she is already lost," Bingley glowered.

"Perhaps not, sir," answered Wilshere. "They have been marked in London as recently as three days ago."

"London? Why London? No other victims were found in London."

"I cannot answer that, but Mr. Bingley, there is another piece of vital information."

"Tell me."

"The young lady," the steward hesitated, "is Miss *Lydia* Bennet."

Bingley's eyes closed as he gripped the sides of the table before him. "Infernal..."

"I have already sent for Mr. Gallagher's assistance—"

"He has replied to our entreaty?"

"Aye, sir, and he is a most willing participant on our behalf."

"Good man," Bingley replied. "His abilities will be very useful. And has Maitland pursued them to London himself?"

"He should arrive there today. As I understand it, the couple absconded quite furtively."

There was a great commotion in the hall—voices and feet stirring. The master and his steward wrinkled eyebrows at each other quizzically.

"Prepare the coach, you and I shall leave at once."

"Of course. And your sisters?"

"I shall make my apologies to Darcy and my sisters and inform them that urgent business beckons me back to town." Wilshere nodded and left the room, more ruckus occurring down the corridor. Bingley paused for a momentary reflection before walking out of the library himself. What he saw astonished him greatly—servants rushing to and from, trunks moving about and, finally, Darcy himself descending the main staircase in nearly reckless haste. "Darcy!" Bingley called.

"I regret to inform you, Charles, that I must quit Pemberley at once for London," he declared gravely.

"For what purpose?"

"A matter of urgent business—"

"Wickham?" Bingley queried.

Darcy stopped in his tracks. "Have you heard and so suddenly? I have just called on Miss Elizabeth Bennet and learned of it from her directly."

"I will go—you must stay here as to not arouse alarm."

"I cannot allow that, Charles."

"Darcy—"

"Miss Elizabeth Bennet may not consent to be my wife, but I shall not see her ruined by a man whose character I should have exposed long ago. You will see, it is a matter of the heart."

"Then let us go together."

"Please—I truly value the gesture as a friend, but it is not your duty to embroil yourself in this unfortunate circumstance. You are on holiday, and you have earned the right to rest, and—"

"There is something of Wickham's nature that I have, myself, concealed as well."

Darcy looked at him crossly. "Whatever do you mean?"

"For months I have believed most seriously that Mr. Wickham is involved in the vile conspiracy which I have endeavoured to end. I have, just this morning, had confirmation of my suspicions. It appears that Miss Lydia Bennet has become his most recent prey. I sincerely apologize that I obscured this information from you, but it was not until now beyond contestation, and I most earnestly did not wish it to cause any hardship on your behalf."

"Then let us fly at once," pronounced Darcy.

Within ten minutes time, the two friends had given their excuses and taken their leave of sisters and acquaintances alike. Darcy took Georgiana aside and made certain that she had no distress as to the cause of his sudden departure. There was much shock and speculation among the remainder of the party as to what might have caused both Darcy and Bingley to depart from Pemberley so abruptly.

Though two of their coaches took the journey, the gentlemen rode together in Darcy's, while their stewards and servants—Bingley's footman Ridley among them—rode behind in Bingley's. They stopped to change horses at Chesterfield, Pinxton, Nottingham, and Costock before riding straight through to Leicester where they delayed only long enough to eat and take on new horses yet again. After countless changes and but one more meal, the party arrived at the Darcy residence at a quarter to seven the following evening, exhausted and battered, but desperate to begin their quest. A meal of ham and potatoes had already been prepared and the entire group—servants included—dined once they had all changed and refreshed themselves.

They were met at dinner by Maitland who made a report with the latest intelligence. It appeared that Colonel Forster had written Mr. Bennet to inform him that Lydia and Wickham departed Brighton under cover of darkness for Scotland where they were to be married. Only later, however, was it learned that they had not be traced past London. Apparently, a Mr. Denny, one of Wickham's peers, reported to Colonel Forster that it was never Wickham's intention to marry Lydia at all. After exhausting all possible inquiries in London, himself, Colonel Forster went to Meryton personally to confer with Mr. Bennet where it was decided that the two of them would return to town the following day to resume their search. Because he was obliged to be in Brighton the following evening, Colonel Forster then departed, leaving Mr. Bennet in town where he would shortly be joined by Mr. Gardiner.

"From the time you recently spent in Meryton, Maitland, did you form any kind of concern on behalf of Miss Lydia Bennet, that she might have been smitten by Wickham?" Bingley inquired.

"Perhaps not in particular," answered Maitland with some hesitation. "It is my own opinion that she was enthralled with the idea of the regiment, more than any one man in particular."

"She and her sister both," Darcy commented glibly.

"Not *Kitty*," replied Maitland. Darcy looked toward him quizzically. "At least, it is not so in *my* humble estimation."

"What possibilities have you explored since arriving in town, then?" Bingley asked.

"We have checked as many carriage inns as possible—I can provide a list—although, if the couple do not remain stationary it may be wise to check all of those again. Our network has been informed of their descriptions, that we might learn if they pass through any of the major turnpikes leaving town. In addition, I greased the pockets of some of ours who might be trusted down on the docks, in the event they attempt to leave the country by sea. All told, I have not slept in fifty-six hours."

"Fine work, Maitland," declared Bingley. "I thank you."

"It is also my understanding that Mr. Wickham has left behind a trail of debts in nearly every place he has been—from Lambton to Meryton to Brighton, and even Hull."

"He is undoubtedly in dire straits."

"Tell me," began Darcy, "typically from the time a maiden vanishes as part of this vile business, how long until her body is discovered?"

Maitland sniffled and cleared his throat. "Her death and her body being discovered are two separate occurrences. It is my estimation that most often, a young lady is murdered within seventy-two hours of her abduction—though her remains are often not located until much later."

"Then time is against us," Darcy affirmed.

"It is, undoubtedly our greatest enemy."

"Mr. Wilshere, when do we expect Mr. Gallagher's arrival?" Bingley asked.

"By morning, two days from now," answered his steward.

"Good," Bingley remarked, turning towards Maitland. "Now, young man, I would like for you to rest this evening whilst we make our first calls—"

"No, sir, I could not possibly—"

"You are in no condition," stated Bingley. "We need you at your best. Stay here, and sleep."

Maitland nodded in worried resignation.

Once they gathered themselves, Bingley, Darcy, and Wilshere set out on horseback into the dark London night to accost a monster.

CHAPTER FORTY-SEVEN

THEY LEFT WESTMINSTER INITIALLY in the direction of Belgravia where they searched a succession of inns and pubs, questioning patrons and proprietors alike, in hopes of procuring any hint as to the whereabouts of the couple. From there they rode on to Chelsea where they continued, with no success, to make inquiries after the youngest Miss Bennet and her beau. That evening, they came back up the riverfront through Pimlico, where they hoped to have the good fortune to stumble upon the man himself—perhaps even, though they prayed that God might forbid it, in the act of discarding her. As the sun rose meekly through a dense haze in the east, the party returned to Darcy's home, only to learn that Maitland had slipped out just hours after they left to resume his own search. Bingley, Darcy, and Mr. Wilshere supped on a small repast of cake and fruit before heading their separate ways within the house to sleep. Just after noon, they were fed and departed once more. To their astonishment, there still had been no sighting of Maitland at the house.

For another six hours they scoured the most disreputable parts of town to no avail. When they returned again to the house that evening, they were greeted with the news that Maitland had returned and, without eating went directly to bed. The two gentlemen dined on lamb and roasted vegetables, while Wilshere resolved to eat in the servants' hall. After a couple glasses of brandy, Clinton, one of Mr. Darcy's footmen, entered the room with a letter from Caroline Bingley. After her brother read it, he excused himself from the study and went to his room to compose a response. It seemed that she, as well as the rest of their party, had learned just hours after the sudden departure of the master of Pemberley and her own sibling, about the circumstance involving Miss Lydia Bennet and George Wickham. Fortunately for Bingley, she gave no indication as to her connecting the gentlemen's departure with the ill-conceived elopement. In fact, her language was nothing but scornful and filled with boasting over what she certainly believed was the final schism which would forever separate her brother from the disreputable Bennet family. To that end she then boasted of the perpetual refinements of Miss Darcy, of her ever-increasing handsomeness, her proper upbringing, and the air with which she carried herself, which so keenly befitted a young lady of her consequence.

Sitting down, and in a furore, he began to craft a response, endeavouring not to divulge neither his personal nor professional interest in the development, nor admit its being the cause of his hasty departure from Derbyshire. He did manage, however, a rebuttal to his sister's haughty condescension, then stopped after having penned nearly a page in even more erratic and feverish hand than was typical of him.

Why on God's good earth am I even deigning to reply? he thought. *I shall not alter her opinions, as they are the product of wilful hubris. More pressing matters demand my attention.*

With that, he crumpled the paper and returned downstairs to his friend. He summoned Clinton, who was passing through the hall, and solicited him to dispose of it in the fire in the kitchen which, due to the summer temperatures, was the only one in the house kept stoked. When he appeared again in the study, he found it empty. He rang for Wilshere, but his man did not appear for a full ten minutes, having been indisposed at the time. After enquiring as to Darcy's whereabouts, Bingley's man returned downstairs. Upon returning once more, Wilshere informed his master that Mr. Darcy had thought that Mr. Bingley was retiring for some time, so he took it upon himself to begin their quest unaccompanied. Darcy had left the grounds nearly a half hour prior.

"What on earth is he on to?" Bingley demanded. "Of all people he should not be singly roaming the most perilous parts of town at this hour."

"The stableboy gave no indication to which direction he had gone," Wilshere answered.

"Insufferable pride," muttered Bingley.

"I prefer to view it through the lens of reckless devotion."

Bingley nodded, and after a moment, ordered their horses to be ready. To their mutual surprise, they were joined by a haggard, but resolute, Maitland upon their departure. Once more, the three men combed through every possible alley, inn, and brothel; and once more their efforts were met with futility. They settled back at the house after eight the next morning, leaving their horses with the stable keepers just as Darcy returned. After declarations of the mutual happiness they felt at the safe sight of each other, the men divulged that neither one had accomplished anything toward furthering their search. It was also learned on entering the house, that Mr. Gallagher had arrived from Grantley Village with much eagerness to be of service.

Three more nights were spent in much the same fashion, though the party did venture to stay together during their raids of London's most loathsome establishments. On the second night, their luck appeared to turn on a word from a tanner in Bermondsey. The man, whose name escaped them all, told them that he had met a George Wickham who was accompanied by a rather handsome, rather young lady in a pub on George Row, by the river wall. Their stated plan was to leave for Scotland in the morning—this had been three nights earlier. The worried party searched not only the pub, but also the bank of the Thames for the duration of that evening, finding no evidence of either Lydia or Wickham. When after sleeping a few hours, they reconvened that afternoon it was decided that, whilst the tanner's story was probably reliable, Wickham's word to him was most certainly not so. Particularly because the couple had not been seen on any of the roads traveling north, it was safe to assume that they were still in town. Wilshere even made the suggestion that their sighting was good news, as it was proof that she had not been summarily dispatched, as so many others had been, but was alive and ostensibly well, just three nights prior.

Eventually, both Bingley and Darcy replied to concerned letters from their respective sisters, requesting the ladies to remain at Pemberley, and advising that their own return to Derbyshire would be imminent once their business had been concluded satisfactorily. All five men were, by this point, utterly fatigued and frustrated, though they dared not consider abandoning their quest. The physical toll was certainly daunting, but the emotional expenditure was far vaster an obstacle. Each one of the men, Gallagher aside, had a personal connection with the Bennet family of some kind, all of them having, at the very least, met the sisters, and at the very most, loved one of them. Yet even the Constable had daughters of his own, and after learning of the evils wrought on defenceless maidens in much the same situation as his own children, he was full of zeal on their behalf.

At dinner that evening, Bingley found it difficult to eat. He sipped his wine and asked, "What are we *missing*, Darcy?"

"I do not understand your meaning," replied Mr. Darcy after wiping the corner of his mouth with a napkin. "They have not left town—it is only a matter of time before they are found."

"I am not so sure as you."

"That they are still in town? Your own men are posted at all the thoroughfares, and there has not been a single sighting of them."

"No, I believe they are still in London, but there seems to me to be a piece of information, one solitary connection, that must be painfully obvious, yet has alluded us all."

"I cannot fathom any connection between our world and *that* man's, Bennet sisters aside," rejoined Darcy with a dash of venom. "Though George Wickham and I grew up as children together, once we parted ways after he left Cambridge, our sphere of relations and friendships wholly and incurably diverged."

"That is perfectly clear, Darcy," Bingley answered. "And all as it should be, but I still cannot accept the idea that we have not overlooked the very thing that would lead us directly to them."

"Do not torment yourself, Bingley. George Wickham is not so bright that it could be imagined he might outwit the likes of us in perpetuity."

"On that account you will hear no dissent from me," replied Bingley. "Which is precisely why it confounds me so acutely—he must be under some person's guidance, someone's protection. That is the only theory by which I can explain his current level of success in evading detection."

"The remaining members of the plot, then?" Darcy asked.

"Perhaps if we spent our vigour seeking *them* out—"

"It is an admirable thought, but not prudent at this late stage," interjected Darcy. "I am afraid the hours are against us and running critically low. We *must* find Wickham and discover him soon. Once we do, he will divulge what information he possesses, that we might eliminate the men to whom he reports."

"Yes, I concur, we should remain resolute and unwavering," said Bingley.

Darcy nodded slowly, then drank what remained of his wine. "I must have you eat, Charles—you are no good to anyone if you are vitiated by malnourishment."

At this word, Bingley's face narrowed in diffident acquiescence, and he raised his fork to his mouth and sombrely chewed what in other circumstances would have been a delectable cut of pork. At that moment, however, he ate only out of obligation to his own body, his thoughts racked by the distress under which his dearest Jane, together with the remainder of the Bennet family, was most assuredly toiling, and the earnest wish to see her suffering alleviated. Several moments passed in relative silence between the two masters before Darcy spoke again: "I do confess, there is one detail that has continued to cause me great vexation these last several days."

"And that is?" posed Bingley between bites.

"Why Lydia Bennet?" Darcy mused.

"I have pondered the same question with much dissatisfaction. She does not fit the mould of the other young ladies to meet similar ends."

"She is an irrational choice, indeed, for she certainly does not lack for protection."

"Quite true," Bingley responded. "All of the others were nearly destitute and without significant cover from their relations. Miss Lydia

Bennet has a degree of connections in society, not to mention being in the charge of Colonel Forster."

"She is not in possession of any kind of fortune, either as was the case not only with my own sister, but also Miss Mary King."

"It seems Miss Lydia Bennet falls somewhere in between, then. Very peculiar, indeed. Would you believe that, perhaps, beauty alone has recommended her for such selection?"

"I would not presume that to be the primary reason for her abduction, as she not half as handsome as her two eldest sisters," Darcy stated bluntly.

"Neither would I," answered Bingley with a wrinkled brow. "Though I might venture to state that it is obvious from the infatuation under many of the officers in the regiment found themselves, that to a particular sort of man, perhaps her... *vivacity* might increase her attractiveness."

"And what sort of men would be seduced by such juvenility and gammon?"

Bingley looked across the table sternly. "Exactly the type of men I have hunted these last two years at least."

Darcy tapped his glass and at once a footman came scurrying with wine to refill his master's goblet. After taking an ungentlemanly gulp he stated arduously, "It is quite the unhappy business which you administer."

"It is indeed," came the reply.

"And to consider after that horrible occurrence involving my sister, I considered George Wickham to be evil then—ha!" Darcy's laugh was then followed by a leaden silence. "With what I know of him now, it seems silly to recall the anger and loathing in which I held that man... that man along with Mrs. Younge who helped him nearly abscond with my dear sister and her fortune."

"What name did you say?" demanded Bingley.

"Mrs. Younge!"

CHAPTER FORTY-EIGHT

Immediately Wilshere and Maitland were roused from their slumber, whilst Gallagher was retrieved from the servant's hall where he was halfway through finishing an onion pie. Darcy's steward, Mr. Perry, was recalled from the wine cellar and questioned as to the location of Mrs. Younge's London residence. He dashed back downstairs to his office but was unable to uncover any address in his various ledgers, as she had resided with the family during her short employment as Georgiana's governess. It was, if you recall, after gaining the family's trust that Mrs. Younge had accompanied Georgiana to Ramsgate and so insidiously allowed the young lady to meet and nearly elope with Mr. Wickham.

"I am exceedingly sorry, sir, to not have kept the address—"

"No, please do not apologize," Darcy broke in. "You may have, and as much as I desired nothing more at that time than full dissolution with such infamy, I may have instructed you at some point to rid us of all connection with that vile woman. And I, for my part, cannot seem to recall any relevant details about her life before she joined the staff, other than that her late husband had been a vicar, but for the life of me I could not tell you where."

"What about any of the maids, Mr. Perry?" Maitland chimed in. "Would any of them have shared quarters with her, or at least had more occasion to become better acquainted?"

Mr. Perry thought for a moment. "Why, yes, Maitland—I do believe she had become rather acquainted with Helena, one of our maids." Darcy's steward then called for Clinton, the footman, to have Helena fetched. The girl entered the room breathlessly, but two minutes later.

"Helena, I understand that you were on familiar terms with Mrs. Younge during her service here?"

The maid cringed at the very mention of the name. "Yes, Mr. Perry, but not after—"

"I understand," he cut in, calming her with the motion of his hands. "We were all quite unhappily deceived by her." The maid managed a nervous smile. "I wonder if you might by chance recall anything of her private details—where she lived, or even in what parish her late husband was vicar?"

"I believe she made mention that her house was in Edward Street," Helena answered, brow knit in concentration.

"Edward Street? That is excellent," exclaimed Mr. Perry.

"There are several Edward Streets all across London," Mr. Darcy remarked. "What about the church, Helena? Can you recall the name?"

Her mouth twisted anxiously as if she were about to apologize, but then her face lit up with cognition. "Yes, she said she had a house on Edward Street, and let rooms to workers for her support, though now looking back, I believe she may have been involved in another sort of business altogether."

"And the church?"

"St. Clement's in Southwark."

"You are *positive*?"

"Without question, Mr. Darcy," she beamed. "She would complain incessantly that the pinchers and rogues would steal from her home, and I remember she would say, 'There's but a single man in all Southwark I trust.' I am absolutely sure of it."

"Thank you, Helena," Darcy said. "Mr. Perry, see to our horses, and see that Helena receives a bottle of wine from my collection as well as a five-pound reward for her assistance."

"Make it ten," Bingley chimed in. "Wilshere, see to it."

Both stewards nodded then left the room.

"Thank you, Mr. Darcy, Mr. Bingley," Helena spoke through welling tears. "Thank you and may God bless you both."

Her departure was followed by Maitland's and Gallagher's. The two masters went and dressed for the evening, before reconvening in Darcy's study in twenty minutes' time. They shared a quick glass of brandy and were met outside by their men and their horses. Wilshere informed them as they mounted that he had just learned that Mr. Bennet had left town and travelled back to Hertfordshire that day, though his brother-in-law, Mr. Gardner was still using what means he had to locate the couple. Both Bingley and Darcy found themselves silently ruminating that they had not the fortune of dispatching him to Longbourn with more favourable news. *I will not see her ruined by such a man as George Wickham.* The journey into Southwark was only slightly over two miles, but through tightly packed and cluttered streets, took much longer than any of them would have wished. Over Westminster Bridge, they rode on down the New Cut toward Nelson Square, where they turned north in the direction of Edward Street.

"How did this possibility escape us earlier?" Bingley asked.

"This is a most perfect, yet inauspicious place to hide," responded Darcy. "I see that quite clearly now."

The streets were surrounded by timber yards, brewers, dyers, and all sorts of trade, but were also littered with boarding houses for the impoverished workers, brothels, and taverns. Even more alluring, perhaps, to a man like Wickham, and an impressionable young lady as Lydia, was its proximity to amusements of all kinds—the Royal Circus, for instance, with all its ballets and performances was mere blocks away. A girl from the country could easily believe she was being treated to the finest London had to offer after a night in such a place and would all the more easily become the prey of a wretch like Wickham. And at the same time, the area was so densely populated that detection could be avoided easily in the faceless hum of the crowd.

Once they reached Edward Street, it was not difficult to obtain the address of Mrs. Younge's house. A child dressed in nothing more than rags was granted two pounds to point out the location which she did with both eagerness and delight. Littered about the place were drifters and drunkards and miscreants of all shapes and sizes. The stench of urine and waste was overpowering, and perhaps worse than in any other repugnant neighbourhood they had searched to that point. The sun's setting only served to make the place more dismal, as long shadows were cast upon the road, turning ordinary objects into protracted monuments to vice and squander. Upon reaching the house, Bingley quickly dismounted only to be obstructed by Darcy.

"Please, Bingley," he said as he climbed down and onto the step. "Allow me the honour."

With a nod of Bingley's head, Darcy turned to the door and knocked loudly. Almost immediately it swung open, and he was face to face with Mrs. Younge herself. Her eyes widened as to nearly devour her forehead upon seeing him, and out of primal instinct she attempted to shut the door as quickly as she had opened it, but was unable to, thanks to the boot of Mr. Darcy. Mrs. Younge found herself stumbling backward into the candlelit foyer; he followed her in.

"Will you not receive a gentleman here strictly on business, Mrs. Younge?"

She quivered and swallowed what felt like a lodged peach pit down her throat. "You can have no business here," she mumbled.

"On the contrary, I do," he replied, "I seek an acquaintance of yours, or perhaps, a business associate would be a more proper rendering."

The fear in her eyes was matched by the trembling of her jaw. "You must be mistaken, Mr. Darcy."

Bingley and Wilshere entered slowly behind Darcy. Their faces being obscured by the light from the street at their backs, in addition to their anonymity to her, caused a cold shudder down Mrs. Younge's spine. Maitland, during this time, went round the back of the building to ensure that their man could not evade them by way of the alley.

"You must know the man we seek," insisted Darcy.

"I have not the slightest idea," she answered, her voice shivering with each word.

"George Wickham," Darcy declared. "Where is he?"

Her lip curled upward, and her brow knitted as her eyes darted to and fro. "George Wickham—how has he offended you now?"

"It is of no consequence to you."

She shrugged her shoulders and said, "Perhaps not."

"George Wickham—have you housed him here?"

Mrs. Younge's hand clutched her chest, and she heaved an audible sigh of relief. "You will excuse me, I must sit," she remarked as she fumbled backward for a chair. Once she was seated, hand still over heart, she let a chuckle out and repeated, "George *Wickham*?"

"For the last time, Mrs. Younge, is he here?" Darcy demanded.

"No, of course not," she answered.

"But has he been?"

"Well, yes and quite frequently."

"Of late? With a young lady?"

"He is *always* with a young lady."

"When was he last here?"

"I am not at liberty to divulge such information," she remarked with a tinge of expectation in her voice.

"How much?"

"Twenty pounds."

"You must be touched in the upper works," Darcy ridiculed.

"*Twenty pounds*, and I will tell you when he was here last."

Being bribed by a woman of such ill repute, particularly the woman who had been involved in one of the most painful affairs in his life, was so far below Darcy that his teeth gritted, and his lip curled in revulsion. Looking about the dismal room he, for the first time, heard the din all around him—the carnal sounds of sin and debauchery echoing down halls from behind closed doors; he smelt the redolence of musk and sweat. For a brief second, he imagined what his father would have thought of him even standing in such a place and felt as though he might retch then and there. The only thing that kept his hands at his side, rather than around Mrs. Younge's throat at that moment, was the sudden recall of Miss Elizabeth Bennet's face. He first remembered her sparkling eyes and her radiant smile as she played and sang before them at Rosings Park, then the tears streaming from those same eyes and the fright in the twitch of her lips in the inn at Lambton, as she revealed to him the dreadful news of her youngest sister's most unwelcome elopement. Reaching into his coat pocket, his heart broke for her all over again, and he determined once more that he would see himself ruined before he saw her disgraced. The corners of Mrs. Younge's mouth nearly touched her ears as she reached out and took the notes from his hand.

"Five nights ago," she began, "he arrived here accompanied by a young lady, rather less handsome than was typical, in my opinion."

"And how long did they stay?"

"Not but a minute, for I turned them away."

"You turned them away?"

"Yes, I had not any vacancy," replied Mrs. Younge. "You see, he arrived rather unannounced, and I was at full capacity."

"What do you mean he arrived unannounced?"

"His typical manner is to send word ahead, sometimes only a day's notice, but I am always careful to reserve a room at that point. Last week, he arrived in a state of near panic, but having no advanced notice of his coming, I had no means of accommodating him, or *them*, I should say."

"How long are his usual visits to your establishment?" Bingley suddenly asked.

"He does not *stay* at all," she answered.

"I do not understand your meaning," replied Bingley, stepping closer to Darcy's side.

"He leaves the young lady here, collects his fee, and off he goes."

"Collects his *fee*?"

At this, a sudden pal came over her face. "I am afraid that I have already said too much."

"Twenty pounds," Darcy offered.

"Darcy, no," Bingley cautioned.

"*Fifty pounds*," Darcy upped his offer.

"As much delight as I take in accepting such a generous offer from a gentleman," she said warily, "there is no amount of your money that could entice me to give up my own neck."

Bingley turned and glared back at Wilshere who stood sentry near the door. "If you turned him away, do you have a notion as to where he might have gone?" he asked.

"I do," she replied, putting her hand out palm up.

"You are mad to think you can have another penny from us, you—" Wilshere suddenly broke in.

"I believe you will have to bleed very freely if it is George Wickham you truly seek."

"Fifty pounds?" Darcy blurted.

She smiled smugly. "One hundred-fifty."

"You are truly mad," Bingley began.

"And you *know* where he is?" Darcy interjected.

"Not with precision, but I can tell you with great confidence where he *ought* to be, if he is in bad bread—unless of course he is already dead, then you would be wise to search the pauper's graves."

Bingley reached in his pocket only to be stopped by Darcy's hand. "You have your portion to be done; allow me to have mine," he said sombrely. With that, Darcy handed the money over to Mrs. Younge. "You have no shame, do you?"

"Why should I be ashamed?" she replied. "My income is not generated from the luck of my forebears and the labour of peasants. Yet should a widow not be allowed a comfortable life?"

"Enough," Bingley chimed in. "What have you to tell us?"

"If Wickham should have half as much brains as he has bollocks, he would hide out in Dover Street."

"And why is that?"

"There are many establishments of, granted, lower esteem than mine but none the less, places where a man might hide away, and cheaply so. It is not a very large street, but the inhabitants are dense and bawdy—*use care*," she ended with a scornful smile.

Darcy's nature caused him nearly to bow before taking his leave, but he caught himself before allowing that woman the courtesy so clearly unmerited. As the three men turned and left, Bingley instructed Wilshere to retrieve Maitland and meet them on the corner of Charlotte

Street. Once the door was closed, Mrs. Younge sat with a glare mixed of hatred and disquiet, bank notes raised to the level of her nose.

CHAPTER FORTY-NINE

Down the lane, Darcy and Bingley sat astride their equines, repulsed into astonished silence by their recent experience at the hands of Mrs. Younge.

"Darcy, I'm sorry—" Bingley finally started.

"It is of no consequence," Darcy interposed. "If it leads us to George Wickham in time to save Miss Lydia Bennet—"

"And therefore, her sisters—"

"Yes, and therefore her sisters, any degree of harm it shall be the most well invested money I should have ever spent."

Bingley nodded in agreement. "It is curious, however, the whole business. If he customarily sent word of his arrival in advance, why not this time? Could it be, perhaps, that he truly intended upon marriage?"

"Impossible," Darcy commented with no lack of certainty. "His debts are great, and he is a man incapable of any notion of love or loyalty. If she did not serve his own purpose in some way, and I am sure you have surmised what purpose she might serve, he would not have absconded with her. George Wickham is selfishness and greed personified, and perhaps, as we have now discovered, even more wicked than we might have ever imagined."

"Here they come," Bingley said, glancing over his shoulder as Wilshere and Maitland approached.

"Mr. Bingley," Maitland called. "There is something I must share with you at once."

"With haste," Bingley answered. "And let us move on while you tell."

"Not two minutes after you had entered the house, I spotted a man exit from the back. He was young and tall, and though it was exceedingly dark, so I could not be sure, I thought I recognized his face, so I followed behind him. His gait was rapid as if he was departing in some urgency. Once he reached the side street, he mounted his horse and under the lamp I caught a proper look at his face."

"Was it Wickham?" Bingley queried.

"No. It was Captain Carter, of the Meryton regiment."

"*Captain Carter?*"

"Aye, and he headed off in this very direction."

"He must be on the hunt for Wickham at the direction of Colonel Forster," Wilshere stated.

"Colonel Forster came to town to search, himself, did he not?" Bingley asked.

"He went to Meryton first and consorted with Mr. Bennet," answered his steward. "Together they searched in town before the Colonel was compelled by duty to return to Brighton."

"Yes, I remember now. Let us be on the watch, then, for Captain Carter—as he might be privy to information we have not yet uncovered."

Once the band reached Dover Street, they turned in to find it a dark lane with degenerates lying all about, many asleep already, or perhaps worse. Broken glass and waste littered the road, whilst small fires burned at seemingly random intervals. Intermittent screams and howls and laughter pierced through the clamour and the smell very much resembled that of Edward Street near Ms. Younge's establishment. A mangy dog chased a rat across the way, and out of sight down an alley.

"Stick together closely," Bingley remarked, receiving subdued nods in return.

As they began their inquiries into the various brothels, dilapidated warehouses, and inns, the two gentlemen began to wonder if they had not been altogether duped by Mrs. Younge. Perhaps she had let the couple a room and simply lied. They had paid her a near fortune and, in actuality, not gained an ounce of concrete specifics in exchange. Had the compulsion of their task, coupled with the lack of sleep, caused them such a fatuous lapse in judgement as to put their trust in such a woman? In each of their minds they considered that the matter could not be settled resolutely until their probe of the dregs of Dover Street was complete. As they exited the front room of one particularly raucous brothel after making inquests about the couple, they realized that Maitland had not entered with them at all. In fact, he was down the lane, waving toward them. The three others joined him with haste.

"I spoke to a beggar who pointed me to an inn in Flint Street," he said hurriedly.

"But we have not concluded our search of this area," Bingley remarked.

Maitland shook his head. "He seen them go in less than an hour ago—it's the Bishop's Whistle, just round the corner," he pointed.

"How much did you pay him?" Wilshere inquired.

"I didn't," came the reply.

"Where is the man?"

"He went off down the alley back yonder," Maitland answered. "He gave me their description—matches perfectly. The man would have no motive to lie."

"Then off to the Bishop's Whistle, no?" Wilshere asked.

Darcy and Bingley exchanged a glance and then both nodded their assent. At that precise moment, Bingley's eye caught sight of a man—much out of place in the current surroundings—leaving an establishment further up the street. It was clear to him that the man was, indeed, Captain Carter. He was studying a piece of paper in his hand, from what Bingley could tell.

"There," pointed Bingley. The other three turned and saw the man, who had his back toward them and proceeded in the opposite direction.

"Let us leave him be," Wilshere said. "I have a notion of something unsettling as regards that man and his quest. Let us find Wickham and Miss Bennet before he does."

With that, they were off toward Flint Street and the Bishop's Whistle.

CHAPTER FIFTY

IT TOOK NO MORE than a sovereign to learn from the innkeeper in which room the couple were stationed. Up the stairs two flights and down the hall to the end. Darcy again took the initiative to knock and knock he did. Inside the room, a scurrying could be heard, accompanied by laughter and "shushing." After a moment, all went quiet. Darcy knocked again, even more firmly than the first time; the response was continued silence. Finally, he called loudly, in a sternness and timbre which Bingley had never hitherto heard from his friend, "Wickham, open this door at once!" Seconds later, the wood-plank door came ajar, a cowering Mr. Wickham behind it.

"I must admit I am astonished to see you at my door, Mr. Darcy, but I am not entirely ungrateful," he said quietly. His chest could be seen heaving under his shirt; his forehead was damp with sweat. "You must help, please—"

"May we come in, Mr. Wickham?" Darcy barked.

"Certainly," the man replied, stepping aside, and bowing as the band of four entered.

"Mr. Darcy?" Lydia called in bewilderment from the table by near the window. "Mr. *Bingley*? What in heaven's name are you doing here?"

"Miss Bennet," they replied in unison, bowing toward her.

"Are you in good health?" Bingley asked.

"Of course!" she laughed. "How could one be in ill health when they are so in *love*?"

"I am glad to hear it," he answered, casting a spiteful glance in Wickham's direction. He took a view around the room to see it in complete dishevelment. The sheets were rolled up and dangled limply off the bed; sullied dishes and mugs covered the table by which the young lady sat, and scraps of paper and clothing were strewn about the floor.

"Mr. Wilshere," Darcy started, "would you and Maitland be so kind as to escort Miss Bennet downstairs for a glass or two of wine, that we might have Mr. Wickham's full attention?"

"Of course, Mr. Darcy," the steward replied.

Lydia followed them out with giggles and squeals and a promise to "be back soon, my love."

"Sit, Mr. Wickham," Darcy commanded once the door was closed behind them.

Wickham obeyed with no protestation other than to say, "This is not entirely what it seems, Mr. Darcy."

"I do not pretend to fathom how indeed to characterize this circumstance," Darcy replied. "It would appear to me that you have at the *very least*, ruined a respectable young lady, along with all her four sisters. At the worst you have signed her death warrant. Even as repugnant as it might be to attempt to sketch your motivations, I can perceive from what I know of your character, why you would abscond with a naive young girl, but I cannot—"

"Mr. Darcy, I am certainly guilty of a multitude of sins and follies, but I would not have you believe me capable—"

"No, Mr. Wickham, *you* will listen," Darcy demanded. "I, at one time, believed you to be a man of loathsome character, but little did I believe you to be suited to outright depravity. Under what manner of demonic influence have you been possessed which could induce you to such a vile undertaking? Has your upbringing failed you so wholly and catastrophically?"

Mr. Wickham stared up at him in mute astonishment. Darcy looked over at Bingley and inhaled deeply; Bingley nodded back at him.

"Are you aware of the violent ends of Sir Eoin Walters of Northumberland, and Sir Andrew Fraser of Grantley Park?" Darcy asked. The seated man gestured that he had. "And of the 'murder' of Thomas Abbott, Member of Parliament?"

"Why yes, of course," Wickham answered.

"And the public killing of Lord Bertram St. John in Naples?" Wickham again nodded. Darcy stared austerely down at him. "And I would not dare reveal to you the following fact, but for the knowledge that you will not have the opportunity to share it with another soul: the man responsible for those deaths is present with you in this very room."

"What on earth do you mean?" Wickham muttered in panicked perplexity.

"Mr. Bingley, or his knife rather, has been the chief means of dispatching such men in the name of all things decent and holy, and you will soon join them in eternal torment—"

"Mr. Darcy!" Wickham cried, rising to his feet. "I am appalled at these vulgar threats—they are far beneath your dignity."

"And your entire existence is beneath the distinction of the courts of law and order, of the crown under whose honour you serve, and even of human decency itself."

The room fell silent as Wickham slouched back into his chair. "I confess, I am at a loss to comprehend you. I readily admit and beg forgiveness for those past sins committed against you and your family, your honour. I even beg forgiveness for those more recent sins of gambling, sloth, and lustfulness, but for all my heart, sir, I cannot begin to apprehend the grave and vicious threats levelled against my very personhood. Enlighten me, sir, what have I done to deserve such an end? What connection links my behaviour to the gruesome fates of such stately men as have been hitherto mentioned?"

"You have abducted an impressionable young lady from her proper relations with the intent to—"

"*But they would have killed her!*" Wickham proclaimed.

"What did you say?" Bingley implored.

"I understand clearly how this calamitous imbroglio must appear, but I simply did not know what other course of action to take," Wickham blurted.

"Explain yourself," demanded Darcy.

"She would have been killed in the most heinous fashion had I not prevailed upon her to elope with me. The only means by which I could achieve this end was to persuade her of my love, and therefore of my desire to enter the marriage state. I left word that we would travel to Gretna Green, but only as a ruse to allow some time to arrange for travel to Boston, however, and most unfortunately, I found that I had neither the means nor the credit to arrange for such a journey."

"Have you any notion of the kind of irreparable damage you have caused?" Darcy challenged.

Wickham's head heaved and slinked down onto his chest. "Of course, but such considerations were of secondary regard and occurred to me only after we had departed from Brighton in such haste."

"A young lady ruined, and *all* of her sisters tainted by association—sisters who, in spite of their charms, have enough obstacles already with which to contend."

"Tell me, then—what was I to do?"

"You could have gone to Colonel Forster!" snapped Darcy. "That would certainly been a more sensible act than being the cause of her ruin!" The room was once again silent for a moment. "And you have been hiding here ever since?" Darcy finally asked.

"Yes," Wickham responded. "I first went to Mrs. Younge's home in hopes that she might have a vacancy, but soon understood that she was a part of the very same scheme that would have seen Miss Bennet murdered."

"Mrs. Younge? —A part of the plot?" Bingley queried. "So, you know about the murders?"

"I only recently discovered it," he retorted. "You see, for the last several months now—oh, where do I even begin?"

"Let me start by asking, have you been delivering unsuspecting young maidens to slaughter all around the country for some time now?"

"I grant that you have no sensible reason to trust me, given my history, but I beseech you now to believe me when I say that I had no knowledge *whatsoever* of the kind of fate that befell those poor, innocent souls."

Darcy stood with his arm resting on the mantle while shaking his head in disbelief as much as disgust. Bingley rubbed his eyes with the base of his palms, then pulled a chair across from Wickham, and sat down opposite him.

"I may regret asking, but what purpose did you believe yourself to be serving?"

"I am not naive," stated Wickham soberly. "You must understand, my debts were *crippling*, and still are. My habitual gambling had cost me dearly, to the point of absolute ruin, if not worse, when I was offered the opportunity to use my youth and charm—I flatter myself—to procure attractive young ladies on behalf of wealthy bachelors. It was my understanding, until recently, that these young ladies caught the eye of men who were either too wealthy or too proud to be seen in such impoverished localities. My task, as it was explained to me, was to act as an agent on behalf of the gentleman, to entice the lady to consent to a marriage which would not only elevate her own status, but which would also ensure her family's wellbeing and comfort. At the appointed time, I would deliver them in great secrecy to whatever place had been specified in my instructions—"

"Like Mrs. Younge's house?" Darcy asked, looking in Wickham's direction for the first time in five minutes.

"When in London, yes—always. I was to send word to her in advance when all the arrangements were made that she might reserve a room. But in other parts of the country, it was always an inn or a cottage somewhere."

"And once you left them there?" prodded Bingley.

"I collected my fee and departed."

"And what was your fee, Mr. Wickham?" Darcy demanded.

"Ten pounds," replied Wickham.

"Ten pounds!" cried Darcy, turning from the mantle, and pacing toward the door before coming back around. "For ten pounds you signed their writ of execution?"

Tears streamed down Wickham's face which contorted in all forms of resistance. "Please, believe me—I *beg* you—I did not know."

"Is it to be expected that you are so cork-brained as to not have suspected any kind of foul intentions?" Darcy barked.

"You must understand the magnitude of my desperation regarding my pecuniary state," he answered while wiping his cheeks with the sleeves of his shirt. "I am positive that a single act of sacrifice could not repay all of the evils I have unwittingly wrought—"

"An act of sacrifice, you would call it—bringing infamy down on a family whose daughter you had no intention of marrying—"

"Is a dead sister more desirable than an untwisted one? And under what pretension do you thus speak that I have no intention of marrying her?"

"You *cannot* be serious," entreated Bingley, eyebrows raised in stupefaction. "Not only have you suppressed any kind of curiosity with respect to your occupation, but you have convinced yourself now to be in love with Miss Lydia Bennet."

"I do not declare myself to be in love," Wickham answered. "But yes, I intend to marry her, as soon as I am able."

Bingley stood and began to pace the room himself. "I feel as if I must have been dipping rather deep—the room is spinning under all this fiddle-faddle. I cannot even begin to comprehend the reasoning behind this assertion."

"Miss Lydia Bennet may not possess the elegance nor the wit of her eldest sisters, but she is not wholly without charm. I feel that, if by marriage I may save her life and some degree of respectability for her siblings, I am duty bound; and though I may not find myself in love with her at present, it is possible that I may, with time and tenderness, grow to love her."

Bingley and Darcy exchanged bewildered glances.

"If you are willing, then Mr. Wickham," started Bingley, "all that it left is to arrange the wedding."

"I am willing, Mr. Bingley, but I am unable," Wickham replied with a hint of shame.

"Unable?"

"My debts, sir, will not allow it, I am afraid."

"I knew it," Darcy said, turning his back suddenly on Wickham. Bingley cast the back of his friend's head a look as if to urge patience.

"What is the sum of your arrears?" Bingley asked with kindness. While he understood fully that he and Darcy were about to be on the hook for whatever the man had run up in terms of the deficit he had managed to accrue, Bingley was thankful that at the very least, Wickham had declared his willingness to accept Lydia's hand, and that her reputation along with that of her sisters might yet be salvaged, after all. He also briefly reflected on Wickham's professed innocence regarding the evil business afoot, and his readiness to do what was required to make some sort of amends. For, while he was surely reckless and, perhaps, intentionally naive to the consequences of his behaviour, he was not in the category of men that Bingley had all but convicted him of being.

"I am ashamed to say it," Wickham answered, putting his head in his hands. "It is upwards of two thousand pounds."

"Two thou—" Bingley's exclamation was cut off by a sudden rush of nausea which forced him to sit back at the table.

Darcy spun from the door and glared directly at Wickham: "If your debt were satisfied, and I promised you a sum that you could subsist on, you would marry Miss Lydia Bennet?"

"At once," pronounced Wickham with confident dignity.

"Then consider it settled—"

Bingley sprung from his chair and approached Darcy. "We should discuss—"

"The matter is fixed, Charles. This burden shall be born solely on my shoulders," Darcy declared.

"*Thank you*, Mr. Darcy," Wickham earnestly answered. "I am well aware of the torment you have suffered on my account and am also fully cognizant of the tremendous encumbrance which you now endeavour to lift from my shoulders. I should not in one hundred lifetimes be able to thank you enough, though *I swear* that I shall endeavour to exhibit my gratitude by the improvement of my character."

Darcy bowed ever so slightly. "It is settled then, and there shall not be cause to broach the subject in future." As much as he loathed the thought of his friend's noble avowal, from the tone of his voice, Bingley was sure that Darcy would brook no reply to the contrary. He nodded his assent and sat back down with a thud. "Now all that is left is to alert Mr. Gardiner and make the arrangements," continued Darcy. "You shall be married from St. Clement Danes as soon as all is agreed accordingly with Miss Bennet's uncle. You and Mrs. Wickham will visit Longbourn that day, from which point you will return immediately to your regiment in Brighton."

"Return to the *regiment*? —No, I certainly cannot," Wickham nervously announced.

"On what grounds?" Darcy asked. "You must have a profession, and—"

"Because not only would Miss Bennet be dead in a matter of moments after our arrival there, but I would be as well." The churning of the two gentlemen's minds was manifest to see in the quizzical glares they returned in his direction. "Is it not plain? —I received my direction from Captain Carter." The motion of their thoughts gave way to illumination. "Captain Carter recruited me for the scheme—it was *he* that I overheard plotting the death of Miss Bennet."

"And who was he speaking with?" Bingley demanded.

"That, I am sorry to say, I do not know. It was through a closed door, but he very thoroughly laid out a plan to—and I shall not repeat it in such revolting details—use Miss Bennet most diabolically, and then have her disposed of completely. It seems that whoever the monster be that employs him is peculiarly engrossed with her. At that moment precisely I made my way to find her and, using the knowledge that she harboured something of an infatuation with me, it was not difficult to persuade her to take flight with me immediately."

"That must be why Captain Carter was at Mrs. Younge's home," stated Bingley.

"Captain Carter at Mrs. Younge's? When?"

"Just this evening, perhaps an hour before we found you," Darcy answered him.

"Then thank God you happened upon us first! Yet still, we are unsafe here," Wickham declared, rising from his chair.

"I agree; I shall have Wilshere hire a coach immediately."

"Yes, and you should remain at my home until all is arranged," Darcy declared.

"I would caution against that, Darcy. Miss Bennet must not be aware of the plot against her—she should remain blissful in her ignorance. It would be better if we put them up in an inn closer to the church in Danes in Covent Garden."

"Then it shall be done."

With that, Bingley quit the room and found Wilshere with Maitland and Miss Bennet in the tavern. A coach was ordered to whisk the young couple away in secrecy, and the innkeeper was bribed to deny the couple's presence at the inn at any time, should Captain Carter inquire there. Upstairs, Darcy remained at the mantle while he tried to reconcile all that he had just seen and heard with all that he once seemingly understood. It was apparent that his friend had much less trouble processing the entirety of the situation, while he, in his relative nascence to such abominable men as were capable of these machinations, struggled to anymore see the world as he had always regarded it to be. And on top of it, Mr. Wickham who, for reasons aplenty he had despised and reviled, appeared to be far less the fiend then he had known him to be.

Once Wickham had collected what belongings they had and packed them away in their trunks, he sat back down at the table, and offered Darcy a drink of cheap liquor.

After a moment's hesitation he answered, "Why, yes, I thank you."

Wickham poured two glasses, while Darcy sat facing him. They raised their drinks and sipped. Darcy coughed upon swallowing the drink; Wickham smiled amiably with the knowledge that the gentleman had never before tasted a spirit so inferior.

"Please forgive my redundancy, but I must from my heart, most cordially thank you again, Mr. Darcy," started Wickham after they drank.

"And I must express my gratitude to you as well, Mr. Wickham."

"Gratitude toward me?"

"Naturally, you are not alone in possessing imperfections, but in spite of your flaws, you have recently acted with valour and magnanimity that do you great credit," Darcy spoke. "You have not only saved a life, but have preserved the possibility of happiness for so many..."

Thinking of Elizabeth, his voice trailed off. Though he prevented himself from the hope that her opinion of him might ever be altered, he took solace in the thought that once this difficult business was resolved, she might indeed encounter true happiness—and even love. He drank again, this time swilling the liquor with no difficulty.

"I remember how we were as children with great fondness," Wickham said with quiet melancholy.

"As do I," replied Darcy with a tender smile.

CHAPTER FIFTY-ONE

HAVING DEPARTED WITH GREAT stealth to avoid detection by the lurking Captain Carter, the group of four men escorted the carriage across Blackfriars Bridge, and west into Covent Garden where the couple were installed at The Silent Lassie, an ironically fitting name, they thought. Next morning, late as it was when they arose, it was decided that Bingley and Wilshere should depart for Derbyshire that day to quell any apprehensions on the part of their sisters. Darcy would remain in London and call upon the Gardiners in order to resolve the details of the marriage, where he would also stay to stand with Wickham for the ceremony. Additionally, Maitland and Gallagher were left in town to learn what they could of Captain Carter's involvement, and potentially discover who he served as master in the scheme. Bingley noted with some curiosity Maitland's unfettered glee at having found the couple and headed off any kind of further disaster. All that night and the following day, a smile remained glued to the young man's face, as if he himself were the one who had been rescued. Bingley and Darcy certainly felt such a measure of relief themselves, though neither of their situations were anything approaching hopeful regarding the Bennet sisters. That being said, not even the humid gloominess of the day, in which rain showers blustered up and spat upon the house windows at arbitrary intervals, could serve to dampen their spirits.

After seeing to some of his legitimate business ventures and having a small supper, Bingley bid farewell to both his men and his friend and set off for the north in the early evening. Through the clutter of London streets and the mud of the sodden country roads, the gentleman and his steward made it only as far as Luton before stationing for the night in an inn. They rose early the following morning and took their breakfast with them on the road. After several hours of something like reflective silence between them, Bingley spake: "Are we *certain* Mr. Hurst is innocent?"

Wilshere looked up from the ledger he had been balancing both mathematically and upon his lap. "Of this particular indictment, I would declare it so."

"How can we be sure?"

"He was not in Brighton," Wilshere answered.

Bingley nodded in acknowledgement. "No, he was not; he was with us in Pemberley. Still, there is a feeling I cannot shake—"

"Your instincts have always served you well, sir, though I would caution you that we have not uncovered a single piece of evidence to suggest Mr. Hurst's involvement beyond mourning for a friend."

"If a man who you knew on a largely superficial level passed on, would it drive you into a nine-month barrel fever?" Bingley questioned.

"Naturally, no, but I venture to say that it would depend upon the man. Mr. Hurst has always displayed a penchant for overindulgence."

"He has, I grant you, but the depth to which he has sunk because of it causes me to wonder all the same."

"You must also take into account, sir, the shock that the very brutality of the act itself may have caused. There are many ways to kill a man, and the intention has from the start been to serve as a warning, and even deterrent, for the rest of the men involved in such unthinkable deeds, but to the general populace, it must be remembered that the violent deaths of noblemen and members of parliament must seem wholly alarming in both their violence and their disconnectedness. With your own eyes have you read the newspapers and how your work has caused general apprehension."

"A completely unintended consequence," Bingley stated.

"Of course, but we must take this response in hand as we consider the weighty imputation of a member of your own family."

"Your counsel has, once more, proven to be very wise."

Wilshere nodded and looked back down to the ledger spread across his knees. They rode on in relative quietude until they reached the carriage house at Kettering where they changed horses once more. The trek slogged on as the weather made a most inhospitable partner in the venture. When eventually they reached Pemberley, they were much exhausted from the trip—poor meals and nearly sleepless nights only compounding the lack of rest from the activities of the week prior—but rejoiced at the sight of the sight of the magnificent house. Bingley mulled the delightful idea of eating his own weight in Mr. Thompson's fabulous apple pudding before climbing into one of Darcy's luxurious guest beds and sleeping till the following afternoon. Unfortunately, his reveries were interrupted at the first glimpse of his sister who happened to be descending the grand staircase when he entered.

"Charles!" Caroline called affably before being afforded a proper view of him.

"How do you do?" he answered, handing his hat to the footman.

"You look like death warmed over," she grimaced upon closer inspection. "And, by God, you smell like it, too."

"Charmed to see you as well, sister," Bingley quipped.

"I am sure having come from town that you were made aware of the most *scandalous* news involving the Bennet family?"

"I confess, I did hear some rumblings of a rumour, but nothing that would cause any particular distress."

"Why should it cause *you* any distress?" Caroline asked with malice lurking under her contentment. "Miss Lydia Bennet eloping with *George Wickham*—I could think of *nothing* more scandalous. Truly, the entire family ought to be considered *ruined* now, should they not?"

"I cannot possibly imagine how one sister's—"

"An utter disgrace—and *George Wickham* no less! Though I cannot with any veracity profess true surprise at hearing the news," she continued on while he stood, hands clasped behind his back chewing the inside of his cheek. "It is something of a self-fulfilling prophecy, is it not? I mean to say that as the most relentless tease I have ever had the..." Caroline's voice trailed off as her eyes searched the ceiling for the best verbiage to describe her feelings toward Lydia Bennet.

"You are aware that they are married?" Bingley pronounced.

"*Married*?" muttered Caroline in disbelief.

"Out of St. Clement Danes."

"St. Clement Danes? In Covent Gardens?"

He nodded his head, moving past her toward the stairs. "Would you have Mr. Perry ask Mr. Thompson to make a large batch of apple pudding, please? *Large*. I shall be down after I wash and change into fresh clothes." Caroline's mouth gaped as she nodded, the rest of her planted like a marble statue.

Bingley had a bath prepared and basked in the sensation of the hot water much longer than was his usual habit. He would not allow himself the convenience of self-deceit in thinking he had not been vexed by his sister's endeavour at gloating over the misfortunate incident involving Jane's youngest sister, but as much as he relished his bath after a long trek, he delighted in his victory, however minute and ephemeral it might have been, after nearly a year of hearing her sneering disdain for the love of his life. When at last he looked down at his fingers, wrinkled like prunes, he relinquished his solitary leisure and proceeded to dry off and dress for dinner. As Burke assisted him in donning his waistcoat, the thought sprung to mind that this whole time he had been at ease, Caroline must have been informing Louisa of the news, and possibly plotting to further disparage Jane's family by whatever means they could, and quite free from restraint, especially as he had been informed by his valet that Miss Georgiana was, at present, with Colonel Fitzwilliam at his family's estate near Prestbury. Bingley prepared himself for such an encounter with the thought that simple acquiescence was his most suitable strategy for curtailing such a distasteful confabulation. And sure enough, he had hardly entered the drawing room before being ambuscaded: "Oh, brother!" Louisa pronounced. "How lovely to see you!"

"And you, as well," answered Bingley.

"Caroline and I were just discussing the latest news from town, and she informed me of what you learned about Miss Lydia—"

"Yes, they are married," he cut in as he approached a chair near his recumbent brother-in-law. "Mr. Hurst," he bowed before he sat.

"Mr. Bing—hiccup—Mr. Bing...," Hurst answered, opening a single eye in his direction.

"I see you are in lively spirits, as ever," Bingley joked.

"As fine as wine," came the boozy reply.

Before Bingley was even settled in his seat, Caroline began once more: "And how is it that the young couple has been wed? You must enlighten us if you know."

"I cannot attest to the details of it, naturally," Bingley replied with a sigh. "But it is a settled truth that they have, indeed, been married."

"And they were married in London?" Caroline challenged.

"Yes, at St. Clement Danes."

"Then they were chaperoned when they departed Brighton?"

"How would I know?" Bingley countered with a bit more pique than he had intended.

"We heard that they eloped from Brighton," Louisa stated with exactly as much hubris as she had intended.

"I am not privy to such details," replied Bingley.

"It really is *shocking*, is it not, brother?" Caroline asked suddenly. When he did not reply, she answered her own question. "After all that was *known* about Wickham—"

"And that is to say *nothing* of your kindly meant caution to Miss Jane Bennet about his character," Louisa pronounced.

"That's right," Caroline persisted. "Of all that was known about him, I cannot imagine more care was not taken in the supervision of Miss Lydia."

"It is as if she was left completely to her own devices, with full knowledge of her *own* wild inclinations."

"I dare say you are correct, sister!"

"It is rather appalling," Louisa continued. "It says as much about the family, as a whole, as it does about the young girl's constitution. Obviously, propriety and caution are not proper concerns when it comes to their own daughters' repute and even, dare I say, their chastity, to say nothing of their *low* connections and—"

"I am in love with her, *damn it!*" Bingley exclaimed, rising suddenly from his chair. Neither of his sisters could tear their eyes from him in light of the horror of his startling proclamation. "I will not be afflicted by your haughty and ignorant presumptions a moment longer! Miss Jane Bennet is the single kindest, most charming, and agreeable young lady with whom I have ever had the fortune to be acquainted. Her family is not one degree more touched in the upper works than mine, and though their situation may not be nearly as fortunate as ours, we must recall that we are but one generation removed from poverty like the Bennet family has *never* known. I may not *marry* Miss Jane Bennet, or rather, she may not marry *me*—and I would not for an instant hold that against her—but I will no longer tolerate such obdurate and wilfully uninformed slander against the lady who holds my heart in the palm of her tender hand. If I should ever have the honour to make her an offer and be accepted, it shall be the greatest single joy I could hope to experience this side of paradise. And should that blissful day come the pair of you will have an important determination to make: either embrace a sister or lose a brother."

With that, he took his seat and flipped open the adjacent newspaper. Caroline and Louisa exchanged thunderstruck glares, both pairs of eyes as wide as their gaping mouths. After only a moment of awestruck silence, Mr. Dennis—Darcy's butler—entered to announce dinner.

"Mr. Dennis," Bingley said in as high spirits as ever, "May I be so bold as to enquire if Mr. Thompson had the time to prepare an apple pudding?"

"Of course, Mr. Bingley," Dennis answered. "As I understand it, he prepared more than a man could consume in a fortnight."

Bingley rose from his seat full of satisfaction and strength and all the delights of the artlessness of youth. "Sisters—shall we?"

Louisa and Caroline stood to their feet and did their best to readjust their mien and reassert their ascendency over Bingley, but they suddenly and simultaneously felt that he might have escaped their control for good. Eventually, Mr. Hurst himself came to the table, where the party ate without a single word being spoken. The sisters ruing their defeat, their brother revelling in his triumph, and Mr. Hurst shovelling venison into his mouth as if he had not eaten in a week. Then, once the main course was concluded came the pudding.

CHAPTER FIFTY-TWO

THE INSTANT THE MEAL was concluded, both sisters coincidentally found themselves suffering from the most egregious of headaches and declared their intentions to retire early, which left Bingley alone in the company of Mr. Hurst, who seemed miraculously sobered by the repast.

"It appears since the rain has moved out, we might have quite the splendid evening on our hands," Hurst spoke slowly.

"Certainly, it does appear so."

"Would you care to join me down by the lake, then? Perhaps a drink and a cigar?"

"That is a fine idea," Bingley replied. Having been cooped up in carriage the last few days, and cooped up in London prior to that, he welcomed an evening taking in such incomparable beauty as the grounds at Pemberley afforded. On top of that, though he did not smoke often, he took great delight in a fine cigar, which of course were the only type preferred by Mr. Hurst. They ordered a bottle of brandy to the table near the reflection pool and sauntered down while lighting their sticks. The sun was low, but not set, casting a golden brilliance across the leaves and ripples in the water. A cacophony of sounds flooded their ears—sounds much more pleasing than the bustle and hum of town, Bingley thought. Across the way a group of egrets waded into the water, croaking at each other lazily. At the same time, the delicate and high-pitched calls of a thousand redshanks echoed across the pond, unseen in the thick brush beyond the water. Only adding to the serene and cheerful ambiance was a delightful breeze that whisked their puffs of smoke high and away into the atmosphere. The two brothers by law sat next to each other at the edge of the lawn, small round pedestal between them. Johnstone, one of Mr. Hurst's footmen, poured the drinks and then was dismissed back to the house, leaving the freshly opened bottle on the table.

"Nothing like a fine brandy after pudding, eh?" Hurst said suddenly.

"Yes, very nice indeed," replied Bingley.

"And on such a fine evening as this."

"Extraordinary, indeed. Particularly after all the rain these last few days."

"Was there much rain in London?" Mr. Hurst asked.

"Aye," Bingley chuckled. "And nearly the entire journey to Derbyshire."

"What an oddity! It only rained here last night and into the morning. In fact, it ceased almost the moment you arrived."

"Remarkable," Bingley answered politely. "Have you much chance to enjoy the weather, then?"

"Whatever enjoyment I am capable of is undoubtedly taken from the outdoors, yes," Hurst said, puffing on his cigar. "I spent a couple days entirely fishing in Darcy's trout stream."

"With any luck?"

"Some, yes, but I find more contentment in the respite and the quiet than I do even from the thrill of the catch."

"I see."

Mr. Hurst sat still for a moment, gazing out across the surface of the water. A butterfly flittered about, and Bingley watched it land on the man's knee without his notice.

"I have not, perhaps, made the best of my life, Charles," he said sombrely. Bingley took a swig of his drink while his mind raced to decipher what could possibly be coming next. He had not, in all his years of knowing Mr. Hurst, ever heard him speak with such apparent and guileless vulnerability. "Your sister Louisa is a fine woman—fine enough. I daresay she is as handsome as a squab like me could hope to inveigle. She is intelligent and accomplished, no doubt, and carries herself with a dignified air, yet..."

"Uriah, I cannot account for where—"

Mr. Hurst put his hand up and nodded. "I am not daft, you know. I realize that for my part, not only was I seduced by her fortune, I was seduced by my own clumpish youth. I had not ambition, nor had I character. Truthfully, I had not any depth to me at all." A large fish suddenly leapt out into the air and splashed back down into the green lagoon, sending golden ripples outward toward the edge. "As a young man, I was only absorbed by the acquisition of wealth—and by marriage preferably, having not a mind, nor a desire, for business. I accomplished as much when your sister was wed to me, and we were happy enough in our delusions of rank and class, and the like. As the years trudged along, I grew rather morose, and used drink to lift my mood. With time I became rather more dependent upon it than was my design."

"I imagine that you understand that we noticed you stayed rather more cup shot than was usual," interjected Bingley, if only to break up the unease he felt at the direction of the discourse.

Hurst took a sip of brandy and a long puff on his cigar. "I am not proud of it, I admit. Yet there was one event last year, however, that awakened me from my malaise."

"Oh?" Bingley asked anxiously.

"The murder of Sir Andrew Fraser," Hurst said, turning and looking Bingley in the eyes.

"I see," he stammered. "You did certainly seem to take it rather—"

"Andrew was my friend, you see. Though he was nearly a decade my senior, at one time we operated in similar social circles. He was a serious man when it came to his duty for his country and his military career, but in more easy-going society he was quite corky—boisterous even, when he was dipping rather deep. Andrew was loved in parties and balls, among the ladies particularly. And though he never, himself married, I can assure you he had more than his fair share of—well, you know. I was never quite as wild as him, but I was drawn to him—you might say I enjoyed my own life vicariously through him."

"Is that so?"

"His violent end sent me sputtering into oblivion, as you might well recall," Hurst continued. "I lost all control over myself. It was a mixture of the depressed state I was already in, along with grief at the loss of a friend, and quite naturally shock and disgust at a crime of such savage inhumanity. I imagined I saw in that act, the descent of all society into barbarity and chaos, as I could not reconcile such a horror committed on our own Christian soil."

Bingley swallowed and averted his eyes from the direction of Mr. Hurst. And suddenly, as if by some work of black magic, a cloud rolled over what was left of the sunset and all at once the pair seemed enveloped in night. A cold shudder ran up his spine and Bingley wondered what could be at the heart of such an oration.

"Uriah, I am terribly sorry about the loss of your friend," said Bingley.

Almost without hearing him, Mr. Hurst continued: "In what moments of lucidity I was afforded, I could not shake the notion that Andrew's demise was in some way personal—to me, I mean. The more I attempted to reason myself out of such a feeling, the more I felt impressed that I must pursue justice in his name. Early on I believed that his estate would persevere in catching his killer, but that conviction waned after it became clear that Fraser's young nephew, upon whom the estate was entailed, was more interested in squeezing what income he could from it and using it for God only knows what other forms of folly. I had heard that he'd hired the volunteer constable, a village cobbler named Gallagher, to track his uncle's murderer, but the cobbler soon became disenchanted and returned home. The nephew made no further attempt at the business, which infuriated me so—I felt it an affront to human decency, not to mention the rules of law and order. Eventually I composed myself enough to investigate the investigator. I found that Constable Gallagher was not only a man of good character, but had made significant strides in the undertaking, though he had been put off by the sheer magnitude of it; additionally, he felt very little support from the estate itself. Together we entered an agreement where he would tirelessly hunt the monster who murdered my friend, while I would reward him handsomely for his work. It seemed that in mere blink of an eye he was in London, following a line of inquiry that he was quite confident would lead him to conclude his investigation. Then suddenly, he was traipsing around Derbyshire, Hertfordshire, and then, without so much as a message to me, he was back in Grantley Village, mending shoes."

Bingley felt his throat beginning to swell as he casually wiped his damp forehead with the cuff of his coat. "Very odd, indeed," he muttered.

"Out of the blue, then," Hurst resumed, not skipping a beat, "I received a letter from the Constable, loosely detailing the guilt of a known highwayman by the name of Garrett Surman, who had just been executed in Doncaster on conviction of unrelated crimes—none of which included murder, I might add. After even a cursory glance at the papers I was sure that Surman could not conceivably be the culprit. Was he violent? Certainly, but he was calculating, and did not act out of passion. Surman's motives were strictly pecuniary and as you might recall, nothing was stolen from Andrew's estate during his murder. Additionally, the Constable never asked for his reward in solving the crime—a lucrative sum for a simple cobbler with a family to feed. Hence, I became convinced that Gallagher had already been paid, and began to wonder by *whom*."

"I do not see where you are going with this, Uriah," Bingley retorted, labouring to conceal his panic.

Mr. Hurst relit his cigar, wafting a plume which floated off in Bingley's direction. "I know what you have done, Charles," Hurst stated, his voice dropping into a low and menacing register.

"Uriah, I cannot—"

"I may not be brilliant, but neither am I a dullard."

A weighty silence ensued, save the sounds of nature which encompassed them. Bingley's mind raced with the complexity of the situation, dozens of explanations and courses of action swirling in a mist of anxiety and smoke. Would he have to drown his own brother-in-law right there in Darcy's lake? And how on earth had Mr. Hurst, of all people, discovered his dark deeds?

"I was sceptical from the very beginning of Fraser's nephew and hired my own investigator to look into not only what clues existed, but also Constable Gallagher himself," Hurst went on. "As I mentioned he did very well early on. Eventually, however, he was followed by my man to your very door in Grosvenor Street, where he departed rather hastily, if you will recall, and quit to his quiet country life in Grantley Village. Once I reengaged him, I found it curious that he had suddenly discovered the identity of the killer—Garrett Surman, supposedly—after being tracked by my man not only to Meryton, but further on to Netherfield Park itself."

"Uriah—"

"I know not what other form of dastardly business you have involved yourself, Charles, but I *know* that you butchered Andrew Fraser... and I want *to thank you* for it."

A noise escaped Bingley that came from bottled dread and adrenaline. He breathed heavily and quickly as Hurst sat, cross-legged and tranquil. Bingley leaned forward in his chair, feeling his pulse drubbing in his neck. "How on earth...?" was all he could muster.

Hurst leaned forward and patted him on the back. "Do not trouble yourself, Charles—your secret is safe with me."

"Uriah, I do not understand," declared Bingley, sitting back up in his chair.

Hurst took a sip of cognac and swirled it lightly in his mouth. He seemed to want to let the atmosphere breathe a moment before he spoke again—for this Bingley was grateful.

"Perhaps two years ago, Andrew entreated me to join him for what he termed, 'a bit of a frolic.' We were at his estate in Grantley with another gentleman—of significant distinction, I might add—and assumed he had hired a few bits of muslin, but as a married man of *some* moral fabric, I naturally declined the invitation. We were all by that point entirely corned, and Andrew had the habit of babbling about when he was in that state—in a very jolly manner, mind you. He went on to inform me that despite his various charms and riches, alongside his perpetual status as a bachelor, which in combination allowed him the company of not a small number of handsome ladies, he had a penchant for the *young*. As he prattled on, I managed to heed very little attention—partly because of inebriation—until he made what, even then, I marked as a most peculiar statement: that not only did he prefer 'inexperienced maidens,' as he termed them, he also preferred them *helpless*. It was this word that seared into my memory: *helpless*. Even as I wondered what on earth he could have meant, the other man in the room snickered along as if he was privy to a juvenile secret among schoolboys. Shortly after that, I retired to my room for the evening. I decided to leave the following morning after breakfast, though I had at first, intended to stay another two nights at least. Andrew, perhaps having no recollection of the previous evening's bibulous ramblings, was near the point of taking offense. I assured him that I had business to attend to which summoned me back to town. I saw him but once or twice in town over the next year, as he disliked London, but our correspondence resumed as normal. The last time he entertained me in Grantley Park was last autumn, not a month before he was murdered. In all honesty, I wished profusely to remain ignorant to whatever indiscretions Andrew was party to, and it was not until a secondary event took place which convinced me that his departure from this world might not have been a random act of brutality."

"And what event was that?"

"The murder of the *other* man with Fraser that evening in Grantley Park."

"Who?" Bingley asked anxiously.

"Thomas Abbott."

Bingley leaned back and breathed in deeply. "I feel sick as a horse," he declared.

Hurst chuckled amiably. "Don't be, Charles," he said, taking a few seconds to puff on his cigar. "It was that connection between the 'victims' which prompted me to initiate my own inquest into whatever business my friend and this bastard were involved in. My man found nothing concrete for months, until eventually he stumbled into evidence that Fraser and Abbott were paying for young maidens to be... well, I do not have to belabour the point to you. During this time, we also uncovered the existence of a guardian angel, a man sent by the Lord who alone had the means, the intellectual prowess, and the physical capability of dismantling such a vile empire. And that man, Charles, was *you*."

Bingley looked on the verge of tears. "Have you made my business known to anyone but yourself and your man?"

"Of course not," answered Hurst. "I will go to my grave with our secret and the sentiment that my brother-in-law is a paladin of justice, virtue, and mercy. I only wish it could be made known to the rest of England, so that our fellow countrymen may comprehend the depth to which we are all indebted to you."

"My quest is not for glory," said Bingley, wiping his eye with the back of his hand. "I have only ever wished to be done with it all and to live in quiet and peace."

"And that, Charles, is why you were selected for such a task."

"Thank you, Uriah," Bingley replied.

Mr. Hurst nodded and rose his glass: "To Mr. Bingley."

CHAPTER FIFTY-THREE

He had just settled in nicely to his bed with a proper portion of apple pudding when his steward knocked hurriedly. "This better be *important*," Bingley called, a bit sarcastically.

Wilshere entered directly and with a hasty bow before he began. "It is confirmed—Captain Carter is the contact."

"We suspected as much," reacted Bingley, scooping a spoonful of pudding into his mouth. "Is that all?"

"Should I arrange for travel back to Brighton?"

"So soon?"

"Mr. Bingley," Wilshere answered, "are you not of the opinion that Captain Carter should be dealt with as a member of the cabal?"

"Of course, he must be dealt with, but in due time. As a member of the militia, whether he is moved to Cornwall or Carlisle will be no great imposition to me. It is hardly conceivable he will be off to fight the French any time soon. Furthermore, am I correct in the assumption that we have not yet unearthed his superior?"

"We have not."

"Then he is at present of no use to us with his throat cut," stated Bingley. "Maitland and Gallagher must keep close watch on him, following him to every tavern, every ball, every—"

"I can assure you, he is followed round the clock."

"Then he will eventually make contact with the evildoer, will he not?"

"I assume so."

"And with Wickham out of the plot, there must necessarily be a temporary reprieve in the acquisition of new victims?"

"Again, I concur with your reasoning."

"Then will you get some rest, and for God's sake, allow me a few days of distraction before we make that arduous journey yet again?"

"Of course, sir. Your time at leisure has been earned most commendably."

"Did you say Brighton?" Bingley asked.

"Yes, the Captain returned to the regiment after four more days of searching for the couple in London."

"Thank you, then, and good night."

"Good night, Mr. Bingley."

Bingley finished his pudding and placed the bowl on the bedside table. He blew out the candles and proceeded to toss and turn for nearly an hour. His conversation with Mr. Hurst, the mystery of Captain Carter's master, and as always, thoughts of Jane Bennet swirled in his mind. Eventually he drifted off, though he was awakened at two different times by two distinct and utterly oppositional dreams.

In the first, he found himself atop a towering bluff, reclining on a blanket laid atop thick grass of the most vibrant green, the sun setting off over the sea. A warm breeze rustled his hair and a familiar, yet out of place, aroma wafted on its breath. Gently rustling footsteps approached from behind him, and delight overtook him to see Jane walking in his direction with all of her grace and charm, a wicker basket hanging by the crook in her arm. The hems of her white gown rippled with every gentle step across the lawn. He scrambled to his feet and bowed, as she approached. With a curtsey she said, "Mr. Bingley."

"Miss Bennet," he answered in glee. She motioned with her free hand toward the blanket, and he nodded his head and made way. Facing the sea, she sat with her legs curled elegantly underweight. Bingley took his place next to her, only the basket between them. "It has been my most fervent desire to see you these many months."

"I confess, I am very glad to hear it, Mr. Bingley," she answered with a warm smile. For all the golden rays of the sun, the white foam of the waves crashing below, the verdancy of the rolling hills behind, he could not take his eyes from her for a second. He swallowed and smiled broadly. "Are you at all hungry?" asked she.

"Famished, yes," he answered. "And I must say that whatever you have brought in that basket smells remarkable."

"Why, thank you," she answered, propping the top open and producing a plate with a steaming slice of pizza. He felt his jaw go slack in amazement. Jane handed the dish over to him before her brilliantly cerulean eyes caught his gaze.

Bingley slowly opened his eyes in the dark. He sighed heavily and rubbed his forehead with one hand. It was a warm night and he had begun to sweat. After a minute's hesitation, he went to the window and opened it. The air was still and not even a breeze penetrated the room. It took him quite a while to dose off again as, aside from the heat, he felt a nearly physical pressure in his chest, as if a large weight was fixed atop it. She had been unequivocally stunning in his dream, but even at this he was sure his memory had not adequately captured the fullness of her beauty. More than ever before he pined for his all-consuming business to be at an end.

The next hours of slumber were unremarkable, until he dreamt again. He was lying alone in his bed in Netherfield Park, when a moaning sound stirred his slumber. He sat up in this dream bed and lit a candle. The eerie groans were emanating from outside his door. The open window beyond the mammoth canopy bed creaked menacingly on its hinge. Just before he reached the door, everything went silent as something wet touched his toe. Bingley lowered the candle and by its luminescence witnessed a pool of thick blood swelling under the door frame. He instantly stepped backward, nearly tripping on his bedside table. In horror he observed the knob turn and a swell of light pierce the room. First a lantern became visible, then the figure of a man, his throat slit dreadfully, blood soaked through his nightshirt and dripping onto the parquet floor where he stood. Though the apparition's eyes were sunken and black, his skin gaunt and sallow, Bingley recognized the face of Sir Andrew Fraser. The ghost's eyes rose to meet Bingley's stare. "You did not think you would get away that easily, did you?"

Just then, Bingley's attention was drawn to the window as it slammed shut violently. When he turned back, Fraser was but an inch from his face, jaws open like a wild dog ready to tear into its prey. Bingley smelled death on its breath and heard a bestial growl before he awoke, back in Darcy's guest chamber at Pemberley. Sitting up with a jolt, he felt the bed around him, his clothes included, soaked in sweat. He rose without thinking and crossed the room to shut the window, making sure to check the lock more than once. Peering outside into the dark, he clutched his heart, endeavouring to cause his panic to subside. After a moment or two of collecting his wits, he crawled back into the bed where he was suddenly unable to control the gush of emotions which flooded over him. Bingley sobbed furiously for nearly a minute, when he was finally able to control his breathing and calm himself to what extent was possible. Over the next two hours, he clutched a pillow close to his chest and eventually watched the sun rise over the grove of beech trees across the park.

CHAPTER FIFTY-FOUR

GEORGIANA TRAVELLED BACK WITH Colonel Fitzwilliam a week later and filled the place with the anticipation of seeing her brother. The Colonel, for his part, awaited his imminent deployment to anti-invasion fortifications on the south coast. It was very much his fervent desire to see his cousin before his departure, as his current orders would keep him occupied for six months at least. So, when Darcy arrived three days later, the place brimmed with happiness and cheer.

In private, Bingley learned that Darcy had attended the wedding of Mr. Wickham to Miss Lydia Bennet and seen them off to Longbourn where they were to stay for nearly a fortnight. With the help of Darcy's cousin Colonel Fitzwilliam, Wickham had been granted a transfer of his commission to the regiment stationed in Newcastle under the command of Colonel Whitacre. Darcy seemed very much satisfied with the conclusion of the business, even though he had outlaid nearly five thousand pounds to have it settled so. Though the sum amounted to nearly the equivalent of half his entire year's income, he displayed no qualms about the money, but was instead, quietly content with the hope that he had prevented utter disaster for Miss Elizabeth Bennet, though he did not at that moment, mention her sister Jane.

Caroline and Louisa made very little of their brother's strong declaration the day he returned. Instead, they spent the vast amount of their time in the presence of Georgiana and for once, not in any kind of effort to have her attached to their brother. Bingley was delighted by this reversal in their comportment and found much peace and solace in spending time outdoors, fishing and hunting in company with Mr.

Hurst and Colonel Fitzwilliam. The men spent several cool evenings down by the lake, smoking cigars and drinking brandy. Mr. Hurst's demeanour had brightened even more since his own confession the night of Bingley's return from London, and for the first time since his marriage into the family, an authentic friendship between the two men began to emerge.

On this particular evening, however, Mr. Hurst had retired early after dinner due to fatigue and an overall feeling of lethargy. Bingley found it peculiar, being that they had spent the entire day indoors due to rain. Nevertheless, as the weather had cleared toward evening, Bingley, Darcy, and the Colonel found themselves out of doors in what was a most pleasant and balmy night. The clouds had parted, and the stars glistened overhead like crystals in a chandelier. When they had been smoking for nearly an hour, a letter arrived from Maitland which Mr. Wilshere received from an express rider. The steward immediately made his way down to the lake where he requested a private audience with his master. Bingley walked with him up toward the house and beyond earshot of the other two men. He was informed that Captain Carter and Mr. Denny would soon be dispatched for Newcastle with the sole aim of snuffing out the life of Mr. Wickham. Unfortunately, according to the letter, no progress had been made in determining the identity of Carter's contact within the plot. Bingley asked his man to prepare for their immediate departure for town in the morning in the hopes of intercepting the assassins, and to have Maitland meet them there while Gallagher remained in Brighton to continue their inquiries.

Bingley strolled back across the lawn and plopped rather heavily back into his chair.

"Is everything all right, Bingley?" Darcy asked.

"Yes, I suppose," replied Bingley. "It seems that business has once more requisitioned my presence."

"*Business?*" Darcy posed with a searching glare.

"Yes, *business.*"

"I hope it shall not keep you long," Colonel Fitzwilliam chimed in. "It is unhappy enough that I shall have to depart Pemberley. It would be a great displeasure for me to have the knowledge that you should not enjoy it in my absence—especially at this time of year."

"Thank you, Colonel," Bingley answered. "I do not know how long I should be detained, but there is even the possibility that I should have to travel further on to Brighton."

"Brighton? What on earth would call you all the way there?"

"Again, my business ventures, it would seem, may demand my attention there."

The Colonel laughed and swigged his drink. "And I thought it might be to pay a visit to your old friends in the regiment."

"Pardon me?" Bingley asked nervously.

"The regiment from Meryton is stationed in Brighton now—were you not aware?"

"Oh, yes of course. I had heard they relocated there."

Darcy looked on trying to conceal his agitation.

"What a lot that is, eh?" The Colonel scoffed under his breath. Bingley nodded politely. "Darcy, after all that trouble, do you think Wickham will finally settle down?"

"I do have confidence in him," answered Darcy flatly.

Fitzwilliam continued: "I find it astonishing that with all that man put us through—particularly you—that you should be able to say a single kind word about him at all."

"Undoubtedly, I would not have heaped much praise upon him six months ago, but of late I have found an improvement in his character that I believe may lead him into a life of decency and modesty, if not peace and happiness."

"I do confess, I am glad to hear it," the Colonel stated. "If only for the sake of knowing how attached you were as children. Now if only something could be done for that scurrilous Colonel Forster."

"*Colonel Forster*?" Bingley piped in. "I found him to be a most respectable man."

"Aye, he would most convincingly give that impression, would he not?"

"Whatever do you mean, Fitzwilliam?" Darcy petitioned.

"He presents a quite believable facade of decency and civility, but oh, he's always been too ripe and ready by half, if you pardon the expression."

Bingley and Darcy looked at each other quizzically. "I confess I have no idea what the expression even means," snickered Bingley.

Colonel Fitzwilliam smiled and had a quick chortle. "I have known of the man for quite some time, and I would not disparage his character, even in private, without some measure of conviction."

"As regards?"

"Did you know he served for nearly twenty years in the regulars?" Fitzwilliam asked. Bingley shook his head. "Yes, and all the way up to the rank of Brigadier, until of course, he was forced into retirement by a few scandals that only powerful allies were able to conceal."

"What kind of scandal?" Bingley asked, leaning forward in his chair.

"I could not say with an absolute claim to veracity, but I have been made to understand that he faced allegations of... *tampering* with some maidens who were hardly of age to even be presented at court."

"What... what is your meaning?" Bingley muttered.

"Only that Colonel Forster has a penchant for young girls, which is the very reason he was dismissed from the Army."

Bingley felt a pressure in his temples and a lump in his throat.

Darcy stared at him in astonishment. "Was he then not arrested?"

Fitzwilliam shook his head and pursed his lips. "As I mentioned, he escaped any form of punishment, though I suspect because the girls' families were compensated, might I say, for their silence."

"And he was then appointed a colonel in the militia?" Bingley asked

"Yes, and then only at the behest of his commanding officer, who vouched for his character."

"Who was his commanding officer?"

"The late Sir Andrew Fraser," Colonel Fitzwilliam replied bluntly. Darcy and Bingley exchanged another awestruck glance before Darcy looked out over the water and Bingley looked to his shoes. The three sat in silence for another moment before the Colonel felt the need to apologize. "I believe I have said too much. I would not wish to have you feel troubled by such revelations about a man you might have considered a friend."

"No need to apologize, Fitzwilliam," responded Darcy. "I am sure I can speak for both Charles and myself in stating that our acquaintance with Colonel Forster was superficial at best."

"Ah, I see," answered Colonel Fitzwilliam. "Well, I am glad to hear that I have not offended you."

"Of course not," Darcy replied.

"Do you know anything about a man named Carter who serves under him?" Bingley asked suddenly.

"Carter, Carter," the Colonel mused. "If I am not mistaken, and you must again pardon me if I venture into scandalous pastures as regards men you know—"

"Of course," Bingley reassured.

"If my recollection serves me, I believe Carter—who is by now a Captain, I believe—is the illegitimate son of Eoin Walters of Northumberland."

"Eoin Walters... of *Northumberland*?" staggered Bingley over his words.

"Yes, I am nearly certain of it," Fitzwilliam confirmed. "It is my understanding that he owes much of his advancement to his own late father's friendship with Fraser, who was able to see him join the militia under Colonel Forster. Obviously, Carter's father wished him to have some form of a career to provide his own means, being that the estate was inherited by his half-brother John."

"I see," Bingley said, finding his breathing pattern heavy and difficult to control. "Most helpful information you have bestowed this evening, Colonel."

"My pleasure, I suppose," Fitzwilliam answered in his usual good-natured tone. "I am only sorry that it may serve to dissuade you from continued friendship with such unsavoury characters. Then again, I amuse myself at the idea of men like yourselves being much acquainted with men of such ill-breeding."

"I suddenly feel quite tired," declared Bingley. "I thank you again, Colonel, for such lively and informative conversation, and Darcy once more for such splendid hospitality. Good night."

With that Bingley nearly raced off toward the house.

"Is he quite alright?" Colonel Fitzwilliam questioned his cousin. "I have not upset him, I hope."

"No, not at all," replied Darcy. "I am certain he will be much more agreeable once he is on the road in the morning on the way to having his business affairs put in order."

Colonel Fitzwilliam puffed his cigar and answered, "I see."

CHAPTER FIFTY-FIVE

"Drive on!" Wilshere shouted as he closed the coach door behind him. Handing his master a tankard brimming with coffee, he sat with a thud, caddy-corner from Mr. Bingley, whose elbow was propped on the window ledge, his head resting in his hand. The master sipped his morning beverage with nonchalant deftness, as though he were incapable of spilling the steaming liquid on himself while they rocked along. It was still dark, save the first streaks of violet which betokened the imminent ascent of the sun. The chill in the air was aberrant for the first week of September, and a thick mist shrouded every turn as the carriage rumbled up the drive leading out of Pemberley Park.

"Can you believe it, sir?" the steward posed as the driver turned the horses out onto the main road—the very same road which led into Lambton from the estate, though they would deviate from it in a southernly direction before reaching the village.

"Once more," Bingley began, taking a sip while he spoke, "in a former life, never would I entertain such rubbish. However, I believe we have safely crossed beyond into a second existence in which there is nothing which would cause me shock."

"Still, it has not been confirmed outright."

"Colonel Fitzwilliam's account of Colonel Forster does, however, elucidate the mystery of Captain Carter—particularly why Maitland and Gallagher were never ever to discover his contact."

"The two could easily speak in confidence without ever venturing from their camp."

"Never an incautious word in a tavern, never a clandestine excursion by dark of night. It was the perfect partnership, and we did not see it."

"I dare say we could hardly be blamed," answered the steward. "And as we have already established, it is very unlikely the operation would be capable of harming any young maidens until the conclusion of this Wickham business."

Shaking his head, Bingley declared, "We *wish* to think it, Wilshere. We hope to God we have done enough. We will soon cause the complete desistance of the whole enterprise, and only then I will be at rest."

Bingley gazed out the window, sipping the last of his coffee. After a moment or so, with enough light to read, Wilshere opened his ledger and began sorting through accounts. The two rode on in silence for quite some time.

When, in due course, they reached the city of Leicester, they were greeted by an express rider who summarily informed them that the Wickhams had departed Meryton the previous day and were expected to stay in a village north of Peterborough the following evening at the curiously named Bloody Bucket Inn. Carter and Denny were to meet them there, murder them in their sleep, and vanish back to London. The killers' room was to be reserved under the alias "Del Patrick." Rather than staying on in Leicester then, Bingley decided that they would ride on toward Peterborough that very eve. Fresh horses were ordered, as well as a meal and a bottle of whisky for the road, and they were off. An express was dispatched ahead to have the Wickhams removed to a neighbouring inn called the Lucky Servant, where Mr. Wickham was warned in no uncertain terms, that if they wished to see the sun rise the next morning, to be sure they remained indoors and out of sight until further notice.

Once they had arrived in the outskirts of Peterborough, Wilshere took a room under a fictitious name in the Lucky Servant. Bingley was clear that he was not to be seen—particularly by Mrs. Wickham—so he was whisked in rather furtively. After some hours of sleep, he and Wilshere rose, took a meal in the room, and devised their plan.

Early that evening, Wilshere headed down to the Bloody Bucket and occupied a table near the bar with full view of both the front door and the staircase. He ordered a couple of scotch eggs and an ale and unfurled a large newspaper to shield his face. When the barkeeper brought his drink, he allowed his peaked curiosity to get the better of him.

"I beg your pardon," Wilshere began.

"Yes, sir?" the man asked as he set the ale down in front of his guest.

"Are you the proprietor of this establishment?"

"I am. George Stoop at your service," the innkeeper answered. He was an extraordinarily tall man whose bald head nearly touched the rafters above him when he stood fully upright. His wide shoulders tapered to a slim waist, and his hands were each large enough to nearly encircle a pint glass completely.

"How do you do, Mr. Stoop? May I enquire after the name of this inn? It seems most unusual."

"Certainly," the barkeeper answered with a proud smile. "But I must know, are you in for a Hookee Walker?"

"Seems I have the time," answered Wilshere with a chortle.

"Very well, then. This building was erected in the year 1628. The first owner, a man by the name of Samuel Dawkins, named it 'The Old Haunt,' because at the time, the little patch of land you might have noticed across the lane—where the well is situated—was rumoured to have been haunted by ghosts."

"Ghosts?" Wilshere laughed.

Stoop held up a finger before continuing on in his deep, resonant voice. "A year or so prior to that, when the well was installed, the patch of land was populated by some very large, old, and as it turned out, hollow trees. Now, as the tale goes, when the townsmen felled the trees, they discovered that some of them were filled with human bones."

"How ghastly," declared Wilshere.

"The popular legend, then, became that the ghosts, on account of having their resting place disturbed, would haunt the well and turn the water to blood."

"Charming."

"Except, then it happened," said the innkeeper with a twinge of fore-boding.

"Whatever do you mean?"

"Just a month after the inn opened, Mr. Dawkins went cross the way to fetch a pail of water, as he had done several times each day he had been in business. When he got back inside, he discovered that the pale was filled not with water, but with blood." Wilshere's face twisted in disbelieving horror. "A very short inquest was held, during which it was learned that a young lad just returned from soldierly duty in Ireland to his mother's house up the street had fallen in and perished. His corpse was removed, and it was found rather badly battered. Some people chalked it up to the ghosts. That was enough for old Mr. Dawkins. He sold quickly and left the village, not to be heard from again. And that very year it obtained its name from its new owner."

"How fascinating!"

"Then, just as the famous old incident threatened to wane into local folklore, the ghosts lashed out once more!"

"I do not believe it," proclaimed Wilshere.

"But, aye, they did," the barman continued. "And exactly one hundred years to the day. Barkeep by the name of Blevins fetches water across the lane, returns to the pub, and finds the blood. Another soldier—this one just returned from Boston in the American colonies."

"Surely this is but a Banbury tale."

"Perhaps," Stoop laughed. "But even so, it's only 1812. We won't expect the ghosts for another sixteen years. And we shall be sure to warn off any soldiers within a full ten miles of the place!"

At that moment, the steward's eggs arrived from the kitchen. Wilshere thanked the man for the tale and commenced his second supper. Once he had consumed his meal, he ordered a second ale and rested back with his newspaper, while keeping a watchful eye on the door. Over the course of the next two hours, he paced his ale consumption while he read, as to keep his faculties intact. Eventually, the door jarred open, and the wind blew in Captain Carter and Mr. Denny. They approached the bar and gave the name "Patrick," after which were shown to their lodgings. With great chary Wilshere rose from his seat and followed them up the stairs at a cautious distance. From the midway point on the landing, he was able to peak over the top step to observe them enter the second door on the left of the hall. When Wilshere remerged downstairs, Stoop was drying a glass at the bar and eyed him curiously.

"Would you like a room, sir?"

"Thank you, no," Wilshere answered. "I am waiting on friends who are expected to stay here."

"Friends?"

"Yes, sir, a Mr. and Mrs. George Wickham—can you tell me, have they arrived?"

"Not as of yet," Stoop replied.

"And in which room are they to stay, if you do not mind my asking?"

"Second room on the right."

"I thank you," said Wilshere warmly. "I have business to attend to but will call upon them tomorrow."

With that, Wilshere left the inn and rode back to the Lucky Servant where he briefed Mr. Bingley. That evening they dined in their room on smoked gammon and summer vegetables. Bingley had two glasses of wine with dinner and a single of brandy once the barmaid had cleared the plates from their room. For all the nerves he had felt on such previous occasions as this, he was calm and steady this evening, convinced of the necessity of the task at hand, as well as his ability to complete it. Wilshere asked him if he felt any apprehension about handling two victims at once.

"You forget, I dispatched two in Naples, and one rather a colossus at that."

Wilshere nodded. "Surprise is a most powerful tool."

"Though, why one any man involved in such filth should be surprised at meeting the swift hand of judgement is beyond what my comprehension."

The two sat in silence as the dark of night took the village firmly in its grasp.

Two hours past midnight, Captain Carter and Mr. Denny crossed the hall furtively, dressed in socked feet that the sound of their steps might raise no alarm. They took a steely glance at each other as they reached the Wickhams' door. Carter took the curved handle and twisted it ever so gently. The planked door opened with the slightest creak and the two marauders entered the room, knives raised in hostile expectation. They each crossed around to opposite sides of the bed and reached down in the dark to identify their victims. The thought had been to dispatch with Wickham instantaneously, though they had planned something a bit more protracted and heinous for Miss Lydia. After all, she had caught *their* eyes first, and there was an element of injustice that Colonel Forster had planned to keep her to himself. Tonight, they would rectify that obloquy. However, their hands rummaged through the blanket until their fingers met each other's in the middle. They both startled and leapt back in shock, knives aloft and panting in the blackness.

"Where are they?" Denny whispered.

"How should I know?" Carter barked back quietly.

"Perhaps their stay was planned for tomorrow?"

"No, they were to have arrived *this* afternoon."

"They could have been delayed and lodged elsewhere."

Carter shook his head adamantly. "*Something* is not right. Let us make haste back to our room. We shall formulate a plan in the morning."

They closed the Wickhams' door, crossing the hall back to their room and shut themselves in soundlessly. The candle still burned on the table in the corner and its light flickered on a cloaked figure seated there in a wooden chair. Carter gave a start when he caught sight of the man.

"Pardon me, sir—have you found the wrong room?"

The man's face was turned down and shielded from view by the brim of his hat. "I would be much comforted if you would sheath your knives."

"Certainly," Carter answered. He and Denny both placed their weapons on the table. "But sir you have entered the wrong chamber. This room is let to us."

"Have I?"

"Yes, I believe so."

"I am not convinced," said Bingley, raising his gaze to meet theirs.

"Mr. *Bingley*?" Denny exclaimed.

"Are you staying in the inn?" Carter asked in astonishment.

"Not for long," Bingley replied, shifting his weight backwards onto the arm of the chair. His legs were crossed in perfect insouciance; his mien relaxed and even chilling.

"Sir, I apologize for our mutual astonishment upon seeing you, if it caused any slight—"

"None whatsoever," he said coolly. "You have no cause to apologize... to *me*."

"May I then ask to what we owe the honour of seeing here?"

"It is indeed an honour to be here," Bingley said, casting his glance casually about the room. "In your bedchamber, and at this very hour, on this particular eve." Denny and Carter exchanged a perplexed look. The single flame cast a menacing and enormous shadow on the plaster wall behind Bingley. "The Bloody Bucket," he continued. "Curious name for an inn, is it not?"

"Very peculiar, indeed," stammered Denny.

"I have heard," whispered Bingley, "that its origin lies in a rather grisly tale of *soldiers and ghosts*."

"It sounds fascinating," Carter blurted.

"We should enquire with the innkeeper in the morning, then," Denny's voice cracked.

"There shan't be need for that," retorted Bingley. With that, he very slowly deliberately leaned over the table, whet his lips, and blew out the candle. "Do either of *you* believe in ghosts?"

CHAPTER FIFTY-SIX

GEORGE STOOP AROSE IN high spirits. Business was good, his son had recently obtained a university post in Cambridge, and he himself had just enjoyed a rousing and unexpected morning romp in the hay with Mrs. Stoop. He set about his daily duties with a smile on his lips whilst she began to prepare for breakfast.

"Mr. Stoop," she called from the back as he flipped dining chairs upright from their overnight resting place atop the tables. "I need water, please."

"Just a moment, love," he called.

"I need it *now*, Mr. Stoop, or the soft-boiled eggs won't be boiled at all!"

"Put some tea on, love," he implored.

"No water, no tea, Mr Stoop!"

He laughed to himself, put the last of the chairs in their place, and snatched the bucket from behind the bar. Outside, he was met with a harsh chill in the air and shivered as he crossed the lane, a heavy fog dangling overhead. Stoop tied his bucket to the rope with a shiver and began to lower it as he had done ten thousand times since he took ownership of the inn, when a ghastly shriek came from the baker's shop across the street.

"Ghosts!" a woman screeched. "*Ghosts!*" Mr. Stoop inclined his head toward the shop when the baker's wife threw open the door and flung a bucket out into the street. Leaving his own bucket on the lip of the well, he sauntered over to see in the spilled contents of the baker's bucket red and curdled across the cobblestones. "Blood in the well!"

By this time, Bingley and Wilshere had already changed horses in Buckden and were within fifty miles of London. The Wickhams for their part, had also departed early and had reached Stamford where they dined and changed horses.

"How do you feel, sir?" Wilshere asked.

"Relieved," answered his master. "Though I still feel the tension of the task as yet being incomplete."

"We shall shortly rectify that," prompted the steward. "And at least it is now confirmed beyond contestation," he added, tapping his fingers on a small stack of the late Captain Carter's correspondence.

"Forster, then Trippier," Bingley mused. "And the head shall be cut from the snake."

"And how, do you think, did it come to pass that Forster would take on Trippier after the death of Lord St. John?"

"If St. John relied half as heavily on his steward as I do mine, then I suppose Mr. Trippier was indispensable. I believe he is in fact the one key spoke in the wheel which we failed to notice, though I wonder how his having been hired to the post of the Colonel's steward evaded the attention of Maitland."

"All of Trippier's letters to Carter are addressed from Ashford, the home of Colonel Forster's estate in Kent," answered Wilshere. "I suppose he has kept busy there running the place in the Colonel's absence."

"I believe your deduction is very likely to prove true."

"Brighton, first then? —Or Ashford?"

"Makes no difference to me," Bingley lamented. "All I know after all these hours and days spent cooped in coaches watching mile after mile pass aeon by aeon, is that when this business is finally over, I shall return directly to Netherfield, and if Miss Jane Bennet will consent to be my bride, I shall not leave Hertfordshire for a decade at least."

"I would not blame you in the slightest, sir."

Eventually, they reached London where they spent the evening at the house in Grosvenor Street. Word awaited their arrival that Mr. Hurst had taken seriously ill the morning they left, but during the night, an express rider bore news that the gentleman had recovered considerably and was thought to be fully on the mend. So, early that morning, they set out for Brighton.

They took the same rooms where they had stayed when the first attempt on Lord Bertram St. John was made—the same night that Maitland saved Mr. Bingley's life. Not long after they had settled in, they were called upon by that very same man. Maitland had left Gallagher with the task of keeping watch over the house of Colonel Forster.

"Maitland, my man!" Bingley called as he stood to his feet and greeted his favoured servant. "How are you fairing?"

"Quite well, Mr. Bingley," the young man answered amiably. "It is a pleasure to see you again, sir."

"The pleasure is all mine," answered Bingley.

"Mr. Wilshere," Maitland greeted the steward with a bow.

"Mr. Maitland," came the reply with an unexpected twinge of austerity.

"Were your travels easy?"

"We were not robbed," chuckled Bingley. "But if I were to be planted in the dirt up to my waist and watered twice a day, I believe you would hear not a single complaint from me."

"I comprehend your meaning," Maitland answered with a laugh.

"What news have you, if any, of the Colonel's movements or schemes?" Wilshere asked suddenly.

"He is increasingly on edge," replied Maitland. "We did not see him out of doors for two days complete after the news of the fates of Captain Carter and Mr. Denny reached him. The camp does not seem to have been alerted, nor do the officers. Each one that remains appears to be largely under the impression that their comrades in arms simply remain away on official business."

"Any unusual visitors of late?" Bingley inquired.

"None out of the ordinary. However, I have confirmed with a particularly talkative corporal that he has sent for his personal steward from his estate in Ashford."

"Mr. Trippier," Bingley blurted, exchanging a knowing glance with Wilshere.

"Yes, how did you—"

"We discovered his new employment arrangement from letters Mr. Bingley was keen enough to nick from the lodgings of Captain Carter."

"Wonderful," Maitland nodded. "And you believe him to be the same steward of the late Lord St. John?"

"I have not a doubt," stated Bingley. "There is additionally no doubt that he is more intimately and centrally involved in the entire business than we ever might have guessed."

"Whilst I may never have suspected him of anything more than cursory involvement on behalf of his master, I cannot declare that I am wholly surprised."

"And why not?"

Maitland bit his top lip and shrugged his shoulder. "If you will recall, I had infiltrated St. John's household staff with some success. There was not a single member of it who spoke favourably of Mr. Trippier. He was known to be quite severe in his treatment of the servants, and even had a scullery maid sacked when she refused to bed him—and now that I think back upon it, I am sure that she was *quite* young."

"We are now of the opinion that Mr. Trippier has, all along, been the impetus behind the plot in terms of daily operations," stated Bingley.

"As I said, I cannot feign surprise at it."

"Have you observed any opportunity in the Colonel's daily routine for me to get close enough to him?" Bingley queried.

"*Perhaps*," answered Maitland cautiously. "He has recently kept himself under guard as inconspicuously as possible, but he is also concerned for the safety of his wife."

"What then? —He stays with her at all times?"

"On the contrary. At the same time he called his steward from his estate, he sent his wife there—and much to her vexation. The house here, is guarded all night—though typically by ponderous men on punishment for drunkenness or the like—and he sleeps in it alone."

"That is fine news, Mr. Maitland," asserted Mr. Bingley. "Now, if you will excuse me, I would very much like a few hours of sleep. Meet us here at nine this evening to dine, and then we will scout our target by darkness."

"Yes, Mr. Bingley," rejoindered the young man.

Wilshere bowed to his master and the two servants left the room. In the hall, the steward asked, "May I have a brief word with you Mr. Maitland?"

"Of course, sir."

Once they were down the hall and in Wilshere's quarters, the steward closed the door quietly behind them. He gave Maitland a cursory once over while nodding furiously as his tongue pushed out his bottom lip.

"I know not how you spend your spare time, Mr. Maitland," he began sharply. "But a single month of your wages ought to allow a young man like yourself to live comfortably for an entire annum."

"Mr. Wilshere, I do not grasp—"

"Is it women? —Or drink? —Or both?" Wilshere demanded. The young man stood before him, brow furrowed in mystery, his eyes darting about the floor in search of some invisible shred of information that might allow him to understand the verbal assault under which he now found himself. Before he could mouth another word, the steward continued his reprimand: "I cannot fathom how a man of good sense like yourself could not only run through such sums so wantonly, but then arrive to his master's door in such disarray. In fact, your appearance, coupled with an astonishing lack of forethought on your behalf, has given me reason to question your judgement entirely—and that not only compromises our ability to bring this task to completion at such a late stage, it also endangers the very life of your master and benefactor."

Maitland stood in silent inscrutability before meekly speaking: "Mr. Wilshere, I would beg your pardon if I knew what infraction has caused such a severe declaration about my character and judgement."

"Your coat, Maitland," the steward pronounced. "Look! —There is a hole worn clear through it!"

"My *coat*?" Maitland demanded.

"As trivial as your appearance might seem to you, if you are to function as a servant of a proper gentleman like Mr. Bringley, such trivialities must not escape your notice."

"Is it likely that Mr. Bingley noticed the condition of my coat, then?"

"For your sake, I would hope not," Wilshere answered. "But it certainly has not escaped *my* notice. And on your wages, there is absolutely no excuse for such a blatant oversight."

"I have not recently kept much, in terms of my wages, sir."

"That is obvious," stated Wilshere, though his tone had softened. "You are a young man, but you must more carefully consider how your wages are spent."

"Mr. Wilshere?"

"Yes?"

"Do you remember when I recounted to you and Mr. Bingley the story of my fiancée, Leticia Yates?"

"Of course, but what does that—"

"Her father is ill, sir."

Wilshere exhaled and closed his eyes. "And you have been sending your wages to Birmingham to support the family."

Wilshere nodded. "At the beginning of April, his son wrote a letter, explaining that Mr. Yates had been unable to work due to a sudden and serious onset of sciatica. During my week of leave I made a hasty trip home to see the family. What I witnessed was truly difficult for me to bear. He has horrible pains which shoot down his leg and tightness in his muscles that forces him to collapse, howling in pain after only being on his feet a matter of less than a minute. In his current state he is no more capable to sweep a chimney as he is to swim the channel. The children were hungry, the house a catastrophe. Since then, I have been living as modestly as possible in order to send every spare farthing to support the family. I would like to apologize for the condition of my coat, Mr. Wilshere—it did not escape my notice, but I had not the means to have it replaced, although I suppose I should have sought out a tailor to have it patched. Mr. Gallagher was kind enough to mend my shoes already."

"Forgive me, Maitland," Wilshere said with kind sincerity. "I should not have reacted as harshly as I did without affording you the opportunity to explain yourself, and I certainly should not have used the occasion to judge your competence."

"Thank you, sir."

"Why did you not come to me when you learned of the condition of Mr. Yates?"

"Sir, you, and Mr. Bingley have been kinder to me than I could have ever dreamed. The wages that I am paid are so far above what I could have ever hoped to earn, that I could not, in good conscience, entreat you for more."

"You are fully aware of his generous nature, are you not?"

"Very much so," replied Maitland. "And as much as he has sacrificed on behalf of the Yates family by avenging their daughter and serving as a guardian of dozens more like her, it would be entirely selfish and cowardly of me to not care for them with what means I might possess."

"When this is finished," began Wilshere, "we shall have it arranged that the Yates family will be well taken care of in an ongoing manner. You have my word."

"It is too much to ask, Mr. Wilshere."

"You have not asked," the steward answered, fishing in his pocket for a bank note. "And here," he continued, handing the bill in the young man's direction. "For God's sake buy yourself a coat."

Maitland took the money with much reluctance. "Thank you, sir."

"Now, if you will allow it, I would also like to rest. I shall see you this evening." The young man bowed and left. The steward flopped on the bed, but slumber evaded him.

At the foreordained time, the three men dined then took hired horses out to the regiment's encampment on the edge of the city. After tying the animals at the post, they met Gallagher in the small room they had taken which directly overlooked the Colonel's Brighton residence. After exchanging pleasant greetings, Gallagher informed them that Colonel Forster had arrived home from dinner an hour earlier and had not had any visitors since. With that, the cobbler was released for the evening.

After Maitland acquainted them with the general layout of the camp and the house, they quit the room and rode round the entire property slowly, making copious notes as they went. It was after four in the morning when they finally returned to the inn where they hatched a plan before each man went off to sleep. This time, Mr. Wilshere fell into repose with no trouble whatsoever.

CHAPTER FIFTY-SEVEN

Twelve minutes after the three o'clock "all-clear" was given, a single rider approached at a leisurely walk, his face concealed by the brim of a hat. He was tall and sinewy and sat casual and confident astride a wonderful beast, as rain fell in persistent and heavy streams. The officer on duty, a Second Lieutenant by the name of Skipp watched as the rider sauntered up the main path toward the house.

"Who goes there?" called Skipp, holding a lantern up to his eye level with a shaky hand. The four privates on watch with him climbed to their feet unsteadily on hearing his voice. An empty bottle rolled off the porch and into the dirt at the bottom of the steps. The rider edged closer still, silent and foreboding in the dark. "Make yourself known!" With this command, the horseman held up a hand and eased to a stop. He was, at this point, but ten yards from the steps on which the guards were stationed. He dismounted with agility and ease.

"Will you inform the Colonel that his steward has arrived, please?"

"And your name, sir?"

"Trippier. Mr. Trippier has arrived with a gift for Colonel Forster."

"And you would... you... you would have me rouse the Colonel at this hour, sir?" the bosky Lieutenant asked between burps.

"He must be informed of my arrival at this instant!"

"Certainly, sir, Mr..."

"*Trippier.*"

"Yes, Mr. Trippier," Skipp replied, turning and unlocking the door behind him after fumbling about with the keys.

"And do not forget to tell him about the gift!"

"Of course—a gift!"

With that, the Lieutenant was inside and the rider out of the rain on the porch. The four soldiers stood there, loosely clutching their weapons, two of them nearly asleep on their feet. One of them sat suddenly and with a thump, then, turned over on his belly with a deep groan.

"You lads fancy a swig?" Though there were only four men, a dozen times the word "aye" was uttered. The rider pulled a large bottle from under his coat and said, "Drink up." The liquor was immediately snatched from his hand and passed around. Even the louse on the floor sat up for a taste. Just then, the wind whipped across the yard sending a steady sheet of rain nearly horizontal through the adjacent trees. The whiskey bottle clanked to the planked floor, rolling toward the steps as liquid poured from the open end. "You are going to lose it," the rider called. Three of the guards scrambled and barely managed to save it before it rolled out of reach. They breathed heavily and then passed it around once more, until it was empty. The lone standing man inhaled deeply and sucked on the top row of his teeth. He heard a rushed and tottering set of steps approach inside the house and watched the door open.

"The Colonel will see you now, Mr.—hiccup—Mr..."

"Enjoy a drink—on me, Lieutenant," said the man as he handed Skipp a smaller bottle from his other coat pocket.

"Much obliged, sir," he responded, taking the bottle, and greedily opening it.

"May I?" asked the rider, with his hand extended toward the key in the soldier's hand.

"Oh, yes of course," Skipp answered, handing the keys over as he slouched against the house.

"And also, this, please," he said while taking the lantern from the guard.

With that, the rider entered, locking the door behind him, pocketing the key.

"Trippier!" came a booming voice from the upper floor. "Trippier is that you?"

"Aye," answered the rider, water dripping steadily down his coat and pooling on the lacquered floor beneath him.

"I hear that you have brought me a gift!"

"I have," he answered, slowly approaching the steps.

"I hope it is news from the north!" bellowed Colonel Forster from his bedroom.

"Perhaps."

"That would be the best gift of all—hearing from you that the Wickhams have indeed been snuffed out!" The rider took each step casually, in no rush whatsoever. The house was dark, and he held the lantern low, casting light solely on the step ahead of him. "Or perhaps George is gone to the diet of worms, and you have brought *Miss Lydia* here for my enjoyment—and after all this time!" The rider silently reached the top step. He held the lantern to eye level and peered down the hall to his left and his right. "Tell me man! —What gift shall I receive?"

"One you will never have expected," replied the rider, following the Colonel's voice toward the bedroom.

"Have you acquired a chill on your journey, Trippier?"

"No, sir. Why do you ask?" the insouciant reply echoed down the hall.

"Your voice is much more raspy and deep than I remember it," the Colonel attested.

"Well, perhaps I have brought in a chill," replied the rider, turning the corner to enter the bedroom. He held the lantern in front of him in such a way that it cast an enormous shadow on the wall behind him.

"Well, whatever you have, I hope you have brought me a fine young maiden! It has been months now since I—" with that, Colonel Forster let out an audible gasp, seeing the shadow and seeing the man—much larger than Mr. Trippier—enter his bedchamber. "Are you the butcher?"

Bingley slowed to a halt and nodded. He then lifted the brim of his hat, allowing the lantern to unveil his face. "Good evening, Colonel Forster."

The Colonel gazed intently, a labyrinth of emotions crossing his countenance. In what was a flash but seemed an eternity, Forster recognized the face before him: "Mr... *Bingley*?"

"At your service, Colonel."

"You... *you*? —Are *the butcher*?"

"I see that my reputation precedes me," Bingley retorted.

"But how? —How is it possible?" Forster stammered.

"Does it not become me?"

"Surely, I would have imagined it to have been a phantom, or a hell-hound of the lowest order."

"Then I surmise that you imagined wrongly," Bingley stated with a resigned smile. "And I admit, as much as your lack of imagination benefits me particularly in my endeavour to remain anonymous, it is perplexing that you have envisioned your phantom as a man of little means, of no morals, and without a doubt bearing an illness of the mind that demands that he should be restrained, if he should deserve to live at all. In short, you have conceived in your tormentor, the very thing you have yourself become. But nay, I am not any of those things. I am an avenger born of your own class—an angel of death sent as a scourge upon devils in human form."

"I am sorry," Colonel Forster blubbered.

"If I was indeed your steward, and I had in fact brought a certain Mrs. Lydia Wickham with me—if she stood before you this very moment, begged for her chastity and her life—would you have heard her pleas? Would you have suddenly altered your state of mind that you might have been capable of the smallest token of mercy?" The Colonel's eyes were as large as walnuts. Frantically, though, he began searching to the room, his head darting back and forth until he settled upon the object on his bedside table. With the ungainly leap typical of a bacon fed man of middle age, he clutched a pistol and pointed it toward Bingley, trembling wildly. The force of his mad scramble left the down quilt and sheets in a crumbled ball on the floor. "Oh, *Colonel*," Bingley said, reaching down slowly and placing the lantern next to his feet. "We can do this *my* way, which while certainly unpleasant, would not inflict upon you nearly the suffering of the *hard* way."

"May I write a letter to my wife?" Forster wailed.

Bingley shook his head and pursed his lips. "This is not *that kind* of death."

Forster swallowed hard, then in one swift motion, shoved the barrel of the pistol in his mouth and pulled the trigger. A blast of smoke and sound filled the room and for a moment, Bingley's ears rang like a bell. Colonel Forster's remains reeled backward and flopped onto the bed, the pistol dangling from his index finger. Bingley calmly put his hand to his ear and flexed his jaw. He spat on the floor, then with the toe of his Marylebone collection boot, calmly tipped the lantern over, sending the flame rolling toward the dishevelled bedding on the floor.

He was outside through the back door, careful to lock it behind him, walked through the drunken camp, and unseen into oblivion like the ghost he was. Within ten minutes complete, the house burned to the ground—the Colonel's corpse with it. The men who awoke from the porch in a vain and jug-bitten attempt to douse the flames were unable to locate the key to gain entry and perhaps save the Colonel—along with his steward—from being consumed in the blaze.

CHAPTER FIFTY-EIGHT

IN ACTUALITY, MR. TRIPPIER had stayed the night in Hastings and set out for his master's quarters the following morning. The forty or so miles could be covered with relative ease, and he might arrive in time for lunch. The news of Captain Carter and Mr. Denny's demise was less of a shock to him than it must have been to the Colonel. After working through the deaths of Eoin Walters and Andrew Fraser, as well as the brutal murder of his own master, Lord Bertram St. John, who was at the time so near to settling what would have been a wildly lucrative contract with the Cardinal in Naples, Trippier had come to expect the worst from the phantom butcher. The ghost had even escaped the clutches of a previous attempt to snare him in that very city. This time, however, with the aid—naive as they might be—of the regiment under his new master's control would be a different story. He was firm in his belief that this trap would be the end of the vigilante. Then, the Wickhams could be dealt with decisively, and the recruitment of other members could proceed without threat of exposure or slaughter in their own beds. He had also just received a reply from Cardinal Endrizzi's nephew who inherited his estate, a man by the name of Iago, who himself, possessed considerably influential contacts within Napoleon's army. As it was, Iago had great interest in reviving the idea of a secret munitions arrangement which might benefit the French on the battlefield but would certainly benefit their own coffers at home. Now, it was only a matter of convincing Colonel Forster of the benefits of such an arrangement for his long-term prosperity. Tripper also had no doubt of his success in winning his new employer over to the idea, as the Colonel was much more easily led than his previous master. The fact that he had worked a twenty percent fee in for his own efforts would remain surreptitiously figured into the final accounts. In preparation for such a conversation, he went over the figures in a ledger once more as his coach approached Pevensey.

The steward was a short and unsightly man, so skinny that whatever clothes he wore hung from his frame like a sack over a fencepost. It seemed that all the features on his face had been squeezed to the center, leaving them crumpled between a long, pointy chin and an expansive forehead replete with pockmarks and wrinkles. His hair, what bit was left of it around the sides of his small head, was greasy and dark. Greenish-yellow eyes harkened back to a childhood full of violence and an adulthood filled with the lust of power and flesh. Though he was not a moral or sensible man, he was cunning, and this may have been his only appreciable trait.

As he again surveyed his work on the munitions agreement with the Neapolitan, a shout was heard up ahead and his coachman reared the vehicle to a sudden halt. *What the devil?* thought Trippier. Glancing out the windows, nothing but dark woods appeared on either side. *Must be an animal or another tree down in the road after the storms.*

Suddenly, the carriage door flew open and in an instant, the small stain of a man was flung from it and into the mud, his papers and articles flapping in all directions. He looked up to see a hooded figure standing atop him. With shock giving way instantly to fear, he pulled his pistol from his coat and fired a round toward the masked man. In the haze of smoke, Mr. Trippier saw not what hit him, but the whole world went dark.

When he came to, all was still black around him, though by the smell and the intimate and scratchy feeling across his nose, he could tell that he was now hooded. There were voices around him, and seemed to be movement, but much more subtle and gentle than a coach or cart. After rocking rhythmically for several moments, he realized he was in a boat. He tried to shake his head free from his hood but was unable to as it was tied under his chin. His small, claw-like hands were also bound behind his back.

"Can you believe after all that trouble you gave me, the bastard shoots a hole in me brand new coat?" a voice bellowed with laughter. Trippier could hear water lapping against the sides of the boat and, by this, determined he could not be aboard any vessel larger than a skiff.

"Where are you taking me?" he demanded in his screechy, nasal voice. The men around him went silent. The diminutive steward breathed heavily. "There is money in a chest on the back of the—"

"We have already seized it," a deep voice cut in.

"Then what do you want with me? Who are you?"

A long pause ensued—only the sounds of the water and a far-off gull—until at last, the deep voice began again: "We are the long arm of justice, Mr. Trippier."

"What the devil do you mean?"

"We are the wind, we are the waves, and we are the storm. You are the sum of your urges, and we are the calamity you have called down upon your own head."

"I do not understand."

"We are voices from beyond the grave—a heavenly chorus of maidens who cry out for justice, mercy, and peace at last."

"You are *the butcher*," Trippier rasped.

"I *was*."

"We are not far off from knowing you. If you kill me, Colonel Forster will no doubt—"

"Your master and I have already reconciled accounts."

The steward was caught off guard by this declaration. "Impossible," he declared. "I had an express from him yesterday evening. He was guarded by five men round the clock!"

"That he was—guarded by five bungling, feckless drunkards," the voice replied. "Not very well thought out on his part, I dare say."

"Then what? —You are to butcher me as well?"

"Luckily for you, Mr. Trippier, I am relinquishing my role as executioner. Perhaps you could think of me more as a constable." Another man chuckled behind him.

"You are a *murderer*."

"A *killer*, no doubt; but a *murderer*, nay. Anyway, that was, as of this morning's sunrise, in a former life. With you in my possession, the last and final link in a chain of evil and disgraceful men, I lay down all claims to justice evermore. From now on, I shall be a citizen, a faithful servant, and someday, by the grace of God, a husband. I shall enjoy the finer things in life—from a proper glass of brandy, to aiding a family who cannot afford a doctor to attend their sick child—I shall have it all. I will dance and I will love, and I will live in peace until the day all things are restored, and all of God's children are safely tucked beneath the shadow of his wing. And on that day, in the hopes of God's great and healing mercy, I shall see you again and even greet you as a brother. But until that day—"

The boat tipped slightly as it bumped against something to the steward's left. "And here we are," remarked another voice.

Trippier was grabbed stoutly about the shoulders and lifted onto dry land. He was walked at a pace much brisker than he was accustomed, up a set of stairs and across what he surmised to be a field of some sort. His shoulder was tugged, and his back was pressed against the trunk of a large tree. Someone said, "Have you the rope?"

The steward swallowed hard. "Am I to be hung like a common criminal?"

"I am afraid you have hanged yourself, Mr. Trippier."

With that, the rope squeezed tightly round his waist and his hood was removed. Night had fallen but he could clearly make out the shape of a Martello tower in the near distance. The men around him vanished off into the darkness in the direction of the sea. Trippier began to shout and holler for help. In a moment's time, lanterns were lit all about the fort and to his relief, a series of redcoats descended on him. Before he was untied, however, the commanding officer picked up a sack from the grass at his feet and removed a letter tied to a series of books. The officer's eyes darted from left to right as he read by the light of a nearby torch. He suddenly looked up at the steward, a mixture of quandary and disgust strewn across his face.

"What are you waiting for?" Trippier cried. "I demand to be untied this instant!"

"What is your name, sir?" asked the officer.

"Trippier! I am the steward of Colonel Forster of the militia regiment stationed in Brighton. I was on my way there but was attacked by brigands!"

"Colonel *Forster*, did you say?"

"Yes, and if you do not release me this instant, I shall personally see to it that you are court-martialled and disgraced!" Trippier searched the man's insignia but could not make them out in the dark. "What is your name, Corporal, that I might recommend such action?"

"Fitzwilliam," the soldier answered. "That would be *Colonel* Fitzwilliam," he clarified as he opened Trippier's ledger books, detailing his munitions plot with Iago Endrizzi. "Take this man into the fort at once, and make sure he is detained securely."

Mr. Trippier was charged and convicted of high treason and was hanged for his crimes against the crown by the week's end.

PART V

CHAPTER FIFTY-NINE

MR. BINGLEY IMMEDIATELY RETURNED to his house in London, though it was not his wish to remain there long. He was overjoyed to receive word that his friend Darcy, along with their entire party—his sisters and Mr. Hurst included, though Miss Darcy would remain in place at the estate with Mrs. Annesley—had left the north and were expected in town the following day. Bingley directed Wilshere to draw up plans for their imminent departure for Netherfield Park and to inform his housekeeper that it should be prepared in such a way that he might stay comfortably for some time. His intent was to spend as many days hunting as possible, when he was not in Miss Bennet's presence, as to prevent him from mindlessly walking the home's various halls. Mr. Gallagher was dismissed to see his family in Grantley Village, though he was considering an offer to relocate to London and open his own cobbler shop—his main investor being Mr. Bingley. Off to Birmingham was Mr. Maitland, with Mr. Trippier's coffer of three hundred pounds for the support of the Yates family, though he had requested, and was granted, leave to visit at Netherfield Park after a fortnight.

To Bingley's dismay, Darcy refused to leave for Meryton on the morning of Bingley's departure, having just arrived in London the previous evening, himself. Darcy informed his friend of several matters of business that demanded his attention, but was positive that they could be resolved with a few days' time. In a most excitable manner, Bingley demanded assurances that Darcy would join him in Hertfordshire at his earliest possible convenience. Having satisfied his friend's want of a guarantee, the two men bowed and smiled at each other before Bingley departed for the country in his coach alongside his steward. Miss Bingley and Mrs. Hurst had resolved to linger in town, in part due to the continued recovery of Mr. Hurst from his illness, but also because, in their time in Derbyshire they dearly pined for both the luxuries and those frivolities furnished by the city.

Though he had much success out of doors, Bingley found himself anxiously awaiting word of Darcy's arrival, as he felt it would be imprudent and, perhaps even foolhardy, for him to make an appearance at Longbourn alone. While he dined on duck the second evening, he received word that Darcy's business in town had been resolved earlier than anticipated and that he planned to arrive in Hertfordshire the following morning at half past ten.

As the coachman guided the horses through Netherfield Park's front gate and up the drive, Darcy could only chuckle to himself at the sight before him: Mr. Bingley, dressed and dapper, astride the ever-splendid horse Quinton, alongside a saddled horse which he naturally supposed was meant for him.

"May I not refresh myself a moment?" Darcy called as the footman opened the carriage door.

"Quickly, man," Bingley hollered, back in the direction of the house. "Some water and towels, and a hunk of bread!"

"And I am to eat as we ride?"

"Or you can wait and eat later," countered Bingley.

Darcy laughed as he approached his mounted companion. "For God's sake, give me ten minutes to don my riding boots and more appropriate attire."

"Ten minutes?"

"Yes, ten minutes—but I must know, for what purpose is the frenetic hurry? —Is the house to be levelled at noon?"

"Darcy," Bingley swallowed a lump as he began. "You of all people must know that I have awaited this moment as if it were a lifetime, or even *two*, in the making—"

"All right, well if it must be *now*, allow me ten minutes."

Bingley nodded from his saddle as Darcy climbed the steps and entered the house, his footmen, as well as one of Bingley's, quickly toting his trunks inside. When his man, Ridley, brought out the items he had required, Bingley himself used the towel to wipe down his beaded brow, and instructed the horses to be given the water to drink. More as a way to distract his quickened thoughts than out of actual hunger, he gnawed on the half-loaf of bread with vigour. Eventually Darcy emerged from the house, mounted his waiting steed, and the two men set off for Longbourn. They had passed through Meryton and were coming down the lane beside the church when a thought suddenly dawned on Bingley: "Darcy?"

"Yes?"

"Pardon me if I have not taken heed of your feelings on the matter of accompanying me on this call."

"Whatever do you mean?"

"In my reverie and anxious expectation of seeing Miss Bennet," professed Bingley with great care in his words. "I seem to have neglected to take into account what your feelings may be about seeing Miss Elizabeth Bennet, or her family entirely, for that matter."

"You have no need to ask my pardon," Darcy explained. "As far as my feelings are concerned, I shall take great delight in Miss Elizabeth's presence—though, perhaps the same could not be said for her in my proximity. I imagine, however, any such lingering distaste she may have toward me will give way to the delight of seeing you and her sister in the same room once more."

"Thank you," Bingley answered. "Though after all this time, I confess, my mind is not at all at ease concerning whether she will even be happy to see *me*. I would not blame her at all—"

"Cease with such thoughts, Charles. We have arrived, and the moment for which you have long pined has arrived with us."

The visit between the two gentlemen and the ladies of Longbourn has been described and in quite astonishing fashion in another source hitherto, so that nothing of consequence might be added, save that neither Darcy nor Bingley left the house with any particular affirmations of the feelings of Jane and Elizabeth toward them. They both endured Mrs. Bennet's tiresome declamations with what measure of grace and civility they could command and were engaged to call upon the Bennet family once more. It should be noted that the renewal of acquaintance had only fostered heightened admiration for the sisters. However, the gentlemen's continued turmoil over the state of the sisters' fondness toward them was such that they very nearly bumped into each other whilst roaming the halls of Netherfield after midnight that evening. It should also be remarked that Mr. Bingley's hopes were considerably more robust than his friends, though during those dark hours, he had not much considered her response were he to reveal the true reasons for his absence these many months past.

The following Tuesday, the gentlemen were received once more at Longbourn, this time as a pair among a rather large assembly. Upon entering the dining room, Bingley's thoughts were a cottage pie of decorum, nerves, and adulation. Mrs. Bennet made it patently obvious that she would have him sit next to Jane, but he dallied, as to not breech propriety and display too great a partiality to her. Miss Bennet, herself, must have felt much the same discomfort at her mother's overt insistence that they be seated side by side, but she set his mind at ease with a glance and a smile in his direction. Just then, his eye caught Darcy's with an expression of half-laughing alarm. Bingley's pleasure in his seating arrangement caused his friend's position at the table, next to none other than Mrs. Bennet, to escape his notice completely. Over the course of the meal, while Bingley and Jane conversed effortlessly and with much mirth, Darcy and Mrs. Bennet exchanged only what words were of absolute necessity, and, and for her part, in a most formal manner at that.

As the evening progressed, Bingley did settle in enough to notice that Darcy and Elizabeth scarcely interacted at all, aside from briefly conversing when she served his coffee. Even though he and Miss Bennet were separated at times, his efforts to be near her when possible were more highly evident and earnest than Darcy's to be close to Miss Elizabeth. Though Bingley had hoped to have the chance to linger longer in her aura, alas, their carriage arrived before any of the others.

The two gentlemen rode back to Netherfield in reflective silence, until Bingley inquired as to how Darcy enjoyed the evening. As it happened, Darcy *endured* it more than enjoyed it, though not with so much displeasure as he might have the previous autumn. Darcy was struck, once more, by the charm and beauty of Elizabeth, and despite all the fortitude he could muster, his heart remained seized between affection and despair. Being unsure of his own situation, Bingley was cautious in his encouragement, but did wish his friend's felicity no matter the outcome.

The pair spent the following days shooting and paying casual visits to neighbours and friends alike, until Darcy had cause to return briefly to town. The evening before his departure they dined at Lucas Lodge at the invitation of Sir William Lucas, where it was clear from the exertions of Lady Lucas, that she wished the gentlemen to be well acquainted with their daughter Maria, who had recently been presented at court. Both men reacted with such courtesy and gentility as might be expected from them, whilst being most scrupulous in neither offending nor encouraging such attentions. Maria, for her part, was charming, though timid—apparently acquiescing to her mother's demands without particular fondness for either gentleman, though if pressed, she would have most likely admitted a preference for Mr. Bingley, as he possessed the more cheerful and easy-going manner out of the two.

Once they were in the carriage and driving toward Netherfield, Darcy seemed contemplative and even anxious very suddenly. "You remember that I shall depart for town in the morning," he said, his eyes focused out the window on the passing scenery.

"Yes, of course," answered Bingley. "I do hope your business shall not detain you for long."

Darcy shook his head and scratched on the window mindlessly with his forefinger. "I hope to return within ten days' time."

"Very well, then," Bingley stated, watching his friend with some concern. After a moment of silence, he asked: "Is everything all right, Darcy? You seem to be in the most ruminative mood."

"There is rather something I would have you know," he began, turning his face to meet Bingley's. "I have always endeavoured to be a kind and sincere friend to you, but I fear that in one regard I have failed in that effort."

"Whatsoever do you mean?" Bingley solicited, himself feeling a dash of Darcy's unease.

"I must have you know, first, that my intentions were *largely* honourable, though I cannot claim to have been as selfless as I should endeavor to be, regarding this particular matter."

"Out with it, already, I beg you."

"Miss Jane Bennet was in town for the better part of the winter."

"She *was*?" Bingley blurted.

"Yes, she was. I was aware of her presence and yet concealed it from you, and for that, I am very sorry. I should not have interfered—"

"You kept me in ignorance of her being in London *intentionally*?"

"I am ashamed of it, but yes," said Darcy. It was now Bingley's turn to stare out at the passing village. "Initially I did entertain designs of keeping her separated from you altogether. It was foolish and selfish of me, I freely confess. I found my own feelings about Miss Elizabeth Bennet in conflict with my pride, and I allowed myself the delusion that in acting on what I quite callously deemed to be your best interest, that I would therefore serve my own best interest and soon forget—alas, it seems ludicrous to describe my own state of mind at that time: that it was remotely possible to *forget* Miss Elizabeth."

Bingley turned back and glowered at his friend. "I hope you will not take great offense at this, but Darcy, you can be a pompous *ass* at times."

The verve and manner with which the pronouncement was declared was such that it forced a laugh from Darcy. "No offense taken, Charles. I freely admit it, though I hope that you will allow me one more word on the subject, and secondly, that you might indulge me in the hope that I might change my ways."

Bingley inhaled and then exhaled sharply, casting a wry smile toward his friend. "I will allow it."

"I thank you," replied Darcy. "The second reason for my action this winter was, in many respects, more noble than the first. As I began to realize the depth of your affections for Miss Jane Bennet, and the futility of my own struggle concerning my feelings of attachment toward her sister, I did not disclose Miss Bennet's presence in town because I wished not to distract you from your duty. As you might recall, during that time in London, you were in the thick of your pursuit of Lord St. John, and as much as I grew to wish your happiness, I knew that you could not attain it until your work was complete. My concern was that were you to be distracted by her presence, you might not fulfil the task before you, and in not doing so, you would be haunted all your life by regret." Bingley nodded and forced a half smile. "I do hope you will take this consideration seriously in your judgement of my actions. I do also hope you will accept my sincerest apology."

"Of course, Darcy," Bingley exhaled. "I have *always* relied on your judgement, and you have never ceased being my most trusted friend."

"Then will you allow me one further unsolicited interference in your affairs?" Darcy asked.

"I shall," came the reply as the coach entered Netherfield Park. "*One more.*"

"You should settle this matter with haste and ask for Miss Bennet's hand."

"I should?" Bingley returned with excitement.

"And as soon as possible."

"Tomorrow then?"

"I see no reason to hesitate."

"And do you believe she will accept me? —That she *loves* me?"

Darcy shrugged. "I cannot, of course, say with absolute certainty, but knowing you as I do—your more recondite past included—I contend that she would be mad to turn you down."

At that, Bingley leapt across the carriage and embraced Darcy tightly. After they had arrived inside, they drank together and then went off to their respective bedchambers. They were by chance joined again, however, in the midst of the night as they both wandered the halls of the great house—Darcy slogging along pensively and Bingley pacing about with all the nervous energy of a schoolboy.

CHAPTER SIXTY

WHILST HE RODE QUINTON to Longbourn the next morning, he suddenly remembered that he had accepted a request to dine with the Robinsons that evening. As soon as it was recalled to his mind, he regretted accepting the invitation, thinking that if all went well, he might certainly be invited to dine at Longbourn. He was not dismayed, however, and even did his best to suppress any doubt that he might, after all, be rejected in his proposal.

The visit was a most pleasant one, but regrettably, he did not find himself alone with Jane at any time during the hour. In one sense he was relieved, as his nerves had him fully in their grip. However, on riding home he found himself melancholy that his hopes were still so unanswered and his love, as yet, unrequited. Having been invited once more the following day and having no engagements whatsoever, he accepted gladly and passed the rest of the afternoon attending to business with Mr. Wilshere before dining with the Robinsons that evening.

When he arrived at Longbourn the following morning then, he could hardly hold in his anticipation. But alas, much time passed without an opportunity to speak with Miss Bennet alone. After tea, however, Mr. Bennet retired to his library and Mary upstairs, and in a most unusual fashion Mrs. Bennet saw each of the remaining daughters—save Jane, of course—exit the room. Bingley sat across from Jane, alone at last, but felt unable to speak. Her beauty was astonishing, her smile like the dawn of day itself. All he could think of was confessing his love, but he felt duty bound to first confess his most furtive and unpalatable deeds.

"Miss Bennet," he began with a shy smile, which she returned in his direction. "May I share something rather personal with you?"

"If you wish to, Mr. Bingley," she sweetly answered.

"I would like to ask a question of you. But before I make a mull of everything, I pray that you make no reply until tomorrow." She suddenly looked like she might be sick. He grimaced, then quickly smiled in a shoddy attempt to reassure her. "I would like to describe a man—his character, as well as his deeds—and then ask if... if it were possible that you could ever *love* such a man." Jane simply nodded, holding her tightly clasped hands across her stomach. "There is a man who is good-natured, honest, and values innocence, purity, and life itself. Inadvertently, this man stumbled into a world of darkness and evil not his own, but a world of other men—wealthy and highly influential men. Their deeds were gruesome, vile, and calculated. There was no question as to their guilt and their wanton disregard for anything save their own pleasure, but there was also no question of bringing them before the courts due to the enormous influence wielded by these same men. So then... this *man*, felt duty and honour bound to carry out justice on behalf of God and those victims who suffered at their hands so cruelly. One by one, this man meted out that justice in a manner which would shock and terrorize the remaining evildoers, until at last, he had succeeded in smiting their plague from the earth." The look on her face might have succeeded in smiting him from the room—she was aghast, overwhelmed, and even mortified, but not afraid. "Before I ask my question and take my leave, I would have you be assured that this man has succeeded in his duty and has laid it aside to live in peace the rest of his life. I would also have you know that this man... thinks very highly of you, and *always has*. There was not a single moment, as he carried out his work, that he did not keep you in his heart. In fact, he succeeded in it only because he could not bear the thought of your innocence, your beauty, and your virtue existing side by side with such wickedness. He even allowed the possibility of losing you in order to help establish a world in which the two of you could exist in serenity, happiness, and *love* together. That has been his fervent and unwavering wish since nearly the moment he first laid eyes upon you."

She was biting her top lip, her furrowed brow wise and strong. "Mr. Bingley..." she whispered.

"I do not expect nor require a response until tomorrow, for it would not be honourable if you were not given time to make a reasoned and thoughtful reply. If you will allow me, then, I shall ask my question: knowing in full what this man is and what he has done, *could you love such a man?*"

Jane looked up from the floor and met his gaze. Her eyes were moist and her breathing heavy. Just then, Elizabeth entered the room once more, and though she paid them hardly any attention, it was too obvious to escape her notice that something rather important had taken place. The next few moments were spent in peculiar silence—Bingley and Jane having come to something of an impasse after such a startling declaration, and Elizabeth too well-mannered to inquire. Finally, after what seemed to him to be a torturous epoch, Jane smiled warmly, looking him directly in the eyes, and asked: "Mr. Bingley, would you care for more tea?"

A swell of affectivity nearly took him entirely off guard as he perceived in the timbre of her voice and the tenderness in her gaze that he had already had his answer. "I would, I thank you," he responded, a sudden moisture rising behind his eyes. He blinked quickly and followed her with his eyes as she rose—graceful, elegant, and kind. From the corner of his gaze, he caught Miss Elizabeth peering at him over her book. He addressed her with an awkward nod; her raised eyebrows betraying the smile she endeavoured to veil.

Once more it would seem that we have arrived at a junction where little can be added to what has already been told long before this particular manuscript came to light, save that Miss Bennet wholeheartedly accepted the good Mr. Bingley's proposal to marriage the next day. She remarked that while she had always been inclined to admire him, knowing his character even more fully served only to enhance her affection.

It so happens that Miss Elizabeth had learned from her aunt, Mrs. Gardiner, of the role Mr. Darcy played in arranging the marriage of Lydia to Mr. Wickham. Since Darcy had laid out such a large sum and had shown the strength of his character through such lavish forgiveness of Mr. Wickham, it was Bingley's firm resolve to keep his own role in the matter concealed. It was only after Darcy and Elizabeth had been married some months that her sister Jane, in fact, informed her of Mr. Bingley's role in saving the life of their youngest sister. From that point, Elizabeth relinquished her grudge against Mr. Wickham, though Lydia's manners and behaviour continued to pique her for years to come. But alas, we have got ahead of ourselves.

One more matter of note, before we may properly proceed: when Maitland arrived in Meryton, he bore with him the sincerest thanks on behalf of the Yates family. Additionally, the young man made a request, rather timidly, of Mr. Bingley—that he be allowed to study the law and establish a career *within* its bounds. Bingley was surprised by the request but was sufficiently impressed by him—not to mention indebted to him with his very life—that he ordered Wilshere to put the plan in motion immediately. As it happened, Mr. Maitland had one final request: that he might take his schooling within comfortable distance of Hertfordshire.

CHAPTER SIXTY-ONE

A WEEK AFTER THEIR engagement, Bingley hosted the entire Bennet family—save the Wickhams who were, by then safely established in Newcastle—as well as his own sisters and Mr. Hurst, who was for the time being, recovered. Having ordered with great anticipation and detail a meal which he was sure would delight and fascinate the entire party, he found himself rather embarrassed at the product Jensen sent up to the dining room. "No," slowly escaped his lips when the meal was presented. Immediately he began to apologize. "This is not *quite* what I had in mind:" warm loaves of bread, topped in juice squeezed from tomatoes and thick slices of cheese. "It is supposed to be... round and... *flatter*." His guests were gracious and, in all truth, even enjoyed the meal, but it was nothing of the glory he had experienced in Naples. Later that evening, when Wilshere caught sight of what remained, he asked the cook the name of such a curious dish. When he heard the answer, he took much of the staff aback by bursting out into bellowing laughter.

In the period shortly after their marriage, Bingley learned from Jane that her most fervent desire was to remain as close as possible to her sister, Elizabeth, rather than her parents. And, as has been well-accounted for in other sources, the lovely Elizabeth Bennet was wed to Mr. Darcy of Pemberley. After the new year, then, which they all spent at Pemberley, the newlywed Bingleys purchased a large swath of land within five miles of the Darcys. Construction began on a home that spring, and by the following Easter, they were settled comfortably, and just in time for Jane to give birth to their first daughter. The new estate was given the name Hope Park.

BRANDON DRAGAN

In the years to follow, Bingley's sister Caroline, having relinquished Mr. Darcy as the object of her future hopes, was wed to a man of good wit and intelligence, not to mention fortune, from Merseyside. His name was Duffy and was related by his mother's side to the very Miss King who had been so fortuitously rescued from Mr. Wickham during his fortune-hunting days. Mr. Duffy genuinely admired Caroline and went so far as to entertain her conceit and hubris with the exact degrees of gravity they merited (which, of course, was none at all). In fact, his humour and indifference to all things vain, in addition to the failure of all her plans, had served to settle her with a dose of humility, however humble that dose might have been. Mr. and Mrs. Duffy settled at his family's estate near Stretton.

The next year, on the day after Christmas, it so happened that Sir John Walters of Northumberland was murdered while leaving Mrs. Younge's establishment in the south of London in an apparent robbery attempt. Less than a week later, Mrs. Younge herself met her end when she was robbed leaving the house with a large deposit of cash. I can assure you most wholeheartedly, these instances were not the result of any whim, plot, or action of Mr. Bingley, nor any person associated with him.

Unfortunately, that same year brought further sickness to Mr. Hurst. At first, he had bouts of illness including fevers, tremors, and vomiting which left him confined to bed for days or even weeks at a time, but as the condition progressed, his skin became jaundiced and itched incessantly. His fingers became alarmingly clubbed at the tips and blood began to accompany his bodily excretions. He saw doctors from York to London, not one of whom could offer a course of treatment that led to any substantial relief in his suffering. One, in fact, prescribed two glasses of wine each night to help soothe the stomach. This was, naturally, his favourite remedy offered by any doctor, but served to only worsen his symptoms. Towards autumn, Louisa had him moved to Hope Park on the insistence of her brother, and over the last three months of Mr. Hurst's life, he spent many hours in the company of Mr. Bingley, and was never in better spirits, despite his affliction. Eventually, he slipped into a coma which lasted nearly three days and passed peacefully into the next life with his wife, sisters-in-law, and Mr. Bingley by his side. After spending three months in mourning in Derbyshire, Louisa was taken in by Caroline and her husband and eventually lived on quite happily, herself having experienced something of an awakening after the death of her first husband.

It should be noted that Mr. Gallagher, the Cobbler-Constable, relocated with his wife and many children to a fashionable district in London and opened what would become one of the premier shoe shops in all of England, and perhaps even Europe, over the next decade. His eldest son eventually inherited the shop and employed sisters and brothers and cousins and children and grandchildren alike for over a century. Gallagher's youngest son, however, became quite the success story in his own right as a founding member of the Metropolitan Police of London. Though Mr. Bingley had invested one hundred percent of the capital which allowed Mr. Gallagher's shop to open, advertise, and thrive, he never took a profit out of the business and even allowed himself to be bought out two decades later, and for far less than his shares were worth.

Most likely, the reader will be delighted to learn that Mr. Wilshere married in the years which followed this tale. She was a fine lady from a respectable family in the village of Lambton. He remained in Mr. Bingley's service for another twenty-five years before his master forced him into early retirement. Bingley's aim in this was to take Mr. Wilshere's son Daniel on as his steward and to take Mr. Wilshere himself on as a friend. In his spare time, the retired steward took quite the fascination to blending his own whiskey, a hobby at which he eventually found a great deal of success. His friends and family enjoyed the fruits of his labour for decades. In time he bequeathed his prescription to Daniel whose own son would inherit it and pass it along down the generations. As they aged, Wilshere, Bingley, and Darcy shared more and more evenings enraptured by the delights of good cigars, home-made whiskey, and each other's company. For many years, Mr. Bennet was often in their company.

Mr. Maitland distinguished himself in his schooling and went on to practice law under Mr. Philips, the brother-in-law of Mrs. Bennet. Over the course of just a few years he became rather prominent and had plans to establish his own practice in Birmingham—only one thing stood in his way. It was a rather unremarkable day when finally, Maitland proposed to and was accepted by Miss Catherine Bennet, with whom he had fallen in love years earlier during his work on behalf of Mr. Bingley in Meryton. Kitty had matured marvellously during that time, though she still had a penchant for all things ridiculous, which happened to be one of the traits her new husband found most endearing.

In an oddly unsuspected, but perhaps peculiarly natural turn of events, three days after her twenty-first birthday, Miss Georgiana Darcy was wed to her cousin Colonel—or should we say, *Field Marshall*—Fitzwilliam. The match might not have been particularly advantageous as far as her prospects were concerned, but she had become convinced that the General was the most handsome and the kindest man she had ever known, admittedly, save her brother and his excellent friend. Darcy, for his part, was exceedingly pleased with the match, if for no other reason than to share in the happiness of two people for whom he cared so dearly. It also so happened that, for his bravery and proficiency during the Battle of Waterloo where he served directly under the Duke of Wellington, Fitzwilliam was awarded a substantial estate in neighbouring Nottinghamshire, so Darcy and his sister were never apart more than fifty miles of good road.

Speaking of the Field Marshall, years down the line through a lengthy chain of events which would, perhaps, constitute a novel in and of themselves, Fitzwilliam came to learn of the identity of the man who arrested the traitor Mr. Trippier, and also of the role Lord Bertram St. John played in the scheme to manufacture faulty weapons for profit on the behalf of the French. When he inquired after the attorney, Mr. Maitland, he was informed after being sworn to secrecy that his good friend Mr. Bingley was, in fact, the responsible party. You might imagine the shock he experienced at hearing this news. By this time, Lady St. John was deceased of natural causes, and due to some rather murky legal circumstances surrounding what heirs had claim to the title, it had gone vacant for a number of years. In light of this, Field Marshall Fitzwilliam recommended Mr. Bingley for the title, and after Mr. Maitland worked tirelessly to clear what hurdles stood as encumbrances, it so happened in the year 1826 King George IV granted the request, making Mr. Charles Bingley the Earl of Canterbury. Lord and Countess Canterbury set about donating most of the estate of Lord St. John to charity, even turning the house in Kent into a hospital for children and the poor. They invested the profits of the estate in various ventures but were purposeful to use the large majority of the funds to help those in need. The new Lord Canterbury even had the St. John house in Brighton razed to the earth and in its place erected houses for destitute families.

The Darcys and the Bingleys lived side-by-side the rest of their lives and raised many children between them. Of those children and grand-children and on down the line, many became titans of industry, as well as titans of charity. Among their progeny might be counted Members of Parliament, surgeons and doctors, writers and painters, revolutionar-ies who secured women's suffrage, as well as conservatives who fought against it. Their offspring included soldiers and sailors, a farmer and a pub owner, a cellular telephone executive, and even a professional footballer, who might just have plied his trade in North London under a certain professorial Frenchman, while earning the moniker of "Invin-cible."

The truth is, though some, or all, or not a scrap of this tale might be factual, what *is* important is that for those of us who care to close our eyes and imagine ourselves within the majestic parks of Netherfield or Hope or Pemberley, the Darcys and the Bingleys abide in all of us—all of us who desire justice, happiness, and love in the world. For us, their legacy thrives as we take the next steps toward the creation of such a world, where people are judged not upon first impression, but on the quality of their character—a world where we are free not only to speak our minds, but to change them.

In one last note—*and I confess, I cannot conceive how this important episode escaped my mind till now*—Mr. Collins was induced to consider a clergy position that happened to be open in Lambton. Some have said this was because Mrs. Darcy herself missed her dear friend Charlotte. Either way, Lady Catherine was in no mood to lose such a servile—*oh, that's not the word*—vicar, that she sent the Reverend Mr. and his wife Mrs. Collins on a holiday to Naples, one of her favourite European cities, in hopes of inducing them to stay on in her employ. Whilst Mrs. Collins enjoyed her time there immensely, by course of an unfortunate event, her husband was prohibited from entering at all. For one reason or another, the name of an Englishman *William Collins* was flagged at every point of entry to the city on suspicion of a double homicide nearly a decade earlier. Though he spent nearly three weeks in a Neapolitan jail, Mr. Collins was released, one stone lighter but without a scratch, after Lady Catherine sent proof of his presence in Hunsford at the time of the murders. He was pardoned just in time to join his wife for their departure back to England. By great coincidence, a cook from a small enterprise in the city's waterfront departed on that very same vessel, bound eventually for Derbyshire, where he had been hired by a great Lord to ply his trade.

—Fin.

ABOUT THE AUTHOR

Brandon Dragan is an attorney in Tennessee and winner of the American Bar Association Journal's Ross Writing Contest. His writing draws on a wide array of influences from modern novelists such as Cormac McCarthy and Richard Yates to classic writers like Fyodor Dostoevsky and Jane Austen. He enjoys a good cigar, road cycling, and is an avid supporter of Arsenal Football Club.

To contact Brandon Dragan for speaking engagements,
please visit brandondragan.com

Many Voices. One Message.

quoir.com.

Made in the USA
Middletown, DE
09 November 2024

64190326R00196